MW01126148

Alien Instinct
By Tracy Lauren

© 2018 Tracy Lauren

All rights reserved. No portion of this book may be reproduced, distributed, or transmitted in any form or by any means, including photocopying, recording, or other electronic or mechanical methods, without the prior written permission of the publisher, except in the case of brief quotations embodied in critical reviews and certain other noncommercial uses permitted by copyright law.

Dedication

I would like to dedicate this book to my dad, Rainer Alfter, who passed away last year at the all too young age of 67. Dealing with loss of my dad, I found myself filled with inspiration--which, finally made me sit down and write.

My dad was the type of man you'd expect to find in a romance novel... probably a cowboy one. He had his own deep sense of honor, ethics, and morality as well as an old soul. He could have easily fit--perhaps much better, in a different era in time.

My early idea of Rennek's backstory was loosely based on my dad, who grew up a bastard in post WWII Germany. I don't mean to call him a bastard in a cruel or harsh way--it's just something that shaped his story. When it comes down to it, love and relationships are what shape all of our stories and my dad had too little or too poor of both, until it was almost like a poison on his entire being. His story was a sad one and I suppose this is my way of giving him a happily ever after.

Chapter 1

Kate

I turn off the T.V. and my crappy studio apartment goes dark, save for the dim parking lot lights peeking in between the cracks in the blinds. I pad barefoot behind the screen that hides my bed from view and set the alarm to wake me just before 6 a.m., then climb under the covers.

It's only 9 o'clock. I should get a full eight hours, I think as I try to settle in. You can just call me Captain Responsible. That's who I've been my whole life. I've had to be, really. It's not like anyone else is going to do my laundry or pay my rent for me. I wish I had a rich great uncle I didn't know about who'd leave me a fortune. I'd quit my job and just focus on school. That'd be sad though, I wouldn't want my fictional great uncle to die.

I wish I would win the lottery, I amend, but I scoff at the fantasy. Shoot, I wish I could at least splurge on a lotto ticket now and then to keep the dream going, but I can't afford to be frivolous. I have an early class before work and need to get my rest. *Work.* My insides twist with anxiety at the thought of going to work the next day.

I want to quit my job. I *need* to quit my job--before they fire me. Neither will look good on my resume. I've only been there a month for Christ's sake but it's been one *long* month. It just hasn't been a good fit, is all. At my last job I was a cashier at a mall shop. I'd always done well handling money, but for some reason being a teller at the bank... I can never get my drawer to balance. The other day I was only a penny off, I was so proud of myself. Unfortunately, the manager didn't share the sentiment. I can still picture the disapproval on her face. There's just so much pressure at the bank. I feel like everyone there is waiting for me to fail.

My coworkers don't seem to like me at all. I haven't been clicking with anyone. I overheard some of them saying I had a bad attitude and hearing that? Well, let's just say it hasn't improved my attitude enough to help me make any friends. In the first couple weeks I had a chance, I think. Some of the girls invited me out, but I couldn't afford it. I made up some excuse because I was embarrassed about my lack of funds. In retrospect, it probably seemed like I was blowing them off. I think that was the beginning of my downfall, or it at least helped me earn my "bad attitude" label.

Maybe I do have a bad attitude. Maybe I'm a sourpuss. An old fart at 22. I sigh.

I thought this job would propel me into adulthood-- that I'd do well and work my way up into something more than just a job... a career. Long story short, being a bank teller isn't for me and now I need a plan. I can't get behind in rent or, god forbid, lose my apartment. The thought terrifies me. I twist my sheets in my hands. In two days I have a rare day off--no work, no classes. I decide to spend it filling out job applications. Not that I have a choice.

Waiting tables might be good. I've never done it before, but I'd get tips. I can't help but picture the needle nearing empty on my car's fuel gauge. Or my bare fridge and cupboard full of ramen. Thank goodness for ramen. A job that tips would be ideal, I could really use pocket cash between paydays. So, I could buy a fucking apple now and then.

School has been my great hope though, even if it has been slow going. I don't have the luxury of living off my parents like most 22-year-olds do. I don't qualify for financial aid because my mom makes too much money. Never mind the fact that she doesn't pay my tuition. The last time she gave me any money was when she lavished me with a twenty on my 20th birthday. She thought I was turning 21. The card said, "first round's on me." I put it in my gas tank.

Most of my friends from high school are graduating college already. Here I am just struggling to take one or two classes each semester at the local community college while I work full time. And forget about a social life. I can't afford a social life. Sometimes I feel like I'm going nowhere and all this hard work and struggling is for nothing and I'll never move forward in life.

But most of the time, that isn't the case. Most of the time, I'm hopeful. I know there's something out there for me, I just haven't found it yet... which is probably why I've taken the widest variety of liberal arts classes my community college has to offer. I mean, I've taken puppet making. *Puppet making.* Who knew there was even a class for that? I know I'll find a place for myself eventually. I'll stumble onto something and I'll just *know.* Until then, we can check bank teller and puppet maker off the list.

"Nothing has really spoken to me yet," I told my mom last time we talked on the phone. "I just want to find something I feel a passion for."

"Keep looking sweetie, the most important thing is you're happy," she told me.

That must have been nearly a month ago now. My not-so-present dad died when I was nine. Sadly, it didn't really hit me hard. He wasn't around much and when he was we didn't really have a *real* relationship. It just felt like we were going through the motions. I didn't ever really *know* him and he never really *knew* me either.

I don't even know myself yet, I think bitterly. But that line of thought will do me no good. I have to stay positive and just keep my chin above the water. Then one day, it will just click. I know it. Hard work pays off. Karma is my friend. She's just late… or lost or something.

Happiness is the most important thing, mom said. Is that true, I wonder? It doesn't sound quite right, but that's my mom for you. She has always been… preoccupied. I have a brother who's 10 years older than me. When he still lived at home things were better. More normal, at least. Then, mom *acted* like a mom. But when he went off to college and didn't look back… well, it always felt like mom was simply done raising kids. Or she had raised her *real* kid and I was just the leftovers.

After my brother Bradley left home, Mom and I turned into something more like roommates than anything else. As for Bradley… I haven't seen or heard from him since his wedding. Which was like seven years ago now. I know he and his wife had kids at some point and mom made the trip up to Palo Alto to see them a few times. What were the kids' names… Jayden? Hayden? Kayden? I won't be winning any 'best aunt of the year awards,' to say the least.

"Okay, Kate. Bedtime," I'm going to shake off these morose thoughts and anxiety and try to relax enough to fall asleep. I stare at the parking lot lights shining through the blinds, creating lines across my popcorn ceiling. I listen to the variety of apartment life rumblings going on outside my thin walls. It's comforting to me. It makes me feel like I'm not really alone.

I listen to the cars driving by, bouncing over the parking lot speed bumps, music blaring an inappropriate amount of bass. A muffled conversation from the downstairs apartment. The T.V. from next door. The neighbors are watching *The Bachelor*. A dog is barking somewhere.

And then… suddenly… everything is silent. It's a complete silence that comes about so suddenly it startles me as much as a gunshot would have.

I freeze, trying to make sense of what's happening. I work my jaw, wondering if my ears are popping. The light shining through the blinds starts to get brighter. And brighter. Until finally it's so bright I wince at all the white light filling my apartment. Then, everything goes black.

Chapter 2

Rennek

"Set controls to cruise while we wait for specs from the lab."

"Yes sir, Captain," Dax replies.

It's impossible not to scoff, "Enough of that captain shit." My childhood friends shoot me laughing glances. "Or at least save it for when we have an audience," I tell them.

I sit in the captain's seat of my new cargo ship, fine tuning a control panel and waiting for a comm from Tennir. Nearby sit two of my four male crew. Dax and Kellen are busy conducting their own work on the bridge and the other two males, Bossan and Da'vi, are on their rest shifts in their quarters for the next few hours.

"Drive set to cruise.... Captain," Dax reports, his eyes on his work, yet still smiling. Always pushing the limits.

"Ass," Kellen and I shake our heads and laugh. Today, Dax sits at navigation, although we often rotate duties. He is likely my best pilot. As a matter of fact, he is a hell of a pilot--both in the air and in the expanse of space.

Then there is quiet and reserved Kellen. Today he is helping me do scans of the ship's processes while waiting to direct the comm signal. Kellen is good at many things, but patience is one of his most valuable traits. I know he longs for a quiet and reserved life, which makes me that much more grateful to have him working by my side.

All but one of my crew are males who spent their internment on Javan with me. We are all "products of war," as they call it. As such, we were required to be raised on an internment planet built to train and mold us into honorable males, capable of making positive contributions to the United Planets.

Our internment was many yets ago; we had since all gone our separate ways. That was until three cycles ago, when I gave my old friends a call. They dropped everything for me, as I would have done for them.

Dax, Kellen, Bossan and I spent our formative yets living and working side by side like brothers on Javan. They understand more than anyone else the importance of being called upon by one's "proper family" and there is not one of them who does not wish for the same honor themselves. When I asked them to join me on my cargo ship there had been no question to it. We were raised together since we were no more than fledglings. We have worked together, hunted together, studied together, and grew into adulthood together. We are brothers, even if we share no blood.

All except for for Da'vi, of course. He is the only one new to our group. I met Da'vi in a merchant spaceport during the days it took me to secure my ship.

Spaceports are notorious for trouble, and trouble seemed to be seeking me on that particular rotation. Maybe the gangs could tell I was retired UPC, maybe they thought I had credits to pinch. Whatever the reason, it was lucky Da'vi had been there. He is a male of principle and honor. In that way, we are cut from the same cloth. He stepped forward to aid me in battle--seeing I was outnumbered.

In the end, the half dozen Canoori punks were no match for the two of us. The fight had been brutal, and though I have been taught not to bask in the rush of a battle, it is always a pleasure to punish dishonorable behavior. In any case, I immediately sensed I had a brother in Da'vi and offered him a job before we even wiped the blood from our hands.

I focus my mind on the ship as Dax and Kellen joke beside me, but I am lost in my thoughts. It brings me much happiness to be working with them again. I am often reminded how grateful I am for my friends' sacrifices. It is my hope that one day I will be able to repay them for putting their own lives and goals on hold for me. I am a truly lucky male to have such friends. I feel the same way even for Da'vi. He has good instincts and knows much about engine and weapon systems. Other than that, however, I know little about him, save for his code of honor. But for me, honor means everything.

In his first days with us we questioned Da'vi about himself: his people, his planet, if he had been in internment... but Da'vi is a quiet one, private. As long as he completes his tasks, it is fine with the rest of us if he does not wish to speak.

Now here we are, three cycles and over a dozen successful transports later. Everything is running smoothly as we continue to become accustomed to our new lifestyles. It is hard to believe it was not so long ago all my efforts had been focused on rising the ranks of the United Protectors Coalition, or the UPC--which acts as law enforcement on-world and in space, serving all United Planets territory. All male products of war are required to enlist in a minimum of four yets of service to the UPC post internment, but I had been drawn to the role of enforcer on a deeper level and enlisted for a full career path.

I was serving on-world on Thaad as an enforcer. I had just begun to gain recognition for my work and had been rewarded for my efforts with a promotion. I was able to move out of the barracks and into my own apartment in an older part of the city. It was no palace, but it was my own and it was the first time in all my 29 yets that I lived alone. The day I moved into the small one room apartment I remember thinking I could never be filled with more pride.

Then I got a call from my proper family. After that, I said goodbye to all my hopes for a future with the UPC, left my apartment behind, and dove into this new career with all my being. There is no greater honor, being a product of war, than being called into service by one's proper family. I would do all in my power to make my mother, brother and sister proud and to earn a place amongst them.

But for now, my crew and I work to navigate this new life as transporters for Tennir. When we aren't learning the ins and outs of this ship, dealing with the cargo, or negotiating the fine line between legal acquisitions and black-market pirating--we make a strong effort to enjoy ourselves.

It isn't hard. Five males, traveling the United Planets' systems and beyond, on a top of the line cargo ship (retrofitted with some pretty heavy-duty artillery) and our chips loaded with Tennir's credits? We have our fun.

We are by no means rich, but we suddenly have credits at our disposal far beyond what we ever dared to dream of as fledglings on Javan, and greater still than what I was earning in my new position with the UPC. Not to mention, the swell of pride we feel for being in the service of my proper family and knowing the work we do is for the benefit of science and the Mother Planet. Pride fills my humble core.

Beep beep.

"Incoming comm," Kellen announces. "Connecting now..."

"Greetings Rennek," the viewing window at the front of the ship becomes clouded, converting into a monitor for the comm. Tennir's image appears in the screen. Tennir is six yets older than myself and though he is a scientist, his build nearly matches my own. We have the same grey coloring to our skin, the same tall, pointed ears, and identical jet-black eyes. That being said, the differences in our appearances are more apparent than our similarities.

While Tennir has tightly cropped hair all over the crown of his head, I have a thick, onyx black mane which dips down between my shoulders. Then of course, there are the more obvious differences. Such as my wings, my tail, the arcing horns on my head, and our legs are markedly different. I can't help but see these differences--when instead I long to see the similarities between myself and my brother.

"Greetings to you as well, Tennir," I reply. "How has the last shipment been acclimating?'

"Very well," Tennir tells me and I can almost see the excitement in his eyes at the opportunity to talk about the latest shipment of creatures he received. Almost. That is if Tennir, the pragmatic scientist that he is, ever showed emotion.

"Quarantine is nearly complete and they will be exiting their artificial habitats soon to be integrated onto the planet. This group seems to be conforming to the new environment well already. There have been no deaths or illnesses as of yet. They reacted well to immunizations, so we are very hopeful about the prospects. Very hopeful," he tells me.

"It brings me joy to hear this Tennir."

"Thanks be to you." Tennir nods his pleasantries, but I can recognize the all business look now taking over his face.

"As you recall from the briefing Rennek, the world the Mother Planet Biological Research Team is populating for this project has a *wide* variety of climate regions. There are both aquatic and dry-land terrains, mountainous regions, deserts," he ticks off his fingers. "The shipments thus far have been exciting for myself and the other scientists…" Tennir pauses, "but we are eager to see variety. This is an *entire* terraformed planet we are populating with wildlife from scratch and for the ecosystem to thrive we need creatures large and small, from great beasts to the smallest insect. Not only that, but we need to account for those who will not survive the acclimation process, or those that will be wiped out due to the newly establishing food chain, and Goddesses only know what else… variety is of the utmost importance here."

"Yes, Tennir. I understand. I know the shipments so far have been somewhat... homogenous." Most of the alien creatures I have seen going through my cargo holds are all roughly the same smallish size and covered in fur. To sum it up, there is a large market for alien pets. I can imagine it is not exactly exciting for a group of scientists who were hoping to be amazed by all the creatures far away planets had to offer.

"It is difficult to know in advance what some of these suppliers will have lined up due to their… ah… methods of acquisition and much of their cargo is aimed at rich collectors who are searching for novelty pets, so the creatures usually tend to be of a certain variety," I explain to him.

Tennir runs a hand over his face. "I know this Rennek. I apologize for my eagerness. It will take many yets to establish the diversity necessary to populate the planet. I am being rash. Just with what you have brought us thus far alone, we have yets of work ahead of us."

"I understand your concerns Tennir, we have two new suppliers in the coming rotations and a meeting with a repeat supplier we have begun to build something of a relationship with. A Ju'tup." I wonder if Tennir knows the Ju'tup race are nothing more than pirates and criminals.

"New suppliers mean new cargo and the Ju'tup... often carry many interesting things... as their captain learns to trust us he may offer merchandise he does not pass along to every client," I inform Tennir.

"Is it a matter of credits..." Tennir begins.

"We offer more than enough, Tennir." I tell him, waving away his concerns. "Pay too much and these suppliers will take you for a fool whose pockets they can leach or they will start dying the hides of common marsh rakes and selling them to you for a profit."

"Yes, Rennek. Of course. You have my faith. Do all you can to inquire about new specimens and I'll trust your knowledge in making these deals." Tennir pauses. "Mother would want me to ensure... are these missions safe?" He asks, making me think perhaps he does know the reputation of the Ju'tup.

I laugh at this, "If Madreed asks, tell her I am no more or less safe than when I was an enforcer. She has no reason to worry over me."

"Yes, I imagine so." Tennir pauses again to take in the appearance of the three males on his view screen. "I see you have decided not to wear the uniforms provided to you."

At that, Dax chokes on his own laughter and Kellen shifts uncomfortably in his seat.

"We... the crew... It would not be advisable for transactions," I explain, rather diplomatically to my pleasant surprise. Especially when one considered said uniforms. There was definitely a reason my team I were out in the field securing new specimens, and the scientists were back in the lab. A fledgling back on Javan wouldn't be caught dead in such a thing. Wearing those ridiculous jumpsuits during transactions with pirates was not on the menu. Not now, not ever.

Tennir nods absently, his mind elsewhere already. "When can we expect you?"

"Just shy of a cycle. That should give us time to make all three contacts and give your team the opportunity to finish clearing out those quarantine habitats. Be ready to process a larger number of specimens, we have never come in with more than two loads thus far. With three, the cargo holds should be at maximum capacity."

"Wonderful Rennek, we'll be ready. You have my gratitude."

"And you, mine." With nods to one another the comms click off and the window clears to show an endless sea of stars.

Chapter 3

Rennek

The first of the new suppliers is unfortunately only able to offer us more of the same old product. Mostly mid-sized cat-like animals that can be domesticated for the rich. I use my scanner to differentiate between cataloged and uncatalogued species. When I find anything that hasn't been cataloged I search the sample cages for attributes that stand out--picking out mating pairs whenever I notice interesting features: a spiked tail, exceptional tusks, elaborate markings.

At the second supplier I press harder for something besides the "pets." After listening to him trying to upsell the fuzzy creatures in his charge, the supplier scratches his head and reluctantly leads us to a large cloudy tank in the back. He explains what is inside is for food and says we likely would not be interested. But I do show interest and suddenly the merchant in him rears up and these small, ugly fish become a "delicacy" on many worlds. This is the part I can't stand. I shrug off the supplier--which is Bossan's cue to step in, negotiate a price, and gather as much information as possible on how to care for the creatures. Which more often than not isn't much, these people are not zookeepers--they are traffickers.

On the way to the third supplier I take stock of the remaining space in our cargo holds. We have already filled one section with a variety of furred beasts. I am not entirely pleased with this portion of the cargo, but at least each mating pair stands out in some way compared to what we have brought Tennir in the past. The true crown jewel of this shipment however, is filling the majority of the ship's two remaining cargo holds. Forty-seven large tanks filled with at least a dozen varieties of smallish fish--all uncatalogued.

They don't look like much in the way of eating, I think as I inspect the tanks. Regardless, this is something I feel Tennir will be excited about, so I purchased the entire lot from the supplier. It was a very good development for us. Now this supplier both knows my tastes *and* knows I am a serious buyer. He will aim to please me in order to make another large sale in the future, and hopefully will continue providing more unique cargo.

The only unfortunate aspect of this acquisition is it leaves little room for the Ju'tup supplier's merchandise. It is a shame because I know if I press the Ju'tup, he will likely produce some truly interesting new specimens. The Ju'tup are gamblers as well as smugglers and often collect large and majestic beasts for fighting rings. I had been hoping to get my hands on some of these creatures at our meeting, but I could not pass up the fish. I hope to still be able to purchase one or two large beasts to further build the trust with the Ju'tup smugglers so at our next meeting I may have better leverage than other buyers.

Beep Beep.

The comms click on. "Rennek, we are ready for entry into the atmosphere. Shall I notify the Ju'tup of our arrival?"

"Yes, Bossan. Please inform the rest of the crew as well," I tell him. "And Bossan, remind everyone this meeting is with Ju'tup. We bring our guns."

***

Our ship lands on a small desert moon in a system just beyond the reach of the United Planets. It is a neutral zone. Not the wild, lawlessness of deep space, but still none of the safety and structure the United Planets sun systems offer. Neutral or not, in a place like this... making deals with pirates... anything could happen.

My crew and I step down the ramp of our ship. Luckily, internment and UPC training has hardened us. We look like the last males in the galaxy anyone would want to mess with. We play it casual, but our hands rest on our holsters and we stay alert. Sometimes you hear of deals that devolve into robberies. It is unlikely in this case, since we have bought from this Ju'tup before. As return buyers, we are worth more than just the credits we bring on this day.

I survey the rocky surroundings and the black and angular ship sitting before us. Bossan holds up his wrist and speaks into a personal comm unit. Seconds later the gates of the Ju'tup ship hiss open and a ramp extends down to us. I lead my crew inside.

Ju'toktah sits at a lone table in the center of a long corridor lined with cages. The table is piled high with inventory lists, a large bottle of liquor and two dirty glasses. Two guards stand behind him waiting for orders to unlock cages, show specimens, and help move cargo from ship to ship.

"My friends! My Friends! Welcome!" Ju'toktah's fat hands and spindly pincers paw the liquor bottle and he fills the two glasses until they overflow, sending the putrid smell of alcohol to my nose.

"Greetings to you Ju'toktah."

"A drink for you," Ju'toktah rounds the table, his heavy form swaying from side to side. He passes me the drink. I do not enjoy drinking. I prefer to stay alert, but to earn Ju'toktah's trust? I will share a drink with the pirate. I throw my head back and swallow the contents of the cup. It burns on the way down and my nostrils flare. Ju'toktah's laughter causes the slimy blubber on his belly to jiggle and mucus drips to the floor with a loud plop. With his own cup, Ju'toktah follows suit and we slam our glasses back down on the disorderly desk.

"Come my friend!" Ju'toktah snorts and bellows through his mucus. "I have much to show you on this day!" clapping me on the back, he begins to lead me past the walls lined with cages in the first cargo hold. Both my crew and Ju'toktah's guards hang back while we captains conduct the business.

As much as I can't stand the Ju'tup, Ju'toktah is our best bet for acquiring more of the items Tennir's project requires. I follow the Ju'tup, studying him. All Ju'tup have three sets of appendages protruding from their bodies: two "legs" that fold out from the sides of their hips and two sets of "arms." The center set are weak and underdeveloped. Other than that, arm and leg pairs are indistinguishable from one another. They have fat bodies and secrete a thick mucus from head to toe. They also stink fiercely because of it. My nostrils flare again as I follow Ju'toktah.

"Allow me to show you the wonders of the galaxy!" He waves his top set of arms and the little ones below them shudder as if desperate to mimic the larger set. Ju'toktah knows I typically buy in bulk and the last few deals he and I squared consisted of exactly what I am *not* looking for on this day. Ju'toktah likely assumes I am a pet dealer on-world somewhere. So, not surprisingly I notice all the sample cages are filled with the usual cargo.

"Jungle cats, from the far reaches of the galaxy! Wild and fierce in their natural environments, but space travel has dulled their animal nature. Perfect now for training, bringing into the home. Good companions. Protection. Shoppers love this," he tells me as if the deal is already made.

"Today Ju'toktah, I have different tastes. I am looking for something special. Unique. Do you have anything like that?"

Ju'toktah swipes a hand across his brow, causing the smaller hand below it to convulse slightly. He motions to one of his guards who fills a cup and carries it to him, drinking it as quickly as the last.

"Different tastes, you say?" he eyes me blinking and I am reminded of the fish back in my cargo hold. "What kind of tastes does an ex-enforcer have?" Ju'toktah says, laughing as if he knows some dirty truth.

"It is not for me Ju'toktah, it is for my buyer and I remind you I am not an enforcer any longer. I am looking for something... "I seek to choose my words carefully, but Ju'toktah jumps in.

"Do not worry yourself, my friend. We have a little something to satisfy *all* tastes here. Come, let me show you something that might be of more interest to your *buyer*," he emphasizes the last word as though he thinks I might be telling some falsehood. He may think what he likes.

Before Ju'toktah leads me through a door beyond the sample cages the guard hands him another drink which is tossed hastily down the pirate's throat. Beyond the door is a much smaller room with two large cages on either side. To my disappointment they are filled with more cats. One in each cage. But these cats are *huge*. Bright orange with black stripes, they stalk their cages showing large fangs as they let out warning growls in our direction. Ju'toktah grabs some type of rod from the wall and shoves it toward one of the massive cats. It roars and swats at the device, showing claws as menacing as its fangs. Both the cats go wild at the sight as it crackles and pops with an electrical charge at the end. I frown.

"Fighters, for the rings. Make you much money these two. Or to hunt, some enjoy testing their skills on large game, as sport."

I did not like either prospect for these magnificent beasts. But I worry on disappointing Tennir by bringing back yet another cargo dominated by homogeneous specimens. "I will take these two, do you have any more?"

"No, my friend, my friend. Sold all the rest this morning. Just these two left." He shakes his head apologetically. This disappoints me, I hate the idea of these proud creatures being sold for awful things.

"Still Ju'toktah, I search for something different...'

He is silent for a moment before he breaks into laughter. The alcohol he has been drinking seems to be making him excrete more mucus. "I have just what you need enforcer! I should have known when I saw you and your crew. I give you something special for long space travel. My males are the same!" He bellows another laugh, "*I* am the same!" He slaps my back conspiratorially. "Come my friend, we have known each other long enough now I think. Let me show you the real merchandise. *This* will please you!" his laughter gurgles and bubbles as slime slides down his face like perspiration.

I might not yet be the most expert transporter, I may not know enough about biology to find the best specimens for Tennir, but in my blood, I am an enforcer. A protector. And I know right away what this pirate speaks of, what his *real* merchandise will be. My blood boils and I take deep steadying breaths and flex my fists to calm down. I cannot keep my wings from fluttering though. Ju'toktah does not seem to notice my agitation, he is hurriedly swaying back the way he came, back through the main sample corridor.

Ju'toktah calls to his guards and asks them to begin loading my purchase onto my ship. Bossan steps forward to deal with payment and catches the look in my eye. He can likely smell the rage emanating off of me. He nods and I know my crew is prepared. Something big is about to happen and they are ready.

Ju'toktah whispers to the Ju'tup guard and they both sneer. The guard types something into the personal comm on his wrist. Ju'toktah takes this as another opportunity to grab a drink and once again offers a glass to me. Apparently, he is happy enough to share his liquor again. I am thankful for his inebriation, it is likely influencing his sharing of information and will make the job ahead of me that much easier.

"If you will excuse us," he bows to the males, "this exhibition might take a bit longer than the last!" he laughs as though his commentary is hilarious, though he is the only one laughing. I follow him down another long corridor with a metal door at the end. Ju'toktah mashes his slimy fingers into the security panel and the door hisses open.

I survey the room. It is easily as large as, if not bigger than, the main sample room. Though this room only holds one large cage. Other than a single worn bunk and a waste receiver, the cage is empty. Not that that offers me any relief. In the center of the room there is a reclining chair. *With restraints.* Mounted next to the main door are more of the electric prods Ju'toktah used on the large cats. There are collars hanging there too bearing the same electric components as the prods.

What worries me the most is that the room itself is lined with metal carts. Each cart holding half a dozen large hanging bags filled with a cloudy white fluid. Disposable cryo bags. Too many to count. Too many to leave here with. Even if I had the space on my ship, I do not have the credits to clear out this number of slaves. Because that is what Ju'toktah is selling here. Dozens, if not hundreds of slaves.

My instinct had been correct. Ju'toktah is violating the most sacred laws in the systems. He is selling sentient beings. And violating them. As I take in the size of this atrocity everything in the depths of my being suddenly goes still. I will not be able to leave here with all these beings. I will not be able to kill all the Ju'tup to liberate these beings. There are too just too many Ju'tup on board. I will have to leave with as many as I can buy on this day and return for the rest. I am enraged that some of these beings might be sold and violated before I can return.

Another door hisses open and a new guard joins us.

"Ah, perfect timing Ju'keef. Let's wake a new batch for our friend here. He is shopping for something unique on this day, so we will let him shop!" Ju'toktah and the guard both sway with anticipation, their secondary arms fluttering. I watch as the guard wheels one of the carts into the cage and pulls a jagged knife from his belt. He slits each bag open, from top to bottom, the fluid spills out unceremoniously and the beings within dump out onto the metal floor, unconscious. The guard steps forward and yanks a thick tube from their mouths--pulling the length of it from their throats. That wakes them.

Chapter 4

Kate

Rational thought isn't possible in this moment. My brain is zeroed in on one thing alone: Ow. Freaking owie, owie, owie. Everything hurts. Then, slowly, I start to become more aware.

I'm on the floor. I'm vomiting. Milk? I'm in a puddle of white milky fluid. How did I get here? Was I out drinking with friends? My heart pounds and my brain works desperately to use what little my tunnel vision is offering me to explain what's happening.

I see my hands. They are wet. I'm on my hands and knees and I'm vomiting. Dry heaving? Did I drown? It's cold in this room and I'm soaking wet. I hear others around me coughing and gagging as well. The lights are bright. Bright, white lights. That seems familiar. Are we in a hospital? The floor beneath me is metal. Why am I here?

Sucking in air, I tilt my head to look around me. There are other girls, like me. We're all on the floor. At least one of them is naked. They're close to me and I'm disoriented, so I just see a blur of arms, legs and hanging heads. Someone is asking for help. Another is crying. I'm still struggling to breathe. My lungs feel like they are on fire and no matter how hard I try I can't get enough air.

There are other sounds around me that I'm becoming aware of now. A low rumble, like a growl. It's constant. And something closer, a strange popping and gurgling sound. I strain my eyes and my head rolls around trying to find the source. I see something. Something fat and green and covered in slime. My eyes connect with it and my adrenaline soars a notch higher than it already was. This something is not human.

It's like some kind of frog-crab monster, the gurgling sound is coming from it. It shifts from side to side and gurgles madly. My feeble lungs try to gasp. I throw myself back towards the other girls, our bodies knocking together. This catches their attention and that's when the screaming starts. And this frog-crab monster... call me crazy, but I think it looks excited. Is that gurgling sound laughter?

We're all still on the floor but I hold my arms out, pushing the other girls back behind me. I feel their hands clutching me like I'm some sort of life preserver. I dimly wonder how the screaming women are managing the lung power it takes to belt it out like that. Unfortunately, I think this is one of those 'you can scream all you want, no one will hear you' situations. I struggle to my feet, my legs feel like jelly but I keep my arms out, in some sort of pathetic attempt to shield these other women.

"Oh fuck, oh fuck, oh fuck," one of the girls is saying. I don't know how she can speak, rational thought is still something I can only aspire to in this moment. 'Bad dream' pops into my head. In dreams you can never tell if you are dreaming or awake, but when you're awake... well it's pretty damned obvious you're awake. I'm wide awake right now. Or maybe I'm dead and this is hell. That's a possibility.

My brain takes another step forward in assessing the situation again. There are bars surrounding us. We are caged. In a prison? Beyond the bars I see two more creatures. A daddy version of the frog-crab thing in the cage with us: bigger, fatter, slimier. Standing next to him is... well... it's a straight up, fucking, gargoyle. And it's growling and baring some massive fangs. Its wings go from being tucked at its back to spreading their full span. It's giant. It's speaking to the daddy frog-crab, but in some language I can't understand. Baby frog looks over at this interaction. I realize it is standing in front of an open door to the cage we are in. And fight or flight? My body kicks in because my brain has checked the fuck out and I rush baby frog. I slam into what feels like sticky, cold pudding and almost lose my balance and fall forward with him. Luckily, his spindly bottom legs crumble beneath him and his bulbous body topples onto the ground just outside the cage. I grab the door and slam the cage shut. Then, I'm instantly embarrassed of my dead-end plan.

I jump back toward the other girls. Some are sobbing. "What's happening?" one asks. Another is repeating her, "oh fuck" mantra. I notice two of them are completely nude. The naked girls are cowering on the floor to cover their bodies. I look down at myself, because I am actually not even sure if I'm wearing clothes or not. PJ shorts and a cami, plus underwear and a sports bra. I feel a wave of relief. I'm soaked and now slimy from baby frog, but it's better than nothing. I hesitate briefly before I tear off my cami and toss it to one girl and send my shorts to the other. The shock is coming off us all now and the others help the naked girls up and try to shield them as they cover their bodies. We are silent, except for the occasional sobs and incoherent mutterings.

I quickly take in everyone's appearance. It looks as if no one has regular clothes on. Just PJs for those of us who are lucky enough to have clothes. In some way or another we are all gripping each other for support or connection or something. Some type of silent camaraderie is going on between us. Without speaking we all scan wildly around the cage for something, anything to help us. A weapon? A back door? I'm not even paying attention to the monsters in the room with us. I am just searching for anything to help. Then the popping and gurgling starts up again. Baby frog is at the gate.

He is watching us, amused I think. I don't know if the noise he is making is speech or laughter, or nothing more than a gross noise. He taps the bars and makes a movement to open the cage. I leap to the door and push hard as I can against it so he can't open it. "Help!" I scream and it takes only a millisecond for the other girls to respond and we are all pushing against this gate to keep the monster out. I look up and I see his wide set eyes. His mouth opens in a toothless smile which stretches to the junction of his jaws on either side of his face. He could probably fit a basketball in his big, gross mouth. He reaches in the cage and runs one of his weird two fingered slimy pincher, hand things across our arms and bodies causing us to falter. Taking that as his opportunity, he pushes the gate open and snatches one of the girls--a blonde one, by the arm and starts to pull her out.

"No!" I scream. She screams. We're all screaming. I try to pull her back, but it's not helping. The other girls try to hold her too. I switch my attention to baby frog and attack him. My balled fists slide over the slime covering him, his gaze turns to me and he lets the other girl go. All the girls fall backwards against the floor now that they aren't pulling against his strength. That's when he grabs me.

I'm out the gate with him before any of the girls can get to their feet. He flings me hard into a chair just beyond the cage and starts to clamp me in. I strain against him and the clamps. I start to think about screaming. It's this weird surreal moment where I waver back and forth over the idea of whether or not I should scream… then I see this *thing* unfold from baby frog's abdomen. It rolls out like a butterfly's tongue and starts reaching, like a snake's body might, up my leg and towards me. This time I don't have to think about it. *I scream.* Just as I do, a deafening crack of thunder shakes the room. A spear or something bursts through baby frog's chest, spraying slime and viscera all over me. And I realize it isn't thunder I hear, the gargoyle has just gone berserk and the sound is coming from him.

Chapter 5

Rennek

I watch as these beings struggle to awaken. It is a pitiful and shameful scene. If I thought I had felt rage before, I knew nothing. I see their forms. They are wet and hurt, but I see their skin, their softness, their manes. I notice one in the front; her mane is a shock of red like nothing I have ever seen before. I recognize these creatures--everyone in the known galaxy would recognize these creatures.

"Ju'toktah! What is the meaning of this? These females, they are Goddesses!" I growl. I don't know that I will be able to control myself for long.

"Eh? The Goddesses? Rennek, my friend! I did not know you were religious! It is coincidence, make good profit though. Everyone want to fuck a Goddess," Ju'toktah laughs. "Take no stock in children's tales, it will ruin the pleasure of this day."

He is ignoring me and focused on the females. Blood is pounding in my ears. Never have I been filled with such rage. I struggle to maintain coolness so I might broker a deal for these females and all the others in the cryo bags. I must play this just right, even though I want nothing more than to kill every Ju'tup on this ship--to feel their necks snap in my hands and to taste their blood. What is happening here goes against all I know and believe in. It is unspeakable, unthinkable. I struggle to collect my thoughts and make a plan. And still the blood in my ears pounds on, a drumming calling me to battle.

"I wish to take them all, I do not want them touched... they must go to my buyer unsullied."

Ju'toktah just laughs. "No one will want an untouched female! An untouched female knows nothing of pleasure, they cry and fight. We break them here, then--much better for buyers. No trouble. *And*," he laughs and rubs his hands together, "it is my joy to take on this burden!"

He pays little attention to me; his eyes are on the females and he does not see my obvious outrage. "No!" I shout, "they must be untouched." It is hard to get further in my argument with the pounding in my ears. It is like the steady beat of a drum. It feels almost as if I will pass out if I do not give in to its call soon.

"Ack! I will give you females fresh from the bags then, and these," he motions toward the females, "will be my treat! A taste, so I know you will be back for more business, yes?" He seems irritated and wishes to swat me off like a fly. His gaze is hungry on the females. He sways, rubbing his hands together. His excitement disgusts me. I feel myself beginning to lose control. I cannot even think of a fair piece of reasoning to talk him out of harming these females. All I want to do is kill, to rip his throat open with my fangs and split him from top to bottom--letting his guts spill out onto the floor. I notice both sets of his hands are roaming over his body and his cock begins to unfurl. He takes joy from watching them being sick on the floor. The sight of his desire makes the drumming in my body pound harder. I growl uncontrollably and my wings extend to their full span.

"What is the cost for the lot?" I growl through my fangs. "I want them all."

"All six? 100 thousand creds. Each."

"No, the entire shipment." This catches his attention, but I am beginning to see red.

"You could not afford such a thing, *enforcer*." He says the last word as if he sees me now. His words become more hash. "Careful now enforcer, or I will not let you play."

Just then the female with the red mane dives at the guard's top-heavy form and knocks him out of the cage. A warrior amongst her people. I am in awe. I worry she will be hurt in this exchange. I cannot keep my eyes off her. I see her protecting the other females. She leads them, she must be their queen. She sheds some of her flimsy garments and offers them up to the nude females, so they do not have to be unprotected. Not that her garments do much, but I assume they feel vulnerable with nothing on. She is generous, this queen. Instantly, I am dismayed however, because now she is wearing less and even more of her soft body is exposed to these filthy pirates. It is unacceptable.

I gather my faculties to try again. It is my duty to rescue these females--all of them. I breathe deeply and try to abate my growling, but my voice is like gravel even to my own ears. I close my eyes to steel myself against the horror these females endure. "I want them all, Ju'toktah. My buyer has an endless amount of credits at his disposal. Name your price. I cannot pay all now, but I will take the cargo and complete the transaction before the rotation is done."

I now gain Ju'toktah's full attention. I have angered him. He turns to me, "So, Rennek? You will take my cargo and not pay me? You think to leave here with such valuable goods and I will wait for you to send me the creds? Shall I suck your cock while I am at it, enforcer? You take my cargo and I wait here while you send the UPC to my doorstep?"

I see from the corner of my eye the guard is at the cage door again, he is toying with the females.

"You misunderstand, Ju'toktah..." I growl out, but he interrupts me.

"*You*, do not understand you filthy mixed breed!" He swings an arm down and I see he is holding one of his electrified prods. He is spitting his words at me, but I am keeping the majority of my focus on the females who are screaming now as the guard tries to pull one out of the cage. I see my red maned female attack the guard again, that is when Ju'toktah jabs his prod toward me.

"There is no UPC in this system you fool, I am not slave to their laws. Here," he waves his prod, "I am *King* and you must bow to my laws. And you, I think Rennek, will make a good fighter for the rings. I think to sell you and your crew for my profit. You think you can even leave this place without my permission?"

His words do not register to me. My red maned queen is being touched by the Ju'tup guard. He drags her from the cage and throws her to the chair. Red clouds my vision and I drop from my hind legs onto all fours. The drumming becomes all I can hear. It is raging within me. Ju'toktah jabs me in the ribs with the prod. I feel nothing. My queen, she screams and I am lost to instinct. My battle cry rips from my throat. I grip Ju'toktah by the crown of his head, my claws sink in and his arms flap uselessly one last time. I rip his throat out with my teeth and he is dead before he hits the floor. I leap toward the guard and swing my tail to drive it through his chest. I fling him aside.

For a small moment we are out of danger. Now that I am close to her, I see she truly is in the form of the goddesses. She looks at me, we lock eyes. Hers are wide with terror and I am myself again instantly--perhaps, for the first time ever. "Are you hurt, my queen?" She does not speak, she only stares.

A great pounding at the door stirs me from my trance. My queen jumps and looks toward the door. I hear the calls of my crew outside. I make quick work of grabbing the guard's knife and I go to Ju'toktah's body. I chop off his hand and use it on the sensor to open the door. My crew nearly falls in. I see their eyes take stock of the situation. I see them eye the females and the cryo bags.

"By the Goddesses..." Dax says, their faces mirror my horror. Then, we hear the scurrying feet of more Ju'tup approaching. Da'vi is the first to move. He rips the cage door from its hinges while I unleash the clamps on their queen. The rest of my crew guards the door.

"I will carry you," I tell her and move to lift her. She flinches violently. I see my hands covered in blood and I realize my face must be as well. She saw the violent death I gave Ju'toktah and his guard. I appraise her and realize the blood of the guard is on her precious skin. She witnessed my kills. I am shamed to show such violence in the presence of a female--this female in particular.

Just then, guns begin firing down the corridor. The Ju'tup are on top of us. "Dax!" I shout, "The females!" I pull their queen into my arms and go to the cage. Da'vi throws a female over each shoulder and Dax follows suit. I try to apologize as I grab the last and hoist her onto my back. Bossan and Kellen send sparse fire down the corridor until I give the word. "Now!" I bellow. Bossan and Kellen take the lead, issuing an unending spray of shots as we run towards our enemy. It is the only way out, so we run into the oncoming fire. I pull my wings down to give as much cover as possible to the small red maned female in my arms.

As we near the end of the corridor a shot skims Kellen's arm. It knocks him back, but he does not falter on providing us cover. We come into the sample room. Three Ju'tup lie dead near the corridor. Two more hide behind cages, only to stick an arm out to send sporadic disrupter bursts in our direction. I hear one yelling into his personal comm. The ramp at the entrance of the ship begins to hiss as its hydraulic locking system kicks on. They are trying to shut us in. We run toward the exit. Dax, Da'vi and myself make our way to the front of the group to protect the females. Kellen and Bossan take the rear to continue providing cover. I bound over two dead guards. My crew likely killed them upon hearing my battle cry. I dive through the increasingly smaller opening to the outside of the ship. Bossan and Kellen switch to running on all fours to make the leap out. They skid in the dust. I clutch the female in my arms, as if holding her tighter will protect her. We are still not safe. We must make it to our ship and exit the atmosphere before the Ju'tup shoot us down. I shift my female to one arm and crouch down to run on all fours… well, three in this case because I hold her in one arm. But I am faster in this mode. I hope the female on my back can hang on as I dig my claws into the ground to gain traction. My ship is close. I must keep this female safe.

Chapter 6

Kate

How does the old saying go? Out of the pot and into the fire. The gargoyle killed my would-be rapist and his boss, or whatever he was. Then, more of these gargoyle like men... and a lizard man... show up and people... or should I say monsters... start firing laser guns at us. I have to make a choice and even though this guy looks like a demon, I think he might have just saved me.

He tries to speak to me, but seriously? I have no freaking clue. He reaches for me tentatively, a question in his eyes. But when the laser guns start he doesn't hesitate any longer, he grabs me and I send a nod to the other girls watching the interaction intently and they allow the other guys to scoop them up, as if we all weighed nothing. Then they run with us *into* the laser gun fire. I duck my head and the gargoyle encircles me in his wings. I close my eyes and bury my face in his hard chest. I don't want to look at anything. I don't want to see more monsters. I don't want to see any of our group being shot. I don't want to see any of us being captured. But I can't look away either, so I just hang on.

We run straight for a few moments and then we turn. I peek out beyond the wings wrapped around me and see cages with animals in them freaking out. I don't get that great of a look as the gargoyle carrying me sprints past them... but these animals look like nothing I have ever seen--like not in a pet shop, not at the zoo and not even on YouTube. They are going nuts over the laser fight, howling and screeching, pacing in their cages. I feel sick at the sight of them. That could have been me. That could still be me if we don't make it out of here.

We bound out of a slowly closing ramp. I see our surroundings. Mars. It looks like we are on Mars. Red and dusty, but I'm breathing... so, not Mars. I look ahead and I see this big metal warehouse or something. The gargoyle tips forward and I think we are about to fall, but he holds me with just one arm and runs like a dog or bear, towards this big metal rectangle building. There are still laser beam shots coming from behind, but I think a lot of it is coming from the gargoyle guys. We make it to the doors of the metal rectangle and one of the other guys uses a control panel to shut the doors. The gun fire stops, but I get the feeling we aren't safe yet because we all continue running down corridor after corridor.

We make it to a large room and the guys set all of the women down and begin to rush over monitors and controls, making these weird guttural noises at each other. Well, almost everyone sets the women down. The gargoyle holding me doesn't let go. He does drop the other chick off his back though. Seems like he is shouting orders at the other guys. Bossy, but you won't see me arguing with him after what he did to those nasty frog dudes back there. Actually, you wouldn't have seen me argue with him before that either.

One of the other men goes along the wall and folds down what appears to be extra seats. Like murphy beds, only chairs. He calls the women over to him, motioning with his hands... er, claws. They stare, because who knows what he's saying, right? He gently pulls one over and begins to strap her in like a baby in a car seat. She slaps at his hands. "Get your fucking hands off me, you aren't tying me down to shit!"

My gargoyle goes to the seat next to her. I see these seats aren't like the rape chair the monsters put me in. These look more like seats for a roller coaster. I don't know why we need to be strapped in. My gargoyle sets me down. He bends to look into my eyes. He clicks or something at me. He knows I can't understand, but I see the pleading look in his eyes. He motions for me to sit and I do. He pulls the strap over my head and secures it around me.

"You're just going to let him?! We don't know what these guys have planned for us. Look at what happened to the last guy who tried to tie you down!" The girl who was swatting the gargoyle says to me.

"Yeah? Look at him. This guy killed the fuck out of him. So, if he wants to tie me down, what can any of us do to stop him? But he isn't forcing us, right? He's asking. And besides," I soften, "I think they are trying to help us. They haven't hurt us yet, have they?"

She huffs her frustration, but the room is giving off vibes of serious urgency. "Yeah, 'yet' being the key word there, Red. Fine, fuck it. Abducted by aliens, might as well roll with it." She throws her hands up to be buckled in. The guy helping her keeps his head down. He looks ashamed or mortified by this interaction. He buckles her in quickly but gently. The rest of the girls follow suit. Then a window opens across from us. My guy sits in a seat big enough to accommodate his large body in the center of the room. I see a shit ton of those frog-crabs swarming our building. That's when it lurches beneath us. At first, I think the bad guys hit us with a missile or something, but then I realize we are lifting up into the air. I see the building we came from. It's a huge black triangle. It looks like a UFO. Then my stomach tries to make a mad dash for my feet. We shoot into the air so fast that in seconds the view outside the window is black. Our *ship* turns and I see... I see stars, just before we shoot into space. The stars blur past us and it hits me. I'm sure as shit not dreaming. I'm not dead or in hell. This isn't a building I'm in, it's a spaceship, and it seems I've been abducted by aliens.

Chapter 7

Rennek

Some of the females sob and whimper. My female does not. She observes, taking everything in. She is smart as well as brave and I am filled with pride at the thought.

I am aware of a sensation within myself… the drumming that began on Ju'toktah's ship. It has not gone away. I thought at first it was rage within me boiling over because of the horrible things Ju'toktah had done. And yes, I *do* feel rage. But I now think this drumming is something else, something more. It is caused by proximity to this female. *My* female. I do not know what it is, but she is affecting me. It is exhilarating and frightening at the same time.

Whatever it is, I need to put it aside for now. We are not yet out of danger.

"I shot into warp after exiting the atmosphere. Sentinels were already trying to lock onto us, but it will be nearly impossible for them to know which direction to go in," Dax reports.

"The Ju'tup will already be fighting amongst themselves to take over the captain's position, they may be too busy to chase us. After all, we only stole six… and you saw their cargo hold. Six are of little value compared to what they still have…" Bossan says. The silence that follows tells me we all feel the pain over having to leave the sleeping females behind.

"We need to send a comm." I say, resolved.

"If they are pursuing us, they will be able to track our location if I engage comms. We *can* wait until we cross into

UPC patrolled territory, it will be safer for..." Kellen says, looking at the females.

We all exchange knowing glances. We are in a difficult spot. We are the protectors of these six, it goes against the grain of all we have been taught to put them in a position where they might be at risk. If we contact UPC to let them know of the slave trade, the sentinels could find us and blow our ship to debris before the comm is even complete.

But, the females we left back in the cryo bags? They have no protectors. The Ju'tup will leave the moons of Magna VII and set up shop elsewhere and when those females are ripped from stasis there will be no one to save them. Even if we get the comm out, the Ju'tup might still be gone by the time the UPC can respond. Do we put these six at risk in an effort to help the ones we left behind? I must be the one to decide our course of action and there is no time to delay. I look to my red maned queen and think of how she protected her people.

"Prepare a comm," I decide. Kellen nods and I begin my recording.

"This is ex-commander Rennek of Thaad, District 17, Unit 2. This is an urgent message. While on a cargo acquisition on the red moon of Manga VII my crew and I uncovered a Ju'tup led trafficking ring. Sentient beings, all females. The Ju'tup are violating them and selling them as slaves. Hundreds are still captive. Requesting immediate response," a violent explosion rocks the ship. Some of the women scream.

"They have locked onto our signal. Beginning evasive maneuvers," Dax reports as Da'vi activates weapon controls.

"The message was dispersed! Everyone in this quarter is going to hear what the Ju'tup have done," Kellen delivers the news we were all praying for. Hopefully a UPC fleet will soon come and liberate the others, but for now we have to worry about the females here with us.

"Bossan! Can you strengthen our shields?" I shout to my friend, who is already bringing the controls up on his panel. "Kellen, give us a visual. How many do our sensors read?"

Kellen adjusts the view window so we see a rear-view image from the ship. Only two sentinels. We are lucky.

"Sensors confirm. There are only the two, Captain," Kellen tells us.

"They may have only sent a handful of sentinels out in different directions. The other Ju'tup are probably fighting over their own ship," Bossan says.

"Can our shields hold up against their firepower?" I ask. Our ship rocks again with another explosion.

"It is a fair match. We have some top of the line stuff... but they have some illegal stuff. We need to take them out before they do some real damage."

"Agreed. Da'vi, fire when ready."

"With pleasure," Da'vi tells me as he adjusts his targets and locks on. The first is gone in an instant. It is as if Da'vi knew exactly where the weak point in the ship was and targeted it precisely. But before he can lock onto the second ship it switches to warp and vanishes the way it came. The honor-less Ju'tup figured we were not worth the trouble.

"Drop us into warp. Get us out of here," I tell Dax.

"Happily," he says as the stars blur and we head out of danger.

Finally, we have a moment to breathe. I turn. All eyes are on me. My crew, the female, but my eyes find my red maned queen and my core seems to march in time with the beat of a faraway drum.

Chapter 8

Kate

Finally, all is calm. I have no idea how much time has passed since I woke up. Everything moved so quickly and my adrenaline's been in overdrive the whole time. Can you ever run out of adrenaline, I wonder? If you can, I must certainly be nearing the end of my supply.

Now that I'm not in fight or flight mode I'm able to really take in my surroundings, alien rescuers included. They are all similar to one another. Except for one, he looks more like he evolved from a reptile. The others all look like horned gargoyles. They are super tall and super built and even look hard to the touch. They all have greyish skin tones aiding in their resemblance to the stone statues from Earth. They style their hair differently from one another, I notice.

I scan them and my eyes instinctively go to *my* hero. The gargoyle guy who killed my captors and carried me out of harm's way through a barrage of gunfire. Well... hopefully he carried me out of harm's way. I guess I don't really know their intentions yet, I think to myself. In any case, *he* is different from the others. *He* has wings. Looking around, I suddenly realize that everybody is looking to my guy, the gargoyle in charge. The only thing is, *he's* looking at me. Our eyes lock. Did he catch me checking him out... er, inspecting him... for... uh, alien... qualities?

"Dang, you guys could just like, get a room. We can wait," the surly girl beside me says and I feel myself turn bright red, finally breaking the intense gaze of this alien-gargoyle guy.

He makes some crazy noises that must be his language and another guy jumps up and leaves the room. Soon after he's back with a handful of blankets. They help us out of the seat belts, because we can't figure them out for shit, and wrap the blankets around us. The guys bustle around helping all the women, but it seems *I* have a babysitter... or maybe the outer space version of a guardian angel. I haven't decided yet. The blanket he puts around my shoulders is a super smooth, thin material, but it's surprisingly warm.

Now that that piece of business is out of the way, all us Earthlings congregate towards each other. Looking at the room, I'm reminded of a middle school dance... all the boys on one side and all the girls on the other, everyone too shy to ask anyone to dance.

It seems the girls are beginning to realize that although everything has settled down, we are still in the presence of a bunch of aliens. I hear tears start again and those who aren't crying are shifting on their feet. I think everyone in the room can feel the tension rising. I take a step forward and stand in front of the other women. I don't really sense danger from these guys, but I still don't want them freaking my girls out. I don't remember what happened to me, and I don't know what happened to them, but they woke up naked and frog boy back there clearly was going to try and rape me. So, I'm in super protective mode right now.

"Tell them to take us home," surly nudges me.

"Okay, hand me my pocket alien dictionary."

"Look Red, that one is paying attention to you..." she points at my hero, "...to say the least. Use it and get us the fuck home." All the other girls are looking to me, eyes wide and welled with tears. I've got to be the strong one. It's okay, I'm good at that. I take a deep breath and step toward my gargoyle. He matches my movement and steps closer to me.

"Um, hello..." I don't know what the fuck to say. I look back and forth between groups. Everyone is looking at me expectantly, like I'm about to bridge some gap. "I'm Kate," I say holding my hand to my chest over my blanket. "Kate" I say again.

"Kate," the alien says fairly well. It sounds a little different coming from him. It's like he makes the sounds deep in his throat and his teeth click a little when he says it. He places a hand over his chest. "Rennek," he says in his throaty, growly voice.

"Rennek," I repeat his name nodding--probably a little too enthusiastically.

He motions toward his friends. "Dax... Kellen... Bossan... Da'vi," he pauses between each to make sure I am understanding him. I expect their names to be more like crazy clicks and things I can't pronounce, but I'm pleased to find I can say all the alien names. I can't do it all throaty like he does, but I can replicate the sounds fairly well in my opinion.

All alien eyes go to the women behind me. I turn and look at the other humans, I realize I don't know their names yet.

"Allison," a girl with long brown mermaid hair supplies. "Clark," says the girl I gave my cami to. "April," says the girl wearing my PJ shorts. "...Viv... Victoria," sobs a mousy brunette with short hair. Everyone is mostly staying back, but my surly friend steps forward and waves, "I'm Reagan," she says.

"Eemmrayyshinn," Rennek repeats. All us girls laugh.

"Sure, he gets your name right and mine gets butchered. Wonder why..." Reagan says sarcastically. "Rayyy Ginnn," She says with heavier emphasis. It doesn't help though, because now all these aliens are trying to master saying her name. It's a cacophony of Rah-shin's and Ray-chin's. "Oh, never mind! What's the point of this? Tell us something useful, like when we get to go home!" She shouts, exacerbated.

And I only feel a little butt hurt. I thought we were making good progress. I shake it off, step forward again and... here we go. "Hi... um, do you guys know any English? Can you understand me?"

The aliens look back and forth to one another. Rennek says something to us and then waits. He looks to his friends and begins to speak, motioning to his ear. The exchange goes back and forth for a minute until my guy approaches me again and lets loose a long string of words. But no matter how slow and deliberate he tries to speak, I'm just not getting it. I shrug. He then tries to pick me up. I squirm away.

"Whoa, whoa, whoa... I can walk!" I hold him at bay with my outstretched arms. Now it's his turn to look butt hurt. One of the other gargoyle aliens laughs at him and Rennek shoots him a pissed look. The one who laughed waves to us and starts walking from the room. I think his name was Dax. He makes some encouraging sounds and continues to wave to us, so we slowly begin to follow him, staying close together as we do.

This guy sure is in an easy mood--despite the situation and all. He talks endlessly as he leads us down the tight corridors, laughing occasionally. He talks even though we can't understand him and it's actually pretty comforting. I lead the humans behind him and my guy, Rennek, presses his way between everyone until he is walking near me... and in the tight corridors of the spaceship everyone notices. Reagan scoffs. I try to pretend I'm oblivious, but I feel the heat creeping up my cheeks.

Following the guys through the labyrinth of the ship gives me a chance to take in their appearances without getting caught staring this time. I notice Dax wears his hair in a long braid while Rennek's is shaggier and unruly. It looks like the mane of a lion--only black. It starts on his head near his, *gulp*, horns and runs down the center of his back. It's so full, it is very much like lion's mane, I think. I notice their tails sticking out from under the loincloth things they wear. It's not a loincloth like tarzan had. It's belted with holsters and the fabric is heavy and well-tailored. It covers their asses and their junk, but leaves their muscular thighs exposed.

These guys certainly don't wear much. I guess I should be happy they thought to bring us blankets at all--they're walking around bare chested, in nothing more than holsters and loincloths. They're even barefoot. Of course, it must be hard to find shoes that fit velociraptor feet. Rennek's tail sways as he walks, catching my attention again. This part of him reminds me of a lion too, but then I remember how solid it must be because Rennek used it to impale frogger back there on the bad guys' spaceship.

We round a final corner and come to a set of doors that swish open as we near them. This room is much smaller than the... I don't know... cockpit? What do they call the part of the ship where you drive, I wonder? Do you 'drive' a spaceship, or would it be 'steer'? Probably 'pilot'.

I shake myself from my thoughts and take in this new place, *and* silently curse myself for not paying more attention to the path we just took. I should have left a trail of breadcrumbs or something, we still don't know if we can really trust these guys yet.

This new room is definitely more sterile than the limited part of the ship I've seen thus far. It's got a high metal table in the center and it's lined with cupboards and drawers. There's a computer monitor thing and a light that can extend down over the table. This is likely a medical bay for the ship. The easy-going guy, Dax, is still talking as he rifles through drawers and cupboards. He locates what he is looking for. He pulls out something like a price tag scanner and sets it on the table then pulls out three small plastic containers, about the size of a golf ball. He turns to Rennek and motions toward the containers and then to us. Rennek looks troubled. They don't have enough for all of us, I take it. Rennek points at me. Dax nods, rips open one of the containers and loads it into the back of the price scanner. He hesitates... then talks for another moment in a much more serious tone to Rennek. *Gulp.*

Rennek approaches me, bending so we are eye to eye. It really emphasizes how tall he is. He must be over seven feet. He's got about a foot and a half on my 5'7. He starts talking slowly in this calm, purring voice. It reminds me of a cross between a cat and someone talking *to* a cat. He motions to his mouth and my mouth. I stare at his mouth. Fangs. Wow, he's got fangs. They aren't crazy though. Not like a saber-toothed tiger. It's a little more than what you'd expect from a vampire, I guess. But all in all, not bad or too scary, I'm thinking... and then I hear snickers bringing me back to reality and I realize his fanged mouth is smiling at me. I guess I zoned out staring at his mouth.

"Yes, go on. I'm listening," I say flushed, waving him along.

He smiles again, a cocky smile and I can't help but reciprocate. He is motioning to our mouths and ears as he talks and points to the price scanner and the side of his head.

I turn to the other girls, "Do you think it's a way for us to communicate?"

"What do you think, Sherlock?" Reagan says. She's pushed her way to the front next to me.

"Yeah, and if we're wrong are you still going to be such a smart ass?" I ask her.

"Until the day I die and *that* thing might kill us, so it might be your lucky day" she tells me smiling. I suddenly realize I like this girl. Her casual approach to all this craziness is somehow grounding. It makes me feel like I'm here with an old friend.

"Yeah, I'm little Miss Lucky today."

"Well, go ahead. Looks like you're the guinea pig," she nudges me forward.

"Wait!" Comes a panicked voice. "It could be anything. It might render you unconscious, it could be poison, it could be a roofie, it might be a communication device that isn't compatible with us and their good intentions could kill you..." the girl with short brown hair is saying, I can't remember her name. April and Clark take a step back and are shaking their heads in the universal 'fuck no' gesture.

"Whoa, chill." I hold my hands up to calm them down. I eye the gargoyles, they are waiting patiently. "Let's try to be objective," I say. "I agree with..."

"Vivian," she reminds me.

"I thought you said it was Victoria?" Reagan asks, lifting an eyebrow.

"No, it's definitely Vivian," she confirms.

"I agree with Vivian, it *does* seem like these guys have good intentions," I emphasize this small point from her mini-tirade, both to calm everyone down and because I'm starting to believe it. "We won't know what *that* is, or more importantly, *what's going on* if we don't have a little faith in these guys. Plus, look around," I wave my hands around at the ship surrounding us, "*this* is all pretty advanced... they must know what they're doing, right?" All the girls nod at this.

"If anyone else has a better suggestion, I'm all ears?" I'm met with silence. "So, I'll be the guinea pig and if something goes wrong, intentionally or not--you'll all know."

"Yeah, but there won't be shit we can do about it," Reagan says.

"That's right." We eye the guys and all scoot a little closer to each other. "They're giving us a choice right now. Let's just trust them until they give us a reason not to, because the alternative does us no good."

"Oh… this is a bad idea," Vivian says and she wrings her hands.

"It'll be fine, I'm sure," April reassures me and gives a tight smile. I smile back and nod. I really do appreciate the encouragement, because I'm actually pretty terrified.

"You got this Red," Reagan tells me, slapping my back.

I turn around and step toward the gargoyles, "Okay, I'm ready." Rennek nods to Dax.

Then Rennek picks me up and sets me on the table. I sit perched on the edge. Everyone is staring at me, waiting, like *I'm* supposed to do something.

"*Seh saghuli*," he says and nods his head. I stare.

"Lay down, stupid." Reagan says.

"Oh," I laugh. "Okay, okay, okay…" but I'm talking mainly to myself. I'm super freaked out. Just a few short hours ago I was nearly raped and now I'm putting myself in this vulnerable position. *Deep breaths*, I think to myself.

Dax, takes a cap off the end of the price scanner. Now, with the lid off, I can see the end is a pyramid shaped blade. "Oh! No, no, no, no!" I pop up. Reagan and Rennek rush to my side. Rennek is murmuring things in a soothing voice. Reagan grabs my hand and puts on her casual face.

"It's cool," she smiles "it just looks strange, but *all* this stuff looks strange. Like you said, check these guys out. They're crazy advanced. You'll be fine." She says it casually, but her grip on my hand is tight. I nod and try not to cry, because for some reason, I want to be strong for the others. I lay back down. Rennek says a few more soothing words and I look into his black eyes. Dax finds a position on the side of my head, near my ear. He is still for the briefest moment, then I hear a loud crack and feel a pain so deep and intense I have nothing to compare it to. It's like a wave of fire. Or lava. This is what lava feels like and I feel it in every cell in my body. Then everything goes black.

Chapter 9

Rennek

Kate's body seizes and then goes limp. Her friend starts shaking her, giving her little slaps on the cheek.

"Stop that," I tell her. "Your queen is sensitive now, she will need rest." I move to scoop up my Kate so Reagan may have her turn receiving the translator chip.

"Wha-ooh buhdee, ghit yeer hanns awf er!" She comes around the table and starts trying to pull Kate from my arms. The other females seem alarmed.

"Whut thugh fuk deed ew dew to er?" she yells at us with accusing eyes.

"You misunderstand. It is the language implant. It is painful to receive, but she will be fine soon. You may get yours next," I try to usher her towards Dax.

Dax pops the cell out of the med-gun and loads it with the next cartridge. We have enough for half the females. The rest can get a neural upload when we get them to the Mother Planet. Dax smiles and offers to place Reagan on the table. She cannot understand what we say, but I hope she understands our intentions and how helpful this will be in communicating.

"Yeer jokeen? Eye ham naut dewing thaht schit!" she recoils towards the other women.

Just then, Kate starts to come to. I set her back on the table. She moans, then rolls her head and vomits off the side of the table. Reagan is beside her again, pulling her hair back. I am filled with jealousy.

"I will do this task," I say and push my way in front of her, taking Kate's smooth red hair into my hands.

"Jeezus, fuhking dikh!"

"Oh my god, my head!" Kate sobs in my language. "It's so bright in here, too bright!" she moans.

"Computer, dim lights," I command.

She pops her head up, only to cringe and rub her temples. "Wait, I think I can...

"Sush, my queen. You must rest until you are feeling well again. There will be plenty of time to speak."

***

Kate

"Well, looks like it worked," Reagan says, "You speak alien now."

"Agh!" I roll back onto the table. "I don't know if it's worth it." I say in English. It's a smooth transition between the two languages.

"Ask them to take us home," Vivian's eager voice is piercing in my current state, but the sentiment clears the fog a bit for me.

"Rennek, we need to get home. Can your ship take us there? Please, we aren't meant to be here. Our planet..." another wave of nausea hits and I gag a little. I feel like I've done nothing but throw up all day. "Our planet," I continue, "we don't even have space travel--nothing like this. We need to get home."

He stares at me; his eyes are jet black. His nostrils flare a bit and then he finally speaks. "Yes, Kate. Anything you wish. We will take you home. What sector of the galaxy is your planet in? We will set course immediately."

I sit bolt upright. I look to the other women. I must be doing a great impression of a fish right now.

"What?" The girls ask, "What is it? Will they take us home?"

"He wants to know what sector in the galaxy our planet is in…"

They look back and forth to one another. Realization dawns on one or two.

"Fuck!" Reagan cries out and starts to bang her fist against the metal wall until she collapses in tears on the floor. Still woozy, I jump down from the table and hug her. Surly as she is, she lets me. I'm pretty sure we just became best friends.

"What? I don't get it..." April says.

"What the fuck is there not to get," Allison says to her, "Do *you* know what sector in the galaxy you are from? Or Earth's address for that matter?" She turns away from us.

"Tell them Earth," Vivian says.

"Earth. We are from a planet called Earth. Do you know where that is?" I ask, looking up at Rennek.

"Is it a member of the United Planets?" He asks.

"No… are there any scientists… or astronomers that might be able to help?" Dax and Rennek exchange looks.

Rennek comes to me and kneels. I take in his legs and feet. He has long feet like a cat or dog--the kind with an ankle high up on the leg and he walks on the balls of his feet. He has three toes with long... talons. Exactly like a raptor from *Jurassic Park*. I'm talking to a real-life alien, I think to myself as he stares at me like he's choosing his words carefully.

"My Kate... you say your people have not yet traveled space?"

"Yes, that's right... well just outside our planet. To our moon and back, but not our whole solar system or anything."

He and Dax look at each other again. They look troubled. "You see, Kate each star in the sky is actually a sun, and each sun has many, many planets surrounding it, and many of those planets have moons."

"Yeah. I got that. Thank you for mansplaining it to me, can we get to the point?" I say, annoyed at how simple he assumed I was.

"Have you ever looked up at the night sky?" he asks with pity in his eyes.

"Yes." I sob, closing my eyes. I get it. We are talking about a whole fucking galaxy worth of planets. Even if we aren't that far away, which direction is it in? And if it is far, and I mean far in comparison to the amount of space these guys can trek, the same question remains: which direction?

Then other questions start to pop in my head. How long was I asleep? How long have we been gone? Isn't there something about time and space travel? Like if you go and then come back more time has passed on Earth than for you traveling in space? Is that real or did I hear it in a movie?

What movie was that? Who was in it? Was it Helen Hunt? Jodi Foster? Now I'll never know, because as advanced as these guys are they don't have fucking Google. I hang my head in defeat.

"Show me a picture of the galaxy," Allison says in a way that makes me feel like we might have hope.

"She wants to see a picture of the galaxy; can you do that?" I ask.

"Of course," Rennek says. He stands and offers me his hand, helping me to my feet. His hand lingers on mine and he searches my face.

"I got it, don't worry about me," Reagan says as she gets up.

He can't understand her, but catches his faux pas. "Do you need assistance Rah-chin?"

She catches her butchered name, "REY-GIN!" she shouts and I put my arm around her, partially to comfort her and partially to steady myself. My head is still pounding.

"Follow me," Rennek leads us all back to the *bridge*. I remembered. It's called a bridge. We move to stand close to the window. Looking out, vertigo makes me weak in the knees. We are in space. Like deep in space. It goes on forever in all directions. It gives me this gut wrenching sense of fragility.

"Bossan, can you bring up an image of the galaxy?" The window clouds and an image of the Milky Way is before us. All of us humans step forward to examine it.

"Ask him to point out our current location," Allison says.

"Can we see where we are now?" I ask and the one named Bossan flicks something so there's a flashing blue light indicating where we're at.

"And the location of the planet we woke up on?" I ask.

"That is too close. On this image, our current location would overlap the Mangan moon," he tells me.

"Oh…"

"I could zoom in?" He offers.

"Just a moment," I look to Allison, she is studying the image. "Anything?" I ask her. She stares for a few more seconds.

"Yeah, I have no idea at all. I just thought if I saw it maybe I'd recognize something," she says.

"Could have warned us not to get our hopes up," Reagan says.

"Whatever," she responds, barely giving her notice.

I sigh. Rennek steps nearer. He's been watching me closely this whole time. It's like he wants to put his arms around me to comfort me, but doesn't know if he should. And he shouldn't, right? That'd be weird. Right?

Some of the girls are still looking at the image, as if still holding onto the hope they'll recognize a landmark or something.

"Can you show us your planet?" I ask.

"The Mother Planet?" he asks.

"Is that where you're from?"

"No… the Mother Planet was an origin world where space travel in the region began long ago. Currently, it is houses the United Planet's Governing Core, but the majority of the planet is allocated to botanical gardens, history museums, wildlife refuges. I lived there for a short time as a fledgling. It used to be the home to many, many beings, but centuries ago the Governing Core decided to preserve the beauty and history of Mother Planet by turning it into what it is today. Bossan, zoom in on the Mother Planet."

"Why did you live there?"

"My mother lives there. She is a member of the Governing Core."

I explain to the girls this is their 'origin planet.'

"Can we see all the systems that make up the United Planets?" Bossan strikes a few more keys on his control panel and a massive region of space is outlined on the screen. I am amazed. It looks like there are hundreds of planets within its borders.

"These are the sun systems they include." Rennek adds something at a nearby control panel. "This is the space the UPC guards and patrols." He shows us a larger area, "We are here now," he indicates our location, "just beyond the border of the patrol zone is where Magna VII is, and our paths intersected on Magna VII's red moon." He shows us a small red dot. I regret not knowing anything about distances in space. It would be nice if I could compare how far we have traveled to the relative distance of things in our solar system, or the size of the territory they've shown us, for that matter.

I try to relay all he says to the other girls as he tells me. "Who were those... creatures back there?" I ask.

"Pirates, smugglers," he says. "The race is called Ju'tup."

"We're humans. What about your race?" I ask.

Rennek looks stone faced. "Our people are products of war." He looks away. Is he embarrassed? I don't get the implications of what he has said. I hope I wasn't accidently rude. I'm not trying to insult our alien hosts. I change the subject.

"And the UPC, is that like military or police? Is that what you guys are? Did you come to rescue us?" I ask.

"No, we were dealing with the Ju'tup--purchasing animals for biological research and we realized they had sentient beings as a part of their cargo," he explains.

I start to relay this to the girls. They double take, "Research on animals? Is that what they intend to do with us?" April asks. My stomach drops.

"Rennek... are we to be used for... um... animal research?" I ask.

"By the Goddesses! No, my Kate! What the Ju'tup were doing is illegal! It is an unspeakable crime! It is simply not done, especially to females. *Especially* to females in the image of the Goddesses themselves!" He waves his hand at us.

"Ok, no on the research," I say to the girls. "What do you mean by that, image of the Goddesses stuff?" I say to Rennek.

All the men look to one another. "You are in the image of the Goddesses, you must be their direct descendants--related to them in some way."

"Yeah, I don't know your people's folklore buddy. Who are these Goddesses?"

"I do not know what is *buh-dee*." He smiles. "I thought all beings knew of the Goddesses, the creators of the universe? You and your people are like them, in form and beauty."

All the guys are looking at us... I take in their expressions and realization starts to dawn on me. I still don't know who these Goddesses are, but apparently, we look like them and because of that they think we're something special. I wonder if this could potentially be helpful to our situation.

Rennek suddenly looks solemn now. "I am so sorry my Kate, it is my deepest shame that I was unable to save the rest of your people. We sent a comm out as soon as we warped from atmosphere, the UPC will go after the Ju'tup ship---but it may be gone before they can arrive."

"My people? What do you mean? Other humans were still onboard the pirate ship?"

"The cryo bags... lining the cargo hold of the Ju'tup ship. I do not know how many..." He starts, but can see on my face I am not getting it just yet. Then, I remember seeing them; all along the walls of the chamber we woke up in. There were large bags, they were white... no, they were filled with a milky fluid. Like the stuff we were covered in when we woke up. I didn't fully take it in as it was happening, but in my mind's eye I remember the room was *filled* with these "cryo bags." How many women did we just leave behind to be raped or worse? Hell, was Earth invaded and did aliens take all the humans? I don't know! I don't remember anything after going to bed, anything could have happened.

"What the fuck is going on?" Reagan asks, likely responding to the horror on my face.

"Yeah, is it like no to the animal research, but yes we will eat you for dinner?" Allison asks.

"This is too much," I tell them. "We need to get more of you understanding their language... there's a lot to talk about... I want you guys to hear it too and I think we need to talk... humans only."

"Oh no, is it bad?" Vivian asks with worry etched so deeply in her face I don't know if she'll ever be able to make another expression.

"Bad compared to what?" I try to say jokingly, but it falls flat.

"Rennek, there are more of those translation things? I'd like... my people... to understand as much as possible."

"Unfortunately, there are only two more, my Kate. Our ship was not equipped for a situation like this. You must decide who would like the implant now and who would prefer to wait until we dock to receive a neural upload."

"Is there a benefit to one over the other?"

"The upload is less painful."

"Well, that's certainly an incentive." I turn to the girls, "Okay, who wants the worst headache of their lives?"

Chapter 10

Rennek

My Kate tells me two of the other females are ready for their language implant. She works to explain all she is learning from us, but there is much to tell and so much they do not seem to know. It is difficult to fill all the gaps in the human's knowledge, it seems the more we speak, the more gaps we uncover. They do not even know of the Goddesses! I wonder if her people are descendants of the creators of life and the universe, or if it is like Ju'toktah said and the resemblance is purely a coincidence.

All the while I battle this feeling building inside me. I am changed in the presence of my Kate. My core beats heavily within me; I am elated with a joy unlike anything I have ever felt before. When my Kate asked that we return her to her planet I thought I would crumble. I would do anything she asked of me, even return her to her home--but surely without my Kate, I would surely be lost. I do not know how I know this, it is as if an instinct within me is awakening. It is the bone deep knowledge: I need this female.

Being a product of war is difficult on many levels--I do not know the traits of my kind and therefore I do not have an explanation for what I am feeling or how it will progress. I think perhaps it is a mating instinct, but I have never before considered having a mate. All my life I have been consumed only with the idea of proving my honor despite my birth, but from the moment I saw my sweet Kate, the queen of her people, I felt a change beginning. It only took the sight of her and I was changed forever. I have become a slave to long buried instincts which are only now awakening within me. I wonder vaguely what set it off, was it her situation? Her distress and the desire to protect her? Or was it her on a biological level, perhaps her scent? I do not know the answers to these questions and there is no one to ask.

Regardless of the cause, I know she is mine and I am hers in any way she will have me. I would forsake all for her. I would follow her to the end of the galaxy and back. I would comb every planet and every moon searching for her home world, if that is what she wanted. I would turn my back on my proper family. I would end my friends if they thought to take my mate from me. I silently vow to do everything in my power to help Kate and her people. It does not matter if she feels the same for me or not. I will pledge myself to her and follow her all the days of my life if she will have me.

***

The two females who volunteer to get the implant are the more outspoken of the group, I notice. They talk much and ask questions to their queen. The language implants will help to make communication with the group easier and lessen the burden on my mate. Of the other three females, one speaks, but I see she is nothing but fear and worry. The last two are quiet. They were nude when they awoke from the cryo bags. I wonder if they were harmed at some point by the Ju'tup. I send prayers to the Goddesses in the hopes that that is not the case.

The two females take their implants. Both are sick, as my Kate was. Unfortunately, this way to receive language is more painful than a neural upload. It doesn't take long for them to recover and while they do I am drawn to Kate's side. I worry about her mental state after all she has been through. I stand as near to her as I can, because it excites the drumming within me, but I restrain myself from touching her. I refuse to touch her on the same rotation a male tried to force his touch on her. It must have been terrifying for my Kate. I shudder to think what could have become of her had I not been there, or if it had been a different set of bags that had been cut open. It drives me to the edge of insanity thinking of these possibilities and how easily she could have slipped through my fingers. She turns to me and I am snapped from my thoughts.

"Rennek, my people and I would like to continue our discussion, but first we need clothing. Do you have anything other than these blankets?" She asks. I am surprised they do not wish to sit and talk more. I would want to know all the answers to my questions immediately. I look at her people-- they are weary, weak from the trauma this rotation brought. Some still sob occasionally, or jump when I move or speak. They need time, rest, and more care. I take note of this, I should have inquired earlier to my Kate how I could help meet their needs. They need clothing. This is something I do not have for them.

"No, my Kate, nothing that will work for you," I see her appraise my body so I stand taller and flex my arms as subtly as I can. We are nude save for the belted strips of cloth that hang at our waists. We carry holsters on our belts or, in Da'vi's case, on straps crossing his shoulders. Of course, we have the uniforms Tennir provided us but, they would be ridiculously too large and heavy for the small females.

"Belts then? Do you have extra belts?"

"Belts we have," I smile. Nothing brings me greater joy than speaking to my female and I am happy to provide her with something she asks for. Watching my Kate, I wonder if she feels the same sensations I do. Could this feeling be natural to her kind? Twice now I have caught her staring at my body and before she received her implant she looked at my mouth in a way that told me perhaps she was feeling something similar to what I have been experiencing. Now that we are free from the Ju'tup we will be heading for Tennir, I hope before we reach the lab there is time for Kate and I to be alone. She might have answers to some of the questions I have.

"We'll also need food and water. We don't want to be a burden on your ship, of course we'll work in exchange for what we use," she says and a wave of shame hits me so hard I nearly step back.

"My apologies! I was not thinking. You and your people shall have all you need. You are welcome to everything on the ship and there is no need to work in exchange for anything. That would shame me deeply. Please, allow me to prepare a meal for you in the dining hall," I tell her.

"Thank you, we'd all really appreciate that," she replies.

"I must warn you, however, the food is not the best. Travel meals are… well… the good news is they are vitamin rich," I explain.

"Uh oh, if that's the best thing you have to say about it then I'm a little scared," she says smiling up at me. Her expression turns sincere. "I haven't had the chance to say thank you yet Rennek. We're so grateful to you and your friends for all you've done for us." She touches my arm as she says this. The sensation is beyond anything I have ever felt. It is electric, it is pleasure and nourishing all in one. It takes all my strength not to take her in my arms in response.

I am thankful when Dax steps in. "You will all need some standard vaccinations first, I'm afraid." I regain my composure, raking my hands through my mane.

The females are nervous when they realize we want to give them shots. We explain all fledglings get them to stave off germs and illnesses which can spread quickly through interplanetary travel. Ultimately, they all receive the shots--with about as much bravery as a fledgling. I chuckle at their fear. After all they have been through on this day a small needle is the least of their worries, especially if they are to eat readymade travel meals after this.

After the vaccinations, I lead them to the dining hall first and show them how to use the food synthesizer. I order some hearty stew, which does not taste as awful as some of the other readymade meals, once it is reconstituted. I also order them some carb sticks and show the females how to break them up and dip them into the stew. I watch as they all eat two servings and drink water as if they had spent the rotation under Javan's hot suns. I am pleased to feed them, but I am filled with shame to think they were so famished and I had not offered to take care of these needs sooner.

I take in their appearances. Their hair is still crusted with the fluid from the cryo bags. I remember Kate had blood splattered on her from the Ju'tup guard.

"Kate, would your people like to bathe?"

"Oh, fuck yeah!" Reagan exclaims. I am stunned.

"There will be no fucking. It is only so you all may clean yourselves," I explain, horrified they think I am propositioning them. The females laugh as Reagan translates.

"She was just expressing enthusiasm, Rennek. She didn't mean it literally," my Kate tells me.

"I see, we use that word only for..." I trail off not sure what to say without offending the females.

"Don't worry, I can guess," she blinks one eye at me.

"Is there something wrong with your eye, my Kate?" I ask, worried.

"Oh boy..." Reagan scoffs.

Kate just laughs, "No, it's like a signal… it's hard to explain. It can be used for different reasons I guess. I was trying to let you know I understand."

"Ah," I blink my eye at her. "I understand."

"Oh geeze." She says. I do not know *geeze* either, but I decide to skip it for now.

"Anyway, where can we bathe," the one called Allison says.

"Follow me," I say, standing. I tap my personal comm and ask that someone bring clean blankets and belts to the showers.

When we arrive at the community showers Kellen is waiting with fresh blankets and belts. Except for the personal bathing unit in my quarters there is only a common shower area. One wall houses a series of hooks for personal items and a long bench. Water spouts occupy the adjacent wall.

"You may place your dirty items in the bin and I can have anything personal to you washed, if you wish," I tell the females.

"Thanks, Rennek. This looks great." Kate tells me, eying the showers.

I pull her aside, daring to lightly touch her arm. "My Kate," I speak so only she may hear me, "if you wish… I have a private shower in my quarters. I do not know the customs of your people, but if you require more privacy I would like to offer it to you."

"Why would I need more privacy?" She looks confused.

"I don't know if a female of your station is accustomed to bathing with your people?"

"Huh? My station?" She looks perplexed momentarily before she says, "Oh! Is that how we're using the phrase 'my people'? I thought you just meant people like me. Other humans. I'm not… they're not *mine*. Is that what this 'queen' stuff is about too?" She asks.

"I apologize, I assumed because you protected and lead them," I tell her and she just shrugs.

"You are a born leader then, my Kate," I tell her and am rewarded with a smile. "The offer stands, if you would like to bathe privately you may have my quarters. To sleep in as well, it has the largest bed of all the rooms. I wish for you to be comfortable."

"Thank you Rennek, I don't need anything special though and I'd hate to put you out."

"Yes, well I will ask again after you see the size of the beds in the spare quarters," I tease.

I show the females how to work the water heating system and step outside while they bathe. I activate my personal comm. "Who's on the bridge?"

"Kellen and Da'vi here, Rennek. May we assist?"

"I will be showing the females their accommodations shortly. Afterwards I need to speak with Tennir as soon as possible. I need to let him know of all these developments as soon as possible and to see if he and Madreed might be able to help with whatever is to happen next."

"I'll send a message ahead letting him know you wish to link comms," Kellen tells me.

"Perfect. Kellen? Do you feel different at all since we brought the females aboard?" I ask.

"Since we brought them aboard? No Rennek," he replies

"Have the others reported anything?"

"Not that I'm aware of," comes his answer.

"Alright, my thanks Kellen."

A long while later the females finally emerge from the showers. I see they have wrapped the blankets around the back of their necks and tied them off with belts at the waist. Now they are gowns. This is a great improvement to the simple blankets we provided them with. I am impressed with their ingenuity. It seems Kellen also brought them a comb, which the females shared. I am grateful to him for thinking of this small luxury. They are clean and properly clothed now and the smell of the cryo fluid is finally off them. When I see my sweet Kate, I am even more taken with her beauty... and her scent.

"What may I provide you with? Anything I can do for you is my pleasure. You said you wished to speak privately? Would you like a meeting room, or would you rather rest first?"

"I vote sleep, anything else can wait a few hours," the one called Allison says.

"I second that," my Kate tells the others. The other females voice their agreement.

"Wise choice, there will be plenty of time to speak before we arrive at the Mother Planet."

I lead them to the section of the ship which provides crew members their accommodations. This ship can hold a crew of twenty or so, but our job with Tennir only requires a small team. It is the large cargo holds of the ship we utilize. Luckily, this means there are more than enough vacant sleeping quarters for all the females to have a private space. Each unit has its own toilet, sink and a small closet. I give them rooms in close proximity to one another and show them how to use the prompters in case they need to go to the dining hall during the night. The females without language transplants will need assistance, but this will work for the time being.

One by one each female enters her own sleeping quarters until eventually it is just Kate and myself in the hall. Her door hisses open and we both linger.

"I would gladly trade chambers with you. My quarters are not luxurious, but the bed is much larger. I insist, for your comfort," I implore.

"Rennek, it's fine. Plus, you would hardly even fit on this bed," she motions toward the small bed before us. My core practically rumbles as I think about the bed in such close proximity to my mate and I. I long for the day I can throw her onto the covers and lick her cunt until she screams my name. I cannot wait to explore her body and find what pleasures her the most. Today is not that day, however.

"If there is anything you need, please call me on the comm." I tell her.

"Will do, Captain." She makes a saluting type gesture and the color creeps into her cheeks again. "Well, goodnight," she says, ducking into her room. I groan and lean into the wall, breathing deeply to regain my composure.

Chapter 11

Rennek

I make my way onto the bridge. Kellen and Da'vi are still on their shifts.

"Did Tennir respond?"

"He's ready to link comms when you are," Kellen tells me.

"Proceed." I hesitate for a moment. "Kellen, Da'vi. I have the bridge."

"Yes sir," they are up and out of the room before the comms even link.

"Rennek, are you well? Is it true the Ju'tup were running a trafficking ring on the outskirt systems. Sentient beings? Females?" comes Tennir's harried questions.

"Yes, Tennir. It is all true. That is the reason I am contacting you. How is it you have heard of it so quickly?"

"It is all over the news, Rennek. This is the greatest atrocity since The Invasion! The UPC have already contacted me and would like to evaluate the beings as soon as you return. There are guards here even now awaiting your arrival at the research facility. The Governing Core is calling an emergency session to decide what is to be done with any beings rescued from the Ju'tup."

I run my hands over my face. "Yes, this will be complicated."

"To say the least, Rennek!"

"Why has the UPC not contacted us and asked to intercept?"

"This is big Rennek, even with your connections with the UPC, they defaulted to your proper family. Just so you know, Mother has stepped in heavily."

"I see."

"How many were you and your crew able to rescue?"

"There are six females here onboard with us. We've vaccinated them and given three of them language implants. The others will need a neural upload when we arrive. The Ju'tup ship, have you received any updates on it?"

"Mother has been keeping tabs on that, as far as I know there is nothing. There was some evidence left on a Mangan moon. Dozens of patrollers have responded and they are combing the area. Did the Ju'tup escape with many captives?"

"Dozens Tennir, possibly hundreds."

"By the Goddesses!" He rakes his face in his hands.

"That is another thing Tennir, these females. They are in the image of the Goddesses themselves."

"You must exaggerate," he says looking into the screen.

"No. They are the *exact* image. It is like looking at the statues at the capital's fountains. They are slightly smaller perhaps, but everything else is exact."

"Incredible. What do they have to say of this?"

"Nothing! That is the strangest part, they know nothing of the Goddesses!"

"How can it be?"

"I am at a loss there, Tennir."

"When will you arrive?"

"Five rotations, three if we hurry."

"I am so grateful you were there to stop this Rennek."

"I have stopped nothing, I was unable to save them all. I failed."

"Rennek, I reject that. You have saved six females who would have been…" Tennir trails off. "You have made a difference for them and have shined a light on this operation. Who knows how long this has been going on. Now rescue missions will begin. Justice will be served."

"There is no fit justice to rectify the damage already done," I say more to myself than to Tennir. "Tennir, I must ask you…" I struggle to voice the words.

"Anything Rennek."

"Is there anything you can tell me about The Invasion? About my people? Any traits you might be aware of?"

"I have never known you to be interested in your heritage. Why do you ask?"

"There is a female among those we rescued. Kate. I am reacting strongly to her. I was hoping you might know something on a biological level that might help me understand what is happening."

"What do you mean, reacting strongly? Are you worried you might harm her?"

"No! Never. As a fledgling I worried how I might behave if I ever felt a mating instinct. I was fearful, but now that I am in the presence of my Kate I know there is no way I could ever harm her. I would die before I let anything happen to her and I would never take something she did not willingly offer."

"And if she does not offer?"

"If all there is to be between us is friendship then I will be content with that alone."

"I do not know much Rennek, Mother would be the one to ask."

"No! I cannot bear the thought of forcing her to recall such a thing. To remind her *I* am a product of that assault. Please Tennir, do not speak of this to her."

"Mother is a logical being and you are her son Rennek, she would help you in this."

"Tennir, it is final! I will not deliver her to the pain of her memories." I have never spoken this harshly to Tennir. I look away from the screen. I do not wish for Madreed to think of the male who assaulted her during The Invasion, I can hardly bare the weight of the shame tying me to such an event. I know she cannot forget such a thing and though I long to, I cannot either. I simply have no desire to remind her of it. Tennir is silent for a long while, watching me.

"A true mating instinct?" he asks finally.

"Yes, she is my mate. I know it," I tell him.

"Tell me more of your reactions to her."

***

I cannot sleep. I have had so many questions my entire life about my people, my kind. Who are we, where are we from? What types of traits and instincts are unique to my people? Never have I had a mating instinct. While I saw other males chasing any female that might give them the time, I focused all my energy into my career and earning a reputation of honor. Now I am faced with the beauty that is my Kate, I feel as if each cell in my body has woken from a deep sleep. I am restless. I have all these questions with no one to ask.

I would be ashamed to ask Madreed about my sire. Likely she knows nothing of who he was, or his kind... *my* kind. If she did have any impression of his instincts towards mating it is unlikely they match my feelings for Kate. My sire hurt my mother in The Invasion. I would never hurt my Kate. I would do anything she asked, even if meant I had to sacrifice every dream or hope I have held in the past, I have but one dream now and it is to be by her side.

Perhaps that is why I cannot sleep. I long to be in her presence. If only I could watch her sleep, or hear her breath, my core might calm enough for me to rest. I sigh and sit up in my bed. It is only slightly less modest than the ship's other quarters, with its own bathing chamber and a larger bed. I hope Kate is comfortable in her room.

I resign myself, I will get no sleep on this night. I run my hands through my mane and strap my belt and waistcloth on. I decide I need a drink. My chamber door hisses open and I walk down the corridors toward the dining hall. I am heavy with the weight of the day and wish sleep would claim me. I round the corner to the dining hall and I see one of the humans inside. Her red mane can be confused with no other. It is my Kate. My core roars to life. I see her fussing helplessly with the food synthesizer.

"May I assist you, my Kate?" She startles at my voice.

"Oh, my goodness! Rennek," She places a hand on her chest to settle herself. "I didn't hear you come in. I didn't wake you, did I?"

"No, unfortunately sleep has been difficult for me to grasp on this night."

"I know exactly what you mean," she smiles and my core melts, "I thought I'd be asleep before my head hit the pillow… but I just can't seem to turn my brain off."

"We share the same affliction then. A head full of questions and with no answers."

Her smile deepens. "Yeah, it does sound like we're on the same boat."

"Ah, my poor Kate. You do not understand space travel yet, this may be a ship, but it is not a boat," I chide her.

Her smile drops from her face like she cannot rid herself of it quickly enough. "I know this isn't a boat, Rennek."

I laugh, "If I take your meaning correctly, I thought you appreciate it when I man-splain to you, do you not? Last time you thanked me."

"You're teasing me!" she laughs. "You bully! Well, I guess I'm glad a sense of humor is universal."

I eye the food synthesizer. "Did you need assistance? I would be happy to show you."

"Yeah, please do help. I'm finding this is an area the translator is less than helpful with. I know my language for food and beverages and I know your language for food and beverages, but I don't know what is what. Not all things translate. I think I need to have actual experience with food before I can figure out the food synthesizer."

"Until then, I am here to help. What would you like?"

"A cup of tea."

"What is *tea*?"

"*Exactly*. You guys obviously don't have tea and I don't know if you have an equivalent in your culture."

I resist the urge to lament the fact I know nothing of my culture and instead ask, "What is *tea* like?"

"It is a drink that can be served hot or cold. Served hot it's soothing and certain types can help you sleep. Like chamomile. It tastes great with honey, but I won't even try to explain what honey is…"

"Well," I cannot help but smile at this female, "I cannot help with *honey*, but I think I can offer you *ceata*. It is a beverage like you speak of. It is meant to be served hot and different spices can be added to help ailments. There are some for sleep." I move beside her and press a few buttons on the food synth, giving it my order. I make ceata for the both of us and add *emon,* a spice with an earthy, warm flavor.

We sit across from each other at one of the tables. I take in her appearance. I need no ceata, I drink her in instead. She is as warm as the emon. Her red mane is clean and dry now and flows over her shoulders. It shines even in the low light setting simulating night in the dining hall. She pushes it behind her ears. She is aware I watch her. I feel the drumming within me quicken. It is my core, reaching for her. I want to take her hand in mine, I want to ask her if she feels what I feel, if she understands it. But I do not wish to frighten her. Her day has been… overwhelming to say the least.

•

Chapter 12

Kate

Rennek is practically devouring me with his eyes. It's strange, but it excites me. I shouldn't feel this way considering everything that's going on, but I do. I'm embarrassed by it for some reason. This is like some form of Stockholm syndrome, only my guy's the hero not the kidnapper. Maybe this is hero worship then. Is that a thing? I know there's penis envy... then I blush. I'm thinking about penises now as he stares at me. I hide behind the hot cup of ceata in my hands and can't bring myself to hold eye contact. His gaze searches me and I realize for the first time that to him, *I* am the alien. Do I look like a freak, I wonder? Am I disgusting? I hope I'm not, though I guess it shouldn't matter at all to me. I'm suddenly self-conscious of my hair. I try to nonchalantly straighten it a bit.

I tentatively sip the ceata, it's sort of like tea I suppose. It has an earthy taste that seems out of place on a spaceship and whatever spice he added to it is something quite like cinnamon. "This is good, thank you," I say. He's still staring, "Do I look very... different from other people, er aliens?" I ask.

He eyes me, taking his time to answer. A smile plays on his lips. He must be very attractive for whatever he is. "You are... unique," he says and then he's silent again. Staring at me.

I give a nervous laugh, "Unique? Is that a nice way to say I'm a freak?"

"No, my Kate. Not a freak. Just unlike any female I have ever seen," his eyes look appreciative for a moment. "Except for the Goddesses." He sips his tea.

"Yeah, you mentioned that. What are these Goddesses anyway?"

"Truthfully? You do not know the Goddesses?" he asks skeptically.

"Yeah, no clue. Is it like an origin story?"

"It can be thought of as such. It is the story of who created the universe."

"Tell me."

"When I first saw your people, I thought surely you must be descendants of the Goddesses." He takes me in again as if staring at me will give him the answers. "You are smaller in size, but everything else is what I know of the Goddesses."

"Well, I hope that's a good thing." I say with a question in my voice. "You've seen the Goddesses?"

"Hmm, there are temples and monuments built for them," he sets his cup down and seems to be thinking for a while. "I can show you one day, if you like?"

"Yeah, I... Well, I don't really know what my future plans are. I guess I don't have any... so I'm certainly free to check out these Goddess temples."

"Plans will be made soon enough. All will be taken care of once we reach Tennir. You and your people will be protected."

I smile, "I hope that's true, but this is just a *huge* transition... I don't know what's waiting for us. Refugees aren't often treated well on my own planet. I don't know what to expect out here." I rub my temples. "How about you tell me about these Goddesses? I don't want to have to worry right now."

He nods his understanding and begins his tale of how the universe was created.

"The Goddesses created the universe and all life. Maia, Asterope, and Pleione." He ticks off each goddess on his fingers. He has five, I notice, but his thumb is set more toward his wrist than mine. His fingers are each tipped by sharp curved claws. They are like a lion's, or the talons on a hawk. "Sisters," he continues, "Maia was the scientist. She experimented and created. She made the stars and the worlds among them. She created oceans, mountains, and trees and set in motion the laws of physics."

"Busy girl."

"Indeed," he smiles. "Asterope had a light within her, she longed to create something to keep her interest. So, she made all beings and took joy in watching their lives. The small things were exciting to her--work, emotions, building, creating. The things all creatures do. She created life and she was happy."

"And then there was Pleione. Pleione watched Maia build all of the universe. She saw Maia's passion for it. She watched Asterope create all life and revel in their daily lives. Pleione longed to find her purpose. So, she searched the worlds. She took to watching the beings and was taken by the idea of love. So, Pleione created the first male."

"So, there were no men before Pleione created one? Just a bunch of women?"

"Females? Yes. All the universe held was the perfect form. The female form. Strong, powerful, beautiful. Each with the ability to create life just as the Goddesses had. Each with the ability to revel in all they could build and create. It was peaceful and perfect."

"Yeah, but was there romantic love?"

"Of course. And that was what Pleione longed for, not for the people, but for herself. This is why she created a male. Her desire was not pure. It was not selfless and it made her creation flawed. He was angry--within him was the capacity for malice: to hurt others, to steal, for jealousy, rape and war. He saw what the sisters had built and was jealous of their power. He was jealous of Pleione too, but she loved him and was blind to his flaws."

"One day he came to Pleione in a rage. He demanded she give him the power she and her sisters possessed. She tried to explain it did not work that way, but he refused to believe her. He killed Pleione and fled."

"Traveling the galaxy, he was like a plague. He whispered in the ears of all the beings he came across, spreading hate and rape and war. He was a poison on all the sisters had created. Maia and Asterope found their sister Pleione, dead, and set out after the first male. They could not undo what he had done to Pleione, but they hoped to save what they themselves had created and to protect the universe from the ugliness of the first male."

"It is said they chase him still, one step behind, touching each place he has poisoned trying to save it. They will find him one day and when it is done the universe will know nothing but peace," Rennek finishes.

"Wow. That's beautiful and tragic... and kind of super negative towards men. I thought Eve had it bad," I joke--though I know the reference will be lost on him.

"Help me understand *men* and *Eve*," he asks.

"Men is equivalent to males," I explain. "In my culture there's a story about the first male and female. The female gets the bad rap though, but that's kind of how it is on Earth overall. Do these beliefs affect the roles of males and females?" I ask and he rubs his chin considering my question.

"I have never thought on this before. It is females who rule in the Governing Core. Females are looked to for wisdom... Males are judged on their honor towards females." He is thoughtful, but then I see his expression darken. "Crimes against females are not common, it is not only illegal--but blasphemous." He stares at me a moment longer and then rubs his hands over his face, weary. "I am so sorry for what you have endured, my Kate."

Now, I watch him. He really is something. He's gorgeous, like an Adonis. He truly looks carved from stone. His weird alien features make him majestic and magical in appearance. He's got these crazy ram horns on his head for Christ's sake. His gaze returns to me and we take each other in. I get nervous and look down at the table--our hands are near one another. I take a chance and reach over, taking his hand in mine. It's huge. My hand is dwarfed by his rock-hard hand. We trace each other's fingers and palms transiently, exploring. I touch his claws.

"These look like trouble," I say smiling at him.

"They can be." His expression is serious.

"How do you do anything with such sharp things on your hands?" He is silent for a moment before he speaks.

"Either very rough," he looks me in the eyes, "or very gentle." He pulls my hand slowly to his mouth and kisses my wrist.

We stay frozen in that moment for I don't know how long, until the ship careens to one side. Rennek and I are thrown to the floor. The lights in the room turn red and a siren starts blaring.

"Rennek!" I scream, but he is there by my side in an instant, lifting me up.

"Are you hurt?" He asks.

"No, I'm fine... are you okay?"

"Come with me," he shouts over the siren.

"But the other girls?" I ask, hesitant to follow him. I should go to the others, right?

"Come! We will take care of them, I do not want you to leave my side." His eyes are urgent, and he is pretty much a superhero in my eyes... so, I find I have no desire to decline. I take his hand and we race down the corridors.

Chapter 13

Rennek

The ship is under attack. This is a strange development, considering we are in protected space. I assume this attack is either linked to the females or there are some very bold pirates attempting to raid our cargo holds.

"All hands to the bridge, I repeat, all hands to the bridge." Various voices reply on the comms and when we reach the bridge Da'vi and Kellen are still at their posts and Bossan and Dax come running in.

I put Kate in the captain's chair and turn to my crew, "What have we got?"

"Multiple crafts. Unmarked. Three, four... I count five, sir." Kellen tells me.

"Confirmed. Five crafts. I'm scanning their weaponry now. I'm seeing moderate fire power." Da'vi punches the control panels. "Correction, the big one's a fighter ship...it's got big guns. The other crafts are the ship's pods and drones."

"What are the weapon systems on a fighter?"

"The main ship is going to have the majority of the power, the pods and drones won't be as much of a threat, but they will try and keep us busy so the fighter can do its damage. The good news is we still outgun them thanks to all our mods," Dax informs us.

"Have they tried to send any comms?" I ask.

"No sir, just came out of nowhere and started firing. Our shields are on full. I began evasive procedures immediately."

"Dax, get on navigation," I want my best pilot at the controls.

"Yes sir!" Dax leaps into the main nav seat and starts to work his magic.

"Da'vi, Bossan, artillery!" But Da'vi ignores me, working his screens furiously. Suddenly he curses and leaps to his feet, running out of the room.

"What the hell," Kate says, holding the armrests tightly as the ship leans heavily from side to side.

Bossan, Kellen and I stare after him. *What the hell*, indeed.

"Kellen, take his place." Bossan and Kellen are on artillery now. "Keep eyes on the fighter." They begin to return fire. I go to the comm.

"This is Captain Rennek. Identify yourselves!" I set the message to repeat.

I hear hollering down the corridor coming our way, Kate whips her head around. I recognize that it is her language we are hearing. Da'vi runs into the room with the one called Allison over his shoulder, flailing her arms wildly and trying desperately to kick at my friend--a pointless effort. Her small form is not likely to do much damage to his massive one.

"Da'vi?!" I am in shock.

"This one was going into cargo hold three!"

"Secure her," I tell him and he moves her to one of the seats against the wall and begins to buckle her in.

"What the hell's going on here?" Kate cries as the ship rattles from another blow.

"I'll tell you what's going on!" Allison fumes. "These fuckers have *tigers* in their cargo hold! These lying sacks of shit said they have never been to Earth! They're in on it! The whole ship is probably full of stolen Earth stuff!"

"What?" Kate looks from Allison to me. "Is this true Rennek?"

"Everyone hold on!" Dax calls as the ship lurches hard. I hang on to a control panel to keep myself upright.

"Sweet Kate, I do not know what *tigers* are," I try to keep patience in my tone, but we have much more important concerns than whatever this Allison is angry about.

"Yeah, and I bet you don't know what *humans* are either you fuck. We're probably just animal research in your eyes! Is this some fucked up test to see how we respond?" Allison shouts accusingly.

"Tigers are big cats Rennek. Orange. Black stripes. Sharp teeth?" Kate explains hastily, a question in her eyes. I know we have only just met but I hate that she doubts me.

"We have many cats in our cargo hold," I tell her, exasperated by this ill-timed conversation.

"From the Ju'tup, Rennek," Bossan yells to me. Ah yes, I had nearly forgotten.

"Yes, yes, yes. We have these *tigers*, we bought them from the Ju'tup and loaded them to our ship before we realized you and your people were aboard. They were going to sell them to fight rings--we bought them so they would be protected." Allison shuts her mouth and crosses her arms. Kate looks to her, but she refuses to make eye contact. When her eyes find mine, she seems to be appeased by my explanation.

"Rennek, are the other girls... er females okay? Can we let them know what is going on?" She asks.

I engage the comm. "You may speak to them."

"Like out loud?" She asks confused. Da'vi clicks his tongue impatiently at her. I growl in his direction. I do not appreciate this strange attitude he is taking on. He has never ignored an order before and his rude behavior towards the females does not match what I know of him.

"I turned on the comms, they can hear you now." I explain. "Da'vi, take over artillery for Bossan. Bossan, try and force a comm link with the main ship." My crew moves fluidly to their stations. I shake the pain of Kate's mistrust away as I focus on protecting my ship and all those on board. I will earn her trust in time with my actions, I vow.

Chapter 14

Kate

"What the hell is happening?" Reagan shouts. We can hear sobs and screams each time the ship lurches.

"Ladies, we are under attack by another ship, but the guys are handling it. Everything is going to be okay. Just sit tight."

"I'm going to be car sick!" Vivian yells.

"Sit tight! Sit tight?" Reagan yells hysterically into the comms before Rennek cuts them off.

"Got it! Forcing link now," Bossan tells Rennek.

Suddenly the window clouds and an image of a creature appears.

"Holy fuck!" I shout.

Rennek and his crew look quickly to me, before they resume their efforts. The alien on the screen slowly begins to laugh. He looks like he's all muscle and by that, I mean he looks like someone peeled off his skin and all I can see are his muscles and tendons that should be hidden beneath a layer of flesh. His face is like a bat's--all scrunched up and weird, and he has teeth like a snake. He looks like something out of a horror movie. I shudder to think his attention is on me in the captain's chair. Rennek steps protectively in front of me.

"Identify yourself." Rennek says in a cold growl and I remember he is just as intimidating. I lean far to the side in the chair so I can watch this drama unfold. Mr. No-skin licks his lips. Yup, snake-like. My skin crawls.

"You," he points at my gargoyle, "I kill you. And your females? Those I take." He spits the words and his red eyes roll in his head. I see he has no eyelids.

Rennek seems to be thrown off by his statement. He has no witty comeback, like they would in a movie, he just swings his wings wide open and lets out a roar that makes me jump and cover my ears.

"Why are you doing this?" I plead.

No-skin's eyes roll again, it seems like this is his version of a blink, and he speaks, "Winged one. Crew. There is bounty. Females, no bounty on females. They just prize."

"A bounty on us," Rennek growls. "Who do you collect from?"

"Ju'tup. You make them angry. I see why," he eyes Allison, leering at her. "You kill wrong Ju'tup winged one. You start war."

For some reason I think Rennek is shaken by this freak's words, but he brings it back in quick. "You will earn no bounty and you will have no prize besides death. Continue to fight and this will be your last rotation. I beg you bounty hunter, stay and fight," Rennek tells the bounty hunter.

The freak throws his head back and laughs again before the comms cut out.

"Fire everything we have. Burn him," Rennek says in a murderous tone.

Our aliens go crazy on the control panels. It's hard to tell what is going on, so I watch their faces to get a read on how we are faring. I try to see what's happening through the window, but we aren't always facing the ships and drones or whatever they are. We make a sweeping spin and then suddenly I see two small objects directly ahead of us. I don't know if these are the pods or drones. Then I see them starting to spit fire at us.

"Prepare for impact," Dax shouts a second before we ram them. Our ship shakes in response. "Drones both disabled," he says and I think I hear excitement in his voice. Oh my god, is he enjoying this?

"Any systems damage reported?" Rennek shouts over the sirens.

"Analyzing... Mild shield deterioration, exterior collision points intact," Kellen reports.

"Round the turrets and lock onto the pods," Rennek tells Da'vi.

The pods prove to be slightly more difficult to deal with. I'm guessing it's because they actually have pilots inside them. Regardless, Dax gets even more creative with his maneuvering and I start praying I won't be sick *again* today. One explosion follows the next and the ship quakes in response. Suddenly, the main ship--the *fighter*, is visible through the window at the front of the bridge. My heart pounds in my chest. I look to Allison, but she doesn't return my gaze. She is staring wide eyed at the massive ship before us. I hope the other girls are alright in their quarters and that they have something to hold onto. Suddenly, I feel very small and alone, but then Rennek locks eyes with me. He looks like the embodiment of confidence and determination and I realize that although this situation is terrifying--I trust him to protect us.

"Missiles," Rennek says.

"He's engaging warp, sir," comes a shout from one of his men.

"Lock and launch," Rennek orders.

I see the bounty hunter's ship turn and start to stretch. It confuses me for a second before I realize it must be an optical illusion or something, from going into warp. Suddenly, the bounty hunter's ship snaps like a rubber band and vanishes just as our ship's missiles speed towards it. Our missile vanishes along with the bounty hunter's ship. Then, far in the distance I see an explosion.

"Scan for life or any escape pods."

"No sign of escape pod activation. No life detected," Kellen announces.

The sirens that have been a constant background noise this whole time shut down and the red flashing lights vanish along with it. Rennek leans heavily on a control panel and hangs his head. The other aliens look just as weary. Allison starts fumbling with her seat belt. Da'vi is by her side quickly and unlatches her. She swats him away and before storming off the bridge she yells to Rennek, "Tell your lizard to keep his damn hands off me!"

"This human does not understand her translator makes it so we can all comprehend her words, just as she does not understand to keep her distance from dangerous beasts. Perhaps her mind was damaged in cryo-stasis?" Da'vi hisses to Rennek as he glares hard at Allison.

"Fuck you," Allison says.

"Da'vi! Allison!" Rennek gives a rumbling shout. Allison storms out, flipping us all the bird.

"Da'vi, it is unacceptable to treat these females in such a way," Rennek tells his friend sternly.

"She is foolish, she was going to get herself killed in the cargo hold," he justifies.

"Enough, Da'vi. Heed my warning. If you are worried for their safety you must teach them what is safe and what to avoid on the ship. They will need to learn these things," Rennek orders.

"Apologies Captain," I can't help but notice Rennek growl at Da'vi's response.

"And Kate," he turns to me, "You and the other females... I must encourage you to stop speaking of mating, it does not seem appropriate at the times you bring it up. Is there a malfunction with your translator that is causing this? Surely Allison did not wish to mate... or you with the bounty hunter?"

"What the fuck are you talking about?" I ask in complete and utter shock, maybe there *is* something wrong with the translator because that sounds like crazy talk to me.

"Ohhh! Wait, 'fuck'? Is it because we said 'fuck'?" All the aliens avert their eyes. If aliens could blush, I think to myself. "That's just like an exclamation or a curse word... it can be used a lot of ways actually. Not just for... mating. Gosh, how many times have we said 'fuck'?" Rennek stiffens and the others all try to look busy.

"I'll tell the ladies to clean it up," I tell him. "Thanks. Wouldn't want to make that mistake again in the wrong company," I chuckle and he nods to me before turning back to his crew.

"We need to notify Tennir of this new development immediately--see if we can get a UPC escort."

"Of course, Captain."

"I said, *enough* with this Captain shit," he shouts, losing control of his temper a bit. The other guys, the ones who look like Rennek at least, all look away as he says this, but Da'vi looks at him, incredulous. They stare hard at each other for a few hot seconds before Da'vi breaks his gaze away.

The calm and quiet filling the bridge is a stark contrast to the chaos of a few moments ago. Rennek approaches me.

"You must rest," he says quietly, so only I can hear.

"The others--I need to make sure they're okay... I need to let them know what happened," I tell him.

"Quickly, but then you rest," he tells me with concern etching his face.

"What about you?" I ask.

"There is much work to be done still."

I want to argue--they all need rest just as much as we humans do, but my survival instincts tell me to shut up and let the space men work.

Chapter 15

Rennek

When I finally make my way to my quarters hours later I am so tired I could fall asleep 'before my head hits the pillow' as my clever Kate said. I check the prompter in my quarters and see all the females are safely in their own quarters. Hopefully sleeping peacefully. I run my hands through my mane. This has been the longest rotation of my life. I guess technically it has been two rotations, only I have yet to sleep.

I am pained we had to end more lives on this day, but I would do it all again. The safety of the females is all that matters. I am troubled by the desire to protect at all costs. I would have destroyed a thousand ships to protect my sweet Kate, but that thought is dangerous. It goes against everything I was raised to honor. Yes, you fight to uphold the law. Yes, you fight to protect the innocent. I have taken pleasure in battle before but never so much it felt like sin. This is stronger. This is different. There is a fire within me. The pleasure I took in this battle and bringing an end to the bounty hunter who dared threaten my Kate? It worries me. What must she think of me after all the bloodshed she has seen? Does she fear me? Does she trust me? Unfortunately, none of that is as important as her safety. I will do what I must, even if it means she comes to hate me.

Even now it seems we are all still in danger--there is a bounty on us. I am not even sure why. I thought the Ju'tup would fight among themselves and move on. If they are not trying to retrieve the human females then why do they bother? I must bring an end to all this danger, for I fear what I will do to keep them safe.

I remove my holster and waistcloth and decide on a quick shower before I sleep. I step into the small personal bathing unit and let the hot water run over me. My mind is instantly brought back to the moments Kate and I were able to spend alone in the dining hall. She let me touch her, let me kiss her wrist. It was bliss to me. I lean my horns against the shower wall. It seems I will forgo rest for one more task. I take myself in my hand at the thought of the sweet taste of her skin on my lips. She was as soft as petals, it makes me wonder how her most precious parts will feel against my tongue.

I imagine Kate slipping into the shower with me and running those smooth hands down my chest and stomach. Would she be as bold in mating as she is with all else? Would she caress my cock? Or wrap her long, smooth legs around my waist and welcome me into her soft, wet folds? I pump my cock harder and think of burying my face in her hair and breathing in her scent as I drive home into her sweet cunt. I long to hear her scream my name and beg me to fuck her harder. My cock has hardened nearly every moment I have been in her presence since we met. It doesn't take long before I am ready to spill my seed.

She will be my mate. I know this in my core. She will want me--no. She will need me, as I need her. It may take her time to realize she and I are meant to be one, but I will be patient. As patient as I can be. I think of the desire I saw in her eyes as I kissed her wrist... her heavy-lidded eyes... the sweet part of her moist lips. I imagine tasting those lips.

I spill my seed with a long low growl, pumping every last drop out. What a waste that it is not filling her warm cunt. How long will it take to seduce my sweet Kate, I wonder? I think of the look in her eyes again and I think it will not be long.

I dry off and lie naked on my bed. May the goddesses be with me and send Kate into my chambers for something. Anything. I would pull her into the bed with me and hold her all night long. My cock is still hard as I drift off to sleep.

Chapter 16

Kate

At first my sleep is so heavy, I have no dreams. But as my slumber wears on I start to dream of bright lights and trying to struggle but being unable to move. I don't know if this is a memory surfacing or just a reaction to the whole alien abduction situation I have found myself in. By the time I wake up it feels like I have slept for days. I feel refreshed, but now I'm starving. I use the toilet and straighten my hair a bit with my fingers then wrap my blanket dress around me and start to make my way to the dining hall. I hastily decide instead to check and see if any of the other girls want to join me. I push the prompter on the outside of the door closest to mine, I remember this room is Reagan's.

"Hey! Are you up?"

"Yeah, come on in." The door whizzes open.

"Did you get some sleep?" I ask her.

She flops down on her bed. Her hair's a mess and she has dark circles under her eyes. "Yes and no. I slept a lot, but I keep having nightmares."

"Yeah, I had some weird dreams too," I say. "Want to talk about it?"

"I don't know. I think I was just dreaming of home. Of people I won't ever see again." She doesn't meet my gaze.

"I'm so sorry Reagan." I reflect for a second. "I feel like I haven't even really had a chance to process that yet. With everything going on I haven't even made space in my mind to worry about it. Were you close to your family?"

"Honestly, there probably won't be anyone who even notices I'm gone."

"Yeah, actually it's the same for me," I scoff at the pathetic realization. "My landlord will most likely be the only one to notice. It'll be months before my mom even tries to call me. I'm usually the one to call her and my job was heading south, so they'll probably just think I quit."

"I haven't spoken to my mom in three years and I just found out my drug dealing piece of shit boyfriend was cheating on me, he'll think I just left him. No one will ever even *know* I'm gone."

We fall into silence, reflecting on our revelations. "Well, look at what a couple of sad sacks we are! Looks like being abducted might be the best thing to ever happen to us!" I laugh, but Reagan sits on that for a second.

"You know, you might be right."

Just then my stomach decides to protest the lack of food in it and growls loudly. "You hungry? Want to go see if any of the other girls want to get a bite to eat?"

"Sure, wait a second while I freshen up?"

"Of course."

I hear water running in the little sink/toilet room. "Hey Kate?" Reagan calls.

"Yeah?"

"You think that's why they took us?"

"What do you mean?"

She steps into the doorway, "Because no one will be looking for us."

"Yeah, that's a good theory. Let's ask the others and see if there are any other similarities."

We check the other rooms, but Clark is the only other girl around and she joins our little posse. The others must already be in the dining hall. I mean, I can't imagine where else they'd be. I start to wonder about Rennek and if he ever got any rest. He was so troubled the last time I saw him. I then I start to wonder about alien abduction rescue etiquette and if I should let him know we are up and about the ship. After I eat, I'll definitely go find him. Just to be polite.

"What are you smiling about?" Reagan asks.

"Huh? Smiling? I'm just excited to eat, I guess." Deflecting, I change the subject, "Oh hey, Clark? Reagan and I were talking and we noticed a similarity that might be coincidence or it might be the reason aliens abducted us…"

"What's that?" She asks.

"Well, neither of us are close to our families and… well, it doesn't seem like anyone will be looking for us, for quite some time at least," I tell her.

"Yeah," she reflects, "I suppose that's actually true for me too. Well, I was close with my parents, but they died a few years ago in a car accident. Then my grandma passed about a year after that. I really only have my cousins now and they won't even think of me until Christmastime."

"Oh, my goodness, I'm so sorry about your parents and your grandmother, how tragic!" I tell her.

"Thanks, yeah. It's been a lot to go through in a short amount of time. Add an alien abduction in the mix and I've got years worth of therapy ahead of me," she jokes.

"I wonder if there's anything else we all have in common?" Reagan asks as we get to the dining hall.

"Now's the perfect time to find out," I say. The other three girls are here, though it doesn't seem like they've been here long because they don't have any food yet.

"Good morning ladies!" I say cheerfully.

"Hey! Maybe you guys can help with this food thing. We haven't been having any luck," Vivian says.

"Vivian and I don't have a translator yet, so we're pretty much useless," April tells us.

"Let me see what I can do..." In a few minutes everyone has ceata with emon and I kind of feel like a champ. Unfortunately, I can't do much in the way of real food. The only thing I know the name of is what we ate yesterday and no one is in the mood for more stew. I still don't know enough about alien food to order anything else from the synthesizer.

"Maybe we should call one of the guys for help?" I suggest. Rennek would be a big help...

"No! Let's try and figure it out ourselves. I could do without aliens for a little bit longer." Vivian says apologetically. "It's just when they're here I can't ignore the fact that we were abducted by aliens. Like this," she gestures towards all of us, "I can pretend this is like... I don't know... a girl's weekend."

"What kind of girl's weekends do you go on?" Allison says in a blank voice which makes everything sound like a burn.

"Anyway, Reagan and Clark and I were talking and we realized, given our family life and stuff back home on Earth, that maybe one reason we were abducted is because no one will be missing us right away. Does that ring true for anyone else?" All the girls give a little info on their immediate family and confirm it will be unlikely anyone will be searching for them.

"Well, that's not true for me." Allison says. "My job will probably be freaking out first thing Monday morning, if that hasn't passed already. I am a crucial member of the design and marketing team at my company. They'll notify my family and my boyfriend right away. I am probably all over the news right now. One of that sad, all-American girl gone missing, great unsolved mystery things."

"Oh, I wonder why they took you then?" Clark says.

"I don't know. Maybe I have the universe's universal blood type or something. But people will be missing me, I'm sorry if that's not true for the rest of you," she shrugs.

"I wonder if we have any other things in common though?" Reagan asks.

Allison looks at Reagan slowly from head to toe. "I strongly doubt it," She says before she gets up and marches over to a comm unit. "We need help with food in the dining hall, thanks." She is either oblivious to or completely ignoring the fact that Vivian *just* said she wasn't ready for another alien encounter. Thankfully, April casually takes a seat next to Vivian, in an obvious effort to offer support. I appreciate the supportive attitude. It seems not all of us share it. When I look at Reagan I see she's fuming.

"And what the fuck is that supposed to mean?" Reagan bristles.

"I'm sorry, what is it you don't understand?" Allison says flatly.

"Look bitch, I don't need or appreciate your dirty ass looks. Throw another one my way and I'll throw a punch to that stuck up face of yours."

"Whoa, guys! Seriously? Calm the hell down! We're like, the only six humans in all of this fucked up outer space nightmare and we're seriously going to be at each other's throats?" I say looking from Reagan to Allison.

"I'm not at anyone's throat. It's not my fault she's upset. I'm just not in the same situation as the rest of you. People will miss me." Allison's tone is calm and she truly looks as unaffected as ever, but Reagan on the other hand looks like she's about to follow through on her promise. I leap in between them to stop Reagan from beating Allison's ass.

At that moment Da'vi stalks into the dining hall. He pauses and surveys us momentarily, reading the tension.

"Great," Allison says retreating to lean against a far wall. Da'vi glares at her and lets a low growl escape his throat. Vivian jumps. I take this as my cue to rally his attention and get some help with the food synthesizer. Let's just change the subject and get food for everyone--stay positive, move forward, I tell myself.

"Hi! Da'vi, right? We're trying to get some breakfast going. Can you help us out?"

"What would you like?" He asks gruffly.

"Any requests ladies?" I ask in English for the benefit of those who don't have translators yet.

"A big, fat breakfast burrito," April says. "Or an Egg McMuffin."

"Oh my god, I'll never have another Egg McMuffin," Vivian sobs.

"Dang, Big Egg McMuffin fan?" April asks her.

"No, I hate McDonalds. I haven't eaten there in years, but now I don't even have the option, you know?"

Da'vi is giving his best impression of patience.

"How about it lizard boy, can you make us breakfast burritos?" Allison asks, barely looking at him.

"I do not know what this is." Da'vi tells us, glaring at Allison. Seems like her attitude is winning her all sorts of friends.

"A breakfast burrito has like, eggs meat, potatoes, veggies sometimes… and it's all wrapped in a tortilla. Which is like a thin, flat bread," I explain as best I can.

He nods and starts to work at the synthesizer. A bowl comes out and he shakes it before popping the lid off. It's steaming. Then, he pulls a pouch from a drawer and pours it over the top of the bowl, it foams up and solidifies. Lastly, the synthesizer produces something looking like a ball of dough. He takes it all to one of the tables and rips off a piece of the dough and kneads it flat. He spoons a helping of the stuff in the bowl onto the dough and folds it over. He holds it out to Allison. She steps forward to grab it, but he pulls back taking a big bite just as she reaches for it.

"Enjoy," he says and he stalks out chewing, without a glance back.

"Hah!" Reagan says.

"Thank you!" I yell after him and we crowd around the strange alien food. We each rip off pieces of the dough and tentatively smell everything.

"Smells okay," Vivian says.

"Might as well start indoctrinating ourselves now." Clark says, "There won't be any McDonald's in our future."

We silently take a few bites, nodding to one another as we eat. It's better than I thought it would be. The foamy stuff is *kind of* like fake eggs and whatever was in the bowl is *kind of* like root vegetables. The textures are all off though and it makes it doubly strange that we are eating it on dough instead of bread or a tortilla.

"No more chocolate," Vivian says, breaking the silence.

"No more guacamole. Or avocados in general," Reagan says a little teary.

"Bacon wrapped hot dogs," April says.

"Sushi."

"Pizza."

"Coffee."

"Root beer floats," I add.

"Beer," Allison says and we all laugh.

"Oh no, I hope these aren't some Puritan aliens who don't drink," April laments.

"This is outer space, not hell. Of course they'll have booze," Clark offers.

"I don't know. Feels like hell to me," Allison says and we eat in silence for a bit after that.

Once we finish eating the conversation goes back to things we all might have in common and Allison leaves without saying a word.

"Bitch," Reagan says once she's gone.

"I didn't want to be the one to say it..." April agrees.

"Come on, this is hard on all of us in different ways guys. Allison is struggling like the rest of us. Let's not make her an outsider," I think of how unwelcoming the people were when I started working at the bank and how it felt like that had shaped my success... or lack thereof.

"Kate's right. Maybe she's just one of those people who pushes others away when they're stressed. We don't know what she's going through. Let's give her time. It's important we all support each other," Vivian adds. Everyone grudgingly agrees.

I realize this is the first time we have all really been able to talk. It's nice, even if the subject matter is a little dark. Turns out, other than Allison, no one is going to be looking for the rest of us. We are all in our twenties, although we range from 20 to 26. We think we were all taken at night. Most of us had already gone to bed, but Clark and April had been showering last they could remember--which explains their nudity when we woke from the cryo bags. None of us have any memories of who took us or how. We are all from the west coast, seems like we were on a travel path for whoever took us. But, that's where the similarities end. Our jobs, educations and anything else we can think of are all unique to each of us. It seems we were just convenient to take and the right age for slaves, I guess.

"So, we have been abducted by aliens and hopefully rescued by some good guys. Now what?" Reagan asks.

"Now we meet this Tennir guy and Rennek's government and they decide what to do with us," I say, but it doesn't feel right to be so passive about this. "We should all think about what we want for our lives, in case we get some level of choice or if we get to make requests. We should be prepared for that, maybe be on the same page. If we want to stay together, that is."

"I don't know you guys all that well, but we're all of humanity that's out here. We *should* stick together," Clark says.

"I agree." I'm filled with the confidence that this is the right move. We must be a team.

"Well, I can't promise to be friends with Allison, but I'm down for sticking together," Reagan concurs and we all laugh.

"I have to say Kate..." Clark begins, "What you did back there for us... I want to thank you."

"What do you mean?" I ask, a little confused.

"With the alien... the bad one," her voice catches.

"You protected us Kate, all of us," April finishes for her.

"Oh! Of course. I just did what anyone would do," I shrug it off.

"But no, you didn't. You did what the rest of us couldn't do. I always thought if I were in a life or death scenario I would be able to handle myself. Or at least if I were in a fight or flight scenario I would *fight*--but instead I just froze. You didn't. Thank you," April tells me and the rest of the girls echo it.

"And thanks for the clothes. It wasn't like anyone had much, but being so exposed was the most terrifying thing I have ever experienced. Thank you for sacrificing what you had to help us," Clark adds.

"Seriously guys, anytime," I tell them all.

"Don't forget she was also the guinea pig for the translation thing," Reagan adds.

"Come on guys! You're making me blush!" I tease, trying to lighten the mood. I'm not used to so much praise.

"Well, hopefully we can return the favor one day," Reagan says.

"Deal, next time *you* get to be the guinea pig," I tell her before Vivian pulls us all in for a hug.

After a minute I put my hand in for a team hand stack, "Team Human?" I say.

"Team Human!" We all cheer.

"Oh, oh, oh and guys! Before I forget! We really need to curb the F-bombs…"

***

Eventually all the girls head back to their rooms. I'm the last to my door... I start to go in, but I hesitate, considering my options. Just then, Vivian pops out of her room.

"Hey, what are you up to?" I ask.

"I was thinking I'd go see Allison. Try to bond or connect or something. I feel like she's more alone than the rest of us."

"That's a really good idea," I say sincerely. "Do you want any back up?"

"Let's see if she does better one on one first. I don't want it to feel like an intervention, you know?" She smiles sweetly.

"You are full of good ideas. Holler if you need help!" I tell her as she heads to Allison's room. I'm glad Vivian is offering an olive branch. Allison needs it whether she realizes it yet or not. I'm also glad because I had been considering going to see Allison myself, but now... I think I'll go see about an alien instead.

Chapter 17

Rennek

My door chimes. I have the lighting set to complete darkness and it takes me a moment to wake up and register the sound. Groggy, I go to my door and open it. There stands my Kate. Is this a dream I wonder? Her eyes go wide and travel down my naked form, stopping at my cock. She turns a lovely shade of red.

"Oh, um sorry, you're still sleeping! I'll just..." Kate turns to hurry away, but I grab her arm. Our eyes meet ever so briefly before we hear Bossan and Kellen coming down the corridor. She looks down the hall and then back to me. Before I have time to think I pull her into my room. The door hisses shut and we are surrounded in darkness and Kate is wrapped tight in my arms. I instantly admonish myself for such an impulsive action, but my sweet Kate surprises me and her arms creep up around my neck. The drumming within me pounds again, it is like a song calling me into action. I can't resist the call and I will not waste such a precious moment. My lips find hers in the darkness.

The feeling of being near my Kate, of having her welcome my touch--it is like I am waking for the first time in my life. I have never been as sensitive to sensation and as aware as I am now, every part of my body reacts to this female. Every cell is alight with the fire she creates in me.

My female is short, so I lift her to meet my lips. Just as I had imagined in the shower, she wraps her legs tightly around my waist. My length rests against her core and I press her back against the wall.

Our first kiss is ragged and needy--desperate. I pull away and nuzzle her nose. Panting, we breathe in each other's air. I run my cheek along hers and smell her delicate scent. My tongue slides along her earlobe and she lets a small moan escape her lips. She is intoxicating, my mate. I growl with neediness for more of her and devour her mouth. Her soft tongue plays tentatively at the seam of my lips, I suck on the tip and tease it with my fangs. Her hands run wildly through my mane, she pulls at it bringing me closer to her, controlling our kiss.

Throwing her head back, she invites me to discover the sweetness of her neck. I lick the long line of her throat and scrape my teeth gently across the space where her shoulder and neck meet. She whimpers at this and our lips find each other's again. She is as hungry for this as I am, I revel. I silently thank the Goddesses for aligning the universe in a way that brought us to this moment. My core swells with the joy and wonder of it.

Her hands begin to explore my body--sliding over my arms and shoulders, up my neck and digging into my mane. Eventually her hands find my horns and grips them tightly. I never thought my horns to be sensitive, but the image of her gripping them is the most erotic thing I can imagine. I growl uncontrollably, barely stifling a roar building in my throat. I feel my sack tighten, even though it was not long ago I spilled my seed in the shower. I feel I could cum simply from listening to the soft sounds she makes in the darkness. It is music to me.

I take Kate's lead and I start to explore her body. My hands find her hips, her wrap dress has spread open from the waist down and I am rewarded with bare skin. There is nothing between us but a thin scrap of material which covers her most private parts--the parts of her that belong to me now. I am eager to taste that sweetness, but there is so much sweetness to my Kate. I will take my time and enjoy every inch of her--slowly, again and again. I knead the curves of her hips and ass. She is all softness. When I grip the globes of her ass she responds by grinding her pussy against my cock and I nearly lose all control. I spin and throw her onto the bed, she rolls so she is on top of me, but pops up suddenly.

"Is this okay? Your wings… is it uncomfortable like this?" All I can do is laugh, my sweet little human mate. I could feel nothing but comfort in her presence. Well, perhaps comfort and lust driven madness. I answer by pulling her back down to me and I feel her smile against my kiss. Her hands play across my chest and as we continue to kiss frantically she begins to ride me as if we are mating. I can feel her wetness through the thin scrap of fabric she wears. The scent of her juices fills the room and my mouth begins to water. I will cum if we continue like this. I grab her hips and lift her up to my mouth, eager to have my female cum before I do.

"Whoa! Times! Timeout!" She jerks off of me. I sit up, unsure of what these words mean. "Lights! Lights! How do you turn the lights on?" *Ah*, she would like to watch me as I lick her cunt. My Kate is as smart as she is beautiful.

Chapter 18

Kate

Okay, that escalated quickly. Rennek turns the lights up so we can see each other. I trip out for a second because I realize I just had a make out/grinding session with a straight up alien. He's all horns and tail and grey skin... and muscles... and complete hotness... Is it weird I think he's so hot? That's a little weird right? I look at him again. He draws himself up on his elbow and smiles at me. It's a lazy, happy smile. He takes my hand and laces our fingers together. Claws notwithstanding, it feels natural.

"Let me lick your pussy now, sweet Kate." He says bringing my hand to his lips--his licks and kisses are like promises. I blush so hard I think I might pass out. I mean, I'm no virgin but I haven't ever experienced such blunt talk before *and* I didn't actually mean to come into Rennek's room and do all this. Oh my god, he's going to think I'm a tease. I hope I didn't mess up anything for the other humans and myself by getting into this mess. I hope he isn't angry.

"Pump the breaks buddy."

"You have mentioned this *buddy*, what is this? And more importantly, tell me what you would like me to pump?" He laughs, sliding his hand up and down my leg that is still draped over his waist. I can't help but laugh. He has this weird way about him, where one minute he seems so sweet and almost naive, but then I catch onto his sense of humor and his guile. I relax into him and he adjusts so I am laying in the crook of his arm. Our hands entwine.

"You wish to stop." He says, it isn't a question.

"I'm sorry. It just started happening faster than I intended... not that I intended, it just kind of happened. And then it was happening fast..."

He tilts his head to look me in the eyes, studying me a moment before he speaks. "You do not owe me anything Kate, you do not have to do anything you do not want or are not ready for."

It feels good to hear those words. "I want you to know I don't usually move that fast," I tell him. "I don't want you to get the wrong idea about me. I haven't been with a lot of guys, plus I don't know how all this stuff works in space. I only know Earth dating rules... Not that we're dating!" I add quickly, I don't want him to think I'm clingy or that I'm under the impression we're suddenly in a relationship just because we messed around a little.

I can't help but reflect on our encounter, though. It's weird for me, because I *never* move this fast. I never chase guys or go looking for them in their bedrooms. Maybe it's because Rennek saved me, but I feel drawn to him.

"Some of the things you say do not translate well..." he tells me. "Kate, I need to know," he sits up a little to look at me with a serious expression. "Have I frightened you? There has been much bloodshed under the circumstances. You have seen me kill." The look on his face is so solemn it's almost cute. He thinks I'm afraid of him because of the things he's done to protect us. I try not to laugh. I mean, maybe you can chalk it up to the fact that I grew up with no parental controls on my TV and I've been desensitized by American action movies or something, but I have *no* qualms over anyone Rennek has killed. I honestly hadn't even thought twice about it. I'll wonder if that makes me a bad person later.

"Yeah... no. No fear at all, don't even worry about that." I tell him. "Rennek you saved me. You saved all of us. Everything you have done since we met has been to keep us all safe. I don't fear you, I trust you completely." He rolls over me and looks deep into my eyes, with a look I can only describe as gratitude, before he kisses me.

"Stay with me here, my Kate," he says against my lips.

"Okay," I tell him, trying to channel Allison's casualness, but inside I'm giddy--like something is starting here, between Rennek and I. We're quiet in each other's arms as he runs his fingers through my hair, playing with it. I think he smells me a couple times too, and god help me, I think it's cute.

"Rennek? What's going to happen to us? Us humans, I mean."

"We will meet with Tennir in a few short days. I am hoping an escort will come and travel with us the remainder of the way. I am waiting to hear back from the UPC, but their communications go through Tennir."

"Why don't they just talk directly to you?"

"Tennir's status. His relationship to the government," Rennek says.

"So, who is this Tennir guy? Is he like your boss?"

"Yes and no. Tennir is my brother. He asked me to help with his scientific studies, so I retired my career with the UPC to aid him."

"Tennir is your *brother*?" I had not gotten that impression at all...

"He is my half-brother, we share a mother. That is his connection to the government--our mother, Madreed, is an integral part of the United Planets Governing Core."

"Wait, what? Isn't that *your* connection to the government too, then?" I'm up on my elbows now, looking at him.

"Not in the same way. I am illegitimate, I am a product of war," he tells me with that suddenly dark expression he gets sometimes.

"I literally have no idea what that means."

He sighs, "Illegitimate means…"

"No doofus, I know what illegitimate means. I don't get this product of war thing."

"It is a shameful thing, sweet Kate. My friends here, my crew and myself, we are all products of war. Products of The Invasion." He pauses and I swear I'm going to lose my shit if he doesn't get on with the explanation. Finally, he begins, "The United Planets is a peaceful union. We favor diplomacy over war. It has been centuries since any such disruptions have plagued our people. We have the UPC as protection, but we were not prepared for any type of invasion. Many yets ago, a great ship of destruction came into our territory. It landed on the Mother Planet and forcefully occupied it. The only beings on the Mother Planet at the time were those who tend the museums and gardens *and* our government."

"Your mother!" I gasp.

"Yes," he nods. "Madreed was trapped there for some time before the UPC was able to retake the Mother Planet. You remember I told you our government is primarily females. The warriors who invaded… they were males and they did what any one might expect in war. They burned buildings, they ruined our historical artifacts, they killed innocent people, and they raped."

I gasp again, but say nothing.

"I am a product of that," he says.

"That's… that's terrible Rennek. I'm so sorry, I don't know what to say."

"It is a shame I carry with me every day."

"No! Rennek, you can't! You shouldn't! You didn't do any of that terrible stuff. You don't own that."

"No, it was my sire. My blood." He says the words as if it makes his own hands dirty.

"So, wait, are you guys treated differently because of this?"

"When young, all males born of this invasion--and this is also true of *any* male with such a birth, were sent to live on an internment planet to learn peace and skills to help integrate us into society. It is done to ensure the safety of the communities within the United Planets."

"You were taken from your mothers as children? Wait, what happened to female kids or offspring or whatever?"

"This is one way perhaps males and females are treated differently. Remember, it is males who have the capacity for acts of war and hate. So, females are treated a blessing and welcomed into their families and males are sent away to ensure they do not develop the traits of their sires."

"Oh my god. That's barbaric. How old were you?"

"I was seven yets, but I entered my internment late. Most fledglings begin at five yets."

"Oh my… that's so sad and tragic Rennek. It's also bullshit. You shouldn't be held responsible for the actions of your father."

"No, my Kate. It is the way of things. What if traits of my sire *did* surface within me? What if I had hurt Madreed or my brother or sister. It would be unforgivable. There is little we know about my sire's people. What if I became dangerous at some point in my maturation process? If an unknown instinct was awoken? This way, young males can be taught and monitored. If there is a problem, no innocents are forced to reap the consequences."

"I can't help but hate it Rennek, I'm sorry. I don't mean to trash your culture or anything, but it's clear you're good. You are a good man, with a good heart. Or a good male, with a good alien organ or whatever you guys have."

"You are sweet, my Kate. You are pure to your core."

I'm quiet for a moment, taking all this in--trying not to be too judgy. "Are you close to your brother and sister?"

"When we were small we would play. It was a good time in my life, but that was long ago. I was honored when Tennir called upon me to join him in his work."

"And you just quit your job? You left everything behind to help Tennir?"

"Yes, and my friends did too. It was an honor."

"Wow. Okay."

"I take it the ways of my culture differ from yours?" He asks amused, despite the serious undertones of the conversation.

I sigh and think about much worse atrocities humanity has carried out. "Yes and no, I guess." I smile at him. "I do think it's weird you just gave up your career. Back on Earth, a career was the one thing I was really searching for. A place that I fit--where I belonged. Something that would be forever... and you just gave up all your hard work and goals to help your brother. No judgement there, it's just surprising."

"Kate, you have somewhere you belong. It is here with me," he tells me and I don't know how to respond, so I stay quiet.

After some time, his arms pull me closer and I feel his breath even out. He must still be pretty tired and I guess I must be too, because I fall asleep shortly after.

Chapter 19

Kate

I wake up to Rennek putting his clothes on... and I use the term lightly. Guy wears little more than a glorified belt.

"You may continue to rest," he says when he notices I'm awake. "Unfortunately, I must return to my duties. We are at a heightened alert considering the bounty on us. I am sure the others are ready for their rest cycles."

"Thanks, but I think I'll get up too and go spend some time with the girls. Bond or something," I tell him as I sit up and try to straighten my hair a bit. "Is there anything I can do to help out around here? Anything any of us can do? I'm sure the others are bored in their rooms now that they've had a chance to get some sleep."

"I do not care about any of the other females," he smiles, "but I would be pleased if you joined me on the bridge." He sits on the bed and pulls me onto his lap so I'm straddling him. He starts kissing and nibbling at my neck. "Mmm, it is difficult to leave your side sweet Kate."

If this were some Earth guy I had just started seeing I would probably make a joke in response. I'd try to come off as cool or causal or something. But here with Rennek, I don't feel like I need to do any of that cat and mouse crap. Maybe I'm becoming more mature. Or maybe it's Rennek. *Or* maybe getting abducted by aliens just puts shit in perspective, you know? Whatever it is, everything just feels real... authentic. And I'm right there with him--it *is* hard to leave his side. So, instead of joking I take his mouth in a kiss and we get lost in it together.

After a bit he growls and sets me down on the bed again. He adjusts himself and takes a second to regain his composure. "Join me soon, my Kate?"

"Definitely," I smile.

He beams one back at me and leaves. But just as the door hisses shut, it hisses right back open again and he wraps his muscular arms around me, lifting me up. This beast is seriously strong. His kisses are hard and full of need. His body feels delicious against mine and I grind wildly against his hard cock, meeting his enthusiasm with my own.

****

Eventually Rennek proves to be the more level headed of the two of us and he marches off to save the day or whatever it is alien spaceship captains do--after I promise half a dozen more times I'll come hang out with him. *Soon.*

I think I have a permanent smile stuck on my face as I make my way back to my room. The door opens and I'm surprised to find Vivian and Reagan there waiting for me. Vivian is curled up and asleep on my bed and Reagan is sitting there with a cup of ceata in her hands and what looks like a black eye on her face.

"Reagan?! What the fuck happened to you?"

"It's not that bad, really. You should see the other guy."

"No, don't tell me…"

"Reagan and Allison got in a fight," Vivian announces sleepily.

"Oh my god! Tell. Me. Everything." I say squeezing onto the bed.

Vivian sits up and makes room. "Well, you know I went to go talk to her... I just felt like she needed a friend or something."

"And surprise, surprise she acted like a bitch," Reagan rolls her eyes.

"It's my fault, she was trying to push my buttons and I let her. This situation--everything is so scary. I already have all these what-ifs running around in my head and when she and I started talking I just got overwhelmed."

"How so?"

"Well, my grandma raised me because my parents weren't around and she got really sick a few years back. Anyway, I ended up taking care of her until she passed."

"I'm so sorry Vivian, that must have been really hard," I put my hand on hers.

She forces a smile, "It was. My grandma was everything to me. I just... I just miss her even more now, and I don't have anything to remember her by here. No pictures, none of her handmade quilts. Her recipes. It's all gone." She starts to cry.

"So, Allison started picking at that until Vivian came running out crying," Reagan interjects.

"What? She was talking about your grandma? What did she even say?" I'm shocked, because it doesn't just seem bitchy to me. It seems cruel.

"Oh, I'm being dumb! Guys, please!" She wipes at her eyes. "That's what I tried to tell Reagan. Allison just asked about why no one would miss me and I told her about my grandma, then I started thinking about what my grandma would be going through if she were still alive... You see, my mom had gotten into drugs and it nearly killed my grandma with heartache worrying about her, until one day we got word that my mom had finally ODed." Her voice breaks again. I look at Reagan, who just looks away--her jaw hard. I don't know what to say, so I just wait for Vivian to go on. I'm not so sure this is as much about Allison now as it is about what Vivian is going through.

And suddenly I feel guilt filling me. It's like a pound of lead in my stomach. Here I am running off, having make out sessions with my big naked alien gargoyle, while I have a group of humans--*my people*--going through the trauma of a freaking alien abduction. These *are* my people. Humans. There's all of six of us and we're probably thousands of light years from home. All we have is each other. *I* have to be there for them. No matter what.

But, for whatever reason my feelings just don't resonate with what Vivian's going through. It's intimidating to be where we are. I have this deeper understanding of how small I am compared to our galaxy... but I'm not tripping about home or anything I left behind. Maybe it's because I never had a close bond with anyone back on Earth, maybe it's because I didn't really have a place there. Don't get me wrong, I'm not super stoked to be an alien abductee... but I'm okay right now.

"Anyway, I lost track of the conversation with Allison and started talking about all this stuff, then I tried to go back to my room and Reagan saw me leaving Allison crying... next thing you know they're swinging at each other," Vivian hiccups.

"She was playing you Vivian! She led the conversation there to upset you!" Reagan tells her and though I wasn't there to hear it myself, I can't say I'd be surprised to find that Reagan's right in this case. "She's a bitch who gets off on hurting others. Period." We fall silent-- lost in thought.

"We can't go on like this guys, we need to pull it together and become a team. Particularly before we end up on this 'Mother Planet. We have to be united when we face whatever it is we are going to face there."

Vivian is nodding, but Reagan looks stone faced.

"What?" I ask her.

"You're siding with Allison on this?"

"Whoa! Let's not get crazy. I'm not on anyone's side," but that's not quite right. "Let me rephrase that: there is only one side. We are in this *together*. I'm just trying to think of everyone's best interest in the long term. We don't know what to expect when we meet these other aliens and we don't want any one person causing damage to our circumstances. Look, I'll talk to her."

"Watch out for her right hook. She's stronger than her princess attitude lets on," Reagan says ruefully.

"Hopefully that won't be an issue for me. But do come running if you hear me scream for help. I've never been in a fight and I'm not looking to start now." I get up to leave, but Vivian stops me.

"Wait! We didn't hear your story yet."

"There's not much to me. Bad job, crappy apartment. Trying to go to school." I shrug.

"No, not that," she says smiling.

"Yeah, we want to hear how you got that hickey," Reagan asks, clearly trying to hold in her laughter.

"Oh my god! Busted!" I bury my face in a pillow in an attempt to hide my mortification. "Is this weird? Am I weird?" I say without looking up.

"No way, they're all totally hot," Reagan says without hesitation.

"And the one with the wings is *so* sweet to you! I mean, I can't understand anything he says… but he seems way into you," Vivian agrees.

"It just feels like I *should* feel weird about it. I don't know, maybe it's because he saved us, but everything with him feels right, we're just clicking. But he's an alien! He looks so alien!"

"What about his junk?" Reagan asks, "Is it as alien as he is?"

"Oh my gosh! Reagan, she hasn't seen his stuff yet! We've only known them a few days!" They both look to me to settle this dispute and I do the only thing I can: bury my head in the pillow again. They scream.

"Well, I only got a quick look… but it's just as big as everything else on them. Like the biggest one I've ever seen. And it might have some extras going on."

"Extras like what?" Reagan arches an eyebrow.

"Like ribbed for my pleasure sort of extras," I smile. "His whole... happy trail, I guess you'd call it, is kind of ribbed too. Like a washboard."

"Okay, as long as they only have horns on one head," Reagan jokes causing Vivian to squeal.

"Oh my god, I can't even!" Vivian screeches.

We break into peals of laughter and I have to say--it feels *so* good. I haven't had this since high school. Girlfriends, I mean. It's just another thing here on my alien abduction adventure that's just clicking. It's funny, I worked so hard to find a place for myself on Earth and I always felt like I was coming up empty. I spend a couple days floating in space and now everything seems to be fitting into place. Hopefully, my good fortune in this impossible situation continues, but I better look around for some wood to knock on, just in case.

We wrap up our girl talk session and I get cleaned up. I'm about to head over to wherever Rennek is, see if I can learn a thing or two about life in space, but I have one thing I need to take care of before I do.

Her door hisses open. She is lying on her bed facing the wall.

"Yeah?"

I came in here thinking about threatening to throw her out of the airlock. But just as I'm about to lay into her, I change course.

"Do you want to talk about it?" I ask.

She sits up and her face looks as blank and unemotional as ever, the only addition to her bored expression is her bruised lip. "Talk about what?"

"Dammit Allison, just cut this 'I'm too cool to be affected by an alien abduction' crap. No one cares and believe me, you aren't coming off as cool."

"Frankly, I don't care what you or your little loser lackeys think."

"Well *frankly*, no one cares what you think. No one cares what trauma you're dealing with, because everybody's got their own. What I won't stand for, what the rest of us won't stand for, is you stirring the pot and hurting people, or hurting our chances to be somewhere safe."

She's silent and I can practically feel the wall she has built up.

"What's your goal here? What's the point of this shitty attitude?" I say exasperated.

"I'm not like you guys. I'm not so unimportant that no one is going to look for me. People will miss me. They'll know I'm gone," she says firmly.

"Yeah, okay. You already said that..." but then I notice the unshed tears in her eyes and I start to hear the question in her voice.

I sigh and take a seat. I haven't been punched yet, so I think I'm making progress.

"You aren't unimportant. I can't speak to the life and people you left behind, but right here, right now? We need you and you're important to us," I tell her this with all sincerity, but she rolls her eyes hard.

"Look, I'm not trying to kiss your ass. Believe me, I have no reason to. I'm stating fact here Allison. There are six of us and we need to combine our skills, knowledge and anything else we've got to make sure we survive this. Who knows what's going to happen once we reach the Mother Planet? And let's not forget there's a bounty on Rennek and his men because of what they did to rescue us."

"You don't think we're safe?"

"I honestly don't want my brain to even go there, but what if another alien ship attacks and our guys don't win? What do you think alien bounty hunters will do with us?"

"Well, what's your big plan? I don't see you doing anything to change your circumstances."

"*Our* circumstances," I correct her. "I'm going to go to the bridge and I'm going learn as much about these guys, their ship, their culture and maybe even their weapons as I can. You're strong. Smart too, from what I can tell. Why waste your time and energy lying around like this? We have to adapt Allison. We are here now."

She hangs her head and the silence stretches on. I'm about to walk out when she looks at me.

"I'm ready."

"Come on then, let's be proactive."

"Fine."

"Awesome."

"I was going to die of boredom if I had to sit around here staring at the wall any longer anyway."

"Look, we don't have to be friends if you don't want to, but we need to be a team," I reach my hand out and after only the slightest hesitation, she takes it. Looks like we have a truce.

Chapter 20

Tennir

I wake up groggy and push myself upright on the couch in my office. I have been sleeping at the lab for four rotations now, ever since I got word about this whole debacle with Rennek. I wait anxiously for his arrival and send prayers to the Goddesses that he makes his journey safely. I rub my hands over my face. I feel responsible for my brother getting mixed up in this dangerous business. I asked him to take this position because I thought it would keep him marginally safer than a career as an enforcer. I also thought it would help to keep him more connected to us, his family. It has seemed the older we get the greater the distance between us gets as well. When I look at my brother, I only see the little boy I grew up playing with back on Mother World. I think though, when he looks at me, he only sees all he did not have. The familiar guilt pools in my core.

"Lights."

The room brightens and I blink to adjust my still tired eyes. I've hardly slept. I wonder how our mother and our sister Kahreen are doing, but mostly I think of Rennek. He is a strong male. He can take care of himself, I remind myself. He always could. Even though he is six yets younger than me, it always seemed he and I were on par. He actually pushed me to work harder so *I* could *remain* on par. Can't have my little brother best me physically... I smile at long cherished memories. Distant memories.

"Time for work, I suppose," I say to no one but myself. I pull on my lab coat over my day old wrinkled attire and grab a protein pack from my desk. Not the healthiest breakfast, but it'll do for now. I will work to occupy my mind while I wait for word from Rennek and then I'll eat a real lunch, I promise myself.

I walk from my office down the halls of the lab. We are located in a small, unpopulated sun system comprised of seven planets and twelve moons which had been reserved for scientific endeavors. There is a moon nearby which serves as a dwelling space for all the scientists, engineers and various professionals who work the system. It is fairly advanced, we even have shops and entertainment. It is luxurious compared to the expeditions on back world planets from earlier in my career.

Our lab orbits a recently terraformed planet which we have engineered to populate with creatures from distant systems. There will be many stages of this research project. Partly, we aim to create a rich catalogue of life forms for study and to cross compare with previously discovered life forms. We are using genetic mapping to determine species links across distant sun systems to gain a deeper understanding of the various ways life might have been spread through the galaxy. Our goal is to build a self-sustaining environment and allow the creatures to live in a naturalistic setting so we may study them in the wild. We learned long ago that caging animals for study corrupts research, not to mention the poor ethics of it.

The cultural values across the United Planets dictates we honor the stewardship we have over environments and non-sentient beings. It is important to study these things so we may care for them better. It seems the more sun systems and cultures that join with the United Planets, the more commonalities we see across vast distances of space. It is deeply interesting to consider how and why this is. Obviously, there are many differences as well… but it is the threads that link us which have always held my attention and sparked my interest.

My mind is already beginning to focus on work as I near the main laboratory. I can see the clouded glass windows ahead of me. I am surprised it is still dark within. I thought I had slept in a bit and hoped a warm pot of ceata would be waiting for me. Perhaps I got less sleep than I realized and I am early still. I punch my code into the panel beside the door, it seems to catch a little as it hisses open. I step inside, but the auto lights do not automatically turn on at my entry.

"Computer, activate lights," I command.

Beep beep.

The sound indicates the computer recognizes my request. I hear some electric whirring noises around me, as if the lights are trying to power on... but nothing happens.

"Computer, engage emergency lighting."

Beep beep.

Now I hear something like a generator kick on and slowly dim red lighting fills the space. The first thing I see is an overturned chair. I step forward to the workstation it belongs to and right the chair. As I bend to retrieve it, I am startled. Lying on the floor is my friend, Goeta. I run to his side.

"Goeta! Are you alri..." but as I place my hands on my friend I can sense immediately that he is gone. I turn him over and am shocked to see the mark of a laser blast across his chest. I stand and back away in shock and horror--only to trip. I find myself on the ground, eye to eye with another friend and colleague, Tismae. Her eyes stare into mine. Unblinking. She is dead.

I scramble to my feet and the silence in the room finally hits me. The animals are making no sounds. I run to the cages. Even in the dim emergency lighting I can see the crime before me. Slaughtered. A pointless cruelty. Whoever has done this could still be on the station. I need to check on the rest of my team.

"Computer," I say quietly, "emergency lights out." I strip off my lab coat and look one last time towards Goeta and Tismae, before I head towards the control room. There is nothing but silence around every corner. My blood pounds in my ears. When I get there, I will scan the station for life signs and determine if there is still a threat aboard. Then I will contact Mother, Rennek and the UPC.

As I journey through the lab station I listen closely for any sounds of life, but there is nothing besides the sound of my own breath. When I finally arrive at my destination I rush inside. The telltale hum of a laser stops me dead in my tracks.

"Looks like we have one last straggler," a rough voice says.

"Scientists. This one should be as little trouble as the rest," another voice laughs nearby.

"I won't be any trouble," I say turning, my hands in the air. But before they know it, I am trouble. I'm the worst kind of trouble. I swing my leg up into a kick that sends the laser flying out of my attacker's hand. Without hesitation, I leap towards the other voice in the darkness and I am on him in a moment, smashing his head into a metal control panel. The first male is diving for the gun, but I am faster. I snatch the laser and swing the handle down hard on the back of his neck. He is on the ground and I pin him with my foot, pointing the laser at him.

"How many?"

My prisoner grunts and I press harder on his neck.

"Five! Five, including us," he growls.

"What are you doing here? Are you bounty hunters?" The male laughs, despite my tight grip. He gurgles a response, but I can't understand him. I loosen my grip slightly so he may speak.

"Do I look like a bounty hunter to you?" He asks laughing. I take in his uniform for the first time... UPC.

"Who sent you?"

"You and your field team stepped on the wrong toes, scientist. We are just cleaning things up, making sure nobody rocks the boat."

"The trafficking? UPC has a hand in that?"

"Look scientist, I'd tell you all about it... but I'd rather just kill you."

At that moment he makes his move and I have to make mine. I need to come out on top, I must warn my brother...

Chapter 21

Rennek

I am excited to see my sweet Kate when she enters the bridge, the joy within me is only slightly dampened to see she has brought the sour one, Allison, with her. I sense much negativity from this human.

I go to my mate's side and pulling her hair into my hand I tilt her head up so I may kiss her lips. She kisses me back tentatively and pulls away sooner than I would wish. Her cheeks flush and she does not look at me. Nor does she look at Allison, who stares wide eyed at her. I can feel the eyes of my crew on me as well, but we do not need to offer them any explanations.

"Hey," she runs her hand down my arm, reassuring me. "Any new developments?"

"No. None." I tell her and she reads the significance of that statement in my voice.

"Is that normal?" She looks to me, head cocked to the side in inquiry. She is so cute, my mate. Out of the corner of my eye, I notice Allison make her way to the control stations.

"I expected to hear from Tennir by now," I tell her. "I had hoped to get an escort for the remainder of the voyage. But we are close now, so it does not matter."

"Is there anything we can do to help?" Kate asks me.

"No, Kate. You continue to rest and relax. You have been through much," I tell her as I stroke her beautiful red mane.

"Actually, Rennek… we're getting a little bored with resting. We're all rested up now," she beams a smile at me. "But, we were hoping to start learning more about your ship or any technology you might be able to teach us…"

"I want to learn your weapons systems," Allison interrupts. "This is it right?" She points to where she saw my crew working artillery during battle with the bounty hunter.

Kellen looks to me and I nod my approval. "They are right, they will all need to learn our ways and technology to assimilate."

"Welcome Allison," Kellen greets her and offers her his chair. "Let me begin by teaching you the names of…"

"No," she waves him off. We all stare at her dumbfounded.

"Him. Lizard boy. I want him to teach me." Since the females entered the bridge Da'vi has appeared engrossed in his work, now he bristles but still does not turn to face the bossy female. The bossy female who continues to insult him.

"Are you sure?" I ask this odd female. Last I was aware she was spitting hatred at Da'vi.

"Yeah."

"Why though Allison? Don't you think it'd be better that Kellen…" Kate begins.

"No. Kellen is going to pussy foot around what I need to know. *He*," she points at Da'vi again, "will not cut me any slack. I want to learn, not have my ass kissed."

Kate swings her gaze to mine, shrugging. She does not appear to have any grievance with this.

"Da'vi, please begin training Allison in weapons and basic ship functions."

Da'vi approaches Allison. Her arms are crossed in front of her and she gives him a cold and unbreaking stare. I was at first worried he might intimidate her with his distant and harsh demeanor, but the more I see of this Allison... the less I worry about *her* being intimidated.

"Follow me," Da'vi tells her.

"Where are we going? I want to learn about weapons?" She points to the control panel.

"You will work your way up to those weapons, human," Da'vi says as he stalks out of the bridge. Her look is defiant, but she follows nonetheless.

"Okay... well they seem to have their own thing going on there, but all of the humans will need to learn about all this... *stuff*," Kate waves her hand indicating everything around us. I remind myself how primitive the world she came from was. There is so much for them to learn.

"Yes, call your humans to join us. We will begin your training right away," I tell her. She smiles at me before she leaves the bridge.

"Why did you not tell her you meant for her to use the comms?" Kellen asks after she is too far away to hear.

"I did not wish to embarrass my mate, she is only just learning."

"Your mate?" Kellen breathes out.

I cannot help but smile. "My mate," I confirm.

"May the Goddesses bless your union, my brother," he says, his voice full of reverence. I nod proudly.

"Check in with Dax and Bossan, see who is available to aid on the bridge. I want Bossan to boost our cloaking system and I want someone running deep scans for the remainder of the trip. I don't want anyone sneaking up on us," I tell him.

"Yes, Rennek."

A short while later all the females are on the bridge. I long to be near my Kate, but I am no teacher and Dax loves an audience. So, Kellen and I run scans while Dax gives general descriptions of all the ship's most basic and fundamental systems. He allows the females to try simple functions at various work stations. Kate and Reagan help one another translate all Dax is teaching. I suspect the lesson is much more difficult for the females who have yet to learn our language. Da'vi and Allison have not returned--I do not know if it means their training is going well or poorly.

"These are the primary communication systems. From here we can create and receive comm links *and* those of us who are really good at breaking into systems can force comm links if a ship is avoiding our hail for some reason."

"Like you guys did with the bounty hunter's ship?" Kate asks.

"Yes, but not all ships are alike, some have more defenses built into their systems. This is true of fighters, destroyers, and anything UPC. They will have more protective measures in place to avoid a force link, but Bossan is a genius when it comes to that kind of thing. He can force link just about anything," he tells them.

"What about you?" Reagan asks.

"I am not as good with computers, I do not have the patience," he smiles. "I am better at weapons systems and I am best at navigation," he says proudly.

"You're a humble guy," Reagan scoffs.

"Why be humble, when I can be honest? You want humble, look to Kellen," he shines his wide grin at all the females and I grit my fangs. I know Dax has been intimate with females in the past, as many are drawn to his charm and good looks. So, when he smiles at the human females I feel an insatiable need to pull my Kate away from him and fold her into my arms.

When I tune in to their conversation again he is quizzing them on which buttons to press to open a live link. Then, suddenly the comm station is alive with some sort of notification.

Beep. Beep. Beep. Beep.

"That's a new sound. What does that mean?" Kate asks.

Dax punches a few keys. "An urgent message is incoming…" he studies the screen. "It's locked and encrypted."

I hurry over and punch in my codes.

"Put it up on the view screen," I tell him.

An image of Tennir is suddenly before me. It is dark where he is--it looks like the lab's lighting systems have been damaged. *Tennir* looks to be damaged, for that matter. His face is bruised and his lip bloodied. Dim emergency bulbs flicker behind him and he begins to speak.

"Rennek, this message is of the utmost importance. I pray it reaches you. Do not, I repeat, do *not* rendezvous with me at the lab. The station has been..." he looks away from the screen, "it is not safe. There is nothing left here. I am on my way out as soon as I finish this comm to you and one to mother. Encoded with this message are coordinates for a new rendezvous point. Do not trust anyone Rennek. Rely only on your crew. I hope to see you soon. Take care of yourself, brother."

The comm cuts out. Kate rushes to my side. Reagan is working to translate and the other females look fearful. I look to Dax and Kellen. I see fury and determination in their eyes. There is a silent acknowledgement between us all. We will protect my mate, and her people, and we will rescue my brother. Kate's fingers link with mine and I meet her eyes. They search me.

"All will be well, my Kate," I tell her.

"That's my line. Are *you* okay?" She asks, studying me.

"Tennir is strong and he is smart, I have faith in him."

I turn to my friends. "Get Bossan up here, I want those coordinates decoded. Everyone else start running scans. Call Da'vi up here, I want him working too."

"Yes sir," my friend says and I try to shrug off the annoyance I feel at any sort of command title. It is not command that bothers me, it is the idea that we are not equals. That I could be above my friends in any way.

"I'm sorry, your lesson must end early Kate."

"Look, I know this message changes things, and you're worried about your brother Rennek..." she looks to her people. "But I don't think the lesson should end now. I think this is exactly where we need to be."

"I do not know if that is best, perhaps you should go back to your accommodations?"

She lowers her voice, "Look, if you send us back to our rooms right now all we're going to do is worry. Here, we can feel proactive--like we have some sort of control over what's going on. Back in our rooms, we're going to feel helpless. *I'm* going to feel helpless. Let us keep learning," she begs. "We won't get in the way, I swear. Kick us out if we do, we just want to watch and learn."

Before I can speak Dax calls the females over to him, "Who wants to do their first long range scan?" He smiles as if it is all fun--a game. But I see the females relax. Still unsure, I look to Kellen and he nods. They stay then.

"Thank you, Rennek," Kate says as she pulls me down and kisses me. There is no longer any timidness about it. When I open my eyes, I see two of the females stare at us with their mouths agape. Reagan and the tearful human pull their attention away.

Chapter 22

Rennek

Bossan works at his touch pad. He has been at it for some time, though he usually is quick to decode. I try not to be troubled by this.

"Tennir, took much precaution in the encryption of this message," he tells me. "He must have been worried about who might get their hands on it."

"He likely had reason to be," I think of Tennir's beaten face.

"But, the thing is, there are not many who have the tech or the skill to decode such a thing. The tech is expensive. If it is pirates he is worried about, they would have to be well funded," he tells me.

I think on that a while, I assumed it was the Ju'tup, but they are frivolous beings. They spend money on entertainment, not equipment. It is more likely they have hired bounty hunters to do their work for them. I do not understand why they would attack Tennir's lab though, unless they had hoped to ambush us. Still, the risk and trouble of taking the science station should have been a deterrent. Why not just come after us directly? Attack before we even reached the science station?

"Got it!" Bossan yells. Even the females who do not understand look to him anxiously.

He reads the information. His eyes shoot to mine. "Dark space. He sent us coordinates for a station in dark space."

"What does that mean?" Kate asks as Reagan hurries to translate.

"Dark space are areas of space that for different reasons interfere with scanners, comms, distress beacons... They are good places to go if you want to disappear or deal in less savory business. These areas are somewhat lawless. Or more accurately, governed by their own laws. The UPC does not even patrol it. I am surprised Tennir knows of such a place."

"It stands to reason that Tennir did not send those coordinates," Kellen postulates.

My stomach sinks, if Tennir did not send those coordinates it means one of two things. Either his message was intercepted and altered, or he created that message under the pressure of a captor. If the former is true, we are being led into a trap. If the latter is true, we are still being led into a trap, but likely my brother is dead.

"No, the message definitely had not been altered. It was too complex and had none of the markers of an altered message," Bossan asserts.

"Okay, so great. Tennir sent the coordinates. How long will it take for us to meet up with him?" Kate inquires.

"It is not that simple, my Kate," I explain gently.

"What do you mean?"

"We all saw Tennir, sweet Kate. He was badly beaten, his lab had sustained much damage," I tell her.

"Okay?"

"He might have been forced to send that message," as I say this realization dawns on her.

"No, he's your brother. He wouldn't do that. He'd try to protect you, he'd find a way to signal it was a trap," she reasons.

"If there were hostages. His friends, his fellow scientists? He may not have had a choice. It is odd he asks us to go to dark space rather than to head directly to the Mother Planet. That he didn't ask us to contact UPC for aid," the questions continue to mount in my brain.

"Well what's the alternative then, if you guys don't trust this Tennir guy?" Reagan asks.

I look to my crew, "Mother Planet. Trying to contact the UPC and the Governing Core."

"But Tennir said not to trust anyone," Reagan adds. "What if you do those things and it gets us killed because we didn't listen to his warning?"

"She's right Rennek. Why would Tennir say not to trust anyone? It seems superfluous if he was being coerced into sending the message in the first place," Kate maintains.

I bow my head to think on what we should do. If the message is authentic and I do not rendezvous with him I could be putting his life in danger. If I go to him and it is a trap I am putting all the females and my friends at risk. But I do trust Tennir and I owe a duty to him. Plus, it is clear he has information we do not have. If I hope to keep Kate and the other humans safe, I will need to know what information my brother has.

"We will go. Da'vi, Bossan. I want you to map the area as best as possible. We will try to find a location to conceal the ship. I will take a pod down and look for Tennir. If I am not back in one rotation, leave without me and continue on to the Mother Planet."

"What? No way!" Kate exclaims. "You can't go down there alone! What if it's a trap?"

"Then it is best that as many of my crew as possible are here with you and your people--to protect you and get you to safety," I tell her.

"You need someone to watch your back," she tries to justify.

"I would rather they watch your back, my little queen," I coo to her, petting her mane to calm her, but I look challengingly to my crew to ensure none of them are *watching* her back. Her delicious round backside is for my eyes only.

She swats my hands away from her mane. "No! I don't want you going alone. It's dangerous."

"Yes Kate, we are in a dangerous situation right now. This is the only way to proceed however."

"Look Rennek, *you* have kept me safe... well, you all have and I thank you for it, but *you* have made me *feel* safe. I'm scared for you to go down there alone. I'm scared to be away from you." I see her eyes light up, "Let me go with you!"

"Absolutely not," I tell her.

"I want to go too," Allison says.

"No," Da'vi and I say in unison.

"Why not?" Dax interjects. "This is life in space, this is where your mate is to be--by your side. It is foolish to pretend we do not find ourselves in dangerous situations every rotation. Let her keep learning, see if she is cut out for this life. And her," he shrugs toward Allison. "Are you going to argue with that one?" He raises his eyebrows.

"Thank you!" my Kate mouths toward Dax, "Look, I will stay out of the way. I'll just be an extra set of eyes."

"We go, the four of us then," Da'vi says. "I will help you take care of the females."

"I don't think we need taking care of," Allison squares to him but he ignores her offense at his statement.

"Wait, I want to go now too," Reagan says.

"No. Reagan, you must stay here. You are the only other human with a translator implant. One of you must remain with the other humans in case there is an emergency," I tell her.

"Wait. Did you just call me Reagan? Like… you said my name right?" She asks shocked.

"Yes. Your name is very easy to say. We were making fun before, but now is not the time."

"Rennek! I wanted to see how long we could keep it going!" Dax laughs and throws himself into a chair in mock dejection.

"Assholes!" She rages.

"It was poor timing for a joke, Reagan. Our apologies," I tell her. "Okay, it is settled then, as long as there are no more objections. We head to the coordinates and hide the ship. Da'vi, Kate, and Allison will come to the surface with me, we will find Tennir and return." My crew and the human females nod in response.

"Dax, lock coordinates and engage. Bossan, Da'vi, start mapping. Find the safest place to leave our ship. Let me know when we have an ETA. Kellen, you and I will continue scans."

"I appreciate it Rennek," Kate tells me. "I know this is all super scary and dangerous, but part of me is excited to see some more of what's out there and... I'm glad we aren't going to be separated." She aims that beautiful smile of hers at me and part of me is glad too.

I pull her to me and breath in her mane. Perhaps I am making the wrong decision. Perhaps I am being selfish. Part of me only agreed to allow the females to come along because I cannot bear the idea of being away from my Kate. The thought fills me with dread. Perhaps I am putting us all at risk. I hold her at arm's length and gaze into her eyes. I am ruled by my core now more than ever.

Chapter 23

Kate

We have been busy since the message from Rennek's brother came in. It seems we'll be in this "dark space" region in a few hours. I feel nervous, but excited at the same time. It reminds me of midterm exams in one of my classes. The only difference is I'm actually confident about the answers for some reason. I feel like I can ace this.

Regardless, I need to do all I can to prepare in the small amount of time I have. I can feel the speed of the ship has increased. Rennek is trying to hurry, in case his brother is in danger. I try to imagine what he must be feeling. Relationships are hard though, unique to the people in them. I think of my own brother. How would I react if he were in danger? How would he react if he were in Rennek's shoes and thought I was in danger, I wonder?

Then I finally start to consider what my family will think once they realize I'm gone. It's the first time I've really thought about it. I feel a deep sadness for them. They'll never know what happened to me. That would be the worst thing, I think. It must be hard for Rennek right now, not knowing what happened to his brother, if he is safe or not.

Da'vi finished his work on the bridge and brought all of us 'females' to some kind of training room. It's like a gym... kind of, but with guns. He gives each of us a hand-held weapon that looks more like a cell phone than a gun and sets us up in front of some targets and fighting dummies, which look *nothing* like Earth fighting dummies, mind you.

He teaches us how to fire a weapon, it's called a charger, and shows us that in close combat it can be used like a taser. We all spend some time practicing on the targets and the dummies. Years of cell phone and remote-control use has made us pretty adaptable to this weapon in particular.

"I don't understand why we are doing this," Vivian says. "You and Allison sure, but we're all going to be hiding here, safe on the ship."

Allison rolls her eyes and continues to practice. I sigh. I don't want to be the bearer of bad news.

"Vivian, sweetie... I think there's a reason why the guys are going to try and hide the ship when we go down to this space station. We're going someplace very dangerous and there's a chance (hopefully a very, very small chance) that it's a trap. If it is, you guys might be in just as much danger as we are *and* you might find yourself in a position where you have to defend yourself," I explain, trying my best to give her the information without freaking her out.

"I don't get it," she trembles. "We got away from those bad aliens. I thought we were just going to their government, like... like refugees or something and they would find a place for us."

"There's a bounty on them." Allison says without looking up. I'd shoot her a dirty look, but she wouldn't care anyway, so I save it.

"Wait, what? There's a bounty on *them*? The bad aliens are looking for *them*, not us? We could just leave and go to the government and we'd be safe? They could deal with all this dangerous stuff and we could go somewhere safe?"

I look at her a little shocked. I mean, they saved our lives and any trouble they're in now is entirely because of us.

"Don't give me that look," she says. "Just look at these guys," she waves her hands at Da'vi... who seems like he could care less about whatever conversation we are having and continues to correct all the other girl's shooting techniques. "They can handle themselves. This is like... their thing or whatever. *We*, on the other hand, are not cut out for situations like this. I'm going to school to become a librarian for Christ's sake! Not to become a... a... space bandit!"

"A space bandit? Seriously?" Allison sets down her charger. "Wake up *Vivian*. You are not a librarian. You will never be a librarian. So, you can put that sad little dream away. We were abducted by aliens. We are in danger. Get that shit through your head. Whether you sit here crying, trying to pretend this is some kind of survival getaway or get your shit together and learn how to protect yourself: *you are in danger*. Bottom line." She picks her charger up and resumes her practice.

"Oh, why don't you just... just... suck it Allison!" And I have to admit, it's hard not to laugh. Even Reagan laughs, and I'm sure she's wanted to tell Allison to 'suck it' too. Vivian throws her charger down on a mat and Da'vi barks at her, only she can't understand what he's saying and it just scares her into another sobbing fit. I'm glad he's chastising her, throwing a weapon she doesn't know anything about is extremely stupid. Throwing a weapon in general is just stupid.

"Hey, come on," April chimes in, pulling Vivian into a hug. "Take some deep breaths."

Vivian buries her face in her hands, sobbing. "What is going on here? I don't get it! Abducted by aliens? Seriously? And here we are learning to shoot and protect ourselves, and there's a bounty? And Kate is having *sex* with one of them?" Everybody's eyes swing to me and I probably turn red enough to pale the nearest star in comparison.

"Whoa, nobody is having sex with anyone," I say in my defense.

"Damn, Vivian. Are you trying to win the title of biggest bitch? You sure you want to go up against Allison for that?" Reagan says and I can hear the anger lacing her voice. I'm starting to really get Reagan, she is fiercely loyal and Vivian throwing me under the bus in front of everyone? Well, it wasn't her place to say and neither of us seem to appreciate the judgement in her tone either.

"I wasn't going to say anything, but what's up with that?" April asks.

Part of me is embarrassed, but mostly just because I have only known Rennek for a few days. I don't want to come off like a slut to everyone.

"Yeah, they were straight up calling you his *mate*." Reagan teases. "Are you guys like alien married now?"

"Haha, very funny. I don't know. Maybe 'mate' is just like alien for girlfriend or something?" I say shrugging it off.

"Doubt it," Allison says, only marginally engaged in the conversation.

"Well, isn't it a little weird. Like bestiality or something?" Clark asks. And now I am completely offended.

"Exactly," Vivian adds.

I'm instantly furious. How dare they say such a thing, or even consider Rennek and his friends to be more like animals than people. Granted some of their features are pretty… let's just say *wild*. But, they are mostly just like us in the ways that count.

"Look, there is something going on between Rennek and I, it's new and I don't know how to define it, but I have feelings for him and he clearly seems to return them. If anyone dares call him an animal again, I am tearing down this human alliance. These guys *saved our lives*. We would have been raped and maybe a million worse things if they hadn't risked their asses for us. We *will* return the favor and if not, you're out. Go fend for yourself."

"I'm so sorry Kate, I didn't mean it like that." Clark says remorsefully. "I'm just still getting used to the changes. Really, I appreciate all they've done and I didn't mean to sound like I was judging your connection."

"That's fine. I get it, we all are still getting used to things. I didn't mean *all* of what I said either," I sigh. "Well, if anyone calls him an animal again, I will lose my shit and I'll get pissed if we don't all try to pull our own weight around here. But when it comes down to it, I'll always be team human."

"I'm sorry too. Bitch isn't in my nature, I don't know what got into me. Team human," Vivian almost begs as she wipes her tears and hugs me. I return the hug. Everyone will take their own time to adjust, I accept that. Who knows, I might be the next to go nuts and have a crazy crying fit where I say a bunch of shit I regret. Hopefully everyone will be as forgiving with me when I do. All the girls come in for a group hug. Except Allison. We stare at her expectantly.

"Yeah, I'm not doing that."

"Get back to work!" Da'vi barks and we all jump.

Chapter 24

Kate

It's time. We are near the coordinates Tennir sent us. The guys are able to gather some data from scans and explain this area is "dark space" because of the composition of a few of the surrounding planets and asteroid belts. Luckily, the geography of this region in space provides us with lots of places to hide the ship without fear of detection. We watch as Dax pulls us into a crater on an asteroid... which is probably the size of Texas. It's like watching a movie, only super scary because it's real. Vivian nearly faints.

The guys continue their work on the bridge, but all the humans go down to the pod bay to see us off. There is lots of hugging... and awkward not hugging in Allison's case. Rennek and Da'vi make sure there are enough emergency suits in the pod, but I'm just going to keep my fingers crossed and pray we don't have to use them. First of all, they are way too big--I don't even know how I'd be able to move in one. Secondly, if I have to walk around out in the open in space, I'm going to throw up and then die from fear.

Once we are on our way, I feel a bit more at ease. Though I do wish I were wearing jeans and a tee shirt rather than this makeshift dress. It's not super functional. Rennek keeps squeezing my hand and looking at me with worried eyes. I guess I shouldn't be surprised when he finally pulls me out of my seat and onto his lap. Allison looks practically disgusted by our PDA and even Da'vi tenses a bit. I just kind of go along with it, because it honestly feels nice and safe. Plus, I don't know alien culture yet, maybe this is a thing. Maybe everybody does this and I'd be rude if I didn't accept. I don't want to be rude, so I snuggle against his solid chest.

It's quiet in the pod as we head towards the spaceport. Finally, we align in a way where I can see the looming port through the viewing window. I gasp. I thought the asteroid was the size of Texas. This space port is… well it's beyond my imagination. I am thankful movies on Earth gave us some kind of preparation for our new lifestyle, a frame of reference at least.

The port looks a little old and hodgepodge. Like bits and pieces have been added on over a long period of time. I start to realize there are many other small ships and pods floating through space around us, heading in and out of terminals. I can see lights coming from the spaceport and it reminds me of high rise buildings in big cities. The specs of light coming through windows are tiny pinpoints and it makes me realize the scale of all this. I wonder how we will find Tennir here. I look at Rennek. His eyes are dark and his body tense. I squeeze his hand.

"Docking locked. Cruise set," Da'vi reports.

The guys relax a bit in their seats. It seems like there is some invisible thread pulling us towards the spaceport. I see a hanger… or a garage, or whatever it might be called. It gets larger and brighter as we quickly approach. I feel butterflies tremble in my tummy, but it isn't fear I'm feeling. Well, maybe it's a little fear, but mostly it's adrenaline. I'm excited. We finally land and through the viewing window I see dozens of aliens moving around, busy and working.

"Is anyone going to recognize we don't belong here?" I ask, "Like humans, I mean."

"There are so many cultures that convene at spaceports no one should notice one from the next." He pauses and takes me in, "Though, many will recognize your beauty is unique," Rennek tells me smiling.

"And if anyone does recognize you as humans we should capture and interrogate them," Da'vi says strapping an extra holster around his waist to match the one around his shoulders.

"What? Why?" I ask.

Rennek frowns, like he knew this too but was trying to keep the mood light and Da'vi spoiled it. "If anyone does recognize you, it may be because they have dealt in the trafficking of your people before Kate. If they recognize you, it is because they recognize you as merchandise," he tells me sadly.

"Oh, yeah. That makes sense."

Rennek pulls another blanket from a cupboard and easily tears it in two with his sharp claws.

"Wrap this around your head and mane. You might also draw attention from those who honor the Goddesses. Though, in a place like this, there are few that do," he says frowning.

Soon, Allison and I have the blanket pieces draped around us kind of like hijabs and we are disembarking from our pod. The bay where we leave our pod is intimidating. There are big open doors looking right out into space. I try not to worry about whatever shield is holding the air--and us--in and hurry to keep up with Rennek's wide strides. He holds my hand tightly in his. I feel for my charger, it's secured to my belt. Weapons are allowed in most areas of the spaceport, but restricted in certain places, Rennek tells me. There are so many aliens bustling around us, at first, I don't notice how *not* human they are. I see lots of creatures with face masks on, they look something like gas masks.

"It is a breathing apparatus. They do not breathe the same composition of air we do," Rennek whispers as we make our way through the crowd.

Many of the aliens wear hearty woolen looking clothing that appears to have seen much wear and tear. There are very few females we come across. Those we do see either look like prostitutes or real bad asses. Allison and I look like neither, but if we get mistaken for anything I hope it's bad asses. We go down a long, wide corridor and there are hundreds of people pushing in all directions. Eventually, we get to an inner part of the port. We step close to a rail and it seems like the levels of this place go on forever in both directions. The men speak in hushed voices and then tug us along beside them. Da'vi grips onto Allison's arm. She, smartly in my opinion, doesn't try to shake him off. It seems easy to get lost here.

We find some good old-fashioned elevators and go up a few floors. Looking around, it appears we've entered a giant market space. It's almost like a mall. There are lots of little shops along the walls and tons of kiosks set in the center of the walk way. Aliens push carts and carry bags whose potent smells assault my nose. Some are delicious, others repulsive. I can't help but look at all the eye candy surrounding me. Everything here is a little dirty and dingy, it doesn't have the shine and presentation of the malls back home, but everything here is also so foreign and amazing. Half of the stuff I see I am completely confused by. Is it a vacuum? Is it a weapon? Are you supposed to ride on it? Who knows! The stuff I can recognize is a joy, because I'm proud I understand anything going on around me at all. Then… I see a clothing store. Rennek feels the change in my body and follows my gaze.

"If the situation allows us Kate, we will buy new clothing for you and your people."

"Oh my god, Rennek. If that can happen, we will totally pay you back. We would appreciate it so much."

Rennek looks at me sternly. "You will never need to repay anything to me, my Kate. I will take care of you and your people." Before I can thank him, Allison interrupts.

"Good to know," she says. "Someone buy me that." She points to a kiosk selling kabobs. I guess it doesn't matter what kind of meat it is. It does smell delicious though.

Da'vi pushes forward and navigates the rowdy crowd easily. He returns with kabobs for both Allison and me. They are as good as they smell and I try to focus on the taste and not let my mind imagine some kind of scary alien rat that I might be chomping into right now. As we eat, I see Da'vi speaking to the vendor. The vendor's bubble eyes shift back and forth and he gestures in a direction with his three-fingered hand. I try not to stare but remember my promise to Rennek, that I'd be an extra set of eyes. I stop looking at all the wonderful things in the shops and start paying better attention to the crowd. I look for anyone who might be watching us too closely.

When we finish eating, the guys bring us down a corridor between some of the shops. The path is not so wide here and the aliens we pass look a little rougher than the rest. Steam pours through grates in the floor and the smell of the air becomes stale. Finally, a plaza opens up and I spy a handful of bars. It's easy to tell these are bars. Even in space the windows are filled with tacky neon signs. Some tough customers loiter around the outside of each entrance and I'm not eager to walk past any of them. Some of them look even bigger than Rennek, though there aren't many of those.

Allison and I are even more out of place here than we were back in the market area. I can feel eyes on us. Rennek puts his arm around me possessively and I remember what a badass I'm with, so I relax a bit. Da'vi indicates one of the establishments and we make our way inside.

The interior is much like the exterior. It is smoky and all of the patrons I can see are male. Rennek leads us to a table in a back corner. I do notice one other girl besides Allison and myself. She is a singer, standing on a small stage a short distance away. She sings in a voice that sounds underwater. I can pick up every couple of words. She is singing a love song. I guess lots of things are universal.

"Why can I only understand part of what she says," I ask Rennek.

"The translator. It is loaded with dozens of languages, but not all. On ports like this, many speak an amalgam of languages because they come into contact with so many cultures."

"Huh. Cool," I tell him.

"Are you cold my Kate?"

"No," I laugh, "just a language thing." He beams a smile back at me. Dang, this guy could be a model I think to myself as I admire his features. But suddenly his face changes and he is looking past me, I follow his gaze. Standing at the bar is an alien that looks like Rennek and his friends. His eyes meet Rennek's and the older alien has to grab onto the bar to steady himself.

I think back to what he told me of his parents. His mother was a politician on Mother World and his father was a soldier who occupied her planet and assaulted her. I saw Tennir, Rennek's brother, on the message he sent and he looked... well kind of standard alien. Grey, no hair, black eyes. Not like Rennek. This guy standing in front of us though? *He* looks like Rennek. There is one thing about Rennek that is different from Bossan, Dax, Kellen, as well as this older alien in front of us... Rennek is the only one with wings.

"Rennek…" I start, but I don't know what to say. Da'vi seems to get the gravitas of the situation and I feel bad for Allison for a second before I remember we are the only people here who understand English. I see she has her hand on her charger, so I figure I better fill her in with the little I know before she starts shooting from the hip.

"I think this might be someone like Rennek," I tell her in whisper, even though it's not like anyone can understand us anyway.

"Well, fucking duh Kate."

"Sorry, I mean he wasn't raised by his own kind," I explain, struggling to find the right words, since I don't really know too much of the particulars. "His mother's side of the family raised him and his dad's side… they were soldiers who invaded and… well, raped his mom."

"Holy shit, Kate." She says and glues her eyes to this new guy, her hand still resting on her charger.

"Yeah, I know. I don't think Rennek has ever met anyone else like himself, except for his friends."

Just then the alien at the bar wipes his hands on a grungy old towel and picks a bottle and some glasses from the shelf and makes his way over to us. My heart pounds in my chest. I have no idea what this means, if it's connected to Rennek's brother or some weird unrelated coincidence. I'm on the edge of my seat here, I can't imagine what Rennek must be thinking.

Chapter 25

Rennek

The feeling inside me has no words to accompany it. I have wondered my entire life about my sire's people… *my* people and here before me stands a being like myself. Does this male have information? Answers? Answers to questions that are now even more salient because Kate has awoken a mating instinct within me. Do I even have time to spend selfishly seeking those answers while Tennir is somewhere here searching for me? Or did Tennir set this up? Could this male have *all* the answers I seek. Those regarding myself and those regarding my brother as well?

As he nears I see him more clearly. Though he is old he is still a force. One horn is badly damaged, broken at the base. That side of his face is scarred. He has no wings, but everything else is like me. He sets a tray with liquor and glasses on the table and crouches before me.

"By the six kings," he chokes. "Your reverence, Sir. My pledge to you: I am your watcher, your protector, now and forever." His voice catches and I see unshed tears in his eyes.

"Get up," Da'vi orders. "You draw attention to us!" He hisses.

"Sit," I tell him and he pulls up a chair. "Who are you?"

"My name is Gorrard. I am from the Grey King's land," he tells me proudly. "Though that was many yets ago… ages ago, but it is still in my core. It is who I am and who I ever shall be." He toys with a pendant at his neck.

"I am looking for someone. A scientist, perhaps you know him. His name is Tennir?" I ask.

"I am sorry, Sir. I do not know him, but I have many connections here. I can quietly find the person you are seeking, if that is what you wish."

"We would appreciate that Gorrard," I tell him.

"Anything for you, Sir." Despite his heavy scarring I can tell he is anxious. "Forgive me, but I must ask. It has been so many yets since I woke from the crash of my ship. I was on one of the scout ships you see, but when I woke from deep cryo the others in my crew were either dead or gone. I was young then, still apprenticing to my master. If I had been older, more experienced... I always wonder if there might have been more I could have done..." he trails off.

"What is it you ask Gorrard?" he speaks as though I should be familiar with what he is saying.

"Where are the others? Did they make it? Did they find Elysium?" He leans forward in his chair, desperate to hear my answer. All the sorrow in me from yets of not knowing who I am and where I come from, I see it reflected in this male's eyes. Silence stretches between us.

"Gorrard, my brother. I do not know of what you speak." I can think of nothing else to say, I can think of no words of comfort. He searches my face for a long while.

"Where do you come from?" He asks finally.

"Rennek," Da'vi sends me a hard look to remind me of our task.

"Gorrard, I would very much like to continue this conversation, but for now I must resume my search for this scientist, Tennir. You say you can help?"

"Yes, of course. I would be glad to aid you in any way I can. Give me a few moments. Enjoy this drink, on the house for you and your companions, Sir." He bows and steps away. Da'vi and I watch him as he speaks quietly to a pair of large Sivoleans. They nod and exit the establishment.

"Rennek?" Kate touches my arms.

"I do not know Kate, this is a mystery to me. One I hope we will have the chance to unravel." Her fingers intertwine with mine and she smiles sweetly at me. For a moment, I think I do not need any answers, all I need is my darling mate. But then I think if we are to have fledglings of our own one day, I want to pass along to them the history of our people--good or bad. It is always better to know than to live with questions in your core.

We sit without speaking. Waiting, listening to the female on stage warble her sadness. An unhappy song, but it is beautiful nonetheless.

Eventually one of the Sivoleans comes back in, he leans over the counter and speaks low to Gorrard. Da'vi and I stiffen and watch their body language, looking for any indicators that our safety might be in jeopardy. I do not know if we can trust these males. I do not want my curiosity to cloud my judgment while dealing with Gorrard. My instinct is telling me he is an honest male, but lately my instincts feel foreign... like they do not belong to me. We will have to wait and see. Gorrard looks to us as the Sivolean speaks. He nods and clasps the other male on the shoulder in thanks. Gorrard hurries over to us.

"You must go to the lodging district on level 134, look for Tranquility. There seems to be a key waiting for pick up for a winged male, if he has a clearance word. My guess is that will lead you to the person you are looking for, but this station can be a dangerous place if you don't mind my saying so. My friends and I can accompany you, offer you and your companions any backup you might need."

"My thanks to you Gorrard. I think we must travel on alone from here, my brother." Gorrard nods, but lingers by our table side.

"May I meet with you again Sir, before you depart? I have questions…" he tells me.

"I have many questions as well, I will try to return so we may speak," I tell him, hoping the opportunity presents itself. It is hard for me to walk away from this male who might have knowledge that no one else in the galaxy has been able to give me.

"I am always here, if you don't see me at the counter, just ask for me and I will come," he bows and begins to walk away, but hesitates. "You know, you look just like your father," he says and my blood runs cold. "Though I only saw him once in person… the day we departed. He touched the shoulder of *every* Vendari boarding his ship. I will never forget that day. It was a day of great hope," he looks teary again and nods before he walks away.

I am so stunned by his words, all I can do is nod to him in return. I watch him walk away. His tail is like mine. His mane is proud and wild, though grey streaks run through it. Perhaps this is how I will look as I age. Though his horns are damaged they remind me of myself, my friends waiting for me aboard my ship and a handful of others who were interned on Javan. This is the only other being like myself I have ever met, the only being that might have answers about who I am and I let him walk away.

We rise from our seats and I numbly follow Da'vi. Though my core and thoughts are heavy I am ever aware of Kate's presence. I see the worry on her face, so I force a smile and pull her close. All is as it should be, I tell myself as I look upon her. I have all I need in the universe.

We make our way to the lifts and find ourselves in the lodging district. I feel uneasy about bringing Kate to such a seedy location. I hope she does not think this is all the United Planets has to offer. There is so much beauty I wish to show her. Even the deserts of Javan offer more "tranquility" than this awful little inn Tennir has led us to.

We pass hordes of beings. Many live full time on the station yet have nothing more stable than rooms rented by the night. We step over dozens who sleep in the streets and beg for creds as we pass. Some of the inns try to offer an air of superiority to the others, but any amenities offered in places like these are tacky and superficial. I want to offer Kate the best… but there certainly is not much to choose from. I suppose Tennir did his best when he chose this place. Though his main concerns were likely safety and discretion, not caring for a mate.

When we go inside we find ourselves in front of a counter. Yellowing poster advertisements cover the metal walls. There is a chair and a lamp in the corner, they are older pieces and made of wood. Usually the furniture in places like this are made of recycled metal, the light weight stuff… aluminum. Someone, long ago, took some care in trying to decorate this place. I'm sure it is an attempt to make the inn seem more warm and welcoming, but it just feels run down. A worn carpet covers the floor. It is cheap replica of the hand-woven rugs on the Inayan moons. I would like to take Kate there one day, I think. They make the most beautiful textiles. I would buy her trunks full of clothing. I look at her makeshift dress. I appreciate her beauty in anything that adorns her, but she deserves more.

Chain link separates us from the innkeeper. She wears a half mask breathing apparatus and I am grateful her eye slits are exposed. I want to see if there is deceit in them.

"There is a key waiting for me," I tell her.

"Name?" She asks, sounding muffled through her mask. I have thought much on this as we came here from Gorrard's bar. It would not be my name or Tennir's, for obvious reasons. Even the name of my ship or Madreed's name could send off red flags.

"Kate," I say.

She retrieves a key, but hesitates before she hands it to me, "Two per room." She nods toward Da'vi and Allison. "I don't care what you do after I give you the keys, but you have to pay for two rooms."

"Gross," Allison says and the innkeeper's eyes light with a smile.

"*Two* extra rooms. Something close," I say as I hand her a cred reader. She winks at Allison, who scoffs in response.

"Up the stairs," she indicates a door beside us. "Floor 7, rooms G3, G5 and G9."

"Which was the room that had been waiting for me?"

"G9."

"Who paid for the room," I eye her.

"Don't know, didn't get rented on my shift."

"Are there any other exits?"

"Roof and through the kitchen. This door is only accessible if I hit the release. We've never had any break ins, don't plan on it either," she says and nods her head toward the wall beside her. She has two blasters and a disrupter.

"Deliveries?"

"Go through me," she says.

She pushes a button and a buzzer indicates we can open the door. We head up the stairs. The walls are covered with more advertisements for local shops, various products, brothels… There are no beings working in the brothels, even out here. Such establishments only utilize sex-bots. It is illegal in the United Planets to deal in sex trade with sentient beings. There is too great a risk for harm or coercion, though not all systems share that belief. I see Kate scan the posters, I hope she knows these are not ads for actual sex workers. She gapes at a particularly raunchy ad and I am embarrassed I have brought her here. It nags at my core.

We reach the 7th floor and head down a narrow hallway. Scanning the numbered doors, we look for the room Tennir had waiting for us. When we find it we quietly move to the door and indicate our weapons to Kate and Allison.

"Oh, should we?" Kate whispers and reaches for her charger.

I shake my head no. "Emergencies only."

She nods, but she and Allison both keep their hands on their weapons, ready for an emergency. They have good instincts despite not being accustomed to using weapons. Da'vi and I position ourselves on opposite sides of the door. I run the key card and swing the door open. A couple of seconds pass and there seems to be nothing but silence inside the room. Da'vi and I nod to one another and I enter the room, my weapon drawn and ready, he follows behind me with Kate and Allison.

The room is sparse. A bed with no windows. There is a prompter across from the bed which serves as a view screen as well. There is a small dresser and a door to the bathroom. I quickly check around the bed. It is clear. The bed does not appear to have been slept in. I catch Da'vi's eyes and silently indicate I will now check the bathroom. I kick the door open and burst inside with my gun aimed. I find nothing I wouldn't expect. Toilet, sink, small shower stall with a warning to not waste water. The sink and shower are dry. There are no signs anyone has been in this room recently.

"Nothing," I say as I exit the bathroom. Da'vi closes the door to the room and locks it. I begin to rifle through the dresser. I find nothing but extra towels.

The females begin to sit, "No, we will not be staying here."

"But what if Tennir comes and we aren't here?"

"We will be down the hall, we do not know if someone else has a key to this room. We will listen to see if anyone tries to come here. If we see someone, hopefully we see them before they see us."

"You still think this could be a trap?"

"I do not know yet either way," I say with some remorse.

We head back into the hall, checking it first before the females step out of the room. I hand a key card to Da'vi and keep one for myself and Kate. We all enter the next room. It is identical to the last. Out of habit, we search this one too. Kate and Allison sit on the bed. Kate sits upright while Allison reclines with a heavy sigh.

"I will take first watch," I tell Da'vi.

"No, I will take first watch. Rennek, you should speak with Gorrard."

"Yes! Exactly!" Kate jumps to her feet, "Oh, I'm so glad I wasn't the only one thinking it."

"There is not time for such a selfish endeavor, maybe when this is all settled we can return…"

"Selfish? Rennek, it would not be just for you, but for Dax, Bossan and Kellen as well. You all deserve to know. And if you and your mate have fledglings? What of them? This is no selfish task, you should take this opportunity before it is ripped from you," Da'vi demands.

Kate begins to speak but chokes on her words instead.

"I should be here, what if there is danger in my absence?" I ask.

"I will have this one's sour demeanor to scare all the danger away," he waves his arm toward Allison. I cannot tell if he is joking or not, Da'vi has never been one to make jokes in the past.

"Whatever," she says. "Which room is ours?" she asks.

"We will take the other one," Da'vi tells her.

"We, as in you and Rennek right?"

"No simple human, we as in you and I," Da'vi scowls.

"Oh, no. Nope. Not happening, not sharing a room with this jerk," she looks at my Kate who sheepishly looks to me and shrugs her shoulders.

"Oh, fucking great. Fine, whatever."

"Well, I vote we go talk to Gorrard. This is an important opportunity. I don't know all the details, but I feel like this has to be fate right? What a coincidence that we run into someone like you. We can't let this chance slip through your fingers. Da'vi and Allison can hold down the fort."

"If I do, you should remain here my Kate," I tell my thoughtful mate.

"No way, I promised I would watch your back," she smiles. "Plus, that would be completely boring. There isn't even a television here."

"What is television?"

"I don't know how to explain it… it's like an electric box that shows you movies and shows-stuff… for entertainment," she tells me.

"Sounds like a view screen, would you like to watch the view screen?"

"What's that?"

I walk to the prompter and swipe it to bring up the view screen options. Usually at inns the viewing selection is poor and inundated with ads, sure enough an ad is the first thing that pops up. It is for prepackaged meals.

"Oh my god, there's TV!" The females are excited by this development. They stand and Kate jumps up and down while Allison presses herself close to the screen. They both seem to get a little teary eyed.

"There's TV, oh my god. I can't believe they have TV." Allison's hands shake a little as she touches the screen.

"Kate! Are you alright?!" I am shocked by their reactions.

"Yeah, yeah... yes. It's just so... so..."

"It's almost normal," Allison says for her. "You even have commercials."

"Right? Just no Simpsons or Breaking Bad." She laughs, "How dumb, I can't believe how excited I am. I can't wait to tell the others."

"How does it work?" Allison asks.

"You can get up and manually swipe it or you can voice activate it. Viewer: channel up." I say. The channels begin to slowly scan. "Slower, volume increase," the viewer responds. But suddenly something catches my eye. "Wait, freeze. Volume increase."

"What, is it like your favorite show?" Allison asks.

"Listen." It is a news report speaking of the trafficking we rescued Kate and her people from.

"Recent reports of the trafficking of sentient beings have been discovered to be a hoax..."

"*Oh my god, what*?" Kate reacts angrily upon hearing this blatant falsehood.

"No evidence has yet to surface in support of these outrageous claims. The UPC has issued an official statement noting this story was initially spurred by the accounts of a former UPC Commander, who, sources tell us, was a product of The Invasion. Motive for the claims are still unknown at this time."

"Former Commander Rennek, is sought for questioning regarding his part in the story that has swept the United Planets, causing the most widespread panic since The Invasion itself. The UPC is also seeking the crew of former Commander Rennek's ship. Please contact local UPC offices if you have any information on the following persons..." The reporter rattles off the names of all my crew. "Communities can continue to rest easy knowing there is no threat to the safety and well-being of sentient beings within our borders," she finishes and I turn the viewer off.

Da'vi's anger is visible, he is stiff and still but his scales flit with agitation. The females look to us, waiting for an explanation I do not have.

"What is this deception?" Da'vi simmers.

"Rennek, you worked for the UPC, right? Can you contact anyone and ask for information? Is there anyone you trust?" Kate asks me.

Kate's words spark my memory. "Tennir said to trust no one, perhaps this is what he was referring to. Whatever has happened, we are missing pieces to this puzzle. We need to find Tennir to know what to do next."

"If we do not find Tennir?" Da'vi asks.

"We will take a new path if it comes to that." I say.

"We need to find a way to contact Madreed. If this is a cover up, she needs to know," Da'vi says.

"If this is a cover up, she likely already has more information than we do," I tell him.

"She could be in danger if that is so Rennek," Da'vi says with concern in his voice.

"No one is more capable than Madreed." I tell him, surprised he even thinks of Madreed in all this. I did not know he knew much of my proper family. "But if Tennir does not show himself, contacting her will be our next course of action."

"Is this whole place going to recognize you now that your face has been all over the news? I mean it sounds like this story has been a pretty big deal," Allison points out.

"This is true to an extent. Here in dark space things operate a little differently. The locals will not care, they live on the fringe and don't abide by the United Planet's laws. Travelers may recognize us, but this only creates a marginal increase in our danger level. As far as we know the Ju'tup still have a bounty out on us."

"Marginal? Seems more like exponential to me! When we were floating around in space a bounty hunter would have been having to look pretty hard… but out there is a whole city that could view you guys as an opportunity," Allison says angrily.

"I did not know you cared, human," Da'vi grunts at her.

"Well don't think I'm getting sentimental, lizard boy. I'm thinking about my own ass."

"Look, Rennek is right. We have been walking around here all afternoon and no one has tried to accost us.

I think we just keep on as we were and adjust as necessary," Kate says.

"That is all we can do," I agree.

"Well, I think this gives us more reason to go back to the bar and speak with Gorrard," Kate extrapolates.

"I do not know if I agree with that," Da'vi says. "It may be better to remain together considering the new circumstances."

"No, wait. Hear me out. We have no allies here. If something does go down Gorrard is a local and seems well connected. He also seemed to be genuine in his desire to help Rennek, maybe we should... I don't know... grease that wheel a bit in case we need to use it," Kate defends.

"I do not know, Kate. We may need to leave here suddenly if something goes wrong. I would not want the group to split up," I tell her.

"You're right. We should have a meeting place incase anything happens," she says, nodding enthusiastically.

"That is not what I said," I tell her.

"The pod?" she asks.

"No, something not associated with us," Da'vi says.

"The kabob place," Allison offers. "That's the only landmark I can remember."

"Good, then if the pod is compromised we can find a new escape route from there." Da'vi adds. All I can do is growl. They look to me. Kate's eyes are full of hope. I resign myself, I can deny this female nothing. What they plan is fair enough, though I do not like being diverted from our original objective.

"Fine. Let us have a respite for a few hours first. Eat. Shower, sleep if you are able to. Then Kate and I will return to Gorrard's."

Kate beams a smile at me. Da'vi and Allison stand to leave. We check the hallway before they make their way to their room two doors down. Then finally, Kate and I are alone.

Chapter 26

Kate

Allison and Da'vi leave and I turn to face Rennek. We are alone in an alien motel room. Just us and a bed. I'm probably blushing, I realize. I don't know what to do with my hands. I wish I was more... experienced so I didn't feel so awkward in this situation. Not that it is a situation... I mean, I'm not planning to do anything. Well, not planning to do much at least, but we do have this nice opportunity to be alone. What would one of those goddesses do if she were in my shoes right now, I wonder? I hope he doesn't expect me to act all goddess-y. Oh my god, I'm getting more nervous and awkward every second. How many seconds has it been since Da'vi and Allison left? Like four? Feels like an eternity. I wonder what he's thinking right now? I wonder what he expects? Is he super experienced? Has he been with a bunch of sexy lady aliens? Look at him, of course he has.

My mind is starting to spin out of control, but then I look at Rennek--I mean, really look at him. I kind of see past the whole half naked, seven-foot-tall, gargoyle with horns and a tail and wings now. I'm getting used to it I guess. I see the man and not the parts of him that are different from me. I see his face. He looks tired, strained. I feel my nerves melt away.

"How are you?" I ask.

He sighs and rubs his hands over his face. "Honestly? Troubled. Confused and many more things I cannot fully put into words."

"I can't imagine," I tell him.

"I think you can," he steps close and pulls me into a hug. We stay like that for a long time, just holding each other. I feel silly for ever feeling nervous, I have never felt more natural and at home with any other man in my life.

"What now?" I ask when we finally pull apart.

"You, my princess... need to bathe. And luckily, I know just the male to help you with that." His cocky grin begins to wash away the weary look that was there a moment ago. His black eyes are playful and shining.

"Princess? You called me a queen before, have I been downgraded?"

He pulls me close and inspects my face, "My apologies, I see now. You are much too old to be a princess. See these lines here... and here... the tired and drooping brows?" He tisks. "Yes, you are definitely a queen."

"Rennek! You jerk!" I laugh, slapping at his hands.

He lifts me easily into his arms and presses his forehead to mine. The teasing air vanishes quickly. "Kate," he sighs, "You are all that is dear. You are my queen, my princess, you are sweetness, you are perfection, you are a goddess incarnate, you are my mate."

While I really want to ask about this whole mate thing, particularly the part Da'vi mentioned earlier about 'fledglings,' I don't want to spoil the mood. So, I just take the compliment. "How about that shower?" I smile.

"Let me help you undress." He sets me down and unwraps the shawl from around my head and hair then pulls my belt off and tosses it on the bed. I pull my hair over one shoulder and turn around so he can untie the knot at the back of my neck holding my "dress" up. He makes quick work of the knot and lets the fabric drop from my body. I'm naked now except for my underwear. I quickly decide to pull them off myself. Not to cut him off at the pass or anything, but they're lacy and literally my only pair. Rennek has some serious claws and I have got to treat these babies like the last pair of underwear in the galaxy, because for me, they might be.

I bend to pull my undies down and I can feel the heat of his gaze on me. I stand and he comes up behind me. His already hard cock presses against my bare bottom. My heart pounds a little faster. His hands run up my arms and I dip my head to the side, inviting him. Gripping my arms, he pulls me tighter against his body, lightly skimming his teeth in the crook of my neck before he gives me a slightly firmer bite. I gasp and he soothes the space with soft kisses.

My pulse quickens again. Rennek excites me in ways no one else ever has before. I turn to face him. He takes in my body. I've been naked in front of guys before, but it's been quick and in the dark. No one has ever really looked at me the way Rennek is looking at me right now. It's like he is devouring me with his eyes. With anyone else I would feel embarrassed, but in front of Rennek, I feel sexy. I feel beautiful. I feel every inch the goddess that he keeps talking about.

He licks his lips and instantly the space between my legs starts to heat up. How can such a simple thing make me so wet? I reach for him now. He lets me tug his belt off and his… I don't know, kilt or loincloth or whatever the fuck it is, comes off easily. I start to toss it away from us, but he takes it from my hands and gingerly sets it on the bed behind me.

"Guns," he says.

"Oh yeah. Whoops," I say, not really paying attention. I mean, it's hard to pay attention to little things like that when I have so many big sexy things right in front of me.

"Tell me what you want Kate," he runs his thumb over my bottom lip.

"Let's see about that shower," I smile and the smile he shoots back at me is so bright, he might have me waxing poetic, trying to come up with metaphors about the sun and the moon if he isn't careful. And then lightning fast, he grabs me and swings me over his shoulder--caveman style. Sexy caveman style.

"Ahh! Rennek!" Now I'm laughing hard, a deep belly laugh that a week ago in my old life would have been hard to come by. Even a few days ago--after I woke up from being abducted by aliens--I would have thought a laugh like that would never happen for me again. But here I am, butt naked, giggling like a mad woman, being carried off to shower and get sexy with my alien boyfriend... or mate or whatever. He sets me down just outside the stall and hits a tile that makes the water turn on. Steam begins to fill the room. It is a bit of a tiny shower... but mostly because Rennek is practically a giant and plus, I doubt it was built for two.

"It might be a tight fit," I tell him.

"Yes, I have considered this," he looks down at massive, engorged cock . "But I think we were made to fit together, my Kate."

"Oh my god, Rennek. I meant the shower." He just smiles that sexy, sure of himself smile and picks me up again, but this time he picks me up so my legs can wrap around his waist. We step into the shower and the warm water feels so good against my body I could moan. But Rennek's body against mine feels even better. He kisses me now, wild and passionate. The teasing playful Rennek is gone, quickly replaced by something savage and hungry. It's easy to get lost in the passion he brings. Soon I'm panting and writhing against him. He presses me to the wall and grinds against my slick entrance.

"Rennek, you feel so good," I breathe. He growls in response and lifts me higher. One of his big powerful hands is cupping my ass and I can feel his claws prickle against my skin as he squeezes. The sensation is enthralling. It feels like I am on the edge of something dangerous. His other hand slides up to my breast and he rubs his thumb in a circular motion around the pink puckering tip of my nipple, then squeezes before bending his head down to my breast. I lean my head back against the shower wall to avoid his horns... but then I get an idea. Instead, I grab those big arcing horns of his and use them to direct his mouth to all the places that feel best. He takes my cue and shoots me that bright grin again before he lets out a deep growl and takes my nipple between his teeth, gently grazing it.

"Oh my god," I moan and he sucks it into his mouth, teasing it with his tongue. It drives me wild and now I am bucking against him trying to find my release, but he has me pulled up too high and I can't connect with the parts of his body I want right now.

"Rennek! Please..."

"This is how I have imagined us," he tells me and I take in his words. "Wet, with your legs wrapped tight around me, calling my name, begging me to make you come. But the feel of your body is softer than I could have ever imagined," he skims his hand over my nipple again and I whimper.

"Your smell is sweeter," he dips his head to my neck again and christens it with his tongue.

"And your taste?" he slides his hand between us and his knuckles run the length of my pussy. I bite my bottom lip and fight the urge to start fucking his hand. Bringing it to his mouth, he licks my juices off his fingers. He can't even finish his thought, it's as if tasting me drives him mad with desire. He growls and attacks my mouth with his. I can taste myself on his lips and I find it intensely erotic. I feel like I could just let go of everything and lose myself in him.

He pulls his mouth from mine violently--pressing his head against the wall. His eyes are tightly shut, as if he's trying to block out his senses. "I know you are not ready," he grits out. "I do not want to push you Kate. This is good for now. We should stop before we go too far."

It was only yesterday I told him I wanted to take things slow. Wow... was that *really* only yesterday? Because today I feel... *ugh*, but he is right. I'm not really ready to go all the way yet. I don't know what it would mean for us if we did. I shouldn't let all this sexy shower stuff cloud my better judgement.

But just because we aren't going to go all the way doesn't mean we can't do some stuff, right? He's been thinking of me in the shower... imagining the things we would do together. I wonder if he's ever imagined *me* tasting *him*? We can start there. I mean, it would be wrong to get him all worked up and just leave him hanging, right? There must be a little something I can do for him...

I push away from him a bit and he sets me down reluctantly. I turn him so he's blocking the water and he tucks his wings in a bit tighter as we maneuver the small shower stall. I study the massive and masculine body before me--his charcoal gray skin, his powerful muscles. I run my hand over his chest. His flesh is harder than mine. I slip my fingers over his nipples and he gives a little moan, bringing my attention to his mouth. I touch his lips, he is soft here. He bites tenderly at my fingers with his fangs. They are sharp, but he is gentle.

I remember his flirting words the first day on his ship. His promises to be gentle *and* his promises to be rough. I smile at the memory.

"Kate?"

"Shh," I scold him. "I'm not done."

"I am all yours. You have my promise of that, sweet Kate."

I return my attention to his chest. I kiss him here, letting my tongue slide across his skin. He grits his teeth and balls his fists at his sides, allowing me to explore him without interruption. All these soft touches are driving him insane. I can't say I don't enjoy the power. I want to touch his wings, but then I see his tail whipping slowly back and forth. I reach behind him and run my hand along his tail and Rennek has to grab onto the wall to steady himself.

"By the Goddesses Kate," he pants.

"Are you sensitive there? Is that something you like?" I ask, though I can guess the answer.

"I have never been touched there before," he says.

"Really none of your other girlfriends have ever touched your tail?" I say a little shocked. Maybe it's taboo or something, though I don't see why it would be.

"I do not know what is girlfriends," he tells me, eyes closed as he relishes the sensations of my touch.

"You know, like a mate," I say. His eyes pop open.

"I have never had a mate before, Kate. You are the only one," he says gravely.

Whoa, is he saying he is a virgin? No. he can't be saying that. "So, has anyone ever done this to you before?" I reach down, gripping his cock in my hand and I start stroking it. It's seriously huge. I mean, it makes sense because he's so big overall, but I have never dated a guy with equipment like this. I can't even close my hand around the thing. He lets out a hissing breath as I slide my hand along the length of him and his heavy-lidded eyes shut again. I smile at his reaction.

I let just the tips of my fingers trace along the veins and ridges of his shaft, then reach down to stroke his balls, feeling their weight in my hand. I notice a few differences between Rennek's equipment and human men. In addition to being larger, he is also hairless down there, which is kind of nice. It makes this part of his body feel satiny smooth, even though the rest of him is rock hard... well, he's still rock hard down there too, I guess. I chuckle at my own lame joke.

The biggest difference between Rennek and human men though are the ridges that run along the underside of his cock and along where his happy trail would be (if he had body hair). These ridged areas feel firm, almost like cartilage or something.

"What are these for?" I ask him, tracing the fine, rippling crests.

"Hmmm," he watches my hand work. "To pleasure you." I look at him, but his gaze doesn't leave my hand. Precum beads at the tip of his cock. I slide my thumb over the tip slowly and bring it to my lips, tasting him. It looks like I just found another difference between Rennek and human men. He tastes completely different. He is delicious. His semen is rich and milky, like a fancy coffee creamer. I smile at the realization and he stares hungrily at my mouth. He's got no cocky smile now, instead he looks dumbstruck. If he likes that I have a feeling I can blow his mind just a little bit more. I kneel before him and bring my lips to his cock.

"Kate..." he begins.

I smile up at him, gripping his cock tightly in my hand. I lap another bead of precum off the tip. He growls roughly and his tail starts lashing from side to side, beating against the walls of the shower. I suck the tip of him into my mouth and his hands grip at the walls. I worry a little that he'll knock a hole through the shower, but he maintains a hold on the last threads of his composure.

I focus on pleasuring him. It is a heady feeling to know I'm the only one to have ever touched him in this way. I want to make this really good for him. He's so big though, there is just no way I can fit all of him in my mouth, no matter how hard I try. But that doesn't mean I don't want to taste every last inch of his delicious cock. So, I start licking and sucking him from base to tip, massaging him as I do.

"Kate," he growls my name. "I cannot take much more of this. I will cum soon if you do not stop."

"Mmmm," I moan as I suck on his head again. I feel him shudder as I hum around his cock. I pull away, still working my hands on him. "I want to taste your cum in my mouth," I whisper, before I take his length back into me. His heavy-lidded eyes go wide at my request. I stroke his shaft, feeding his cock into my mouth hungrily. He throws his head back and I'm sure I hear the sound of tile breaking against his horns. One of his hands still grips the shower wall, but he takes the other and pulls my hair back so he can watch me. A deep growl is building within him and he struggles to keep from pushing into me with his hips. I work hard to take in as much of his delicious cock as possible. One of my hands grips his length and I use the other to pull his hip towards my mouth, encouraging him.

I am so turned on by his arousal, it makes me feel like I could cum soon too. I slip a hand between my legs and I run my fingers over my wet clit, trying to reach my O as I suck and jerk Rennek's cock. I moan around him again and he lets out a wild roar as he cums. It's thick and syrupy in my mouth. I've never been one to swallow in the past, but with Rennek I find myself wanting to suck down every drop. I keep pumping him until he has spent every last drop of his seed. I'm so close cumming, I can almost finish--but before I know what's happening, he grabs me and effortlessly lifts me up, pressing me against the wall of the shower again.

He holds my wrists over my head stopping my masturbation. "No," he tells me.

"Please, Rennek. I'm so close!"

"No," he growls, and then he is licking the fingers I had been using on myself. Oh my goodness, he is so dirty. "Mine." He tells me before he picks me up and carries me, legs around his waist out of the shower, both of us still dripping wet. I whimper at the sensation of his body pressed against my pussy, but before I can grind my way to release against his abs he tosses me down on the bed and dips in close to me. He kisses me again and oh those kisses are so addicting. I'm practically raising up off the bed to keep our lips locked together, but he urges me down and pulls my legs over his shoulders.

"It is my turn now, Kate," he tells me. His voice is husky like gravel and I practically swoon at the sound of it. His hands explore me and he drags his claws over my flesh as he slowly kisses me from my lips all the way down to my cunt. I am absorbed in watching him. He is magnificent. Not animal-like, as April and Vivian said, but he is a beast... an unmistakable force. In a way, I can't believe someone like Rennek is interested in *me*, 'Captain Responsible'. He is foreign and wild, like nothing I have ever experienced. I feel a call within me. It tells me to let myself go... to be wild and free and confident like him. Maybe that's just me being lost in the moment.

I dig my hands into his thick black hair, wet from our shower. I watch water drip down over his broad shoulders.

His wings are slightly unfolded behind him and even like this they tower above us. I wonder vaguely if he can fly, but then I can't think at all because his mouth finally reaches my core. He spreads my legs further apart, exposing my wet and ready pussy to him and he licks me deeply.

He is savage and uninhibited, it is like his need to taste me is as bad as my need to cum. I arch into him, wiggling my hips to bring him to my clit. But instead he licks at my folds, teasing me. Every so often he circles my core and dips his tongue inside. I lean into him--enjoying the ride and wanting more at the same time.

Finally, he works his way to my clit and I scream, grabbing frantically at his horns, grinding against his face. I won't last like this. He starts circling and tonguing my clit feverishly, flicking it with his warm tongue and sucking it into his mouth. I'm just about to find my release when he suddenly moves back to my core.

"No, Rennek. My clit," I beg and I hear him laugh against me.

He's teasing me I realize, but he doesn't make me wait for long. Just as I asked, he returns his attention to my most sensitive spot. He takes his thumb and toys with my clit, careful of his claws. He uses his tongue to thrust inside me hard, again and again. It pushes me past the edge. I'm cumming. I'm riding his face and calling out his name. I can feel my pussy clenching around his tongue. He growls and works me harder, giving my clit long, slow strokes until I'm limp against him. When I'm done riding out the last waves of my orgasm he slides up so his face is pressed into my neck. We both pant, trying to catch our breaths. His hand goes to my breast and I laugh. All men are the same, even in space.

"You are pleased, my Kate?"

"Yeah, super pleased," I say with a goofy grin on my face. "Never been more pleased," I tell him and it's true. I've never really had much luck reaching an orgasm with past boyfriends. It's strange, with Rennek I was so ready--even from just pleasuring him. Maybe it's the situation, we are on a super dangerous outer space spy mission. I've never done anything remotely as adventurous as this. Maybe that's making whatever's going on between us sexier? Or maybe horns and wings are just my thing? I smile and drift off to sleep, surrounded by my alien's arms.

Chapter 27

Rennek

Kate's breathing slows and becomes heavy with sleep. I rise carefully from the bed so I do not wake her. She is beautiful, how I ever found a mate as giving and sweet as she I will never know. I watch her for a moment. Her red mane splayed out across the pillow. I briefly wonder if our fledglings will have such extraordinary manes. But now is not the time to think of such things. There is work to be done.

First thing is first. I go to the prompter and slide across the selections until I find the correct sales branch of the merchant market here on the station. Within in minutes I place my order and set the delivery to be made to the pod. I hope I have gotten enough of what is needed. I do not have much expertise in this area.

Then I dress, take one last look at my sweet goddess Kate and head out into the hall. I make a pass of Tennir's room, but it does not look like anyone has been there yet. So, I head to Da'vi's room and quickly check in. Allison sleeps and Da'vi keeps watch of the hallway. All is well, so I head over to the stairway and make my ascent to the roof of the building. From here I will watch the passages below.

***

Kate

I wake up some time later. The blankets are wrapped around me and I'm nice and cozy. I blink at the room and briefly trip out on the fact that I'm not in my awful little apartment, but countless light years away on an alien space station with my alien boyfriend. I look around... okay, no alien boyfriend.

"Rennek?" I call out. No answer. I pop my head in the bathroom. Empty. Then it dawns on me.

"Son of a bitch! That jerk went without me!" I hurry to pull on my clothes, cover my head and hair, and fasten my charger to my belt. I'm so mad he left me behind. I am getting sick and tired of this 'you need to rest, Kate' bullshit. Like I'm anemic or some shit.

I try to just be mad, but I'm worried too. I know Rennek has gone to speak with Gorrard and I do really feel Gorrard is trustworthy, but I also didn't want to split up. I feel safer when I'm with Rennek *and* I promised to be an extra set of eyes for him--to watch *his* back. What if we are wrong about Gorrard and it's an ambush or something? Or what if bounty hunters see him and try to take him away or kill him?

I know I don't have many skills that are super helpful in this situation. I don't know karate or anything, but I have a charger and a set of eyes. I might be able to help, if Rennek really needed it.

I hurry out of the room, keenly aware I don't have a key to get back in, but I figure if I don't find Rennek at Gorrard's place I can just come back and knock on Da'vi and Allison's door. I decide to sneak as quietly as possible past their door on the way out though. I don't want Da'vi to try and stop me. If someone tells me to rest one more time I'm going to scream.

I hurry down the stairs and into the hotel lobby. The alien woman there glances up but her eyes quickly return to her magazine. I try to act like I know what I'm doing, like I belong on a space station just as much as the other aliens do. I walk out of the lobby and into the wide-open passageways which lead to the other areas of the station. I head for the elevators, passing throngs of every kind of alien imaginable, and many aliens that are unimaginable.

Now that I'm out here I feel vulnerable. I try to walk with confidence, even though there is fear pulsing throughout my body. I keep one hand on my charger and scan the crowds of aliens as I push my way through them. Once I'm at the elevators I wait in a long line with others trying to move around the station. When it is finally my turn I board the elevator. I put my back to the wall so I can keep an eye on the other passengers. I notice all the other passengers are male... or as far as I can tell at least. I guess that isn't really surprising considering there are so many more males than females on the station, but it still makes me uncomfortable to be the only girl in a confined space like this.

As we get closer to my stop I could swear the creature next to me leans over and smells me. When the door slides open, I'm quick to get out. I hear the creature that smelled me say something to another guy and when I glance back I see them both exit the elevator. I quicken my pace. Maybe it's just a coincidence they got off here too.

I keep heading towards Gorrard's, weaving in and out through other aliens all headed to their own destinations. I stumble over some blankets and boxes, earning a hiss from a down on his luck alien lying along the side of the alley. I mumble my apology and keep moving. I find the thin alleyway that leads towards Gorrard's. I recognize it because of the steamy grates with the funky, stale smell. When I look back again my view is obstructed by the steam, but it doesn't seem like I'm being followed. I sigh my relief.

I notice it's noisy up ahead and that sort of registers as odd to me. The alley opens up and I take in my surroundings. Okay. Definitely not in the right place. My stomach sinks and my heart starts pounding. First of all: holy shit, I'm lost in space. Second of all: I think I just stumbled into the red-light district.

The little back alley I took dumped me out onto a crowded thoroughfare. It's darker here. Neon lights hallmark the atmosphere of this new place I'm in. The buildings remind me of Amsterdam. There are all kinds of alien women--and men for that matter, standing exposed in the windows of the different...er, um... establishments? They try to entice the customers to come in. Others stand in the doorways calling to aliens as they pass. Okay, Kate... just turn around and go back the way you came.

I start to take a step back when someone grabs me tightly by the arms and a rough hand slips over my mouth. I instantly kick and flail, but I am held tightly and hauled off in another direction. I try to scream, but the sound is muffled by the hand over my mouth and drowned out by the hum of the god-awful place I stumbled upon. I desperately try to make eye contact with someone else in the crowd, but I am quickly being pulled away from them, away from anyone who can help me.

Before I know it, we are in a quiet little recess between buildings. It's just another back alley in this awful labyrinth of a place, only it reminds me of a sewer or something. It's dark and there are lots of pipes and mechanical looking things filling the narrow space. The monster holding me throws me to the floor and I bang into the wall hard on my way down. My charger goes sliding out of my reach and the fall knocks the wind out of me. I struggle to regain my breath.

Looking up, I see the aliens from the elevator standing over me. They make some clicking noises. My translator doesn't recognize their language, I guess, because I can't make heads or tails of what they're saying. Doesn't really seem like they're talking to me anyway. One of them unhinges his mask and reveals his face. It's like spaghetti on the bottom with two little beetle eyes on top. He starts to come at me.

"Oh no, not going down like that." I'm not sure if I said that out loud, or just felt it really strongly… but I push myself to my feet and use the wall to propel myself into spaghetti face's torso. I catch him off guard and he falls back into some of the columns of pipes lining the wall. I scramble to run, but alien guy number two grabs me by the hair and flings me back. I hit the pipes with a crack. I cling to the wall, struggling to stay on my feet. They are clicking at me like crazy now, likely pissed. Don't need a translator to tell me that. One of them turns me around and holds my arms to my sides. The other starts coming at me again. I'm kicking and screaming with all my might, trying to swing my head enough to headbutt one of these mother fuckers.

I notice that, even with all the noise I'm making… it's oddly quiet. It's like you could hear a pin drop. I can hear the sounds of their clothes rustling as the one in front of me approaches. I can hear the soft hiss of steam spilling from a nearby vent and I can hear clicking. Only, it isn't the clicking of these creep's language. It is something with a rhythm to it. Click clack, click clack, click clack… it's getting louder. Then I hear an ear-splitting scrape--like nails on a chalkboard.

All three of us turn our heads down the passage from where we came and I'm so thankful for what I see. Rennek comes bounding up on all fours, coming to such a screeching halt, his claws tearing up the metal floors. His wings are spread to their full span and his tail lashes madly. We all freeze at the sight of him. Talk about silence. Then, he roars. It's like the sound a lion would make and even though he's here to save me I tremble at the sound of it. The creep holding me drops me to the floor. Rennek is charging. Using his horns, he slams one of the alien guys into the wall with a nasty crunch. He stands at his full height and from my vantage point on the floor it looks as though I am staring up at a giant. He stalks to the other alien who clicks feebly at Rennek. Rennek grabs him by the throat and lifts him high. The creep's legs swing helplessly searching for solid ground.

"Are you hurt, my Kate?" He asks me without breaking eye contact with my attacker.

"No. I'm fine. Just scared, but I'm okay," I tell him.

"You are lucky she is not hurt," he tells my attacker. "Your death will be quick." The spaghetti faced guys' eyes bulge and I hear a wet popping sound before he goes limp. Rennek drops him in a pile on the ground. He turns to me, lifts me to my feet, and presses me against the wall.

"*What were you thinking*?" He growls as he starts to roughly inspect me. My hair is loose and free now. I must have lost my wrap somewhere along the way. He pulls my hair aside to inspect my neck. He grabs my chin and turns my head to either side. Looking at my face.

"You could have been killed. Raped. Taken away by these monsters! *Taken* Kate, and I would have never been able to find you!" He grips my arms gingerly and turns them over, looking for injuries. I can see the red marks turning into purple bruises already. His words hurt more though. It isn't just his tone, it isn't even that he's saying something mean-- because he isn't, he is stating fact. Maybe it's just the reality of it that's hitting me, but tears start to form in my eyes. I want to hug him, to have him hold me and tell me that he'll always be there to protect me, but another part of me wants to be strong and to not need to be taken care of.

Is this my life now? Professional damsel in distress? And does Rennek really want to be my keeper? What if he doesn't and he moves on? Will I be kidnapped by aliens five minutes later? Because honestly, my track record isn't looking so good right now.

He puts a massive muscled arm on either side of me and leans down so we are eye to eye. I try to look anywhere else. I cross my arms over my chest.

"Can we just go please?" I ask.

"Kate?"

"No, can we just go? I don't want to be here with this," I motion towards the dead aliens a few feet from us.

He takes in our surroundings and wraps an arm around me wordlessly. Then, to my surprise he lifts me up and starts scaling the wall. With one arm around me and the other clutching pipes or digging claws into solid metal, he makes his way to the top of the building. Setting me down, he glares angrily at me. But I can play this game too. As a matter of fact, I am the queen of this game. I send him my coldest stare.

"You will speak to me!" He yells finally.

"Oh? Will I? Fine, let's speak. Where did *you* go? What were *you* thinking? I thought we had a plan, that we were partners here and *you* took off on *me*. My dumb ass was coming to protect you."

"You came to protect me here?" He gestures furiously at the alley below, disbelief in his voice.

"No! Of course not. I went looking for you at Gorrard's, but I… I overestimated my navigational abilities," I cross my arms, pissed, remembering why I was out here in the first place.

"I was not at Gorrard's! What made you think this?"

"Ummm, I woke up and you were MIA. I figured you went without me."

"*EMMM EYE AYE?*"

"Gone, Rennek. I woke up and you were gone. What was I supposed to think?"

He huffs out a breath and appraises me. "I would not have gone without telling you," he says finally, his tone softening.

"Excuse me? Wouldn't have gone without *telling* me? My, how gracious of you!" I say sarcastically. "You should be saying you wouldn't have gone without me, period."

He covers his face with his hands, shaking his head. Slowly I hear his laughter bubbling up, but I'm really not in the mood. "Yes, that too, my mate. *Unless* I had great reason to change plans. You are my partner Kate," he pulls my hands to his lips, but I resist. It's hard for me to let my anger subside.

"What is wrong, my Kate? Is there something more?" He asks.

I let out a sigh. "I just don't want to be a victim anymore Rennek. I want to be able to protect myself. I want to be able to help you."

"I will protect you Kate, always. It is my job," he assures me.

"No Rennek, you don't get it. *I* want to be strong and capable. I don't want to feel like a burden or to be afraid to leave your side. Not that I don't appreciate you saving me, but the past few days--I've been so utterly helpless. That's just not me. I've been taking care of myself since I was a kid and to now be in a situation where I have no control over my own safety and wellbeing... well frankly, it sucks. Then on top of that, to feel like I'm incapable of helping anyone else? I can't stand it Rennek, it goes against everything I am."

He stares at me for a long while, taking in my words. Then he silently stalks over to the edge of the building, looking out over the edge to the cavernous space station surrounding us.

"There is a story," he begins. "Of two Havash birds, born of the same egg. If the Havash ever truly existed it must have been long ago, but they are in many ancient tales. You see, the Havash are meant to live among the stars, but they are born of the planets."

"The first, Teeka, was wild of spirit. Eager. The second, Aerine, was born without functioning wings. But in her core, she knew she would take her place amongst the stars. Havash birds are night birds," he explains. "They cannot be exposed to the sun. After they hatch they fly in the night to the heavens, following the path of their ancestors."

I'm failing to see the point of his story, but I go stand next to him and look out on this terrible and amazing place we're in.

"Teeka begrudgingly agreed to wait for Aerine, who found a mountain. Since she was unable to fly, Aerine decided to climb that mountain and simply step into the stars once she reached the top, but it was much work for her. Teeka grew exceedingly impatient with Aerine. Restless and overeager, she decided to leave her sister to make the climb alone. She crept away, but as she flew, the sun rose and she was burned before she could reach the stars."

"Later, Aerine found Teeka and her spirit became as wounded as her wings. She feared she would not be able to go on, now more than ever. She looked to the top of the mountain far above and wept. The mountain had been watching and took pity on the young Havash and spoke, she told her that over many, many yets she had watched travelers climb to her peak and so she shared a great secret with Aerine."

Rennek looks at me now. "In every step we take, there needs to be a moment of pause. A rest step. We cannot rush our journey or we will burn up before we arrive, but if we take a moment in each step of our journey to rest, to gain strength for the steps to come, to honor all the steps which have brought us this far..." he sighs heavily, "You cannot rush the journey Kate," he tells me with eyes full of empathy.

"Did Aerine ever make it to the stars?" I ask, swiping at a stray tear on my cheek.

"I do not remember. Probably," he shrugs.

"Rennek?!" I laugh, pushing my big guy hard on the shoulder. "What the hell? You can't tell a story like that without remembering the ending! What if Aerine ends up getting eaten by an alligator or something, or decides she's cool with just living on the mountain forever?"

He is smiling now too, bringing me close to him. "It is not the story that is of importance, but the moral my little Havash," he says, kissing my forehead.

"Yeah, well thanks for the pep talk Aesop," I tell him and I mean it. Sometimes all you need is for someone to remind you to have a little perspective.

"What is an Aesop?" He asks.

"Don't worry about it," I say and I relax into his embrace, feeling a little more centered--all things considered. "But wait! Where were you? Why weren't you there when I woke up?"

"I wanted to let you rest and I needed to scout the building. I was on the roof when I smelled your scent and saw you pushing through the crowd. By the time I made it to the elevators you had already gone down and I had to wait for the next to follow you," he explains.

"Wait, you smelled me from the roof?" I ask, horrified.

"Yes, your delicious scent is unmistakable, my Kate. Especially after I licked your cunt." He purrs into my neck, bringing back memories of enjoying each other back in our room.

"Wait, wait, wait. Can other people smell me too?"

"Yes, your arousal is like a perfume," Rennek tells me, matter of factly.

"Oh man, those guys… one of them on the elevator smelled me. Is that why they attacked me?"

"No." His demeanor becomes more serious. "Your scent is like a perfume and it speaks of arousal, but no male should interpret that as an invitation to take what has not been offered," Rennek says icily.

I'm reminded now of the jerks lying dead in the alley. "Um, so do we need to get out of here before police or enforcers or whatever show up?"

"No. Space stations in dark space essentially police themselves. There is an organization to their lawlessness. If you commit a criminal act or wrong someone, no one is surprised if a punishment is dealt out."

"Oh, okay. That's good… I guess."

"Now, *my partner*, perhaps we should take this opportunity to go pay a visit to Gorrard," Rennek smiles and squeezes my hand.

"I'd like that. Can we grab my charger before we go? I dropped it down there."

"Of course, my mate," he says and holds me tightly with one arm while moving to the ledge to climb down.

"Thanks, Rennek," I tell him, looking into his black eyes. He kisses me, sweet and gentle, full of both passion and affection, before he effortlessly climbs down the side of the building.

Chapter 28

Rennek

Together, Kate and I make our way to Gorrard's. Her head wrap was lost in her struggle with the slime who tried to assault her. Now her beautiful red mane is on display for all to see. I am even more on edge because of this. Males stop in their tracks when they see her. I am not worried she will be attacked again though, not with me walking by her side. I glare and growl at all those who stare and though she holds my arm tightly, her features are brave and stoic. My mind is focused on all that surrounds us, but within my core I am aware of my swelling of pride, that I have such a beautiful mate on my arm, that she chose me.

When we enter Gorrard's establishment he is not at the bar, but one of the Sivoleans nods to me and goes up the back steps. I lead Kate to the table we sat at earlier. The same female still sings on the stage nearby. She is a species I am not familiar with. Thick blue tentacles fall from the crown of her head and she sways along with her melody. It is a beautiful song.

"Do your people dance, Kate?" I ask my mate. She raises a brow at me.

"Yeah, we dance. Do *your* people dance?" She asks, the surprise lacing her voice causes me to laugh.

"I do not know of my people, but I dance. Does that surprise you?" She leans back and appraises me from head to toe.

"Hmm, well I was surprised to find out there were aliens. I guess I shouldn't be surprised there are dancing aliens," she jokes. "But, no. I don't think I'm surprised you dance. You're like the perfect boyfriend. Of course you dance." She pauses to reflect. "But if you tell me Da'vi dances you'll blow my mind."

I chuckle at the image that brings up. "Yes, that would 'blow my mind' as well." I look at my smiling Kate. It is grounding to have her by my side, it makes all that is difficult so much easier to bear.

"What is 'boyfriend'?" I ask.

Her cheeks flush and she begins to mumble a response, but just then Gorrard emerges from the stairs and after scanning the room he heads towards our table. I stand.

"Brother," I say in greeting and we clasp arms.

When we sit silence quickly falls upon our party. I have too many questions to know where to begin. Gorrard seems to be waiting for me to take the lead. Kate senses my hesitation and places her hand on my leg. Her touch comforts me, but I still struggle to put my questions into words. I realize I still fear what the answers will be.

"Please, can you tell us everything?" Kate asks. "From the beginning?"

"You were born after the migration then? I suspected as much, you are young still. But your father? He never told you our history?" Gorrard asks with a questioning expression.

"There was never… an opportunity," Kate answers for me. Gorrard takes this in and hangs his head in his hands.

"It is a sad day to learn such news. Your father gave our people such hope. Something to live for again," Gorrard tells us.

"My father..." I grit out, clenching my fangs, but Kate stops me before I can tell Gorrard exactly what I think of my father.

"Please, Gorrard. From the beginning, there is so little we know," Kate requests.

"Yes, of course. Our people, the Vendari, are a very old race. We are from a very old and desolate region of space. The stars around us were dying. Our scientists struggled to find new ways for us to continue on despite our expanding sun. Our planet was becoming cold and hard with no life coming from within. Our ways were dying. Everything. Our culture, our beliefs. They were dark days. We feared even having fledglings... not knowing if they would..." he trails off and looks away momentarily.

"The Six Kings convened and brought with them the most intelligent minds in all of their lands. A decision was made, to look out into space and find a new home. Some thought perhaps that as a people we had run our course. It took time to get all to agree there was more out here for us. In the end, the Vendari longed for the old days and to resume our way of life. Starting new elsewhere was the only solution."

"However, it was difficult to say goodbye to our planet. So, we looked for something that felt similar. It was called Project Elysia. Sensors ran for seven years, until finally we found our new home, or we hoped we had. It was a great distance away, and the sensors couldn't provide us with complete assurance. But it didn't matter. We were out of time."

"Massive ships had been built. Six of them. One for each King and his people. A beacon was sent ahead to guide us. We were all to be placed in cryo for the long trip. Even at great speeds it would take many years to reach

Elysia. Some of us were set to wake early, myself included, so we may scout ahead and decide if this planet we were headed towards was truly meant to be our Elysia," Gorrard toys with the pendant at his neck again.

"I was there briefly, on our new planet. I found myself alone after the crash. Injured. Our equipment was obliterated. I had to seek out medical attention. I was lucky to be able to get a pod to function and I left. The beacon was never activated. I couldn't have activated it, even if there was time--I had no key or code..."

"What would the beacon have done?" Kate asks.

"It would have called the six ships. Let them know the planet was all we had hoped. It would have activated the thrusters and begun the wake cycle for the cryo units," Gorrard explains.

"Wait, what? So, everyone from your planet is still out there somewhere, frozen and asleep in space?" Kate asks horrified. My mind reels and my stomach feels as if it is going to empty itself onto the floor. Gorrard nods painfully.

"When I first saw you, I had hoped it meant the other ships arrived somehow. That our people found home and they were safe." Gorrard searches my face. "But you are a mystery to me, my King."

"I am no King," I tell him.

"You are your father's son," he insists.

"How do you know Rennek is the king's son?" Kate inquires.

"The wings. None but royalty have wings," he tells us. Kate's eyes go wide at Gorrard's response and though I admit it would explain why I am the only one with wings, I know my father was no king.

"You called him the Grey King? What can you tell us about him," Kate questions.

"He was my king. My family followed the greys for generations. He was of great intelligence. It was he who encouraged the plan for Project Elysia, our whole planet would have died and all our people with it, if it hadn't been for his leadership."

"Where are our people now, Gorrard?" I ask, breaking my silence.

"I have not been successful in locating them. The first thing I did after I was healed was gain employment so I may secure deep space, long range scanners to begin the search. I have eight now, on surrounding moons and planetoids. It has been thirty years since my crash and based on my estimated speed and trajectory calculations, they are still approximately ten years out."

"What happens if the beacon isn't activated? Will they just arrive in ten years and wake up?" Kate questions.

"I do not know," Gorrard shakes his head. "I do not know if they will remain in cryo… suspended and waiting. I worry too that if they are not awoken they might be discovered by slavers or pirates. We hadn't anticipated how much more populated this region of space would be, I do not know if the migration ships were programed to manage attacks. These questions, the fears, have plagued me for years. The fate of every male, female and fledgling has been in my hands alone. It has been a terrible burden and your presence only brings more questions," the old and scarred Vendari's shoulders sag.

"You are no longer alone, brother. Can we hack the beacon?" I ask.

"You honor me, my King." Gorrard says, sincerely and humbly. "I did hire a hacker once in an effort to try to activate it remotely, but it was expensive and she was ultimately unable to sync with our technology. This seemed to be a dead end, so I placed more of my efforts on the scanners."

"You will have to show my friends and I your data from the scans. I believe we will be able to help. The person I am here looking for might be able to offer resources as well," I tell him.

"Who had keys or access codes for the beacon?" Kate questions.

"There were two senior officers on board our scout ship, they had the code. Each king had the code also," Gorrard tells us. I cringe at this. My father was out raiding planets rather than caring for his people, the people he supposedly encouraged to journey out into the stars. It makes little sense to me.

"My crew, they are Vendari also," I tell him.

"No…" shock covers his face.

"Half-breed, like myself."

"I do not understand how…" Gorrard raises his arms in shock--just as a laser blast flashes towards us, connecting with the older Vendari's arm.

Chapter 29

Kate

Gorrard's arm seems to explode before us. Blood splatters my face. There is a strange and surreal second where my brain struggles to process what just happened. We were sitting and talking only seconds ago... and now chaos. Everything was silent and then... the silences shatters violently.

Rennek's chair shoots out from under him as he pushes forward onto all fours. He lets loose one of those deafening lion's roars. His body is so massive, especially with his wings spread, he seems to cover both Gorrard and I completely, shielding us from danger.

I dive forward as Gorrard falls from his chair. He is nearly as massive as my man, so it's a struggle to help him gently to the ground. I have to help him. I look at his arm. It's hard to tell what's going on there, it's a mess and bleeding profusely. I need to make a tourniquet. I start ripping at my hem and I'm vaguely aware of the sounds of lasers whizzing past us. Rennek flips the metal table over to cover Gorrard and I before he bounds away. I hear screams in his wake.

"It's okay, it's okay. You're going to be okay Gorrard," I tell the Vendari man over and over. He growls viciously in response. I work madly to tie off his arm.

"Our people, long ago..." he breathes hard. "We were warriors. We fought with honor and only to protect the weak. It was our purpose. To serve, to watch, to protect." He tells me as he watches me work. "Generations have passed since we were last able to follow those instincts. To live by the old ways is an honor. To die by them is a privilege." I look up into his eyes now, confused by what he is saying.

"Take this," he pulls the pendant from his neck. "It has the coordinates of Elysia and a chip with all my scanning data."

"Gorrard, you're going to be fine. We just need to get you to a hospital," I tell him, but he forces the pendant into my hands.

"You will make a wonderful queen. It has been my honor," he says, then he is up on his feet. He lets out a battle cry before he drops down onto three legs and leaps into the fray. Laser shots are still flying past me as I crouch behind the table. I cover my head and ears, but my eyes go to the other side of the room. The singer, the blue one with hair like medusa and a voice like water, lays sprawled across the small stage... a hole in her chest.

I fumble frantically for my charger. The table flies out from behind me and Rennek is there. He throws me onto his back, between his wings and I grip him around his neck. We are escaping.

The noise fades as we race through a kitchen in the back of the bar, but as soon as we exit the building we see the chaos from within has spilled out into the plaza. Rennek shoots two aliens as we speed past them, his tail whips and slices three more. He keeps running.

When we get far enough away, Rennek sets me down and we walk side by side, hurriedly through the crowd. He keeps his grip on me tight. We walk like this for a few paces before I venture to find my voice. "Where are we going?"

"The rendezvous point. We have been compromised, it is not safe to return to the inn," he tells me and I think of Allison.

"Maybe it was just us? Bounty hunters happened to recognized you and thought to turn you in?"

"It was not," he dismisses.

"How do you know?"

"The males I killed, the ones who fired on us. They were UPC." His face is unreadable as he tells me this.

"How could you tell?" I ask. "I mean, I didn't see much, but I didn't see any uniforms."

"Their weapons, their training. I know it well enough."

"I don't understand... did an off-duty officer recognize you or something?" I reason. "I thought they just wanted you for questioning."

"There should be no UPC in dark space. They do not patrol here. There is some other reason those men were here Kate, a reason they attacked us. I do not understand yet, but it is not safe to go back to the inn."

"But Da'vi and Allison?"

"We must trust them to take care of themselves," he says pulling me along. He's walking quickly, which means I'm running to keep up.

"Wait, Rennek. I need to catch my breath for a second," I beg. I feel a little dumb, since he carried me ninety percent of the way. To be fair though, his legs cover a lot more ground than mine do. He stops patiently and places a big hand on the back of my neck. He kisses my forehead before resuming his watchful survey of the bustling crowds around us. I notice we are back in the section of the space station that has shops. We must be near the kabob place.

"That was scary," I tell him. "Do you think Gorrard..." my voice catches. Rennek strokes my hair but doesn't answer right away.

"He aided me in protecting you. He bought us time to escape. His sacrifice will not be forgotten. Come, Kate. We must keep moving."

I swallow a sob at his response but the words steel my resolve and I press on.

"Look, is that the kabob place?" We see it just ahead of us. I scan the surrounding area. I hope to see our friends waiting for us, but I don't see Allison or Da'vi. But... I do hear them.

Laser shots erupt ahead of us. The crowd parts and everyone begins to scatter, running to safety. Rennek crouches low and throws me onto his back again. I feel a little bit like a rag doll. I cling to his neck and peek over his shoulder. As the crowd parts, I see Da'vi and Allison running full speed towards us. Da'vi is firing in the direction they came from and I see at least half a dozen aliens in pursuit.

Rennek kicks over a nearby kiosk to block us and starts firing his own gun--providing cover to our fast approaching friends. Allison actually beats Da'vi to us. She slides to a stop and dives behind the kiosk with us.

"We've got good news and bad news," she shouts. "The bad news is a little obvious--" she nods towards the fire fight.

"What's the good news?" I shout. Just then Da'vi reaches us, but he isn't alone. Rennek's brother, Tennir, slides in beside us.

"To the hanger, now!" Tennir commands and we are up and running again before we even have a chance for introductions.

"Why does she get a ride?" Allison complains and before she can finish her sentence Da'vi throws her over his shoulder and continues to run, seemingly unburdened by his load. "Whoa! I was kidding!" She shouts, but he doesn't put her down, and she doesn't try to fight it either.

Tennir is leading the way now and most of the gunfire has died down, but there are still a few pursuing us. Every so often one of the guys pauses to shoot a couple rounds behind us. I'm recognizing where we are now. I can see where the pods are just up ahead. Red lights flash along the walls and a siren blares. The previously crowded area of the station now looks like a ghost town. Everyone has taken cover to avoid our little party.

Just before we round the final corner leading to our escape a new batch of pursuers cut us off. We screech to a halt--literally, because Rennek's claws drag big gauges into the metal floors. Before our guys can do anything to defend us, another bunch burst through a doorway. We're finished. There are too many of them, I think immediately. But then a miracle happens. The guys who burst through the door don't turn their guns on us. They spread out between us and our hunters and start laying down cover. Rennek and the guys don't even question it. They just run. I look back to try to make sense of what's happening. Then I recognize two of the men protecting us. They are the guys from Gorrard's bar. My heart had been ready to give up, I thought we were dead. I struggle to breath without sobbing my relief. We aren't dead yet. We might still make it.

I see the pod. The rest is a blur. Everyone scrambles aboard. The men are shouting. We are buckled in. Then, the speed we hit makes my stomach try to cuddle with my spine. The men worry we'll be followed, but the seconds tick by and nothing happens. Gorrard's friends saved us. We hustle to the ship and Rennek is shouting orders to everyone. Dax jumps on navigation and we rocket the hell out of Dodge.

Chapter 30

Kate

Rennek strides over to me and starts inspecting me from head to toe. He is practically shaking. I haven't seen him like this. In all the life or death stuff we have been through, I've seen him angry and wild and brave and courageous... but never shaken.

"I'm fine," I tell him. "Are you okay?" He presses his forehead to mine and lets out a long exhale. When he pulls away he smiles at me. That cocky smile that makes me want to slap him and kiss him at the same time. I can't help but laugh.

"I do not like you being in so much danger in one rotation," he admits to me.

Rennek swings around and finds his brother. Reaching out to him, he clasps his shoulder--like I saw him do with Gorrard. Tennir pushes his hand away though and pulls Rennek into an embrace. I see Rennek's shoulders sag, like a weight has been lifted and he can finally relax. I hear the pair speaking quietly to one another, but I can't make out their words. When they release one another, I see tears in their eyes. I can't help but think their brotherly love is insanely adorable--but I keep that to myself.

"We must all talk," Rennek says. All his men are already on the bridge, so Allison and I assemble the humans via the comms. When they make it to the bridge I'm met with hugs from everyone while Allison stalks away before she has to engage in physical contact with any of us. I get teary when Reagan hugs me and I see she does too. BFFs. I knew it.

"Oh my God, we were so worried," Reagan says wiping at her eyes like a criminal trying to hide the evidence.

"Was it scary?" Vivian asks.

"You have *no* idea. It was also awesome and wonderful too, but I think you're going to hear all about it and then some…" I tell them before all us humans pile onto an outcropping near a control panel that creates a little bench-like seating space. We snuggle into each other like kids at story time. I look around at my girls and smile. It's weird how glad I am to see them again. It's like this whole alien abduction situation made instant sisters out of all of us. April reaches over and squeezes my hand and deep down inside me I have this sense that everything is going to be okay.

"We are all in grave danger," Tennir says, deflating my ballooned sense of security. "The Ju'tup you rescued the human females from--their leader, Ju'toktah was the nephew of Ju'tok Mah'goh." The men nod knowingly, but we humans need someone to fill in the blanks.

"Ju'tok Mah'goh?" I ask.

"A leader in interstellar crime. Very rich, untouchable," Dax explains.

"He is garbage. The scum of space," Kellen adds.

"And the head of a massive trafficking ring, which he had foolheartedly allowed his nephew to participate in," Tennir continues. "Ju'tok Mah'goh was angered by the death of his nephew and at the loss of slaves as a result of the death. It is he who placed the bounty on you."

"So those were bounty hunters back there who attacked us then?" I ask.

"No, those males were UPC," Tennir replies.

"I thought as much," Rennek adds. "Why were they on a space station in dark space?"

"They were in my lab as well," Tennir reports, but Rennek and his crew look skeptical.

"The UPC broke into my lab and killed every living thing, including all the animals within my study."

"Impossible. The UPC is an honorable organization..." Kellen stands, outraged at this accusation.

"Any organization can have corruption, even the most honorable ones," Da'vi puts in dryly.

"It is true," Tennir says, steel in his voice. "I... interrogated... one male before I evacuated the station. That is how I obtained much of this information."

The men all look grief stricken, even the usually jovial Dax looks inconsolable. In the short time I have known Rennek and his friends, I have come to understand that proving they have honor is vital to them... sins of their fathers and all. It seems the UPC, and what it represented, was a big part of their identity and this new revelation has them deeply unsettled.

"So how does the UPC fit into all this?" Allison asks.

"It seems Ju'tok Mah'goh was giving large credit deposits to a corrupt faction of the UPC in exchange for protection--to keep their operation from being discovered by those who would fight against the trafficking," Tennir explains. "It is they who reached the Mangan moon first and destroyed any remaining evidence. They have swayed the media as well, which sadly, was an easy task. No one wants to believe such a thing could happen in the United Planets, so they choose to believe any alternative."

"And the acceptable alternative is that we are dishonorable, spouting falsehoods? That we are criminals like our fathers?" Rennek says with a harsh voice. "Because *that* is easier to believe."

My heart aches for him. "People believe what they want to believe, Rennek. That doesn't say anything about you, it just means people like to feel safe," I tell him.

He sighs heavily, raking a hand through his wild black hair. He looks like he has been through hell and back. I slide out of my spot, surrounded by my human friends, and go to Rennek's side. He wordlessly pulls me into him.

"Besides, it doesn't matter what anyone else thinks… *we* happen to think you guys are awesome," I say. The strife melts from his face.

"Hear! hear!" Reagan seconds.

"There's an old saying on our planet, that always helped me when I felt overwhelmed by other people's negative energy," Allison says and we all look to her for some much-needed words of wisdom to help the men out of their funk.

"What is it Allison? We would love to hear more of your human culture. Share with us your axiom," Rennek asks.

"Haters gonna hate," she shrugs and we humans erupt in laughter.

The guys on the other hand don't share our humor and just seem confused, but too polite to say anything. I try to ease their confusion.

"It's just a simplified way to say people with hate in their hearts are going to look for something to hate and if it's you they focus on, don't take it personally because it has more to do with them than it has to do with you."

"These are wise words to remember," Rennek says.

"What is the saying again? Haters are going to hate? Yes, I like that. 'Haters' do hate me!" Dax proclaims. "I like that very much. I will use this human saying."

"Wow, the first major contribution of humanity on the galaxy: Haters gonna hate. Good job everyone," Reagan laughs.

"You are right my Kate. The only thing that matters is your opinion of me," Rennek says looking into my eyes in a way that makes the butterflies in my tummy go crazy.

"Tennir, I have not properly introduced you to my mate. This is Kate."

"She is to be your mate then?" Tennir asks, looking more at me than at Rennek. I feel like he is expecting me to chime in. Too bad I really don't know how to respond to that… and I'm starting to feel a little nervous about the fact that I have been sweeping this whole 'mate' thing under the rug. The title seems even more serious now that he's using it to introduce me to his family. I'm nervous so, I do the only thing I can do: smile and nod.

"Blessings be to you and your union. May you be prosperous and fertile in your lives together. Congratulations my brother." I gulp as Tennir gives hugs to both Rennek and myself. When I look at the girls everyone's eyes are wide. "Madreed will demand a blessing ceremony," Tennir laughs.

"I had not yet thought of that, it sounds pleasing. Perhaps we could include some of your people's customs at the ceremony as well?" Rennek suggests.

"Just to give you a fair warning about Madreed though, she will want a hand in planning," Tennir tells me with laughter in his voice.

"We've been in space for what, like just over a week and you already have an alien mother in law?" Reagan laughs, "The good news is she sounds just like a mother in law from Earth. The bad news is she sounds just like a mother in law from Earth," Reagan says in English and the girls all laugh. I laugh too, but probably a little too strained for it to sound normal.

"We have other news too!" I blurt out.

"What? Are you pregnant?" Allison says, actually breaking a smile... though it is likely at my discomfort.

"No!" I shriek, "I mean, no. Rennek met someone on the space station..." I look at Rennek and he becomes somber again.

"It is true. There is more to discuss." He looks at each of his friends, his fellow Vendari. "I met a male like us. He called our breed Vendari. He told me of our people," This statement causes Dax to fall back into his chair, and Kellen and Bossan jump to their feet.

"There is bad news though, I must tell you that first. I do not want you to get your hopes up. Our people are lost, missing in space. Gorrard, was searching for them... but he died ensuring Kate and I made it off the space station. Any further information he had was lost with him," Rennek tells them and the pain on their faces is palpable.

"Rennek, no! I'm sorry, I didn't have the chance to tell you." I pull Gorrard's pendant from around my neck. It had gotten tucked up into the neckline of my dress. "He gave this to me. He told me it has the coordinates of Elysia and his data from the scans on it." Bossan is up and snatching the pendant from my hand before I know what's what and Rennek scoops me up and hugs me so tightly I could pop.

"My Goddess! Words cannot express my gratitude. You are my salvation, Kate, in so many ways," he exclaims before kissing me. All this weird pressure about 'mates' aside, his kiss feels so *right*. Something about this all just clicks and I sink into my gargoyle's kiss, feeling enveloped in his joy.

It comes time to split up. The guys are all hunched over the computer screens, multitasking between ensuring our safety and assessing all of Gorrard's information. Allison already took off to go eat and knock out, so all the other humans are relying on me to fill them in on the details of our adventure. We gather in the dining hall and they show me some new foods they have been trying out while I tell them about my harrowing attack in the alleyway and the war-like scene that broke out in the bar.

I start crying when I remember how Gorrard saved us and the terror I felt when his arm was shot. Vivian cries too and everyone hugs me. I also tell them how badass Allison looked running from the bad guys, like she belonged in an action movie. Everyone is entranced by my description of the space station and all the different aliens on it. Everyone except for Vivian that is, she just cries some more.

Dax chooses that moment to come in. He is carrying a huge crate on his shoulder. "Do not cry tiny human female!" He shouts, "I come bearing gifts!" He slams the heavy crate down onto a table.

Vivian swipes her at her eyes, unaware of Dax's words. "Ugh, I thought they were all supposed to be looking at data or something," she says meekly, looking embarrassed by her tears.

"Yeah, what's up? Don't you guys have some homework to do or something?" Reagan asks Dax.

"Such work is not for me. I have too much energy to sit still for so long. I will leave it to the professionals," he laughs.

"Too much energy or too easily distracted," Reagan teases.

"Ah! But it is easy to be distracted with so many beautiful females on board! In fact, it is my favorite type of distraction," he beams proudly.

"So, what's in the box?" I say and my mention of it seems to remind him he came in here with a purpose.

"Oh, this? It is nothing much… You probably will not like it. In fact, I will take it away. Perhaps it will fit in the trash compactor," he moves to take the crate away.

"No!" we all beg. "Come on Dax, what's in the box?"

"Okay, but only if you show me a smile, sad little human," he says to Vivian, ignoring the fact she cannot understand him. She blushes, unsure why he is staring at her.

Reagan just laughs. "Smile for him Vivian," she translates.

"What? Why?" Vivian asks flustered.

"Just do it, otherwise he won't show us what's in the box," Reagan explains. So she pastes on a tight fake smile, but it's gone before anyone can blink.

"There. Now, what's in the box?" she asks.

"I want a better one, a real smile," he demands. His eyes are still smiling, but there is something about his request that doesn't sound so much like the playful side of him I have seen thus far. None of us translate as he continues to stare at Vivian until a blush creeps up her cheeks. She doesn't quite smile, but her eyes soften and that seems to be enough for Dax.

He smiles and saunters over to the crate like he just won a bet. Slowly he moves to unlock the latches. He watches our expressions. He almost seems more excited about the big reveal than we are. "Inside this box... there are..." he swings the lid open, "new garments." There, inside the heavy crate, are stacks and stacks of neatly folded articles of clothing.

"Oh my god!" are the only intelligible squeals to be heard. We attack that box like wild animals, pushing Dax out of the way. "Oh my... thank you, thank you, thank you!"

"Do not thank me. Rennek purchased it on the station. He only just remembered he ordered the garments and had them delivered to the pod. I simply offered to bring them to you. I am no good to anyone on a computer, but making females smile is one of my specialties," he shoots a beaming smile to Vivian.

"Okay, now tell him to go away so we can try these on," Vivian says making a shooing motion with her hands.

"I can stay if you like. I would love to learn more about human fashion, or answer any questions you might have about these foreign garments," he says with teasing eyes on Vivian.

"Oh my god, get out. You're like the annoying older brother we never wanted," Reagan says, throwing a belt in his direction.

"Fine, but if you need me, do not hesitate to call," he says, winking at Vivian before he leaves.

"*What was that about?*" I ask.

"Nothing," Vivian says quickly.

"Oh yeah, nothing at all," Reagan says sarcastically. "He's been following Vivian around the past two days trying to lighten her up."

"It's just because I've been so emotional lately. I'm not normally like this guys, I swear," she says apologetically.

"Don't even worry about it Vivian," April tells her. "I'd be lying if I said I didn't cry myself to sleep most nights. This has been hard on all of us," she says sympathetically.

"Yeah, well Dax seems to be trying to bring out Vivian's less weepy side and I'm the poor chump that gets to help translate everything. We really need to get these girls their own implants or downloads or whatever. I didn't realize I was signing up to be the freaking narrator around here."

"Hey, at least you know what's going on all the time. I feel like I'm watching one of those novellas on the Spanish channel. It's like, you know drama is going down, but you have no idea what or why," April says.

"Oh my god, I love to watch novellas!" Clark thrills.

"How cool, you speak Spanish?" I ask.

"No. I just like my novellas," she shrugs.

"Fair enough. Okay, someone pass me some clothes. I'm tired of wearing a damned blanket," I say.

"Right there with you. Just about anything else would be an improvement compared to a blanket," April agrees.

"Should we call Allison?" I ask.

"No," Reagan quickly answers. So, I give her 'the look.' "Okay, fine. I'll call her," she rolls her eyes and makes her way to the comm unit.

"Earth to Allison. Earth to Allison," Reagan says. "Come in Allison."

"What is it? I'm sleeping," comes a groggy reply.

"No big deal, just a delivery of real clothes in the dining hall. But if you're busy sleeping…"

The comm is silent.

"Allison? Honestly though, there's some new clothes down here for all of us if you're interested… Hello, Allison?"

"Did someone say clothes?" Allison says bursting into the room panting.

"Dang girl, did you sprint?" Reagan laughs.

"Shit, I'd have been here sooner if I didn't have to wrap this godforsaken blanket around me one last time."

And soon, for better or worse, we have all ditched our blanket dresses and found some real clothes to wear. Rennek did a great job of picking a variety of things and there is even enough for all of us to have two or three different outfits. Not surprisingly everyone chooses to wear pants and the few dresses and skirts that are left in the box will just have to wait for their day in the sun. Now, we just need to figure out where we can get some shoes. This whole barefoot thing is really starting to wear and tear on my feet.

As we start to walk back to our rooms I can't help but think about what's going to happen next. The danger we are in seems to be growing and compounding. I look at the others with worry building in my gut. Everyone is so pleased with the fact that we have clothes now, they are all smiles and laughter. Even Reagan and Allison are getting along. So, I keep my mouth shut. I sure as hell don't want to be the one to ruin the moment.

Chapter 31

Rennek

After hours of heated discussion and planning I take my leave of the bridge. When I get to my room it is dark and silent. Kate is not here. I huff and stalk out. When I get to her room she is sleeping soundly. I lift her into my arms and head back towards my room.

"Rennek… What's going on?" She asks trying to sit up.

"Nothing, sweet Kate. Sleep. I am taking you to bed," I tell her.

"Oh… sorry. I thought about going to go to your room, but I wasn't sure how long you'd be. Or if you'd be in the mood for company," she tells me sleepily.

"It is *our* room Kate and I will always crave your company."

When we get inside I lay her gently in the bed and slide in next to her, she drapes her arms around my chest and it brings me a deep-seated peace in my core. She is still and silent, I assume she has drifted to sleep and I plan to do the same, until she speaks.

"I'm almost scared to ask, but what now Rennek? What's our next move?"

"You do not need to worry about such things, my Kate." It is quiet for a tick before she speaks again.

"What is that supposed to mean? Of course I'm going to be concerned with what's next," she says, with fire lacing her voice.

I laugh. She is all fire, just like her mane. "I simply meant to alleviate any fears or concerns you might have about the safety of you and your people," I explain. "I will take care of such things."

"I'm sorry, when did this turn into 1950's America? I'm not some passive housewife. I want to be involved," she tells me.

"That will not be necessary in this instance. I have decided we will head straight to the Mother Planet and present ourselves to the Governing Core. They should be able to sort out this mess." Now that it is settled, I close my eyes so that sleep may take me.

"Wait, what?" She says, indignant.

"We have set course for Mother World and once we get there my crew and I will surrender ourselves to the UPC and offer you and your fellow humans into the care of the Governing Core. Once you are able to give testimony it will corroborate our stories and I am confident that all will be set right."

"*Wait, what?*" she emphasizes and sits bolt upright next to me.

"Come sleep, my mate," I say, pulling her into me. She slaps at my hands.

"Rennek, are you fucking kidding me?"

I groan and sit up. I encountered arguments from my friends and brother, but somehow, I did not anticipate any from my mate.

"This is the best course of action, Kate," I say with tired conviction.

"Bullshit. The UPC tried to *kill* you and your brother and you're just going to hand yourself and your friends over to them?"

"This is the best way to ensure you and your people are delivered to safety."

"I sincerely don't believe that."

"Well you must. The UPC is filled with honorable enforcers. We will be well. All will be well."

"No freaking way. We're not splitting up. Even if I wanted to, I don't think I could talk the other girls into it. Literally everyone else we have met has tried to kill us or turn us into sex slaves…"

"To be fair, I wish to make you my sex slave as well…" Rennek lets out a deep rumbly laugh that would make me melt into him on any other occasion, but right now I'm too mad.

"Rennek! Now's not the time to be cute. I don't like this plan and I can't believe the others even agreed to it."

I bite my tongue and look away from my mate's piercing eyes.

"Oh my god! They didn't agree, did they?" She shrieks. I pull her down on top of me so fast she doesn't have time to protest.

"It is a blessing and a curse to have a mate who knows me so well," I say as I bite her neck softly.

"I see what you're doing! Don't you try to distract me with sweet talk! We aren't done talking about this. What were the other suggestions?"

"It is unimportant," I tell her.

"I'll decide if I find it unimportant, thank you very much."

"We have already set course Kate. None of this will change that." At my words she jumps up out of our bed.

"Oh no. Let me explain something right here and right now." She jabs her finger at me as she speaks. "You have been throwing around all this 'mate' talk, and to be completely honest I'm not really sure what any of it means, but if you plan on being together, with me, in any way, *this*," she indicates she and I, "This, Rennek, is a *partnership*. Decisions, particularly the big ones, will be made together and that is non-negotiable."

"For the most part, I agree. But on this issue Kate, I am sorry. I will not bend. I *must* protect you."

"How can you protect me if you leave me? How can you protect me if you give yourself over to the UPC and they kill you?"

I hang my head in my hands, my mane spilling over my eyes. "You do not understand, I *must* protect you. I would do anything if it meant you would be safe. I would die to protect you. It is all I can think of, it clouds my thoughts. From the moment I saw you, a fire was kindled inside of me. You awoke some buried part of my core. I *need* to do this Kate, I need to know you are safe."

"What about what I want? What about how I feel?"

"You cannot live in a world of constant danger, I would go insane."

"Then take me to a different world." Her eyes light up. "That's it! Take me to Elysia," she says. I look away. Tennir suggested this as well.

"I do not know what awaits on Elysia."

"But we *do* know what awaits us on the Mother Planet. We know we would be separated. We know the UPC and the media have painted you as a criminal. There are a lot of unknowns with Elysia, but more importantly there are too many things we *do* know about the Mother Planet. We *know* there is danger there."

Beep Beep. The comm interrupts. Kate glares at me passionately.

"Rennek, we have incoming ships on radar," Tennir voices through the comm.

"Evasives. Full shields. Cloaking if possible. I'll be right there."

I turn to Kate. "Stay here, I will return."

"Rennek, I mean it. This is a partnership or it's nothing. Take it or leave it," she tells me and her voice quivers with such sincerity, I have no doubt this is her line in the sand. So, I take my tiny human mate and throw her over my shoulder.

"Rennek! What are you doing?" she squeals.

"I am taking it. I will need your help on the bridge, my partner."

Chapter 32

Rennek

"Seven UPC ships, coming from the direction of the Mother Planet. They have not made any attempts to hail us," Kellen reports.

I study the monitors.

"Orders?" Kellen asks.

A battle inside me wages.

"They will be within firing range in ten seconds," Dax shouts.

Kate's eyes search me.

"Five seconds."

"Set course for Elysia. Maximum warp," I tell them and even in just speaking the words I feel my core resonate with the rightness of this decision. It is as if some part of me knows we are finally on the proper path.

But my peace is quickly shattered. There is a resounding boom that shakes the ship, the lights cut out and I hear Kate's scream. I struggle to maintain my footing and grip blindly in the dark at my captain's chair.

"Kate!" I bellow.

"Engaging warp!" Dax shouts over the sound of bending metal. Sparks start spilling from the control panels illuminating small pockets of the room.

"Rennek!" I hear Kate's voice calling to me and see the small shadow of her form. I dive to her and envelop her body in mine. I feel the ship shifting, the loud hum of the engines revving up into a roar.

The ship has been badly damaged and we are about to enter warp. I know the everyday risk in warp, it becomes exponential in a compromised ship. In this moment, I am thankful Kate comes from such a primitive planet that she does not know the extent of the danger we are in. I breathe in the scent of her hair and clutch her close to me. These might be the last sensations I ever have... this ship may not survive the next few seconds. *We* might not survive the next few seconds.

Everything seems to bend and twist around us, there is no up or down. We lose gravity stabilizers and I push off from the ground to get Kate and I to a hand hold to keep us steady. The sparks and flames from the control panels seem to suddenly move in slow motion and the flames billow out into orbs.

My hand hits the wall and I punch into it with all my might, digging my claws into the metal. This ship would have to tear in two before I let go of my Kate. She clings to me just as tightly. Then, there is the telltale snap, like a band of rubber, and gravity kicks back in. Kate gasps out a small scream and I swing us down to the floor.

"Dax! Report!" I yell, praying to the Goddesses that my friend still lives, that all my friends still live.

"I am driving blind Rennek! We lost the majority of our systems."

"Are we alone? Did the UPC lock onto us before we engaged warp?"

"I cannot tell for sure, but considering we are not dead yet I think we made it. They sent an array of missiles when they anticipated we were going to make a run for it."

"Our shields?" I ask.

"Blocked some and failed for others, non-existent now," he tells me. "We are lucky we are not dead in the water. We are running on only one backup engine now and frankly, I do not know how long it will last."

"Kellen, can you give me a read on all life signs aboard the ship?" I ask but there is no reply.

"Kellen?" I shout.

"Rennek, over there!" Kate says as she runs to Kellen's side. He has been thrown from his post, there is a gash on the side of his head oozing blood. Kate pulls off one of her new garments, leaving only a thin strapped top underneath. She holds the cloth to Kellen's wound and elevates his head onto her lap.

"I am… alright..." he groans and I breathe out a sigh of relief.

"The others Rennek, can we check on them? Are the comms working?" Kate pleads.

"Da'vi, report? Tennir? If anyone can hear me please respond." I say, but I am met with silence.

"Dax, do we have any indication where we are? Are we anywhere near Elysia?"

"We will have visual in less than a minute, from there we will have to guess," he tells me as I grab the nearest bottle of flame retardant and begin spraying down the stations. I am able to extinguish all the flames, but sparks still fly from the equipment.

"Is there any way to cut power to these systems so another fire does not ignite?" I ask.

"You have to speak with Bossan about that, the links on my unit are all nonfunctional," Dax tells me.

"I will head to med bay, gather supplies and retrieve the others," I say.

My eyes scan the chaos and disarray on the bridge. Dax works furiously at the controls. Kellen seems to barely cling to consciousness in Kate's lap. My poor goddess looks like heaven amongst all this hell. She is my glimmer of hope when all else seems lost. Her fiery mane is tangled and she sweeps it out of her face, tucking it behind her ear. I see a bruise developing across her precious cheek bone. Her arms are smudged with dirt and blood. She nods to me, giving me a weary, but determined smile. It gives me strength like I have never known.

I slam down into the ground and race on all fours. I head first to the living quarters, grabbing a sensor as I go. Sprinting down the halls, I come across Da'vi and Allison first.

"Tennir and the human called April went to check on the animals in the cargo holds," he tells me. "Bossan is already headed to the bridge."

"Good. The other females?" I ask, but before he can answer we hear their calls.

"Help! A little help over here!" We hear Reagan yelling nearby. We race toward the sound of her voice. She and Clark stand in the hall clawing at a malfunctioning door. "Vivian is in there!" She yells when she sees us. I push my way through them and they give me the space necessary to free the door. I dig my claws in and peel the panel away. Vivian, the one who cries often, lies motionless in a heap on the floor--her arm bent behind her in an unnatural position.

"Oh my god," Reagan gasps and the human females start speaking wildly in their native language. Tears spill from their eyes and I do not blame them, if it had been one of my friends… Allison pushes me aside and quickly sets to work on Vivian.

"I feel a pulse guys! She's breathing, but it's shallow. Can anyone do anything to help?" She looks up at us with pleading eyes. I take the scanner and run it over the injured human. Her arm is broken, as is her collar bone. She has a head injury, a mild concussion, but she will live.

"She will be fine." I tell them and Reagan collapses into Clark crying. "She will be in pain when she wakes, but she is likely unconscious due to a head injury. We will need supplies from medical. Da'vi, Allison. Can you secure what we need and meet us on the bridge?"

"Yes sir," Da'vi replies.

"Kellen has a head injury as well," I tell them.

"We will meet you there shortly," Da'vi says before they race away. I bend over and scoop up the injured human, relieved she lives.

"Follow me," I tell the other humans and we head back to the bridge.

When Kate sees us enter, with me carrying the unconscious female, she covers her mouth in horror.

"She is only injured," I tell her quickly.

"Oh, thank god!" she exhales. "Is everyone else alright?"

"Yes, there are no other significant injuries," I assert.

"Oh, poor Vivian," she says as I lay her injured friend near her and Kellen.

"We will need to set her arm before she wakes," I let her know. "I will need help. Someone to hold her body steady while I fix the position of the bone." We all look to Reagan who lingers nearby, but she turns pale and grips a control panel to keep upright.

"I don't think... I can't..." she shakes her head vehemently.

"Here, trade me. Keep Kellen's head elevated and pressure on his cut?" Reagan considers this and finds it more palatable than the task I offered her. She takes Kate's place with Kellen, gingerly tending to his wound. Kate helps me as I set the bone in Vivian's arm. The human does not wake, but her flesh becomes a sickly color and sweat covers her body. Soon Allison and Da'vi are here with supplies and they help with our two wounded. Tennir and April join us, but there is no time for an update on our neglected cargo.

"We have visual now on Elysia. Everyone is going to want to see this," Dax hollers.

Kate and I are drawn together as the view window before us fills with the lush blue and green hues of my people's planet. It is the world they dreamed of seeing. I feel unworthy, a bastard son gazing upon this symbol of hope. Kate's fingers entwine with mine and it settles my torrid thoughts. I may not be worthy, but I can work to become so, as I have done my whole life. I look to my friends; their faces are filled with reverence making me that much more determined.

"Can the ship make it through the atmosphere?" I ask, fearing the answer.

"It will be close. If she does make it she will be scrap after," Dax estimates.

"We will have to split the group and send as many as possible in the pod," I say. "The males will remain on the ship and all the females will..."

"Whoa, slow down there. You can't send us alone in the pod. First of all we can't pilot it. Not to mention the fact that we wouldn't know what to do on the surface alone. Second, Vivian is injured. She needs to be with someone who can care for her medical needs," Kate challenges.

"Why don't we all take the pod?" Reagan asks.

"There is a limit on the capacity," Dax tells her. "It could take you females and possibly two males, three max. But even then, there would not be enough harnesses for everyone to wear during entry."

"I'll stay with Vivian. She needs someone to translate once she wakes up," Reagan offers.

"There might be a way I can manually create a language upload without the chip implant," Tennir suggests while Reagan works to translate to the other females.

"Whale eye wahnt too stay wit heem!" One of the human speaking females says.

"Okay, well all the non-alien speaking girls want to stay with Tennir now," Reagan laughs.

"It's only a possibility. I can try my best, but cannot make any promises," Tennir explains.

We all go back and forth over who should take the pod and who wants to be paired with who until I am crazed with how particular everyone is being. They should all be fighting for a place on the pod. They could die upon entering the atmosphere in this ship. I pace madly and rake my claws through my mane, trying not to snap at the minute requests being brought up.

"Okay, so it's settled. Me, Kate, Rennek and Da'vi will take the pod down and everyone else will stay with the ship," Allison says.

"What?" I roar, "I will not allow it! As many females as possible must take the pod!" Kate and Allison give me weary looks. I search their faces confused. Kate pulls me aside.

"We get it Rennek, everyone gets the danger," she says in a hushed tone.

"Then why are not more of the females agreeing to board the pod?" I ask astonished.

"They have the right to choose. They have the right to stay with who they feel the closest to. To not leave a friend behind," she looks at Reagan and Vivian. "They even have the right to downplay any danger in their minds, if that's what makes them feel better about their choices."

"I cannot board the pod. We should all remain together then," I say resolved.

"No, they want the four of us to go because we are the strongest and most capable if anything goes wrong. We can help with any injuries if the ship does sustain more damage when it lands. Remember, it's not just about us, someone also needs to find the beacon for your people."

"No… I do not agree to this," I tell her.

"Rennek, the beacon is paramount. Gorrard is dead, no one else knows about the beacon. If it's never activated what will happen to the Vendari?" She tells me in a furtive whisper.

I growl low in my throat. I know now that my friends all think this as well. It is true, we must ensure the survival of someone who can work to activate the beacon. The females, as intelligent as they are, would not be able to explore the technology the same way we would be able to.

"The injured should go down on the pod at least, to have a more stable journey to the planet," I try to bargain for the safety of more.

"The injured must stay with me Rennek, I have the most medical training out of anyone here. The human female still needs to have her bones repaired, do you know how to do that?" Tennir asks pointedly. I do not respond.

"This is the best we can do Rennek," Kate tells me.

"Fine, but we will look over the ship first. Let's do all we can to ensure your journey is safe."

"No arguments there," Reagan says.

"Dax, can the ship handle a moratorium while we manually check all systems relevant to landing?" I ask.

"Captain, sitting still and waiting is the one thing this ship *can* handle right now," he laughs.

"Please, none of this captain shit right now," I tell him through gritted teeth.

"Enough!" Da'vi slams his fist into the wall silencing the room. His eyes flash with anger and his tone makes me want to challenge him, though I do not know where this outburst is coming from. The bridge stills and everyone looks to him.

"Whether you like the title or not, Rennek, *you* are our Captain. *You* are the male we follow and that fact has nothing to do with titles."

My anger swells, but as I survey the room the heated emotion escapes me. All eyes are on me now, expectant. I release a heavy sigh. "I am not above any of you, my friends. You are my brothers, all of you. I want no title that suggests otherwise," I say humbly.

"That is one of the reasons we would follow you anywhere," Kellen says as he struggles to raise himself up from Reagan's lap to speak. I nod to him and search my friend's faces. I see now, for the first time, the request in their eyes. I have been blinded for so long by my shame. Shame for my father, shame surrounding my birth, about being sent away from my family… about the very blood coursing through my veins. But I am not my father, I am not his crimes. I am Rennek. I have earned these friends, their respect, and my place in this life. They want me to lead. So, I shall.

"I will be the leader you deserve then."

Chapter 33

Rennek

Hours pass and we work as a team to test all the ship's functions crucial to landing safely. Even the humans find small ways to help. The process is slow, many circuits were completely fried and we are having to cannibalize less important systems to make the repairs. I make sure everyone gets rest in shifts, but we all stay close to the bridge--sleeping in an unoccupied room which was originally meant to be a conference room or an office. I do not want anyone too far away, we cannot predict if there will be anymore fires, door failures, or--goddesses forbid, problems with the air filtration systems. So, we remain close together.

When we have finally done all we can, we gather all the ship's supplies that might be useful on the surface including blankets, food, water filters, clothing. After the females express wariness to go barefoot on the surface we use the prompter to synthesize footwear for them. This causes a significant uproar, as apparently, they had wanted footwear sooner and did not realize we could simply make some for them. My sweet primitive Goddess and her people, their world really must be quite simple, I think to myself.

We divide the supplies and make our way to the pod. The females exchange quick, tight hugs, but are otherwise silent. The mood is heavy and solemn. In such times, words are not necessary.

I decide to pilot the pod myself. Entering this planet's atmosphere feels sacred to me. Luckily, the pod sustained no damage during the missile assault on the ship, so entering the atmosphere is uneventful. When we pass the cloud layer I see the glory that is Elysia. Kate gasps at the marvel below us.

"Wow, it's... it's so much like Earth in a lot of ways," she says.

"I know, I was thinking the same thing," Allison agrees.

"Your planet must be magnificent," Da'vi comments.

"It really is, I never appreciated it until I was ripped from it though. Seeing this... something so blue and green... it's... I can't..." she trails off. I notice Allison turn away from us. I am sorry that the humans miss their planet. I think of what it must have been like for the Vendari to leave their dying planet behind, all on a hope, a dream, a gamble.

It is easy to think of home on a small scale, the walls that surround you. I think of all the homes I have known... the glass house I lived in as a small child on the Mother Planet, back when I was cared for and loved by my mother Madreed. Only to be shipped away to be raised in the mud huts on the dunes of Javan, of which I grew to love deeply. Nothing can compare to the beauty of a Javan sunset. I think too, of my small apartment on Thaad. My home there was one I *earned* on my own merits. It was the first place I had ever lived that was my own choosing rather than a result of my birth.

To leave a home, particularly against one's will, is a tremendous agony. But, to choose a home... I can think of few things that are an equal symbol of hope and joy. Kate's hand finds mine and we watch in awe as we fly over the terrain far below.

We entered atmosphere near the coordinates given to us by Gorrard and our computer systems scan for any residual ship materials from his crash as well as any electrical impulses that may be coming from the beacon. We find the spot easily enough, but the nearest place to land without compromising the crash site is perhaps a two-day hike if we travel at a pace comfortable for the females. I run scans to assess any danger on the planet. Though sensors indicate there is no civilization, there seems to be many lifeforms in the dense forests below.

We land and I use my personal comm unit to connect to Dax and Tennir on the ship. Luckily, they report there have been no changes to the stability of the ship's systems since our departure. I send our coordinates and direct them to make a landing attempt in our vicinity.

We gather our packs and step out of the pod. The first thing I notice is the fresh air. After being in space for cycles on end it is always restoring to breathe in fresh air. The sun is bright and warm on my skin and there is much vegetation surrounding us, adding a natural perfume to the air. Here in this meadow, we are knee deep in grasses that are peppered with wildflowers. Long purple and white flowers curl up from their stems. I see Kate examine them with much interest.

The only sound we can hear is the hum of insects and a gentle rustling as a breeze drifts through the grass. In the distance, trees dot the meadow, marking the beginning of the forest. I can see massive trees looming above the sloping hills before us. That is the direction we must head.

I set a pace that is brisk for the females after loading all the supplies for Kate and myself onto my back, but I notice Da'vi has hoisted a heavy bag onto Allison's shoulders.

"You mean to have her carry all of that?" I ask in shock.

"She is not my mate, she is my apprentice. I will not dote on her," he says harshly.

"But she is still a female, it is our duty to care for them..." I argue, but I am met with two pairs of human eyes set on destroy. I believe that if looks could kill I would likely drop dead at this very moment.

"I do not mean to say that Allison is not capable," I explain. "But..."

"Just stop there," Kate says holding up a hand. "Don't even try to finish that next sentence, you'll only hurt yourself," she says with a teasing note in her tone.

"I'm capable of wearing a backpack, thank you very much. I can hike and carry my own supplies. And I sure as shit didn't ask Lizard Boy over here to train me because I was betting on his doting abilities," Allison says with *no* teasing note in her tone.

"I am capable of doting," Da'vi points out gruffly.

"Save it for someone who gives a shit," Allison dismisses and I see Da'vi's scales flick in irritation.

"Um, Rennek? Sorry if I am asking a question with an obvious answer here... but I'm a little confused. Where are we going right now?" Kate interrupts.

"We are clearing the area. Dax will make a landing attempt soon and we need to be far enough away from here to be safe, in the case that the ship has difficulties," I tell her.

"Well, wouldn't we want to remain close, in case that happens?" She asks looking concerned.

"The ship might lose control, if there is a crash scenario we do not want to be in its path," I tell her.

"Oh," she says thoughtfully. "That makes sense."

"The real worry is that if they do crash, the warp engines could blow," Da'vi tells the females, not pulling any punches. I shake my head disapprovingly at his bluntness.

"What happens if the warp engines blow?" Allison asks.

"It would not matter," he tells her.

"I think it would matter," Kate stops in her tracks, "it would be devastating to lose everyone."

"It would not matter because the blast would be so large it would kill us all," he finishes.

"Oh. Okay, so fingers crossed then," Kate says in a tight voice as we resume our brisk pace.

"We can make it to a safe enough distance where we can be shielded fairly well. There is nothing to worry over," I try to reassure them. "Da'vi exaggerates."

"That is very unlikely, Rennek," he says, eyes ahead on the tree line. I whip him with my tail and it brings him mentally back into our conversation. I shoot him a look to shut his mouth and he dutifully complies.

"On second thought, Rennek is correct. All will be well." I am relieved now that the females will not be worried. Both Kate and Allison look at one another and shift their eyes in a rolling motion. I wonder at the meaning of this expression.

"While there is no impending danger, I would like to get beyond this ridge as quickly as possible," I tell them.

"Shit," is the only utterance I hear as the females quicken their pace, scrambling over large stones and pushing through thick brush. I realize I must have underestimated their speed capabilities, because we make it to the tree line much quicker than I had originally anticipated. As the females pant and gasp for air I study my scanner before we proceed.

"There is a large stone deposit a ways ahead, I would like to make it there before Dax makes his landing attempt," I tell them.

"Just point the way, babe. Just point the way," Kate says and the females are up and ready to travel again.

Chapter 34

Kate

I'm on an alien planet. A world probably a hundred light years from the shitty little studio apartment I called home. I'd really love the opportunity to explore and take in my surroundings, but Da'vi and Rennek basically informed us there is a good chance we could all die in some uber explosion if the ship crashes. So, we have been hauling ass trying to get as far away as possible from the landing site.

From what I've seen so far, this planet has many qualities that are very Earth-like. There are meadows, grasses, trees, rocks. The plants, however similar to their Earth counterparts, are still like nothing I have ever seen before. Back in the meadow there were these long curling flower stems, that towered above me, covered in bell shaped buds in just about every shade of purple imaginable. The palest were so light they were almost white with the slightest bit of lavender mixed in. They were utterly amazing.

I'm most excited to enter the forest ahead of us though. The trees fan out like an oak does, but look bigger than a sequoia. The branches twist and curl, reaching out as wide as the trees are tall. These would make perfect climbing trees if the next set of branches were just a little closer to the ones below them. I appraise the distance. Rennek could do it, I think to myself. Especially with those killer claws of his, he could just take to the trees and build a whole city spanning across the branches, I bet.

We are just about to enter the tree line when we hear a hooting noise. Rennek and Da'vi pause and look at one another. Farther, in the distance, we hear another series of hoots in reply. The guys look a little wary at this, but we continue on regardless.

Very quickly the sprawling branches from the trees block any clear path on the ground.

"What now," I ask.

"We go up," Rennek tells me. He hops up onto a limb and turns to grab my hand, effortlessly hoisting me up with his muscular arms. Up in the limbs of the tree I start to get a better picture of the forest around me. Even though I'm only a few feet off the ground I feel like I have a whole different perspective. Branches from trees intertwine and spread out as far as the eye can see in all directions, vertically and horizontally. In most places, the canopy of the trees high above completely blocks out any view of the sky. I get a little vertigo as I look up. These trees are like skyscrapers.

"We must keep moving," Rennek says, pulling me away from my moment of awe.

"It's beautiful here. Your people chose an amazing planet," I tell him as I follow his steps over the wide and winding branches.

"My thoughts are the same. There is so much to explore and discover," he says, and the excitement in his voice is clear.

"It *is* exciting," I beam at him and I'm rewarded with that cocky grin of his.

"Exciting and dangerous," Da'vi chimes in. "Listen to the sounds of the forest. Learn them. Pay close attention to the absence of the sounds you are familiar with. Silence means danger."

"Why would silence mean danger?" I question.

"It means *something* scared everything else away," Allison says.

Gulp.

"Also, be careful to watch your surroundings closely. Many creatures have camouflage and will strike out if you accidentally disturb them," he adds. "It is easy to focus on a larger predator and miss the smaller poisonous insect that is right under your nose."

"Great. Great, great, great," I murmur, my mind now on poisonous alien bugs.

"You have no reason to fear, my Kate. I will always protect you," Rennek assures me solemnly. I feel some of the tension dissipate instantly. I believe he *will* always protect me. I look up at him like a lovesick teenager and I see his eyes twinkle in response, like he can read my thoughts and I blush wildly.

"Didn't you say we have some place we're headed," Allison interrupts.

"If we continue to follow this slope, there should be a rocky mountaintop whose peak rises above the trees. If we can make it there we will have some protection if a blast occurs, as well as a visual of the valley," Rennek explains.

"Let's do it then," Allison says and we all continue on, walking along the massive branches of the trees. The path they create is like a labyrinth. Every so often we need to ascend to a higher level to maintain our course. The branches are a good four to six feet wide in most places, so I'm not too worried about falling off, but I'm also not trying to look down either. I watch the vines spiraling up the trees instead, making sure there aren't any crazy spiders or poisonous lizards or anything.

Finally, we get to a point where the mountain juts up into the trees. The rocks pushing up out of the ground remind me of the wild formations out in the Joshua Tree National Forest, only these are covered in moss and have ferns bursting from any and every available crack in the stone. This is definitely more of a rainforest climate, there is certainly no shortage of greenery here.

We follow a branch that leans against the rocky mountain. It appears we now have only a short climb before we reach our stopping point. Rennek sends Da'vi up first and instructs Allison and I to watch his foot and handholds, so we can mimic them when we make our ascents. Rennek remains behind to catch us if we fall. The climb isn't actually that strenuous at all, Rennek is just being overprotective, which is totally fine with me in this scenario. We quickly make it up to a small plateau without any issue.

Once all four of us are up, we finally have a moment to take in the view. For the first time in my life I feel like I really get why people say something takes their breath away. This world is incredible. The forest seems to go on forever, rolling with the hills and mountains like an ocean before us. Puffy white clouds accumulate high in the sky and mist hangs like a veil in the valleys. Farther still, there is a mountain range so tall that it fades into the clouds. The peaks spike up from the ground like spears. I count at least six waterfalls disappearing down into the greenery below. As a matter of fact, I think I can hear the sound of rushing water. There is likely another fall somewhere nearby.

"Look," Allison points out in another direction. "Is that an ocean?" She squints. We all look where she indicates.

"I think you're right, it looks like there are some islands along the coast," I agree.

Just then, a loud noise breaks through the peaceful scenery. It's like a screech and a witch's cackle had a baby… an ugly baby. I jump about ten feet in reaction to the horrific noise. The men burst into their warrior stances, but we quickly find the culprit receding farther and farther away into the distance. It is a large black bird. The size reminds me of something you would expect from Jurassic Park, but it is covered in drooping black feathers. It looks more like a muppet than a dinosaur to me. We see it join three more birds just like it.

"That was the most awful sound I've ever heard," Allison says.

"Right?! That scared the shit out of me," I exclaim.

"Quiet," Da'vi reprimands Allison and I, "we do not know if they are birds of prey. It would be unwise to call their attention to us." Allison nods, unfazed by his harsh tone.

"I will check in with Dax now," Rennek announces. We turn our attention back toward the direction we came. I see the meadow in the valley below and am surprised at how far we came in such a short time. I mean, it wasn't easy getting all the way up here, but the valley seems much farther below us than I expected. The pod looks like nothing more than a tiny white dot.
I also notice that in this direction the sky is clear and the flora changes significantly. I think I can see a herd of something in an open meadow, but it is too far away to be sure.

"Report your status Dax," I hear Rennek saying into the personal comm unit he carries with him.

"We need to move in on a landing now boss. We have lost hull integrity in a few areas of the ship and had to put air locks on the doors. Luckily, they were all non-crucial locations, but I want to get this over with before she falls apart on us, if that is alright with you," comes Dax's voice from the comm.

"Transmit projected landing path, we are ready when you are," Rennek tells him.

"This way," Da'vi calls and I see him waving to Allison and myself. We make our way over, but my attention is on Rennek. We round a rock formation and once on the other side I see that Da'vi has found something like a small cave… or more like a large hole between some rocks.

"This will shield us from a blast," he tells us. Allison squeezes in without hesitation.

"I'll wait with Rennek," I tell them, but before I can make my way over to him there is a noise like a sonic boom.

"There!" I hear Rennek yell.

I shield my eyes and follow his line of sight. I see the ship hurdling through the air, tiny at first but growing larger by the second. A trail of smoke follows it. Something snaps off and goes spiraling behind the ship. Actually, I see a series of somethings break off. The first of which falls into the ocean where I can see a great white splash shoot up from the water. It's obvious they are going to overshoot the meadow. Just as I realize this, I see debris from the ship raining down on the place where we parked our only means of leaving this planet. The little black dots of the herd in the distance turn and dust kicks up as they make their escape.

"Take cover," Rennek shouts, his eyes fix on a point behind me. He is talking to Da'vi, who grabs me like a rag doll, dragging me back to shove me into the hiding space. I don't fight him, but keep my eyes on the ship as long as I can as he pulls me along. The last thing I see is the massive ship skimming the rocky top of a mountain before Da'vi pushes me into the hole and uses his body to shield Allison and myself.

My mind is reeling, I can't think straight enough to worry in specifics… about Rennek, about myself, about everyone on the ship. My heart pounds and my mind is blank, save for fear. This is how a rabbit must feel when cornered. I expect us to be engulfed by an atomic blast, but silence stretches on. I blink a few times as my heart starts to relax a bit, and then I hear it. The chirp of the comm unit. We pile out of the crevice in the rock.

"Whooo!" comes an ecstatic holler from the other end of the line. It's Dax. "I won't leave you in suspense my friends, we are all alive and well!"

"Thank the Goddesses Dax," Rennek exhales.

"There is some bad news though, Captain." I hear Dax say through the excited cheering and chattering going on over on his end.

"What is the bad news?" Rennek asks.

"The ship is dead. Zero power, no control to any of the systems. I will not know if we can get things running again until Bossan has a chance to poke around. Also, I believe we have landed in a swamp."

"Can you transmit your coordinates through the personal comm units?" Rennek asks.

"Yes sir, those are independent systems and are still functioning fine. Sending them now," Dax replies. There is the telltale beep of an incoming message. Rennek studies the information on his unit.

"Does the swamp pose any immediate threat to you or the ship?"

"The water is not so deep that we will sink. Tennir and Kellen are doing manual scans of the area now, but it is likely our landing caused any nearby creatures to scatter," he tells us. "There are significant ruptures to the exterior of the ship, but if any predators become curious enough to poke around, we have blasters."

"Would you like our assistance?" Rennek asks.

"Honestly Captain, although there is much work to do here, there are more than enough able bodies to do it. I suggest you and the others continue with your goal and we can rendezvous at a later time. If the situation changes we can always communicate via the comms," comes Dax's easy voice.

"That is true, however, we will be more than a rotation's journey from you. If you are in danger it will take time for us to return to you for backup," Rennek challenges.

"We are eight bodies strong, we have blasters as well as the safety of the ship. It is more likely that *you* will call us in need of assistance," Dax laughs. Rennek looks at us with appraising eyes.

"Somehow, I think that will not be necessary," he shoots me that gorgeous cocky smile and flicks his untamed black hair. I eye his wide, muscular shoulders and the V of his hips. I think we'll be just fine too.

"It is agreed upon then, my friend. We will proceed to the beacon, scouting the surrounding areas as much as possible. Safety checks at sunrise and sunset," Rennek tells him.

"Yes sir. Good luck, my brother!" Dax says cheerfully.

"May the goddesses be with you," Rennek replies before turning back to our group. He paces in front of us, like a jungle cat. His eyes are wild and full of amusement in a way I have never seen before.

"Are you ready brother?" He bounces a little in place and takes a couple playful swings at Da'vi, who blocks him methodically.

"I am ready for anything, Captain." Da'vi responds.

"And you, my mate?" Rennek stills and looks at me intensely, waiting for my reply.

"Like the man said, I'm ready for anything, Captain," I give my best salute and Rennek scoops me up, laughing heartily. It's exhilarating seeing him like this, so easy and playful. I can't help but laugh along with him.

"Allison, my sour friend? What about you?" He asks, nodding to said sour friend.

"I was born ready," she says, unaffected by the barb.

"Good! Because now our adventure begins!" he bellows.

"What the hell have we been doing up until this point…" Allison mutters as she walks away. Rennek doesn't hear her though, he's too busy nuzzling into my neck and giving me kisses that are almost a bit too sultry for company. I don't know what has gotten into him, but I'm going to go on the record here and say that I like it.

Chapter 35

Rennek

I feel a sense of elation I have never experienced before. The past few rotations since Kate came into my life have been in a constant state of peril: running from pirates and corrupt UPC, searching for Tennir, being attacked by bounty hunters and criminals. But now, we are hidden from all this danger and conspiracy. All my friends, my brother, my mate and her people are all safe and well. That is more than any male could ask for in a lifetime, but the Goddesses have granted me even more. They have granted me what I once would have considered the greatest gift of all: answers to the questions I have had about myself and the history of my people. Answers to questions I have held in my core my entire life. I know and accept that in this endeavor I may not find all the answers I seek, but never in all my dreams did I expect to have *any* of my questions answered. To know anything at all is a gift beyond imagination.

Truthfully, I had been too fearful to even speak the questions I coveted. Now I find myself on the planet my people had hoped would be their home, with my own mate no less. I may even be in a position to help my people--to rescue them from their purgatory in space and deliver them to their new home. If it is not some type of magnificent fate that has led me to this point, then I do not know what it is.

But there is more than just that. There is so much more, it feels as if a veil has been lifted and I see my path clearly now for the first time in my life. My friends have asked me to lead them and I have finally agreed to take on this role of "Captain." In the past I always pushed the title away, but now that I have chosen to embrace it and it feels like a second skin. My methods of leadership have not changed, but now there is a peace inside of me surrounding it that I have never known before. It is as if my core, my very being, has suddenly come into focus.

I think there is something nearly magical about this planet as well. Perhaps it is simply the fresh air, or maybe it is that I enjoy being in the wild again after so many yets. Javan was like this... an untamed world. Living in the wild makes one feel free in a way nothing else can. It is truly a beautiful thing to live amongst nature and to find your own place within it.

I look forward to all the work ahead of us. We will need to hunt and create shelters. I will teach my Kate how to make her own weapons and to build a fire. I sense she is as excited about this place as I am. Oh how I look forward to working alongside my mate! But, if she does not wish to do such things, I will gladly tend to all her needs instead. Perhaps I will build us a home with a soft bed--a *large* bed-- and if she does not wish to hunt and work? Then she can rest all day in the covers so that she may have ample energy to mate with me late into each night. Either possibility pleases me greatly.

I watch my mate hungrily. Since the moment Dax informed me everyone was well the entirety of my attention has been able to shift back to my sweet Goddess, Kate. Blood pounds in my veins and the drumming from within threatens to take me. It is like a song leading me to my female. I want nothing more than to take her against the trunk of one of these old trees. Now that there is no longer a threat absorbing my mind, it is as if all I can see is her. I can smell her sweet scent, I can almost taste her on the air.

She looks out at Elysia, taken by its beauty. But it is her beauty that whispers in my ear. I am aware that Da'vi speaks in the background, making plans... but it is of little importance to me. Instead, I stalk my mate. I wonder if there is time before we resume our journey to steal her away and lick her cunt until she cries my name. The breeze catches her fiery mane, bringing with it a fresh rush of her scent and I nearly go mad with desire. I pounce on her before I can think twice about it.

"Rennek!" She squeals my name as I scoop her up into my arms. I bury my face in her neck, savoring her sweet smell. She wraps her arms around me and I am in heaven.

"Do you like it here, my mate?" I ask--*no*, I nearly plead. I want her to love this as much as I do.

"Oh, Rennek! It's just stunning. It really is. Back on Earth I never imagined I'd be able to travel. I wouldn't have been able to afford it, but I always wanted to see the rainforests. It was a dream I never let myself entertain, because I didn't think it'd ever be possible. Now look at me, not only am I in a rainforest, but a rainforest light years away from my own planet! Now that's some serious traveling," she laughs and it is like music to me.

"That pleases me," I tell her, pulling away just enough so I may study her face.

"How do *you* feel? I mean clearly, you seem pretty happy... but I know this place must hold a lot of layers of meaning for you," she asks, studying me. Her small forehead creases with concern. It is adorable. My sweet mate's features are so expressive, it is endearing. I shake these thoughts from my mind so I may give a truly contemplative response to her question. I let out a long sigh, truly trying to focus on her concerns.

"I feel... I feel like kissing you until you are breathless and begging for more," I laugh.

"Dang, tiger. What's gotten into you?" She chuckles, but I see her eyes shine in anticipation.

"Oh my god, Da'vi, teach me how to... I don't know... use a divining rod or something. I'm going to barf if I have to listen to any more of this crap," Allison complains.

"Yes, Da'vi. Show her your divining rod. I must speak to my mate privately," I shout as I carry Kate down into the privacy of the trees. We head further into the forest ahead of us, dropping down a few limbs until we can no longer see the rocky plateau, or hear Allison's complaints.

"Seriously though, I want to know what you're thinking," Kate asks as we make our way to a secluded spot. "What's this like for you?"

"You are correct in thinking there is much on my mind," I tell her as I press her back against the smooth bark of a tree. I want to touch every inch of this female, but I settle first on her face. She has the face of a Goddess. I push a lock of her mane back and she smiles at me.

"I find I have many hopes for this place. It is strange. Two rotations ago I did not know it existed. I did not know anything of my kind, save that my sire was a rapist. Now, I have met another like me who proved himself to be an honorable male. Gorrard has given me hope that I might have a culture and a heritage I can be proud of, regardless of my parentage. I hope to find the beacon. I hope to unlock its secrets and call my people home."

"I can hardly imagine how life changing this all is for you, Rennek. I'm so happy for you," Kate beams. I can feel her sincerity.

"There is more on my mind though, my Kate. This place... it could be our home too." Her smile falters a bit as she takes in my words and she pauses briefly before she speaks.

"I don't want to be that guy who brings up worst case scenarios, but... are *you* entertaining any worst-case scenarios... you know, before we start planting roots here?" She asks with a pained expression.

"I know this may be all I ever have. There is a chance we will fail to understand the technology of the beacon, we may never understand how to activate it. It is entirely possible I may never know more about my people than I do in this moment, but *just this* has been a gift I am grateful for. *And*, even if my people are never found, this planet is a gift. It is fertile and safe--"

"Well, I'm not sure if we can declare it safe. We don't know much about the animals who live here yet," she counters.

"I am the only wild animal you will ever need to worry about," I lean in and tease her neck with my teeth. "Wildlife I can handle, other males attempting to take you from me, attempting to harm you? *That* is the danger I wish to avoid," I explain. "But this place can be more. Think of the other humans."

"Reagan and the others--" she begins.

"No, the ones the Ju'tup escaped with. How many more are being taken from their homes right now? How many have been sold since I rescued you? Humans who have woken from their cryo bags alone, with no one to save them?" I could continue, but I can sense her pulse quicken and her body tense. She is affected by this. I am a bit surprised by how sensitive I am to her emotional states.

"What can we do?" She asks.

"This could become a safe haven. We can search for and rescue as many as possible and create a refuge here for humans," her eyes well up with tears, but she smiles.

"For humans and Vendari," she tells me. We look into each other's eyes, sharing together the joy of hope.

"Now, my mate, no more words. That is, unless you wish to scream my name," I say before I take her mouth.

I am hungry for my Kate and she returns my kisses with equalled passion. When we are connected like this, it is almost as if I can feel her emotions. She is weary and finds peace in my caress. It is as if every flick of my tongue pushes away the fears and doubt within her. I wonder if all Vendari become this connected to their mates?

My hands find the globes of her ass and I pull her against me, pressing her body against my hard cock which strains to escape my waistcloth. She moans into my mouth and I feel her giving in to me, releasing any hesitations. Deep inside she knows this is right, that we are right for one another. She may say she does not understand what it is to be mates, but I feel the truth in her embrace.

She becomes more frantic now in her kisses, wrapping her arms around my neck, willing me to lift her so she may grind her eager pussy against my cock. Of course, I can deny this female nothing. Once I lift her into my arms her legs tighten around my waist and her hands begin to desperately search my body. She runs her fingers madly through my mane and digs her feeble claws into my shoulders before skimming my nipples with her graceful fingers.

Her focus is drawn to my muscled chest. Kate's soft mouth works my flesh as she licks and kisses me there, before working her way along my neck and collarbone. She whimpers and moans with every touch I administer to her giving body. If I could not smell her arousal, the sounds she makes would reveal all her secrets to me. We are evenly matched on this front, I think. Her every touch lights me with the same fire.

She rolls her hips enticingly, causing me to imagine what that will feel like once I am buried deep inside her cunt. I can taste her smile against my own. She has never felt this free and uninhibited with me before.

"Rennek, I want you," she pants between kisses. The scent of her desire is thick and my mouth waters in response. I step back and lower her to the branch. Kneeling, I unwrap the tie at the waist of her pants and begin to pull them off her body.

"Did I not buy you dresses," I growl at this inconvenience. She laughs in response and tries to help kick off the pant leg stuck around her boot. We free her a moment later and I pull her leg up to my mouth. I lap up the sweet juices dripping down her thighs.

"Mmmm," she moans. "Oh God Rennek, you make me so wet," her hands go to my horns and she bucks her hips up to reach for my desirous tongue. My arms go under her legs and I pull her to my face, sliding my tongue into her folds I nearly cum simply from the eroticism of it all.

I tune into her emotions again and feel how needy she is for me. She bucks and grinds against my mouth, impatient for her release, but eager to be filled with my cock. My own desire threatens my control. I long to bury my cock deep inside my Kate, to fuck her until she is spent, sweating and smiling. I imagine how her pussy will look with my cock pushing into it, filling it. The image causes a low growl to escape my throat.

Her hands tear at her blouse until it is gaping at the front. She uses one hand to steer my horn and the other to tease her own nipple. I need no further enticing. I reach up and bat her hand away. I will be the one to play with the pink tips of her breasts. She bites her lip to stifle a groan.

"Rennek, I want you inside me. Please, I need you in me now," she begs.

I cannot help but laugh against the delicious flesh of her mound. She whines in response. I sit up on my elbows and appraise my mate. She looks dazed with lust. I smile, deeply content, even though I have yet to spill my seed.

She wiggles lower until her face is below mine and her cunt spread and pressed against my cock, with only my waistcloth separating us. She reaches for my belt and I allow her to undo it. My cock springs free. She grips my length in her hand, pumping and caressing me. Now it is my turn to moan. My forehead falls against hers and she throws her legs around my hips. My cock rests against her entrance. As wet as my mate is, it would only take the slightest of thrusts to enter her warmth. I lift my head up to gaze into her heavy-lidded eyes.

"I will not fuck you here in a tree my mate," I tell her.

"Huh?" She says, blinking and trying to make sense of my words.

"I will not fuck you here in a tree," I repeat, kissing her gently across her brow.

"Yeah, sure you can. It's cool," she tells me.

"No, I will not. Though I mean to fuck you in many trees during our lives together, I will not let our first time be as such," I explain. She throws her head back, pained.

"Are you serious right now?" she groans, eyes closed.

"Yes, very serious. In fact, I promise to fuck you in many, many trees," I tease. She opens her eyes just to roll them at me. I am starting to understand this gesture, I think.

"Our first time together will be in a bed, Kate, where I can make love to you the way you deserve," she softens at this explanation.

"This might be a dumb question... but have you ever..." she begins, only to trail off.

"You are my first everything. My only. I never felt desire for a mate before I saw you," I tell her. She is silent as she processes my words.

"You're right. A bed will be perfect," she smiles. "Wait! Rennek, where are we going to find a bed around here? There's not exactly a Banner Mattress up the road," she worries, her voice laced with panic. "I mean, I can wait... but, how long are we talking here?"

"Have no fear, my Goddess. I will build us a bed. We will not have to wait long."

"So... are we talking like a couple days... a week?" she gages.

"Keep begging for my cock the way you were and I will begin building a bed this very night," I laugh, lying down next to her.

"Oh, don't think we're done yet," she says climbing on top of me.

"Believe me, I have no intention of being done yet," I say, watching the sweetness that is above me. I run my hands up her thighs and squeeze her full hips. I think when we do make love this will be one of my favorite positions. From here I can watch her expressions alight with pleasure. I reach up and caress her breasts. I appreciate the way they bounce with even the slightest movement on my part. Yes, I will enjoy this position very much.

My Kate begins to roll her hips, mimicking love making. The feel of her against my cock is unreal. She reaches down and wraps her fingers around my length. Her touches are slow and teasing. She wipes a drip of precum from my tip and sucks it off of her fingers. Her pink tongue licks her lips and I am amazed to find such a simple motion so utterly sensual.

"I was kind of hoping we could try something…" she smiles mischievously.

"There is nothing I could deny you, my mate," I tell her.

"I was hoping you would say that," and she moves to get up.

"Do not go," I tell her.

"Relax, I'm not going far," she leans down and kisses me, slowly at first, but then bringing us back to the passion of moments ago. She moves to get up again and reluctantly, I allow it. But she is true to her word and does not go far. Instead, she turns around and straddles my face. I gladly dive into her pussy. Reaching up behind her, I grab her ass and lead her in riding my face. Her hips rock and wet folds slide against my tongue. Her scent is intoxicating. Her taste is delicious. I spread her pussy lips apart and tease her clit.

"Oh my god! Oh fuck, oh fuck, oh fuck! Rennek--that feels so good," she pants. Her hands slide down my sides and her nails play over my abdomen before encircling my cock, I freeze for just a moment as I realize how smart and sensual my mate is. She leans forward, pussy still positioned over my hungry mouth and licks the tip of my cock. I understand now, we are both to pleasure one another simultaneously. I did not know such a thing could even be done.

I am mad with lust. Never has anything been so arousing than this moment and never has anything been so delicious to me as my mate's sweet cunt. Her nectar overflows and drips down my chin, I try to savor each drop. I am lost between the thrill of eating her pussy and the arousal of her ministrations to my cock. She pumps and sucks and licks and pulls me deep into her mouth.

The eroticism of this moment makes me see stars, but I refuse to cum before my mate. Determined to bring her pleasure, I find her clit and am careful that my claws do not drag against her soft flesh. I begin to circle and tease this spot that seems so revered by my mate. I feel her body shiver and she begins to moan--my cock still in her mouth. The vibrations push me closer to the edge. My tongue seeks out her center and I push it inside her entrance. She releases my cock to let out a scream of ecstasy.

I fuck her with my tongue. We are both frantic now, eager and greedy in our adoration of each other's bodies. It matters not if the others hear us. Let the entire forest hear our passion. We move as one, her body synchronized with my own. She whimpers and moans around my cock. Just the sounds my mate makes when aroused are enough to make me cum.

I struggle to focus on her release and just when I think I cannot last another second her body quivers with an orgasm. I can feel her pussy contract around my tongue. I instantly think of how good that will feel when it is my cock buried deep inside her. My release is but seconds behind my mate's, waves of her orgasm still rock her as I spill my seed into her hot mouth. Her body goes limp, but she still grips my cock, lapping up every last drop of my seed.

"Lay with me Kate," I say, tugging at her. She lazily twists around so we may wrap our arms around one another. Her eyes are closed and her smile is wide. Her head rests against my chest. She breathes in deep and I notice she is smelling me, I laugh heartily at this.

"Shhh!" She says, "They'll hear us!"

"Who will hear us?" I ask.

"Duh, Da'vi and Allison," she whispers, causing me to laugh aloud again.

"You did not seem concerned with them hearing us moments ago. Indeed, you were *screaming* as I licked that tight cunt of yours," I tell her, still laughing.

"Oh my god, do you think they heard us?" She asks, her eyes wide now and her expression mortified.

"Yeah, we heard you! Are you guys done yet? Pretty sure we have shit to do before nightfall. Wrap it up!" Allison shouts.

Kate's eyes go wide and her face takes on a reddish tint, "Oh em gee," she says burying her face in my chest.

"Are you ready?" I ask.

"I'm going to need a minute… and maybe a paper bag to put over my head before I go back up there," comes her muffled voice from against my chest.

"Come," I hoist her up.

"Aren't you embarrassed they heard us do all those dirty things?" She asks, whispering now.

"You may be embarrassed for the both of us if you like, sweet Kate. I will choose instead to be proud of how well I satisfied my mate," I grin and throw her over my shoulder and begin to make my way back up to the plateau.

"Wait! Rennek! Clothes! Clothes!" She whisper shrieks at me.

Chapter 36

Kate

After making the walk of shame back to the others we all decided it was getting late and we should begin to think about shelter and dinner for the night rather than continuing on our journey.

"Should we just go back to the pod to sleep?" I ask.

"We can," Rennek tells me. "If that would make you an Allison more comfortable this evening, but the rest of the nights on Elysia will be spent in the wilderness. Tonight will be our last opportunity to return to the pod."

"No, I don't want to double back," Allison says definitively. "I'd rather move forward, not back."

And even though Allison was so assertive in her response, Rennek looks to me for my answer.

"Yeah, no. That makes sense. No reason to make the same trip twice, especially if we are going to be roughing it from here on out," I tell him. "Plus, it's not like the pod is super luxurious or anything." He studies me a moment or two longer, like he is trying to make sure I'm not just taking one for the team. I smile to assure him it's fine and he nods before getting to work.

"We will eat our evening meal here before going down into the trees to sleep for the night," Rennek tells us. "I will hunt and return shortly." He gives me a hard and happy kiss before bounding down into the trees.

"Is there anything I can do to help with the hunting," Allison asks Da'vi.

"No," he says curtly. "Tonight, you work on fire. *If* you are successful, then tomorrow I will begin to show you how to track," he tells her.

Allison gets to work and I sit and watch the world around us. I stare off into the direction of the ocean. The sun, which appears to be the same color as Earth's sun, if perhaps only slightly larger in the sky, starts to dip towards the horizon.

Rennek is back in no time with the carcass of... I don't know... a little ugly bear or something. He flicks his hair back and holds the creature high to show me. I give him a thumbs up and try not to be too grossed out by the thing, after all I'm going to have to eat it.

Da'vi helps hold the ugly bear while Rennek works to skin it. Allison watches the process closely... I try to look literally anywhere else. A lot of chopping starts happening, so I examine some rocks, and a leaf, and the bottom of my boot, and then the leaf again. I'm vaguely aware in my peripheral vision that Rennek makes a long cut down the center of the animal.

"Wait," Da'vi directs Rennek, who looks confused by the halt in their work. "You. Remove the offal," he commands Allison.

I look up in shock. Allison is quick to step up though. Rennek moves hesitantly aside and I see him shake his head at Da'vi. Da'vi's scales flick and he refuses to meet Rennek's gaze. And even though this is likely the grossest part of the whole thing, I watch. I feel like it's my only way to support Allison. Solidarity.

She struggles a bit at the neck and Da'vi grunts at her... I'm not sure if it is meant as encouragement or disapproval. Her hands slip, but she adjusts her grip and rips the guts out. She is bloodied up to her elbows and her clothes have gotten a little dirty as well.

"Now you will bury it," he tells her.

"Great job Allison!" I beam, clapping. I mean... someone's got to give her credit. She nods in acknowledgement but her eyes stay on her task. She and Da'vi descend down the side of the plateau which we originally came from. I stare after them for a bit.

"Your assistance, my goddess," Rennek calls to me. His hands are as filthy as Allison's. He motions to a water pouch and I open the lid and pour it out over his hands.

"She wants this?" He nods after Allison.

"It appears that way," I shrug.

"Hmph," he grunts, kissing me atop my head before getting back to work.

The rest of the evening my thoughts are consumed with our time in space and here in the wilderness. In space I felt like I needed to step up, but here on Elysia? I don't know, I don't feel the same sense of urgency to perform. Part of me wonders if I should be more gung-ho about learning all this survivalist stuff Allison has been trying to pick up on. But another part of me is starting to relish being taken care of. I've never had this before, not with a boyfriend and not even as a child with my family.

So... I let Rennek carry the pack, and I let him start the fire, and put a blanket around my shoulders. I even let him feed me a little bit as we sit around eating dinner together. There will be plenty of time to learn all this stuff, I think to myself. It's not like we're going anywhere anytime soon. Right now, I'm just going to bask in the attention and care Rennek is giving me.

Allison, on the other hand, sits a few feet away struggling to make her own fire by rubbing two sticks together. Is that even real, I wonder? Did Tom Hanks do it that way in *Castaway*? I try to remember, but end up thinking about Wilson. Da'vi sits a ways off, his back to us all, eating ugly bear.

"Allison, it's getting chilly. Why don't you come sit with me?" I offer.

"No thanks," she mumbles without looking up.

"At least eat," I tell her, but she completely ignores me this time.

Another twenty minutes or so goes by. Rennek stares at Da'vi's back and huffs a few times. Finally, Rennek gets up and stalks over to Allison.

"You must eat now. Darkness is fast approaching. We will leave to find a resting place for the night soon. There will not be another chance to eat until morning," he tells her this sternly--probably taking a hard stance under the assumption she might refuse. She stills briefly before throwing her sticks angrily away. She finally pulls herself to her feet and grabs some ugly bear meat. But, instead of sitting with us by the fire she goes and sits alone, staring off towards the ocean. I watch her.

Rennek returns to my side. Wrapping his arm around me and shielding me with his wing, he hugs me against his body. I know he can sense how much this distance Allison is creating bothers me. It's pointless, I've spent so much of my life in self-imposed isolation. Now that all this has happened to us--the abduction and everything since, life has really been put into a different perspective for me. Why waste time being unhappy, or alone, or struggling when you don't have to?

Sure, Allison doesn't have a big sexy gargoyle to take care of her, but she has other humans... she has me. I can't hunt for her or anything, but I can hear her out. I can listen to what she is going through and be there for her. She doesn't have to be alone in this.

"It's time," Rennek says, giving me one final squeeze before standing and extinguishing the flames. The sun has already sunk and there is only a bit of light left, peeking at us from the horizon. We rinse our hands and faces with some water from one of the pouches Rennek carries and we all take a bathroom break before we slip back below the canopy and onto the branches. The light is even more faint here, so I rely on Rennek to hold my hand and show me the best footholds as we move from tree to tree.

Soon we approach the wide branches that Rennek and I... enjoyed... earlier in the afternoon. I notice it seems a little warmer under the trees compared to the mountaintop, so Rennek spreads a blanket on the branch and we lay on top of it. I watch Da'vi yank a few vines until they hang with greater slack from a branch above. He twists them around one another a few times in a braid like motion and climbs inside. He has made a little makeshift hammock. Allison takes a blanket from her pack, wraps it around her shoulders and leans against the massive trunk of the tree.

"First watch," Da'vi calls.

"Wake me when you require rest, my friend," Rennek tells him. Da'vi grunts his acknowledgement.

Slowly the last warm light from the sun fades and we are surrounded in darkness. Rennek holds me close to him and the warmth of his body chases away any chill that might threaten to make my slumber anything less than comfortable. I snuggle into him and can't help but smile against his muscled chest. I try to look up towards the sky. I want to see the stars on this new world, but the trees block much of my view, and before I can find a tiny prick of light peeking through the leaves, sleep whisks me away.

Chapter 37

Rennek

When I next open my eyes I can see that the moons have risen. The forest around us is filled with the milky light of Elysia's moon system. Kate stirs beside me. I caress her back in the hope that I will soothe my sweet mate back to sleep. I look up towards Da'vi and see he is no longer in his perch.

"No sudden movements," he whispers to me.

My eyes search in the direction of his voice and I see him on the branch nearby, crouching low. His blade glints in the moonlight. My hand finds my blade as well. I sense Kate stiffen next to me. His words have roused her to awareness.

I carefully roll to my stomach so that I may more easily follow his gaze. Then I see it. There, climbing atop Allison are four arthropod creatures, roughly the size of marsh rakes. They look agitated. They hold long, segmented tails up in the air above their bodies. I can see stingers at the tips. I watch them closely. They congregate near her booted feet. Da'vi makes a few slow and stealthy steps forward and the creatures seem unaware. Kate tilts her head so she can see what is happening. I see her hand fly over her mouth when she sees what is atop her friend.

Da'vi and I both inch forward together. This time however, Allison stirs and one of the creatures climbs higher up her legs and onto her lap. We freeze as Allison's eyes open slowly and then go very wide. She looks to Da'vi and he motions for her to wait. Da'vi clicks, once, twice, he pauses and on the third click we both pounce. He knocks two of the creatures off and I send the other two flying off the tree limb.

"Holy shit!" Allison exclaims as she moves to get up, a look of relief rushing over her face for just the quickest moment--before pain sinks into her features.

"Agh!" She screams out. She flings the blanket away and there beneath the covers is one more of the arthropods, stinger stuck deep into Allison's leg. Da'vi does not hesitate. Before I even know what is happening, he has skewered the thing with his blade. Its legs are still writhing when he tears its tail from her calf.

"Ow, ow, ow! Careful, don't twist it!" Allison begs.

"Sit!" Da'vi commands and he helps her lower herself to a position where we can examine the wound. I move to use my blade to cut her pants, but he grabs it from me.

"I will do it," he grits out.

Instead I hurry to my pack to retrieve a lantern and the scanner. When I return Da'vi has cut her pants up to her knee. I can see the wound is on her calf. It is red and swelling. I hold the light close, some of the stinger is still lodged in her leg. Da'vi looks angrily at Allison.

"This will hurt," he tells her, just before jamming his knife against the wound at an angle--this pushes the stinger out along with a spurt of blood and venom.

I turn my attention to the lifeless arthropod and begin running scans on the creature to determine how poisonous it might be and to see if we have any meds to counter the effects. Kate has joined us and sits beside Allison. I am surprised to see Allison grab for my Kate's hand. She must truly be in pain.

As the results are processing I survey the scene. Da'vi looks down at Allison and Kate loathsomely before stalking over to inspect the dead creature. Its back is hard, it's color a deep greenish blue, with three sets of legs and a long, flat tail that tapers toward where the stinger once was. He flips it over to reveal it's under belly. Underneath there are thousands of small legs that are almost hair-like, leading up toward a mouth and a pair of ventral eyes.

It is undoubtedly ugly, but does not look like a creature that poses much of a threat. Appearances can often be deceiving, I suppose. Da'vi seems as unimpressed by the creature as I am. He turns his attention instead to the place that Allison had made her bed for the night. I hear him huffing and cursing under his breath.

"There is a nest here, human! You made your bed on a nest!" he bellows. Allison refuses to meet his gaze but Kate looks at him, incredulous.

"You say you wish to learn skills to survive, but you make such a foolish mistake as to sleep on another creature's nest! I cannot teach you! Tomorrow you will be as this one--" He waves his hand at my Kate. "I will carry the supplies and possibly you as well. I will feed you and keep you warm by the fire each night. You will not concern yourself with learning any longer."

"What?!" Allison says as if a blow has just been landed to her core.

"How dare you!" My Kate stands and her tone is enough to level any warrior.

"You are *goddesses*," Da'vi stresses. "I should have never attempted to teach this female," Da'vi tells her.

"How about instead of reprimanding the *student* for not knowing what *you* didn't teach her, you reassess your teaching skills. All I've heard you do so far is point out the things you think she isn't ready to learn. And that's only half the time, the other half you completely ignore her and don't even help with the things you have agreed to teach her."

"You should be working *with* her, pointing out as much as possible rather than faulting her for not *already* knowing how to survive in a damned rainforest. If she already knew these things she wouldn't need your ass to teach her in the first place!" Kate bellows accusingly.

Though the situation is a heavy one I cannot help but smile at how fierce my mate is. This is why she is the queen of her people. Hard headed Da'vi however, only flicks his scales in response.

"I will not be responsible for this foolish endeavor any longer. She is going to get herself killed if I allow it to continue," Da'vi says firmly.

"*Allow* it to continue? Who do you think you are? Maybe Allison doesn't need you to be her teacher anymore. You aren't the only one with survival skills around here. Rennek could teach her, Rennek could teach us both," Kate tells him.

"Absolutely not," Da'vi commands.

"Hello! You don't own her! If Allison wants to learn, it doesn't have to be from you, and I'm starting to think it *shouldn't* be from you!" Kate yells and she jams her finger into Da'vi's chest as she speaks.

"She indentured herself to me!" Da'vi begins to argue.

"*Indentured herself to you*? What are you saying, she's like your slave now?" Kate interrupts, scoffing at him.

"I will not let another male…" Da'vi bellows into the face of my mate, but I have had enough of this. I tackle Da'vi with all my might, catching him off guard and sending both of us careening over the side of the tree limb into the darkness below.

"Rennek!" I hear Kate's scream from above.

Da'vi and I come crashing down to a branch a few levels below the females. I work quickly to pin him against the tree. He fights hard against me, but is unable to free himself.

"I see what is going on here, my brother," I tell him in a hushed voice, so the females do not overhear.

"You will not let her continue this! I won't allow it! She will fail…" He declares ferociously, still trying to fight against me. Finally, his body slacks and he hangs his head.

"If she tries and she fails Rennek, if she is hurt or killed… it would end me. Even now she sits up there with poison in her system…"

"The scanner results finalized while you argued with my mate. It is a mild venom, she will have swelling and pain around the wound for a rotation, maybe two, but she will not even need any meds to counter the effects of the venom. She is fine Da'vi," I tell him knowingly. "The larger wound is to her pride."

"Her pride," he laughs ruefully. "She may be fine now, but she cannot continue like this. I will lose my mind Rennek! She is so stubborn! She will let me do nothing for her."

I release my grip on my friend and we sit side by side on the branch, our feet dangling into the abyss below.

"I know exactly how you feel," I assure him.

"You do not, Rennek. You could not possibly know how I feel. Your mate..." he sighs. "Your mate is your mate. She is yours and you are hers. The way she looks at you... Allison will never look upon me with such affection. That female is incapable of it," he says disheartened.

"You are too quick to give up, my brother. When I first laid eyes upon my Kate I knew in my core she was my mate. That there would never be another for me. Never in my wildest dreams did I dare think she would return my affections. I believed I was doomed to follow her as nothing more than a friend and guardian for all the days of my life. But I would have gladly done just that. Be grateful for what you have and maybe from that, something more will grow."

"Do you truly see Allison returning anyone's affections?" He says with disbelief and anger lacing his words.

"Right now, all I see is two stubborn fools. Which of you will be the one to bend first?" I ask. "Kate is correct. You have been a poor teacher, especially if you wish for your student to one day be your mate."

He breathes a long sigh at my words. "She will never be one to bend, will she?"

"And what of you?"

"I do not know that I can."

"Then that is something you must consider. Oh, and Da'vi?" He looks me in the eye and I hit him square on the jaw so hard he nearly topples over the edge of the branch. "Do not ever raise your voice at my mate again or I will rip your throat from your body."

"I apologize, my friend. I have not been myself," he says rubbing his jaw.

"Yes, you have been even more bad tempered than usual," I agree. "Take the rest of the evening. Think on where you wish to find yourself and what path you must take to arrive there. I will stand guard over the females," I tell him.

He nods solemnly and I climb back up to my mate, leaving him to his thoughts.

Chapter 38

Kate

"Shhh! Quiet, I think I hear them," I tell Allison and we both still, listening for sounds from the men.

"He's right. I will fail. I'm a failure," Allison says with resignation.

"Bullshit," I tell her, holding Rennek's lamp over the side, trying to get a glimpse of what's going on below. The moon does a decent job of lighting the forest, but visibility doesn't go very far.

"I'm sorry, I should have just let the guys do everything. I was so caught up in trying to find a place for myself, I put myself in danger and that puts the whole group at risk. I was being selfish."

"That's dumb. Don't say that," I tell her.

"You must have been a damn inspirational speaker back on Earth," she says with anger filling her words rather than her usual dismissiveness.

"That's funny, I was thinking the same thing about you," I turn the light at her and smile, but I'm really checking for signs she's dying from that nasty scorpion centipede thing that stung her. "How are you feeling?"

"My leg hurts. It burns and itches, and the skin is so tight it feels like it is going to split open, but other than that, not too bad. No dizziness, no fever. I'm not hallucinating or anything else," she tells me, but I don't hear a lot of confidence behind her words.

"You're scared," I say. It isn't a question.

"Wouldn't you be?" She asks.

I sit down next to her. "Yeah, I would be, and I'm scared for you now." I see tears stream down her face. This is a rare moment for sure: Allison exposing her vulnerability. I watch her and try to think about what she needs in this moment and how I might be able to be there for her.

She really is beautiful, even dirty in the forest. She has that long brown mermaid hair and the kind of looks that make you hate a girl for no good reason. The kind of looks that make you assume life just fits neatly in place for this person and they've never had to struggle before, or work hard a day in their life.

"Talk to me, Allison. Please? I want to be there for you, but I just really don't know how to do that without you letting me in." She wipes her eyes and looks away shaking her head.

"This is just who I am. Or who I was at least. I work hard, harder than anyone else, and I succeed. I climb ladders and I just keep going. There isn't time left over for... for other things. Trivial things. This is just *who I am*," she repeats.

At first, I don't really get it, and then suddenly I do, because it actually sounds kind of familiar. "I thought if I could just keep going... shut out all the white noise, work hard... it'd be the same as Earth. I'd kick ass and climb that ladder. I'd have the sense of security that comes with success, but I don't know if I can succeed here. This isn't a marketing presentation for a large account, this is life or death survival shit and I'm afraid Da'vi is right: I will fail."

"Am I white noise in this scenario then, me and the other girls," I smile, trying to show Allison I take no offense. I just want to understand.

"No offense," she says confirming my assumption.

"Tell me then, why is it so hard for you to admit you're like the rest of us?" I don't say the words though; the words Reagan and I used the first time we had this discussion with everyone. Allison saves me the trouble.

"Why is it so hard to admit that no one will miss me? That no one will be looking for me or even notice I'm gone? That if I miss a day at work there are ten people in line waiting to snake my job and bad mouth me the first chance they get?" She does something between a rueful laugh and a sob, "What bugs me the most is that they'll all just assume I couldn't handle the pressure. That's the part that drives me crazy."

"Why didn't you just tell us that?"

"What I don't get is how you guys can even say it out loud. Aren't you embarrassed? Isn't it humiliating to know that no matter what you were doing in life, no matter how hard you were working, or how much success you garnered, that no one really gave a shit about you? To know you were utterly replaceable at every level?"

"Hmm, well when you say it that way…" We both laugh lamely. "I don't know what to tell you. Yes, it's painful to know that no one will notice I'm gone. But I wouldn't go so far as to say no one gave a shit about me. The people in my life… my family in particular, well, they just cared for me in their own way. It wasn't the best way, and there were many times in my life I wished for more, but it was all they were capable of, you know?"

"Well fuck that and fuck them," she says. "I don't do anything in my life half ass and I certainly wouldn't half ass my friendships or my family."

"As far as I can tell, you 'no ass' your friendships," I remind her of the distance she continues to place between herself and the rest of the women.

"Like I said, I don't have time for white noise. This is a whole new world we are in Kate, if I don't devote myself entirely, who knows what could happen."

"So, you aren't giving up then?"

"As long as this injury doesn't kill me, then I guess not. I can't. I don't have it in me to give up."

"Well, I'll count that as a win and we can just work on being friends another day," I tell her. She scoffs in response. "But I agree Allison, this is a whole new world. Don't waste the opportunity to be more," I tell her.

"I'm trying as hard as I can Kate, there isn't room for more."

Just then, Rennek climbs up onto the branch, startling the shit out of us both.

"Oh my god! Rennek, what the fuck was that all about? Allison's here injured and you guys decide it's a good time for a round of grab ass?" I say irritated.

"*Grab ass*?" He laughs heartily before turning his attention to the matters at hand. "I apologize for the delay Allison, the results from the scanner came in. The venom was mild, the effects should be localized to the wound and should dissipate within a day or so."

"You couldn't have told us that before you and Da'vi... did whatever it was you did down there?" I ask.

"If Allison had been in danger that would have been my first priority. Since she was not, I had to make it clear to Da'vi that he is not to raise his voice to my mate--no matter how loudly she howls at him," he tells me frankly and without regret.

"*That's* why you tackled him? I thought you were reprimanding him over the way he has been treating Allison!" I exclaim.

"That matter will have to remain between Da'vi and Allison," he says, his expression serious and knowing. All I can do is grumble in response.

"Wait, if Da'vi refuses to continue to teach Allison or..." she eyes her friend, "...if Allison no longer wants Da'vi as her teacher, will you help her learn to take care of herself?" I ask. I have to know this answer, I feel like *Allison* needs to know this answer before she decides what to do next. She needs to know if she has options.

"In the morning Allison and Da'vi can decide together how they would like to proceed. If their agreement comes to an end, know that I will always do everything in my power to aid your people, my Kate," he nods to me and to Allison.

"Thank you," Allison tells him.

"Now you both must rest. I will remain on watch until daylight," he says firmly.

At first, I don't think I will be able to sleep after all the adrenaline and worrying of the past hour or so, but sleep seizes me before I realize it and seemingly minutes later Rennek is waking me for the day.

I wipe the drool off my chin and blink my eyes a few times to adjust them to the daylight peeking through the branches above us.

"Are you hungry, my mate?" Rennek asks.

"Mmm, yeah. I just want to check in with Allison first," I tell him, getting to my feet. But when I stand and look around Allison is nowhere to be seen. "Where's Allison?" I ask alarmed.

"She and Da'vi left," he tells me simply.

"Left? What the fuck do you mean, left? Left where? When will they be back?" I demand.

"They did not include me in their conversation, but it seemed they had reached a mutual agreement," he shrugs and digs into his pack to get some space MREs out.

"When will they be back, Rennek?" I ask, starting to get angry.

Smart fellow that he is, he catches onto my angry tone and brings his focus onto me. He wraps his arms around me and nuzzles my hair. "They have their own journey to make, my sweet mate. They will not be back here. They will either join us later at the beacon or seek out the others on the ship."

"So, they just left? Allison didn't even wake me to say goodbye or let me know what her plans were," I ask surprised... well, *kind of* surprised.

"You are upset at this?" He asks, his voice sweet and concerned.

I sigh and think about my response. "I don't know. Maybe. Yes? I just wish she would have talked to me before she left. It's okay she decided to go with Da'vi and all, I wouldn't have judged her or tried to talk her out of it. I just wish she would have said something before leaving. At least a goodbye. I don't know, I'm being stupid I guess," I say rubbing my temples, trying to push away my feelings.

"You care. That is not stupid. It is generous," he kisses me on my head and looks into my eyes for a long while. "Come, let us eat and then we will continue our journey." I join him, but my heart is reluctant to let go of the disappointment over Allison not letting me in. I keep thinking I'm making progress and then we're back to square one.

"So, how far is the beacon?" I ask, trying to steer the conversation to a brighter topic.

"Depends on how we travel. Two days, more if we would like to take our time and explore a bit. Would you still like me to teach you survival techniques?" he asks.

"Huh? Oh god no, I was only going to do that so Allison would have a buddy," I tell him, causing his deep laughter to reverberate through the surrounding trees. "I mean, I'd like to pick up on stuff. Like, do point out important information so I can start becoming aware of things I should know. Like if you see poisonous bugs or a nest or something I shouldn't touch, let me know. But as far as the hunting and gutting animals? I'm just going to let you do your thing. That is, if you don't mind," I tell him.

"Of course I do not mind, my mate. It is a singular joy to care for your needs," he tells me with sincerity.

"Well, promise to let me know if you feel like I'm not pulling my own weight. That being said, it's really nice to be taken care of. I've never had that and I just want to kind of revel in it for a bit."

"You and I are on parallel journeys, Kate," he says.

"Yeah? How so?" I ask.

"I have the sense that before we met, in a way, you and I were both lost. Since we have come together, our lives have been bound toward something profound. It is as if fate carries us along," he tells me, sharing his attention with those MREs. He reads the labels and chooses one for each of us. "What we lacked in our lives before, we now have in abundance." He squeezes the food pouch he has chosen for me, kneading it in his hands, then pops a stick-like utensil off the front… it's like a lone chopstick. He opens the MRE, steam escaping the bag, and hands me my chopstick. He then does the same with his meal. We sit next to each other on the edge of the branch. His solid muscled arm rubs against mine. It is such a familiar and simple touch. We sit in silence and I turn his words over in my head for a bit. He's right.

"This is nice," I tell him.

"It is," he smiles at me. I realize again just what a hunk my alien gargoyle is. I'd have never snagged such a hot guy on Earth. I poke at the meat and veggies in my food pouch.

"This is the first chance we've had to really be alone," I point out.

"Alone and not in imminent danger," he nudges me with his shoulder. "It is nearly a cause for celebration."

Silence falls and my mind immediately goes to the topic of conversation I have been sweeping under the rug for so long. I take a deep breath. I shouldn't push it off any longer. This is our chance to figure things out. To figure us out.

"So… maybe we should talk about this mate thing?"

Chapter 39

Rennek

When the sun rose on this day I knew in my core it was the beginning of something wonderful. Da'vi and Allison took their leave of us and I am grateful for it, though I know it troubles my mate. Da'vi and Allison have their own work to do and Kate and I have this day. For today is the first day of the rest of our lives.

It seems as if my senses are alive in a way they never have been before. I trust our path, both the literal one before us, and the emotional one between us. With each passing moment I feel my core entwine more deeply with Kate's. We are woven together so intricately now that I know we can never be taken apart. To be without her would be a death sentence for me.

It is no wonder that on this first day of our forever, my mate brings up the topic of *us*. I am pleased to discuss it. Today is a day of vows.

"I was under the impression we were finished discussing it," I tease.

"Is that right?" She smiles up at me.

"I bent to your iron will and agreed to be your partner. Has anyone ever told you what a pushy female you are?"

"Haha. You think you're being funny, but you have no idea how pushy I can be," she laughs.

"It will be my burden to bear then, to have a female so demanding. You demand I take you to new worlds, demand I hunt for you and feed you, demand I fuck you each night until you swoon in ecstasy..."

"Pfft!" She snorts. "*Wow*, you take some liberties, don't you?"

"Hmm, perhaps I do. Or perhaps I find no shame in speaking the truth," I tell her. I finish my meal and place the packaging aside, she does the same.

"On a serious note though... I would like to understand the meaning of 'mate.' What does it mean to you, or for us..."

"Perhaps it would help me if you described what mating is like on your planet. Then, I could tell you if it is the same or if there are differences," I suggest.

"Oh gosh... that's a loaded question. Well, it depends on if you're talking about mating as in sex, or dating relationships in general, or something more serious."

"What is dating?" I ask her.

"Dating is like slowly getting to know a person and deciding whether or not you like them and if you would like to pursue more from a relationship with them," she explains.

"That is definitely not what I mean when I call you my mate," I tell her. "We are beyond that."

"Oh we are?"

"I already know I *like* you, my feelings for you are much stronger than *like*. Though I do look forward to getting to know more about you."

"Ditto. Er, I mean, me too."

"What is more than dating?" I ask.

"I don't know… cohabiting? Like two people living together. Or maybe engagement, which means a commitment has been made to spend forever together, but it doesn't become official until marriage," she clears her throat and has difficulty meeting my gaze as she says these things.

"We do live together. You agreed to share a bed with me."

"I didn't know if that was a permanent arrangement or based on convenience."

"Both," I tell her. "Mating must be very complex on your planet," earning me another of her beautiful laughs.

"So, we're cohabiting then? That's what you mean when you say 'mate'?" she asks.

"Being mates means that and more. It is a commitment, as your earth engagement is. What is marriage?"

"Marriage is a big deal. You make that commitment not only to your partner, but in a ceremony in front of all your family and friends as witnesses. You say vows to love, honor, cherish… in sickness and in health for all the days of your life. It's like two people deciding to be family," she finishes.

"That is the meaning of mate." I tell her. "We have a similar bonding ceremony, though not all mates choose to have the event. But as Tennir mentioned, Madreed will likely insist." She looks a bit pale at my words.

"On Earth there's a bit more to it…" she stammers.

"Tell me."

"Usually the couple dates for years before they decide to get married," she tells me.

"That is foolish." Why would one wait so long for what they already know, I wonder?

"Not really… it gives the couple time to really live with each other and get to know all the annoying habits they have… it helps develop trust…"

"You have already said you trust me and you will be happy to know I possess no annoying habits at all." My mate smiles at me and I see laughter in her eyes.

"Well, you're right. I do trust you in a lot of ways, I guess. But maybe I should be the judge of your annoying habits." I know she jokes, but her words wound me.

"You should trust me in all ways." My tone causes her to still momentarily.

"I didn't mean it like that. I trust you in many ways Rennek. I trust you to protect us, I trust your instincts and your knowledge. I know you are a good friend, a good captain and a good son. I trust your sincerity with me…"

"But there are ways in which you do not trust me?" I cut through her words, feeling burned in my core at her insinuation. The drumming comes to life again, rolling like thunder within me, but this time it hurts. It is like all the air escapes me.

"I don't mean to say that. What I mean is… relationships are hard and you might feel one way at the beginning and those feelings change over time. I'm not saying I don't trust your feelings toward me, I'm just saying we don't know right now if you'll feel the same way in a few weeks or a few months or a few years."

I am dumbfounded at her words. I do not know whether I am angry or hurt. All I know is that she is wrong and I must reveal her error to her. I must somehow get her to understand that I knew from the moment I saw her she would be everything to me until the end of time.

"Kate," I take her hands in mine. "When I call you my mate, it is forever. Those feelings will never change."

"I believe you mean that Rennek, but there is no way of knowing. Don't people get divorced in your culture?"

"I do not know what this is," I tell her.

"It is when a married couple, or mates, decide they don't love each other anymore and they agree to end their relationship."

"Why?" I ask her aghast.

"I don't know, lots of things… people grow apart, money problems, infidelity. On Earth like half of all couples get divorced. My parents got divorced when I was little, most of my friends growing up had divorced parents. Wait, Tennir and your sister have a different father? What happened to him?" She asks.

"He *died*! What is this infidelity you speak of? Do you believe I would be unfaithful to you? Or that *you* might be unfaithful to me?" I bite back a growl at the thought, but my tail betrays me and whips angrily against the tree.

"No! No, I would never! I'm not a cheater!"

"But you think that I might be?" I ask incredulous.

"Of course not," she says without conviction.

"Speak what is on your mind Kate!"

"Oh god, I'm doing this all wrong," she shakes her head and covers her eyes for a moment, collecting her thoughts. "Do you know why I was taken Rennek? Why I was abducted in the first place? The best I can tell is that I was abducted from my home because no one would miss me. No one would come looking for me or even notice I'm gone. Forgive me if I don't trust that relationships are forever, because I don't have any examples of relationships that last forever."

"Both my parents were unfaithful to each other. They probably only had me as a last-ditch effort to save their marriage and *surprise...* it didn't work. My dad checked out when I was little. He didn't care about a relationship with me and even though my mom got custody of me in the divorce, she had checked out too. I hardly ever even saw her as a kid because she would leave me home alone and go spend weeks on end with her flavor of the month boyfriends."

"I had to do everything myself: cook dinner, clean the house, do my laundry. Once, the checker at the grocery store called CPS because it freaked everyone out that an eleven-year-old came in every week to do the grocery shopping all by herself."

"What I'm saying is, relationships are complicated. You don't know what the future will bring and even the love that is supposed to be the strongest can fail. It's not that I don't trust you, it's just that we can't know, there's just no way anyone can know. And that's why it's a good idea to take relationships slow."

I take in her words. I think of Kate as a precious child, left all alone to care for herself. I think back upon my own youth. I remember how horrified she was when I told her Madreed had sent me away to Javan as a fledgling, but I was not left alone. Javan is where I met my friends. There were teachers and advisors guiding us through every day and every lesson. There were people who were close to me, that cared for me and took care of me. Kate did not have this.

"I hear you my sweet goddess. I will work to earn your trust as a mate and with each passing day you will come to know that what is between us is forever… for all the days of our lives." She leans into my embrace.

"I do trust you Rennek, probably more than I've ever trusted anyone, and whatever this is between us, it's something I've never felt before. I need time though."

"You may have all my time," I say, stroking her fiery mane. "We will take our time getting to the beacon as well. We can explore, run scans on the environment, discover what the best creatures for hunting are..."

"Find wood that might build a good bed?" She adds.

"I like how you think, sweet Kate."

I smile, content with my mate in my arms. A handful of days will be just what Kate and I need to continue to nurture what it is that grows between us.

Chapter 40

Kate

I feel a tremendous weight off my shoulders. Rennek and I finally had the "mate" talk and he was super chill about it. Part of me worried that if I wasn't on the same page as him he would change or get angry, but he didn't. He was just normal, positive, reassuring and accepting, Rennek.

Now, to be fair… it isn't that I'm exactly on a *different* page than he is. It's just that everything in my life is happening super-fast right now. It's a lot all at once. I do want to be with Rennek, I do. It's just he is very… *official* with all this mate talk. It sounds very… *forever*, and although I want to be with Rennek for the foreseeable future… I'm just not sure if I believe in *forever* and I get the impression he really does. I don't want to be the asshole that ruins that for him. He deserves someone who can give him his happily ever after.

Also, I don't think it's a good idea to commit to a lifelong relationship after only knowing each other a couple weeks. It just doesn't seem smart, especially given all the crazy shit that has happened to me since I met him.

I wonder if all alien men move quick like this? I wish Reagan was around so I could have some girl talk with someone about it. I suppose we'll get the chance in a few days anyway. Until then, I'm just happy Rennek and I are in a good place.

Even though we are off exploring on our own, Rennek uses his personal comm unit twice a day to check in with both the ship and Da'vi and Allison. The conversations have been brief. It seems everyone is doing well and finding their own stride. I got to speak with Reagan a couple of times, though it was just for a minute or two. She told me Tennir was able to fabricate translators for the other girls.

They are a little different from ours, but they work, and I guess that's all that matters. It's good news for the girls, because now they can communicate with everyone, and double good news for Reagan, because now she doesn't have to translate every single little thing. I can imagine how frustrating that must have been.

My days with Rennek are a mixture of exhausting and exciting. We do a lot of walking... and hiking, and tree climbing, and mountain climbing and... well, basically *every* outdoorsy thing possible. At the end of the day I'm sore in muscles I didn't know existed, but it really has been so much fun. It's like going on a road trip and seeing a sign that says "World's Best Pie, 200 miles" and you just go for it because why the hell not. We see a ridge that looks neat, or a waterfall, or cave and we go check it out.

There's just so much to see here. The views are beautiful. At night, three moons light up the sky, one large and two that are so small they are little more than pin pricks, outshining the surrounding stars. I wonder if they are actually nearby planets.

A couple semesters ago I took an Intro to Botany class. I wish I remembered more of what I learned. Not that much of it would transfer to an alien world. In any case, all the plant life appears to be what I would consider megaflora, or close to it. Yesterday we stumbled across some pink flowers the size of cabbages! Subsequently, much of the fauna appears to be supersized as well. I wonder if the ugly bear thing we ate the first day was this planet's version of a mouse.

We see more of the muppet like pterosaurs from our first day here too. They do appear to be carnivorous. Luckily, they tend to stay closer to the ocean and our path has taken us further inland.

We also notice there are a great deal of shallow cave systems at the base of the trees, forming out of the earth and the massive twisting roots. Rennek keeps a close eye on these when we descend from the trees. He explains creatures likely nest in the caves and he doesn't want us to stumble upon anything dangerous or predatory. I try to make mental notes of all this helpful stuff he's sharing, but I really just count on his tough guy skills to get us through the day.

I was in the middle of a Geology course when I was abducted, and though we were only three weeks into the semester, I do remember some of that stuff. So, I pay close attention to the landscape. Many of the rocky ridges we traverse are filled with large crystalline inclusions. Some of them are as big as fire hydrants, making the place feel like fairy land or somewhere you'd expect to find the seven dwarfs. I wonder if these are made of quartz or if they are actually diamonds or some other precious stone.

Yesterday we came across a rocky cave carved out of the side of a mountain. There were beautiful stalactites and stalagmites stretching from floor to ceiling. Deep inside the cave we could hear rushing water, but I freaked out when a family of squirrelly salamanders ran around my ankles. At the time it was repulsive, but once I had the chance to really look at them, they were kind of adorable. They had bodies like squirrels or ferrets, but their flesh was a depigmented pinkish color and smooth like an amphibian's. Then, Rennek suggested we eat them and it got repulsive all over again. For whatever reason, it feels less creepy to eat things with fur or feathers. I'm sure all my vegan buddies back home would not like to hear that, but frankly, eating alien creatures is super weird and I'm just dealing with it as best I can.

"Hey Rennek?" I ask at breakfast the next morning. We are down to our last MREs, but haven't been hurting for food since the forest is so abundant with wildlife.

"Yes, my goddess?"

"We've been having some protein heavy meals lately; do you think today we could try and find some fruit or vegetables? Can your scanner tell us if things are edible?"

"Hmm," he grunts. "That is a good idea. Have you been getting bored with our meals?"

"Yes and no," I laugh. "Eating anything here is far from boring. But, to be honest, I have been craving Earth food. This is cool too though, it's like Bear Grylls extreme."

"What is it you crave?" he asks.

"Oh man… things I'll probably never have again. Rocky Road ice cream. Brownies. A carnitas torta. Some really good salsa." I try hard to remember the last good-enough-to-drink salsa I had.

"Rocky Road?"

"It's a cold dessert. Chocolate, marshmallows, nuts. What kinds of things do you eat, I mean, when you aren't in space or backpacking alien planets?"

"On Thaad you can buy flavored ices. It is similar I think. Though, I do not know chocolate or marshmallows."

"I keep getting surprised by how many things are similar across our cultures, even though our planets are light years apart," I say getting a little lost in thought. Rennek is silent. "You've been a little quiet today."

"Quiet? No," he smiles at me.

"Okay, not quiet… introspective perhaps?"

"Introspective... Your words bring to mind the Vendari. I wonder if I will have anything in common with them."

"You are Vendari too," I tell him, but instead of responding he helps me to my feet and smooths my hair down, admiring me.

"Today is an exciting day," he says, his eyes shining.

"Why's that? Did you find a shower?" I tease.

"Better... well perhaps not better, I do enjoy you and I in a shower together," he says leaning in to kiss my neck.

"No!" I laugh, "I'm all salty and gross!"

"Mmm, no you are just... potent... ripe," he says leaning in again.

"Ew! No, get away! That's like the least sexy thing ever!" I say trying to swat him away through my laughter, but he pulls me close and kisses my lips and I relax into him. "So, why is it an exciting day?" I ask.

"We will reach the beacon today."

"That's wonderful Rennek! So, what's the plan? Will you try to activate it or what?"

"I do not believe that activation will be a straightforward process, otherwise Gorrard would have done it straightaway. I will take scans and send them back to Tennir and Bossan, see what they can uncover. But I am picking up some interesting readings on my scanner."

"What do you mean?"

"There is something like a structure in the vicinity of the beacon…" he begins.

"Whoa! A what? I thought this planet didn't have any civilization!"

"It does not appear to have any sentient life forms. The planetary scans we did before landing did not pick up any such life forms or modern structures," he tells me.

"But you think there is a structure up ahead?"

"It is too uniform to be a natural formation," he says.

"Could there be people living there?"

"No, my scanner does not detect anything besides native wildlife."

"Then what could this thing be?"

"It is a mystery," he beams.

"Well then, what are we waiting for?"

Chapter 41

Rennek

When I first noticed the structure on the scans I was troubled. Though this development is an exciting one, it may lead to danger. It is my hope however that it may instead lead to more information about what might have happened here yets ago when Gorrard's scouting ship first arrived.

I worry over having someone as precious as my Kate with me. I try to brush away these thoughts. She has proven herself to be a formidable traveling companion, but bringing my mate into situations where there are so many unknowns… it agitates me. Hearing Kate's excitement however, brings me back to my center. It reminds me of my fledgling days on Javan with my friends: going on adventures, getting into trouble, testing our limits.

"We can detour back towards those denser trees there," I point in the opposite direction of the beacon. "There is a better chance of finding fruit bearing plants in that direction. The forest thins towards the beacon. It may be less likely for us to find the food you crave if we continue on," I explain.

"Huh? Oh screw that. Let's go for the beacon! We can go look for pineapples or whatever later, this is way more exciting!" She exclaims before she starts making a path along the branches of the trees. When she sees a better route, she drops down a level and continues on. I follow her, watching her movements, amused. For such a small frame she is sure footed, focused, and strong. She has gotten quite comfortable here on Elysia.

"You are very adaptable," I tell her.

"That's the most romantic thing anyone has ever said to me," she teases, batting her eyes.

"I mean to say that you have been fitting in well here," I tell her.

"On Elysia?" she asks. "Yeah, I guess so. It's kind of like a camping trip."

"And on the space station as well as on the ship, when we first rescued you and your people..." I say, trying to find the right words. "Some of the other females. You adapted."

"Thanks. I've actually thought about that quite a bit. It's weird. It was never like this for me back on Earth. There, it seemed I could never find a place that fit for me--yet here, or since the abduction I mean, everything just feels right."

"That is wonderful," I say encouraged by her words.

"It is and it isn't," she says, surprising me.

"How could that be bad," I ask and she pauses her steps to answer.

"I feel kind of guilty about it. Almost like I need to keep it a secret or something. The others all miss home and the things they left behind. They are having a hard time… transitioning. I feel like I should be having a hard time too and instead I get to make out with a sexy gargoyle alien every night and go on exciting adventures."

"I think I may be too biased to discuss this with you fairly," I smile and she leans up to kiss me… but I hear the snapping of branches. I dart my gaze in the direction from which the sound originated.

"What is it?" she asks.

"Perhaps nothing," I breathe deeply through my nose. "Smells like there is an animal nearby." We both visually scan the trees around us. Just then, a small pack of primates swing through the trees above us, hooting wildly as they pass.

"Holy shit! Did you see those things? Oh my god, wow!" Kate laughs. "Were they up there the whole time?"

"They likely spend their time on the upper canopy, they may have heard us and became frightened."

"They were beautiful! We have creatures kind of like that on Earth, but those colors were unreal! At first, I thought they were freaking parrots or something. Those are big colorful bird on Earth," she explains as I survey our surroundings.

"The branches become more dispersed up ahead, now is the best time to descend to the ground level of the forest."

"Aye, aye," she says. I jump down to a lower limb and reach for her. She slides down off the branch and into my arms. "Do we have much farther to go?"

"No. Just around this bend we should be able to see what the scanner is picking up." She jumps down ahead of me to the level below. I follow behind, hurrying to get ahead of her. I jump down another branch and slide off into the leaves on the forest floor, turning to catch my mate.

"Gosh, it's humid down here!" She says, plucking at the collar of her shirt. "The air is a lot fresher up in the trees."

"Perhaps then I should build you a home in the trees," I tell her.

"Hey, if it has a shower and a toilet you can build it anywhere you please." We both eye the hillside ahead of us. We look at each other. "Race you?" She asks, taking me by surprise.

"I think instead we should approach with caution," I tell her.

"You said no sentient life is here? The scanner isn't picking up any technology or energy sources except for the beacon, right?"

"Both of those statements are correct."

"Well then… hey what's that over there?" She asks, pointing behind me. When I turn to look, she bolts in the direction of the beacon. It only takes a moment for me to recover from her rouse and I chase after her. I overtake her easily, scooping her into my arms and hoisting her onto my back. I fall to all fours and run the rest of the way, laughing with my mate as she clings to my neck. The decaying leaves covering the forest floor kick up as we pass the caps of giant mushrooms and bright green ferns with long and curling branches. Fallen tree limbs occasionally litter the ground, slowly being swallowed up by moss. Roots from the massive trees sprawl out before us, but they do not slow me down.

As we round the bend, I stagger to a halt. Kate disembarks from my back, her mouth agape. I stand to my full height and take in this mystery before me.

"This didn't show up on the scanners from the air?" she asks shocked.

"No. These are all natural materials, made from the same stone as the mountains… the overgrowth may have interfered as well. Even now, all the scanner picked up was its uniformity."

We stand before a long stone wall, covered in moss and vines. Even with all the overgrowth I can still see the wall beneath is ornate. In the center is a wide arched gateway leading to an interior courtyard. My guns are holstered but at the ready. I run one last scan while Kate watches, but the data has not changed. We are alone here. Kate's hand finds mine and we proceed through the arch.

Directly across from us is a temple of sorts. It is tall in the center, as if it has multiple levels within, and long on the sides. It is made of stone just like the wall surrounding us. To access the building there are three sets of stairs leading up to a long open corridor with arched windows, looking down upon the courtyard. The primary staircase is set on the north side and two secondary sets lie on the east and west ends. In the center of the courtyard there is a massive fountain. Within it is the dilapidated statue of an avian female. Her face is gazing upward toward the sky. Her stone wings are tattered and her nose, or perhaps beak, is missing... broken off over the yets. She stands among stone flourishes and her own broken pieces. Though it is wet, the fountain is not filled with water, instead dirt and plants overflow from it.

"It's beautiful," Kate breathes out. All around us I begin to notice carvings in the stone, remnants of statues and sculptures, all depicting these winged and feathered females.

"This is either the image of the builders or an image of their Goddess," I tell Kate as she admires the form.

Exploring further, I notice the ground was once paved with stones, but they crumble and are covered in a layer of soil in most places. There are benches and seating areas throughout the courtyard. The walls are lined with more fountains, though the others are less ornate than the central one. Though the trees are much sparser here, they still grow out of the crumbling stone. Thankfully, the air is less humid, likely because this space is open to the sky.

I get closer to the long corridor running the length of the structure. Through the large arched windows, I can see the wall beyond is lined with doorways. Kate makes her way to the west stairway and I follow her up the steps, inside the corridor. It is covered here, offering protection from the frequent drizzling rainstorms. The view of the courtyard is a powerful one. It is designed so that one could sit on the ledge and watch everything in the space below. Or even talk to friends lounging by the fountain. I imagine what this place must have been like when its civilization flourished. Kate begins to peer inside one of the doors.

"Careful, let me check first," I tell her and she rolls her eyes in response, but acquiesces. I retrieve my handheld lantern from my pack and shine it inside the first room. It is empty. We continue down the corridor, looking into each doorway as we pass. They all seem to be fairly uniform, square rooms with an indentation along the back wall. Leaves mound in the corners and there is evidence animals nested here at one time or another. Any doors were likely made of wood or cloth and have long ago rotted away. Kate knocks her foot on a small piece of something that clatters across the stone floor.

"Huh, wonder what this is?" She asks, picking it up to examine it.

"It appears to be a small piece of pottery, yes?" We both look at the floor. We see more shattered pieces, as if a vase or some type of receptacle had been dropped, only this did not happen centuries ago. I go back and examine the rooms again more thoroughly.

"What are you thinking?" Kate asks.

"Look here…" I point to a few spots in the first room. I see signs confirming my assumption and I look more closely at more of the rooms. It appears as if long forgotten items once belonging to the builders of this structure sat in these rooms for many yets. We can see the outline of items that have at some point, in more recent history, gone missing. "It looks as if raiders may have found this place and pillaged it. Though it appears that was some time ago."

"Interesting. Do you think this could be linked to what happened to Gorrard and his crew?" She asks. I shrug, but it would make sense. If Gorrard's ship arrived unexpectedly, the raiders might have viewed them as a threat and fired on them.

"Let's look for more evidence before we draw any conclusions," I say as I see a shadow darken the courtyard. I move quickly to one of the arched windows and peer upwards.

"One of those big birds?" Kate asks, but I see nothing.

"Perhaps."

"Want to check out the main room?"

"What's that?" I ask, still distracted by the unknown origin of the shadow.

"The main room? Big building in the center," she points.

"Ah, yes." I say, bringing my attention back to Kate.

"Upstairs or downstairs?" She asks.

"I hold no preference," I tell her.

"Okay, let's start up and work our way down."

"As you wish."

We make our way down a short stairway to access the long one that is at the center point of the courtyard. At the top are columns holding open the front half of a large domed room. We can instantly see this room is significantly more elaborate than any of the other rooms we have seen thus far. The floors here are a tiled mosaic and instead of grey stone walls, it is a smooth marbled stone. You can faintly make out murals across the ceiling that have been fading for centuries. The view from this room is amazing. It looks down onto the courtyard on one side and across the forest beyond the rear wall on the other.

"This is absolutely stunning. There are no words for…" Kate says, trailing off. I pause a moment to appreciate the awe in her eyes.

"Look! A stairwell." She notices in the back of the room. I lead the way and we follow the spiraling staircase down using my lantern. We hear water dripping before the stairs open up into a large and humid room. Luckily the back wall of this section of the structure has the same arching, open windows allowing light and a slight breeze in. Thankfully so, for the humidity in here is even more dense than when tucked under the canopy of the forest.

"What on Earth… or Elysia. Let me try again. *What on Elysia*?" Kate mocks a gasp mirthfully.

"A bath," I say impressed, admiring the intricate mosaic tile covering the room. I can see the walls are lined with a series of small fountains. Some have vines spilling from them. This culture thrived because of their access to water and their ability to harness it. It makes sense that they decorate liberally with water features throughout their temple.

"A bath?" Kate parrots. "That's more like a pool! It's practically an Olympic sized pool!"

"It needs a little care," I say, examining moss and mold growing along the walls as a result of the humidity from the water. "I think we could have it back in usable condition in about five to ten rotations."

"Wait, we could really turn this back into a working bath?" She asks.

"Absolutely," I smile at her. "And those spouts along the back wall," I point to the dark side of the room, "they appear to be a type of shower head." Kate says nothing but loudly breathes in a long and drawn out breath of air. Surely a sign of her surprise and excitement.

We move to the windows and look out together at the view from the rear of the structure. I can see crumbling wall lines far in the distance. "Likely there was a village out that way, fields for farming perhaps."

"It's so humbling to walk through this place. It feels sacred or something."

"It is a blessing Kate. This place will be ours, a home base for the humans. It has everything we need. There is much space here and room for growth, to build something more. I know there is work to do here," I see her eyes go to the vine filled fountains, "but it could be beautiful."

"No, I see it. It *is* beautiful, and with it cleaned up and a little... *pruned*... I can totally see it. This could be something really amazing," she agrees and my core soars. We look out again to the forest beyond the bathing room. Something nearby catches my eye and I jump down, out of the window.

"Hey! Where are you going?" Kate yells after me. But I am back before she can chase after me--with a large yellow fruit as a prize. "Oh, please tell me I can eat that." I run a quick scan which tells us there are no toxic compounds within this fruit, so I dig my claw in and crack it open. The meat of the fruit is yellow and the center is filled with puffy orange seeds.

"Oh, please let it taste like mango, please let it taste like mango." She takes a bite. "Bummer. Papaya." She scrunches up her nose. She sounds displeased, but continues to eat.

"Try a seed," I offer and she grabs a few, popping them into her mouth.

"Oh sweet! It's kind of like a fruit we have on Earth called pomegranate. Oh man, these are good. I could eat this part all day. It's good, try it." I taste both the seeds and the meat and find that my preferences are opposite of Kate's, which we agree works out quite well.

"So... what do you say we find that beacon?" Kate urges me. I grunt in response.

"Have you been stalling?" She asks.

"Only very slightly. But I am ready now. I would like to report back to the others as soon as possible to give them an update."

"Do they even know about this place yet?" she asks.

"I did give Dax our coordinates this morning and I let him know we may have discovered some ruins."

"You'll have a lot to talk about tonight, I guess."

"Let us hope it is all good news."

Chapter 42

Rennek

Kate and I make our way out of the ruins and continue on toward the faint signal the beacon is emitting. It is but a short walk from the ruins. I immediately see signs of a crash, where a ship ripped through the trees and dug heavy gouges deep in the soil. We follow the path Gorrard's ship dug out.

"There!" Kate says and I see it too. Scraps of torn metal. I inspect some of the larger pieces.

"What are you looking for," Kate asks.

"A reason," and the reason is easy enough to find. "See these marks here? This discoloration?"

"Yeah, what is it?"

"Plasma blast," the ship was shot down. We spot a seat from the ship, sprawled out on the ground amongst the metal. It is covered in old, brown dried blood. Kate covers her mouth and I see her fingers tremble.

"It was raiders then?" she chokes out.

"Likely. This planet must have sat forgotten for centuries. Unfortunately for Gorrard and his crew, their timing was tragic. The raiders might have thought Gorrard's ship was... I do not know, competition perhaps, or UPC patrollers, and simply shot them down, no questions asked." I search the ground for more clues, but this is an old crime scene and there is little more I can learn from these remains.

"Do you think they might come back, the raiders, I mean?"

"Unlikely, they took every artifact of value yets ago."

We continue walking past the debris of Gorrard's ship, following the beacon's signal on my scanner. We journey deeper into the forest again. Eventually, we reach a clearing encircled by trees. In the center is a metal post, about half my height, covered in intricate carvings and symbols. A small blue light pulses on the top. We stop at the outer circle of trees and stare in silence at the beacon.

This device could call my people home. My feet are as heavy as my core and it seems all I can do is gaze upon this relic of the Vendari. Finally, Kate's soft fingers slip in between mine. I look down at my mate. She urges me forward. Together, hand in hand, we walk to the beacon. I focus my scanner on it and see if any of the readings have changed now that we are close.

"Is it safe to touch?"

"I believe so," I tell her.

"What's up with the crop circle? It's not radioactive is it?" She asks, still unsure.

"Residual, from its landing impact. The plant life here was probably scorched and is only just now beginning to grow back. The beacon will not harm us." We return our attention to the metallic pillar.

"It's beautiful… both what it is *and* what it represents for you guys," she says. I squeeze her hand. This female knows me so well. We both bend to inspect the details on the beacon. There is no obvious control panel or interface. We circle the device, but I see nothing but the swirling artistic designs. I wonder if this is the written language of the Vendari, but even if it is a language, there is no way to know what it means without Gorrard to translate.

"I don't suppose that flashing light is a button?" She asks. I push at it with my claw, but it does not give as I press it. It is nothing more than a light.

"Does not hurt to try," I tell her, shrugging.

"These slots here, could these be anything?"

"Slots?"

"Yeah, these six slots here? Kind of looks like a USB port," she says.

I do not know what she speaks of, but I examine the space more closely. It does indeed appear as if there are slots… perhaps a keyhole of some kind.

"What now?" She asks.

"I will let the others know we found the beacon. Bossan and Tennir will likely have some insight into how to activate it. They will begin running tests. It may take some time."

"Will we just leave it here then, until the others meet up with us?"

"It should be fine here. It has survived many yets in space and nearly thirty or so here on Elysia. Another few days are hardly of consequence."

"Bummer. That was a little anticlimactic," Kate pouts.

"What did you expect," I laugh.

"I don't know, a secret button that we would discover and it would… I don't know, send a big flare up or something."

"A big flare to wake the Vendari from stasis?" I cock an eyebrow at her.

"Yeah, well not a flare. But something big, figurative fireworks."

"Let us go choose a room back at the ruins and I will give you all the fireworks you can dream of," I pull her close and wrap my arms around her. She melts into me.

"Are you good? Did you expect more from this moment?"

"I knew that we would not make much progress on this day. If it were a simple design, Gorrard would have activated it yets ago. We have located the beacon though, we have discovered a place where we can create a more permanent camp, and I have my mate by my side. This is more than I ever expected. I am content in this moment."

"My Rennek, so patient," she sighs, hugging me tightly.

"I *am* yours," I tell her and she tilts her head up to look into my eyes.

"I know."

I revel in my mate's loving embrace, but I smell something in the distance. I inhale deeply.

"What is it?" Kate asks with her brows furrowed.

"I believe I smell the primates from before. There may be more in this area."

We stare up into the trees, but see nothing.

Chapter 43

Kate

Now the fun part starts. Is it weird that I think this is the fun part, I wonder? I mean, this is where the real work begins and I'm excited by that. This is what I can see myself dedicating my life to. And I have Rennek to thank for that. Now, not only do I feel like I have come to peace with my place in life, but I also feel like I have purpose.

We are going to start by cleaning up the ruins and making it into a home base. When the others join us there will be lots to talk about. Our goal is to find a way to keep searching for more humans, to rescue them and bring them here. I need to see who is on board to help and who wants to just live the quiet life. Heck, the other girls might eventually want to go live on a less primitive planet, but to me Elysia feels right.

I can see us building a village at the ruins. We can bring a little technology in, make it more livable, with some lamps and hopefully some toilets. We can farm, lead a simple lifestyle--safe and away from traffickers and bounty hunters. It's perfect. And it all starts with Rennek and I deciding which room along the corridor will be ours.

"This is so exciting! It's like we're moving in together and we're on an apartment hunt," I chatter excitedly. Part of me wants to play it cool, but I'm giddy. "Sorry, this is a first for me and I'm super excited. I've never lived with a guy before." Luckily Rennek doesn't seem to mind. He just smiles and lets me fuss.

"The rooms are all very similar. Did you have a preference when we looked earlier?"

"I think I might actually. You see the room there, it's closest to the stairway that leads up to the large... I don't know, throne room, or whatever it was up top. It seems like we could repurpose that room as a headquarters where we could coordinate things and meet with people. I think it'd be good for you to be close to it. Especially once we crack the code to this beacon and the Vendari get here. You might have to take on a… a… role that…" I see him stiffen and I trail off. I feel like I really stepped in it. I know Rennek is not fond of titles and he still harbors some serious negative emotions towards his father. Gorrard said he was a king, but I really don't know if that's a role Rennek feels linked to. Or even *wants* to be linked to.

"Regardless of whatever your role is, people will want to meet with you to discuss what went wrong," I recover… but just barely.

He grunts in response. "A good choice for a room. It is farthest from the outer walls, it is safe. If an animal breeches the walls and attacks we will be farthest from any entry point."

"Do you really like it though?" I ask and this seems to snap him out of the funk I accidently caused.

"Anything I share with you is perfect, my sweet Kate," he tells me with soft and caring eyes.

"Well, then let's get cleaning! First thing I need is a broom."

I watch as Rennek fashions me a broom out of a long branch and some ferns he packs tightly and then binds together. He is quick in his work and once he's done I take it for a spin. It works surprisingly well! I feel a swell of pride in him… and even a little lusty. I never thought I'd be aroused by a guy just making me a broom, but I'm finding his handiness is shockingly sexy.

I start sweeping the small stuff out of the room while he takes out big armfuls of dead leaves piled in the corners.

"Are we going to do the other rooms too?" I ask.

"I will take all this and burn it in the courtyard so it does not attract vermin. We can let the others clean the spaces they choose. When we are done here we should focus on rehabilitating the common areas."

"That's a good idea. Oh man, it's a lot of work though! I hope the others get here soon to help, especially with the bathing room. I'm thinking that can be more of a guy's job. Or at least, that's what I was hoping," I throw him my biggest doe eyes in hopes of getting out of cleaning that old, soupy water.

"No, we will need you females to clean out the ducts. Our hands are not the right size, but human hands are perfect. You will need to climb in and feel around the bottom of the pool in search of ducts and then reach in and pull out all the solid matter," he says scooping up the last of the leaves. I stop dead in my tracks.

"Oh my god, you're kidding right?"

"I would never joke about such a serious matter," he tells me.

"What's so serious about cleaning out the nasty swamp water?"

"The eelworm of course."

"Holy fuck, tell me you're kidding. We need to make some damn tree houses or something, because I cannot live in a place with something called an eelworm."

"Do not worry about the eelworm," he says, brushing away my concern… before his eyes go dark and serious. "If you do… they can smell it and they will slither out of the water and come for you," he says to my horror, but slowly I see the twinkle in his eyes.

"You jerk!" I swat his legs with my new broom. "You're going to give me nightmares talking like that!" But he just laughs and carts the last of the leaves and junk out of the room.

"Freaking eelworms," I mutter. I start sweeping the back corner and send flurries of dust swirling towards the door. As I do, I notice the indentation along the back wall. "Huh… I wonder what this is for?" I squat down to get a better look. Directly above the indent, built into the wall, is an open hole.

"What is it, my mate?" I hear Rennek ask as he comes back to our new room.

"It's like a hole… a vent? Do you think this is a fireplace Rennek?" I ask. He joins me by the hearth and examines it.

"It appears to be," he says, focusing his gaze up into the vent. "Can you bring me my hand lantern?" He asks.

"Sure!" I run over to his bag and dig through it. When I bring it back to him I see that he has shoved his whole arm up the damned vent.

"Rennek! Don't do that! It could be filled with crazy bugs or something!" I gasp, thinking of that one scene from Indiana Jones. It makes my skin crawl, but he just laughs.

"It seems clear on this end," he tells me. I notice he is looking at the ground with some concern. "With as much rain as this region gets I would expect there to be signs of water flow on the ground here. I believe there is a clog somewhere higher up the line. I will go to the roof and check."

"Need help?"

"No, it should take but a moment. You continue your work here," he says before bounding out the door like a happy puppy with a crap ton of energy. I chuckle to myself… he must be as excited about this as I am. Maybe more so, at least he has more reason to be. I resume my sweeping. What I really wish I had was a bunch of wet rags so I could wipe down these dusty walls, but I don't want to sacrifice any of the clothing or blankets we have to do that.

"Kate!" I hear Rennek's voice echoing through the vent.

"Yup! I hear you. Is there a clog?"

"No! It is ingenious for the primitive capabilities this civilization had… There is a type of cover that vents along the sides. It seems to both block--"

"Okay! Okay! Tell me about it when you come back!" I holler to him.

"I see something in the distance, I want to get a closer look. I will return soon!"

"Wow, a fireplace. Now that's cozy," I muse, smiling to myself and admiring our hearth. I start to look around the room. In my mind, I'm already beginning to formulate a plan on how to make the place more homey. I could put a long and narrow table against the wall by the hearth and create a kitchen area. We could put baskets underneath to store things. I wonder if Rennek could come up with a way to make some floating shelves to go above it.

A little kitchen table and a couple of chairs could go in front of it. And then on the other side of the room Rennek could build that bed we're both so eager for. It would be so nice to spend our nights in bed cuddling in front of the fire. We could put up some peg hooks for our clothes and a trunk or a dresser could go in the corner. Maybe an armoire would be best. That's as close to a closet as we'd get here. Then all we would need is a door. Well, that and maybe a nice throw rug and some rainforest decor. Hopefully one of the other girls knows how to macramé or something. Too bad we can't do a shiplap accent wall, I think to myself and start chuckling again.

Chapter 44

Rennek

When I get to the top of the roof I am impressed by these ancient people who left us the gift of their ruins. There is no problem with the vents. They are all capped with still functioning chimneys, designed to keep out both the elements and small animals. This means Kate and I can build a fire in our new home this very night.

I take the opportunity of being at a high vantage point to survey the surrounding area. In the distance, I notice a long artificial form… something like a wall perhaps? This peaks my curiosity enough that I set out for a closer look. I jump over to another portion of the structure I am on, only to be met by a rancid smell. I realize immediately an animal has died up here. I must dispose of it.

It does not take long to find the carrion. It is large and I cannot decide if it is a wingless bird or a two-legged rodent. I kick at it, trying to determine the best way to get rid of the thing, but then I notice something strange. It is a fresh kill, but it appears dried out… almost mummified. Its fleshy face is sunken and pruned. I kneel to get a closer look, searching for the cause of death. Perhaps it became stuck up here and perished, but I do not see how a creature such as this would be able to mount the rooftop in the first place.

Moving its fur a bit I am able to see what caused the end of this creature. There are a series of puncture wounds over its body. I scowl at it and look around for the tracks of a predator, but other than some scuff marks, I find none. I grab the poor creature and drop him off the side of the building and follow it down. I will have to carry it far enough away so it does not attract scavengers, a minor burden that will give me an opportunity to explore the wall I saw from the rooftop.

Once I am rid of my smelly friend, it is not much longer until I find that which I spied from the roof. Coming down the mountain, it is not a wall, but a canal. I notice a tree branch has fallen across it and hardly any water trickles through, instead it spills out making a muddy mess everywhere. I reach in and hoist the branch out. This blockage doesn't seem like it has been present for too terribly long, and now that the branch is out, the water gushes down the path of the canal.

I run a scan on the flowing water and find it is within safety limits for drinking. It also tests negative for parasites. I begin to follow the canal back towards the ruins. Another day I will trek to the canal's source, but today I will follow it back home. *Home.* I smile to myself. As I get close to the ruins the flowing canal drops down into a wide pipe in the ground. Using a type of sonar on my scanner I follow the pipe. It leads directly under the ruins.

"Rennek! Rennek!" I hear my mate's scream. It rips the air from me and my vision becomes like a tunnel. I tear into the ground, my claws propelling me forward towards her cries. I round the front gate and charge into the courtyard. Kate stands leaning out of a corridor window, her face flush with excitement.

"Look! Rennek! Look at that! Oh, my god! It's all of them!" She shouts pointing. It takes a moment for me to stop seeing red. I stand on my hind legs and struggle to make sense of what she is saying. Then I see it, the fountains have bubbled to life.

Water shoots up in small flourishing geysers from the stone ornamentation the winged woman stands amongst. I look to the fountains along the perimeter. Water pours from stone mouths and stone flowers and cascades down stone wings.

I move to the central fountain and run a scan again to see if anything has contaminated the line underground. The water mixes into mud in the basin, but data continues to show it is potable. I look at the murky mess. What I would not give for a shovel in this moment.

"Find something to scoop with. We better clear this before it fills," I call to my mate as I begin to tear out the plants and dirt from the fountain. She squeals in excitement and hastens down the stairs. A moment later she is beside me, holding a long, heavy leaf. She hurriedly fills it with handfuls of wet dirt, and when it is full, she dumps it on the ground beside my pile of dirt and plants.

"Promise me there are no eelworms," she begs. I cock my eyebrow, laughing in response.

We work like this for what seems like hours. The longer we take, the muddier the water becomes. We dig our hands in and mud cakes our arms and chests, soon we are covered from head to foot. Eventually Kate goes to get herself a new leaf and one for me as well. We are able to get much of the dirt from the fountain. By the time we are done we are soaked to the bone and the remaining dirt in the fountain has already begun to settle on the bottom. The courtyard is a mess, but we now have a functioning water source in our own front yard. We sit on the muddied ground with our backs against the fountain's base.

"My water filter can strain out the rest. Though it will likely take a full rotation, the filter is small and meant for personal use, but perhaps as early as tomorrow evening the fountain will run clear."

"So tomorrow we can do laundry? Amazing. You're amazing. I can't believe you found a still functioning canal!"

"It was nothing more than luck. I have had tremendous luck this past cycle."

"It looks like we made a bigger mess than we cleaned," she says, slapping her hand in the mud beside her.

I grunt in agreement.

"Soon I will make some tools for us. A shovel, a wheel barrel…" I tell her.

"I've been thinking about furniture and things for our room. A table for the kitchen to prepare food on, a table and chairs to eat at, shelves, a wardrobe, and that bed you promised me," she says the last in a sing song voice that has us both grinning.

"I have not forgotten my promise. I will build you our bed and all the other furniture you desire. You just tell me what you need to make our home comfortable and it will be done."

Kate leans her head back and watches me with a smile across her face.

"Share your thoughts with me," I say.

"You have a little something… right... there…" she smears more mud across my cheek. I grab her and hoist her onto my lap, pinning her hands behind her. She laughs sleepily, leaning her forehead against mine.

"You will pay for that, human," I tell her, nipping at her lips. It is the only place not caked in mud. "I should bathe you," I pause, looking her over. Our eyes lock.

"Later." She claims my lips with hers. I can taste the saltiness of her sweat and the bitter soil, but beyond the seam of her mouth there is nothing but sweetness. My mate's taste thrills me like nothing else. It sweeps me away from this world until I am lost in the drumming again. Before I know what has hit me, we are locked in a wild embrace. Her hands greedily try to touch every inch of my body. She bucks against me and we roll into the mud making loud and wet, slapping noises. But, just as quickly, the ridiculous sounds coming from our bodies slapping against the mud breaks the spell. We both crumble against one another in laughter. The sun begins falling and the courtyard becomes grey with the remains of the day. We lay there, too tired to move. I stroke her back as we listen to the sound of the gurgling fountains, until I notice my mate shiver.

"Come," I tell her.

We survey the mud and uprooted plants spread before the fountain.

"Man, I don't know if my broom is going to be able to handle that."

"That is a problem to be solved tomorrow," I say, pulling her along with me.

Once we are back in the room we now share, I place our hand lantern on the floor, illuminating the space.

"It looks much better in here. You did well," I tell her, proud of my mate.

"Yeah, I wish I had some more cleaning supplies. But it is a pretty big improvement, huh? I can really see all we can do with the place now that it's tidy."

"Wait here. I will gather supplies and return," I tell her, handing her one of the last protein bars. I remove the last of our supplies from our pack and take the now empty satchel with me as I head back out into the quickly darkening forest. I first go to the fruit bearing plant we discovered earlier and fill the satchel with it. On the way back, I grab a thick branch for firewood and some smaller pieces for kindling. By the time I return, darkness fills the courtyard, but I can see the glow of the light from our room. Kate's smile is wide, even though she shivers. It is hard not to laugh at my mud-covered goddess, I suspect the only thing that keeps me from doing so is the joy filling my core. I am content.

"First, we must get this fire started, then we must get you out of those clothes," I say.

"Do you need help?"

"Will you hand me the flint?"

"Square metal thing?"

"No, oval metal thing."

"Got it," she says bringing me the tool I requested.

I take the large branch and snap it into smaller logs that will fit into our hearth. I arrange them with the kindling, setting extra pieces aside for later in the night. I strike the flint and light the small dry pieces. Soon our home is illuminated with a warm glow and filled with the crackling sounds of the fire.

"Oh, that feels so nice. The stone in here really makes it chilly," Kate says inching closer to the fire.

I retrieve a small bowl from the pile of our supplies. I add water to it from my pouch and place it near the fire.

"We can take turns washing with that," I explain.

"How nice! What a luxury warm water is after a few days of washing with ice," she laughs. "Can you imagine what it will be like when we get the bathing room functional?" she asks excitedly.

"I would give you any luxury you desired, my Kate," I tell her as I search for a scrap of cloth to clean my mate with.

"I'm more than happy with life's simple luxuries, thank you. Save the diamonds for the next girl," her voice is jovial, but her words tell me she still does not understand what my core tells me is true.

"There will be no next girl," I say as I dip the cloth in the warmed water. I pull my mate close to the fire and help disrobe her. I assess the damage. She is filthy. I begin to scrub her face and arms. I long to make this bathing session one of romance, but my poor mate is caked in dried mud. It will be a task to clean her.

Her eyes examine me as I work. "Oh, Rennek! What are we going to do with *you*? You have like ten times more area on your body to clean and your hair is *full* of mud!" She exclaims trying to pick at my mane.

"Hmm, this is true," I agree. "I will douse myself in the water outside."

"That doesn't seem very fair, that water's so chilly."

"It is not a problem, my sweet Kate. You seem to be impacted greater by temperature changes than I. But, if I do become cold, you may have the task of warming me."

"That I can do," she smiles and shivers.

"Are you still cold?"

"No, I'm good. The fire is perfect. The breeze from the open doorway just got me," she tells me.

"Yes, a door shall be one of my first priorities. We will require our privacy once the others arrive."

She chuckles. Finally, I have her body as clean as I can get it. I spread our blanket out on the floor before the fire and break open one of the fruits I gathered from outside, handing it to her.

"Thank you," she says going for the seeds first.

"I will return," I tell her as I remove my waistcloth. She blushes at my form and I intentionally flex my muscles to impress her further. I steal a glance on the way out to the fountain and her eyes follow me. I smile happily. I will win her yet, I think.

At the fountain I dip my hands in the now full pool of water and splash myself repeatedly, rubbing the crusted mud from my body. It is cold, but my body does not prickle in response to cold temperatures as my Kate's does. I dunk my head in the water to rid my mane of the mess. Flinging my head backwards, I shake and wring it to rid myself of excess water.

I hurry back to my mate, but hesitate by the door, taking in the beauty of the scene. My mate sits nude and cross legged before the fire. Her skin glows and her mane looks even more like a wild blaze than ever. Hers is a beauty that cannot simply be admired from afar. I am drawn in. I grab another fruit and sit, adjusting my wings so that I may lean against the wall. When she sees I have returned she pulls in beside me, nestling into the crook of my arm. We eat our fruit in silence for a while.

"We will have to name these things you know," I tell her.

"Wow, that's a big job," she ponders. "All I can think of when I eat it is papaya and pomegranate, but it doesn't seem right to steal a name from something it doesn't quite match up with."

"Perhaps a papayagranate then? Or a pompaya?" I offer.

"Wow, I'm so tired I can't tell if those are terrible or genius."

"I will save you the trouble then, sweet Kate. They are genius, all my ideas are genius."

She laughs heartily and snuggles into me while I continue eating.

"I can hear your heart like this," she says.

"I am not familiar with this term."

"Um… which part?" She asks.

"Heart," I tell her.

"Oh, ahh this," she says placing my hand over my chest. I can feel the gentle drumming within, the drumming that I have felt since the moment I saw my mate--that only she has the power to make rage within me.

"You know what this is?" I sit upright with shock.

"What do you mean? Yeah… like your heart. It pumps blood… makes you live." Her face reflects her confusion as I am sure mine reflects my surprise.

"You have one as well?" I ask.

"Yeah, right here." She places my hand over her chest. She is right. I feel the reverberations within her as well.

"I have done this to you?" I ask excitedly, she has been having the same response all this time!

"What do you mean?" She says with a mixture of confusion and amusement.

"May I listen?" I ask. She eyes my horns.

"Yeah… we can uh…" she stands and maneuvers her body so she may reach my ear and not be poked by my horns. I listen. I hear the clear and steady drumming of her *heart*. I put my hand to my own chest. They beat in time with one another.

"Ha!" I laugh out loud and am up on my feet with adrenaline rushing through me. I grab my mate and hug her to me. "This is amazing!" I tell her. "This is some sort of magic!"

"I think it's just anatomy, but I'm glad you're psyched about it. I don't get it, Mr. I fly around in a spaceship, how do you not know what a heart is?"

"Anatomy was not one of my points of study on Javan. But perhaps more importantly, my *heart* as you call it, only just began to drum when I met you. It drove me mad the first days we were together. I had no idea what this thing was inside of me--ruling my emotions and my choices, driving me."

"Your heart never beat before? How does your blood circulate then?" She asks perplexed.

"That is a question better suited for Tennir."

"It really never beat before?" She asks.

"It reacts strongly to you. When you have been in danger, like earlier today when I heard you scream, when we kiss, when we do other things…" I purr the last words and bring her close to me once more.

"Wow. That's pretty amazing." She places her hand on my chest and feels the beating of my heart.

Beep beep.

"The comm, give me a moment." She nods and sets down on the blanket again. I take the comm and step outside.

"Rennek here."

"Bossan. Do you have news of the beacon?"

"I do, brother. We located it in the forest. As we suspected, it has no obvious interface but Kate did locate six oddly shaped slots hidden amongst some tribal markings. I will leave it for you to uncover any further secrets."

"That is wonderful news."

"We also located ancient ruins and it appears we may have discovered the cause of the fate of Gorrard's shipmates. It seems raiders may have been in the process of looting the ruins and shot them down."

"Are there any signs they have been here recently?"

"No, all indications of a raid are many yets old."

"Then it was simply a tragic twist of fate?"

"That appears to be the case." Bossan is silent on the other end upon hearing this.

"When you are ready, I would like the group to join us at the ruins. I will ask Da'vi and Allison to retrieve the pod. They can make trips transporting everyone and our supplies. Bring all that you will need to work on the beacon. I would also like the ship's water filtration system and all the padding from the beds brought here as well. Does the synthesizer still function?"

"We might be able to get it up and running for a short period, what did you have in mind?"

"At least one more filtration system, a smaller one will do. We will also need certain tools and building materials. I will send you a list of specifications tomorrow. It is late and I must still contact Da'vi."

"Rennek, there is much to report on our end as well."

"Is everyone well?"

"Yes, but--"

"Then it can wait one rotation. I have had a long day and I am tired my friend."

Bossan and I end our conversation and I connect to Da'vi and tell him of the situation. He is hesitant to return with Allison. This either means he is making progress with her and does not want that to end or he has not yet made any progress and hopes the tides will still turn. I allow him one or two more rotations before they head back to the pod. This will give Kate and I more time together and I am as greedy as Da'vi when it comes to spending alone time with my female.

When I get back to the warm glow of our room Kate is fast asleep on the blanket. I do not have it within me to rouse her. I tuck myself close to her body to block her from any wind that may steal into our room from outside. I can see her skin prickle and she unconsciously folds her body into mine. I wrap my arms around her. I will keep the fire burning through the night. Tomorrow I will build a door and perhaps I shall start our bed as well.

Chapter 45

Rennek

I wake as dawn breaks. I feel rested and eager to begin the mountain of tasks before me. Last night was the first night since we arrived on Elysia in which I was able to sleep deeply. Sleeping among the trees, one must always be wary of predators, but in the confines of our room, I allowed myself to relax.

For Kate, I add a log to the red embers in our hearth and tuck the blanket around her. I hope to bring her a fresh kill before she wakes, but I have not seen as much readily available game in the past rotation. I may need to begin setting traps.

I dress, then step out into the courtyard to survey our mess from the night before. Something seems different to me, but it is hard to tell what. I walk to the fountain and get the scent of those primates again. I scan the area but there are no signs of them. Surprisingly, there are no tracks in the mud either.

Likely the creatures were curious and explored the changes made to the ruins while we slept. It makes me uneasy to know something snuck so close to where we slept last night without me having taken notice. I will be glad once the others join us... and once we have a door.

I splash some water in my face and make my way to a young tree growing near one of the smaller wall fountains. I inspect it. Along the trunk are long, thick, fibrous strands. These will work perfectly. I begin ripping off the long strands. Once I have a fist full, I comb them straight and begin to braid a length of cord. I then cut a small patch of material from my waistcloth, poking a hole on each end. I cut my cord into two equal pieces and tie them to the holes in the material. Outside the gate to the ruins, I toe the soil until I find a few rounded stones, I place them in a small hip pouch, and head for the trees.

I ascend the trees and crouch low near the trunk, waiting for the call of birds. Birds are undoubtedly one thing this planet has in abundance. Soon enough I see a small flock with feathers of red and grey roosting nearby. These creatures will make a perfect breakfast.

They have feet seemingly too large for their bodies and long legs leading up to a fat, oblong body. The torso is a deep, claylike red and the only color variation on the birds lie in their grey collar feathers, which are much longer and hang down low towards their disproportionate legs.

They coo and clamor together. I place one of the rounded stones in my new sling and take aim. I swing my arm around hard, with my eye on my target. My aim is true and the bird falls silently to the forest floor. The kill was so seamless the others in the flock do not even startle. I load my sling once more and take another down for good measure. Then I move to retrieve my kills. I pluck, clean, and gut them before I head back towards the ruins, grabbing some sticks as I go. We will have to think of a name for this place. It will not do any longer to think of it as ruins.

The sound of my return rouses my mate.

"Oh, man… did I sleep in?" She sits up and rubs her eyes. The blanket falls away revealing her still nude body.

"Rest all you like, my Kate. Breakfast should take some time yet. Would you like some pompaya until then?"

"So, we settled on *pompaya* then?" She questions and I send her a cheerful shrug in response. "Looks like you've been busy," she says, noticing the food I have brought. "What do you have there?"

"A bird of some kind. Would you like to name this one?" I ask.

"Let's just call this one chicken and pray that that's what it tastes like." This must be an Earth reference I do not understand, I think to myself.

I squat at the hearth and lay out the sticks I brought with me from the forest. Kate stands and begins to dress, but I can feel her eyes on me. I turn my body so she may watch as I prepare both birds for the spit.

The last two sticks I have brought fork at the end. I prop them with rocks in the pit with hot coals. Because of the size of our fire pit we can only cook one bird at a time. I lay the meat across the spit and arrange the coals so heat seems to be radiating evenly. I position our small bowl beneath the meat to catch any grease. When I turn, I find Kate watching all of this with intensity.

"How did you hunt them?" She asks.

"A simple sling, they were the first weapons we learned to work with on Javan." I show her.

"Do you think Allison's learning this stuff?"

"I do not know how Da'vi was trained. He may be teaching her such things, or something similar at least." She looks thoughtful, but does not respond. "Will you help me with this while I gather some supplies for my next task?" I ask, interrupting her thoughts.

"Yeah of course, what do I do?"

"Watch that the coals heat evenly. Keep them low, but stir them if necessary. I will return before it needs turning."

"What's your next task?" She inquires.

"A door." She squeals her delight making me laugh aloud.

"It *is* true then, it is the simple pleasures you wish for. I have heard of males courting their females with precious gems or the pelt of a powerful beast, even flowers. It seems the males I have been speaking to have it all wrong." I slap her butt appreciatively, making her squeal again, and turn to head out.

"Wait," she calls after me. She approaches and runs her hands up my arms and over my shoulders, pulling me into an embrace. I shiver, her delicate touch has such power over me. It is as if my vision blurs and everything fades away except for my Kate.

"We've been so busy… and last night I fell asleep before we could…" But she does not need to continue. I have my mate down on our blanket before she can finish her thought. Her legs wrap instinctively around my waist.

"Is it weird that I miss you? I mean, we only skipped one night of cuddle-time," she rationalizes. I answer her with my kiss. It is not weird to me, every moment I am not touching my Kate is a moment that is missed. If I could survive on her kisses alone I would spend the rest of my days in her bed… a bed that I must make soon if I wish to remain sane.

Kate's arms wrap around my neck and her fingers intertwine in my mane. She pulls me into her. I dip my head to her neck and slide my tongue along her delicate jawline.

"Sorry, I'm probably all salty."

"You are delicious," I assure her.

"Psh, you'd say that no matter what."

"I would, and I would mean it." She smiles up at me and continues to play with my mane. Her smile is so precious, I cannot help but taste it. Her tongue teases mine. I suck on her full bottom lip and she nips at me, gently at first, but then with more urgency and need. I can feel her desire not only in her kisses, but in her body as well. Her legs tighten around my waist and she arches her back. Through her clothing, her breasts rub against my body, but it is no substitute for the feel of her skin on mine. I push myself up and begin to tear the shirt from her.

"No! Wait, I'm running out of shirts!" She protests and I allow her to pull herself far enough away so we may get her garment over her head and off of her warm body. Once her soft skin is against mine we resume our kiss. The drumming in my core quickens. I know now it is the beat of my heart and that it beats for my Kate. I press close to her, trying to feel her heart against my chest.

"Mmmm, Rennek. I can't stand not touching you," she moans as her hands skate between my wings and back. My tail lashes wildly, so I curl it around her thigh.

"I live for your touch," I tell her. It is true. I live for her touch, her voice, her laughter, her fire, and her spirit. She reaches up and grabs my horns, pulling my mouth to her breasts. I skim my claws gently across her pale and rounded flesh. I hear her suck in her breath. Her pink nipples pucker in anticipation. I stroke the tight buds with my thumbs.

"Kiss me babe, I want your tongue on me." Using my horns, she directs my mouth to the place she wants it and I oblige. I circle the tip of her breast with my tongue, sucking and teasing at her teats until she is grinding against me.

My waistcloth is useless against my straining cock. I quickly unbuckle it and toss it aside. Silently, I regret not tearing her pants from her body when I removed her shirt. She must be having the same thought because she begins to tug futilely at the waistband. I help her pull them down, over her full and fleshy behind, taking care not to rip them. I know how precious these garments are to her after having gone so long without. She kicks her pants off the rest of the way and wraps her legs back around my waist. Now that she is naked, the scent of her arousal becomes more potent. My cock twitches in response, slipping against her wet folds. Her scent alone brings me close to the breaking point. My heart drums faster and my senses seem to cross circuits.

"I want you inside me," she whimpers and I have to fight myself to keep from thrusting into her cunt. "I feel so empty. I want this," she reaches between us and wraps her fingers around my length and begins to pump... slowly, rhythmically. I freeze and let out a slow growl, biting back my own need for satisfaction. "It's going to feel so good to finally have you inside me. How much longer are you going to make me wait?"

"Not much longer if you keep speaking like this," I grit out. She gives a throaty laugh. My mate is trying to push me over the edge I think. She slides the tip of my cock against her entrance, coating it in her juices and then begins massaging the crown, her fingers slipping and sliding over the wetness. I remain as still as I can, grabbing fistfuls of blanket on either side of me to keep from touching her. Touching her in this moment would surely send me over the edge.

I bite into my bottom lip hard and squeeze my eyes shut. I attempt to regain my control, but her tongue is playing with my ear and I hear every breathy moan that escapes her lips. She arches her back again and rubs her soft breasts against my hard chest. The sensations are overwhelming. I battle between the desire to make love to her and the desire to fuck her.

I am close to coming when I notice my mate slip her other hand between her legs. She plays with her clit before pumping her fingers inside her cunt. I will not have my mate pleasuring herself, not when I am so eager to bring pleasure to her. I do not trust myself in this position though, with my cock so close to her entrance. I grab my mate's wrists and pull her hands away.

"Hey!" She whines. But before she can protest further I flip her over onto her hands and knees. She braces herself against the wall and I roughly spread her knees further apart with my tail. Her pussy is exposed to me and I can see for myself how wet and needy she is. She can hardly hold still, she arches toward me and begs under her breath.

"Louder," I growl and that is all the encouragement she needs.

"Fuck me, Rennek. Please. I want you so bad. I need you, I need you inside me. It will feel so good Rennek, I promise. Please Rennek, please fuck me," she whimpers and begs, her body writhing in effort to make contact with me.

I grab her hip with one hand, kneading her flesh. With the other hand I slide my knuckle along her slit. She bucks into me. She wants something inside her, but I am not ready to fuck her just yet. So instead I push my knuckle into her, always careful of my claws. I hear her gasp in delight. She begins to ride my hand and my knuckle pushes in and out. Her tight cunt sucks and grips at my hand. I am mesmerized by the way her body moves, by the sound of wet skin on skin.

"Oh, fuck. Rennek, that feels so good. Do it hard, fast. Please Rennek, please," she begs. I will not deny her this request. I pump harder and bring my body close behind hers so that I may reach around with my free hand to work her clit. Her knees weaken when I start to tease that precious nub and I have to hold her to keep her from falling over.

"Just like that, don't stop. Don't stop. Don't stop," she repeats her breathy mantra. I lean forward and sink my teeth into her neck. She lets out a scream of passion before she starts cumming, bucking wildly as I feel her pussy quiver around my knuckles. I keep pumping into her, letting her ride out her orgasm. Her juices drip down my hand and onto her thighs. When her tremors finally subside, I lick the juices from my hand and spread her ass to lick every last drop from her sweet and waiting cunt. She moans and I notice her weaken again, another orgasm rocks her. I lap at her cunt, giving her pussy long, deep licks.

Even when the wave of her orgasm is done, I am not yet finished licking her. My mate has other ideas however. She flips around and knocks me to the floor, pouncing on me like a fierce predator. I throw my head back and laugh out loud. Straddling me, she pauses. Her hands wash over my chest. Her eyes are wild, shining and full of lust.

"You're so hard everywhere, Rennek. You're like stone."

"And you are soft everywhere," I reach up and caress her breast, giving it a squeeze and running a thumb over her nipple. "Like the petals of a flower." She gifts me a smile in approval of my words.

"I want to make you feel good too," she says.

"It will not be difficult," I smile. "Everything you do makes me feel good. Gazing upon you makes me feel good." I tell her, and it is true. Even now, looking up at her with her flame colored mane wild around her face, her lips pink and swollen from our kisses, her eyes heavy lidded, satisfied. And I am satisfied.

My little human is every inch a goddess and more. She leans down and places a kiss to my lips, but she does not linger there. Instead she begins to make her way lower, kissing every part of me as she moves downward. Those soft lips of hers play at my collar bone, her tongue tracing my throat. Even after her orgasms I can sense she still hungers for me. Her hands alone tell the story… it is as if she must touch every bit of me, every dip and swell of a muscle.

For a moment, I think I might go insane and lose myself in the joy of all this stimulation. I throw my head back again and try to ground myself. When she gets to my hips, and her hot mouth teases at what is to come next, I begin to growl wildly in an effort to control myself. I hear my mate giggling and I smile through the wildness of it all. This is joy and pleasure at its most primitive, I think to myself.

Finally, after all the teasing I can take, she wraps her fingers around my thick shaft. Bringing her face close to the head of my cock, she pauses just before placing her mouth on me, looking up at my face. Her eyes are sparkling and mischievous, a smile plays on her lips. I see her pink tongue dart out of her mouth and she gives the tip of my cock a lick. I groan and she smiles wider, but the teasing is done and she sucks the head of my cock into her mouth. Her fingers pump my shaft. Her grip is tight and it makes me imagine what it will be like to slide inside her warmth.

I reach down and pull some of that red mane out of her face so I may watch her pleasure me. I can feel the precum dripping from my tip and I see that smile spread across her face again. She tastes my seed and she enjoys it. She lets out a moan, with my cock still deep in her mouth. The rumbling vibrations bring me one step closer to the edge. With her free hand she explores me, gripping my hip, sliding her fingers over my ribbed abdomen, clutching my thighs. I had never thought these to be erotic places on my body, but given the right circumstance these touches alone could cause me to spill my seed. It is the hunger in them, her need for me is electric, sending pulsing signals through my body. We are connected. My thoughts scatter and the sensations rock my body in waves. I try to will my body to be still, but I cannot control my hips and I begin to thrust into my mate's hand and mouth. I catch myself, but she moans again and pulls my hip towards her encouragingly. She enjoys this.

I prop myself up on one elbow so I may watch her more closely. Still holding her hair back, I allow myself to let go--to lose myself in all that she is giving me. Pumping into her mouth, I begin to cum and her moans become more frantic. She pumps and sucks at my cock, hungry for my release. The sensations overcome me… her hot mouth on my cock, sucking at my seed, her moans of pleasure, the drumming within me, harder and faster, harder and faster, until finally… I am spent and fall back onto the floor.

My body was coiled like a snake waiting to strike moments ago and now I am limp with pleasure. My mate licks the last bead of cum from my shaft and then curls her body next to mine. Her arm goes around my chest and her leg drapes over my waist. I can feel the wetness of her cunt against me and smell her arousal in the air. Life with Kate is pure joy. She nuzzles my chest and I bury my nose in her hair and breathe in deeply. I could remain like this forever.

"Okay big guy," she says. "Back to work." She is up before I can protest, but I pull her back down to me. Her naked rear end falls into my lap.

"You are done with me then?" I laugh, cupping her face and bringing it to my lips for a kiss.

"You know what they say," her hands go around my neck and she kisses me back, "no rest for the wicked."

"Hmmm, and what we just did was very, very wicked."

"Exactly." She bounces up to her feet and I allow her to go this time. Even though I would rather spend the rest of the day finding new ways to pleasure her, my mate is correct. There is still so much work to do. I want to prepare our space so it is safe and we can sleep easily at night. I want to provide her with some basic luxuries to make her day to day life easier. All that takes much work however, and the days are not long enough to get all I wish done. So, with one last kiss, and another slap from my tail to her perfectly rounded behind, I head out to gather supplies to make a door.

Chapter 46

Kate

I clean up Rennek's mess from making the spit, but soon after he is in our room again tossing even more supplies to the floor. He lifts his wings up so he can sit comfortably and begins tearing up a fibery tree trunk to get enough threads to weave into a long, thick cord. Looks like I jumped the gun on tidying up.

I watch him as he works. The muscles on his back move as he rips at the tree. He is the type of man an artist would want to use as a model, I think to myself. It's easy to admire him. Then, he rips a bunch of tangled mess from the tree and tosses it aside as if I didn't just sweep in here. Men on any planet, I shrug. At least he's pretty.

I turn my attention back to our neglected spit as he works. He gives me tips here and there about keeping the coals even and when to turn the meat. Soon, the bird is looking tasty and smelling pretty darn good too. Fat and juices drip off the meat and into the drip pan Rennek set up. My mind starts to wonder about spices and seasonings. Luckily, we have the scanner so we can determine if the local plants are hazardous in any way. It sure would suck to have to use the trial and error method to find out what was and wasn't edible around here.

Rennek has about a dozen long, straight branches he gathered from the forest floor. They are all fairly uniform in size and length. Once the cord is done he begins to bind them together. It looks kind of like he is making a raft, but I know when it is done it will be our door.

I wonder how he is going to attach it to the stone doorframe and if there will be any type of locking mechanism. The door begins to take shape quickly now that the cord is done. I admire how agile his fingers are with the braiding. It gives me all sorts of ideas. Maybe we can weave some baskets, I wonder if he can braid my hair. Then I have some other, less practical, and much more sexy ideas. I chuckle to myself.

As he works he tells me stories about growing up on Javan with his friends, about hunting and learning how to survive. It's impressive. He laughs about Dax jumping off a tall rock, into a pool of water far below, that all the older boys were afraid to jump off of. Then there was a time when Bossan got caught in his own trap and hung upside down for hours before the guys found him and cut him down. Apparently, they still tease him about that one.

I find myself slightly envious of his wild childhood and his closely-knit group of friends. My childhood was spent at home alone. The TV kept me company. There were no adventures. I snort a little at my own melancholy thoughts. Well, I certainly made up for lost time in the adventure department.

"It sounds like you enjoyed living on Javan. What made you leave there?"

"It is a place for learning only, for fledglings. You graduate and move onward. Post internment it is required that one spends a minimum of four yets with the UPC. They station you anywhere males are needed. Could be a back world, could be a large city. I ended up on Thaad, it was very different from Javan. When I was young I enjoyed it, but now I think I would not like it so much. It swarms with people from many distant worlds."

"Like the space station?" I ask.

"Nothing like the space station. I was sorry to take you there, it is no place for a goddess."

"Luckily, I'm only human," I tease. "I don't know, I kind of liked it. I mean it was gritty, but it was also mind blowing."

"It is a poor first look at what this sector of the galaxy has to offer. Thaad is a metropolis. It is a city so large that it is built up into the skies. The richest of people live high up in glass towers, like crystals growing up towards the heavens. In the evenings the setting of the sun illuminates them, breaking up the light like a prism shining down upon everything in the city."

"The cultures all blend and the streets smell like the delicacies of a dozen worlds. There are cultural centers, universities, and shops selling all sorts of amazing items. But, like any big city, it is crowded and there is much petty crime. It was good for a time, but being here reminds me of life on Javan. I too enjoy the simple pleasures," he pauses his work and smiles at me. "It is much better to raise fledglings in a place like this. With much fresh air and open space," he says and I'm sure I blanche at his words. I think he notices my reaction and changes the subject. "Tell me of Earth."

"Huh? Oh... Earth."

"Do you miss your home?"

"Hmm, my home? That's a big fat no. But my planet, yes. There's a lot of beauty to Earth. There are all kinds of different climates and regions: deserts, mountains, rainforests, beaches. They all have their own unique beauty, not that I ever got to see much of them. I mean, I've been on a couple camping trips with my dad when I was real young, but just local stuff. I've been to the beach, but only the Southern California ones, none of the really pretty tropical ones. That, plus one trip to Vegas, covers the extent of my traveling. It's a little sad that I'll never get to see any more of what Earth has to offer, but when I compare it to this place...

it doesn't bother me so much. I've seen more in the past couple of weeks than I have in my entire life. I consider myself lucky," I tell him and he is quiet and thoughtful for a while.

"You did not have the chance to experience much of your home planet. It does not have to be so on this world. Tonight, we should climb atop the ruins and watch the sunset. There is much to discover here together Kate, we will make it our task to uncover all the beauty Elysia has to offer."

"The sunset sounds like a really great place to start," I agree. I can't help but feel the flutter of butterflies in my stomach. It almost feels like being on a date with a guy I'm really into. I try to think back to the guys I dated back on Earth. Did I still feel this giddy a few weeks into the relationship? I wonder when this fuzzy, new feeling is going to wear off.

Once the door is finished Rennek leaves again and returns a while later with another big log and some smaller pieces of wood. I don't bother cleaning up after him this time because I figure he still has a mess to make.

The first bird is done cooking by this time and we remove it from the spit and place the waiting bird over the fire. I start to pick at the cooked one a bit and silently wish for plates or bowls or something. Luckily, the meat is delicious, and with some seasoning it could easily become my new favorite meal. It's not chicken, but it is what it is. I look forward to making this again once the others get here. I tear off pieces and feed them to Rennek, telling him about Thanksgiving. He beams at me, licking and nipping at my fingers with each bite I serve him.

Rennek splits the wood using the big knife he keeps on his hip and a large rounded rock. Unfortunately, we don't have an axe or saw. The backside of Rennek's knife is serrated though, which is better than nothing. He hacks at little pieces that need to be removed. It leaves a rough edge, but doesn't diminish the overall product.

I see that with these pieces he is making a frame for our stone doorway. He, rather impressively in my opinion, cuts the wood to just the right size so that it can be pressed into the doorway. It fits so tightly in the space that he has to hammer it in with the rock. Then he gets to work whittling, making wooden hinges. I thought braiding the cord took forever, but this whittling business takes the cake. After much of the day is done, he hammers the final pieces together and hangs our door.

"Tomorrow we will find clay and fill any cracks," he says opening and closing the door, making sure everything is up to his standards. I notice he has a ton of braided cord left over.

"Wow, our little home is already starting to take shape," I beam at him.

"The simple things," he says, lacing his large clawed fingers through mine while we admire our new door together.

The rest of the day is filled with more supply gathering. Rennek collects and prepares a stock pile of wood for the fire: to cook with during the day and to heat our chilly stone room at night. He makes a long list of things we need and sends it over to the ship. I give him my input, suggesting plates and bowls and different things to cook with, towels, supplies to hand wash our clothing, buckets or jugs to hold larger amounts of water, and crates to store things in. We talk about creating a metal arm to go in the fireplace, one that we can hang a pot on. The synthesizers can easily whip one of those up… if they are functioning that is. If not, we can cannibalize some of the ship to make something work. There are so many things we need, but my mind keeps going to useless things, like a cool area rug. I'm just really excited to make this place homey.

Rennek is super busy. He knows all the things that need to be done to survive and to make the day run smoothly. I want to help, but I don't really know what needs to be done and I don't want to keep interrupting him. So, I try to be as useful as possible. By now I'm familiar with the small water filter Rennek carries for us and I fill all our pouches with fresh drinking water. Rennek disposes of the bones and waste from our Elysian chicken meal and adds spices to the list of things we will ask the others to bring. When we cross paths back in our room I see he has hung some pegs in the spaces between stones on one of our walls. Now we can hang our pack and our clothes up, instead of just tossing them on the ground--though hanging up clothes mostly just affects me. All Rennek has to hang up is his loincloth.

Rennek lets me go behind the ruins and collect some more pompayas on my own, but he makes me take the charger with me. It's sweet that he makes such a stink about my safety, but I assure him that I can do such a simple task on my own. On the way back, I come across a dead animal. It's hard to tell what it was, and I'm not so curious as to poke around to find out. Instead I see a cluster of those giant pink cabbage looking flowers and it easily distracts me from the yucky dead thing. I rip one from the stalk it grows on and bring it back with me. I'm curious if it's edible.

I ask Rennek to do a scan on it for me. When he does I see a little blue light appear on the screen, that must be good, I imagine bad would be red or something. It's unfortunate that the language implant in my head only helps me speak and understand alien language, it doesn't make me literate in it. My guess is confirmed however. He tells me it safe to eat and when we break it open to inspect its center, we find it is filled with something like seeds or nuts. The scanner tells us this plant is also a wonderful vitamin source and I'm super excited I found something useful. I just hope it tastes good. In all my excitement about this new leafy prospect I forget to mention the dead animal I saw.

As it gets close to sunset I sweep the room one last time and organize our food, water, and firewood. The pack hangs from a hook by the door. I straighten our blankets to make our sleeping area look neat, if not cozy. I mean, the blankets are a thin material so you can only get so cozy lying on a stone floor. I look forward to when the others arrive and bring pillows and mattresses from the ship.

As I tidy up I keep stopping to admire our little space. Even though we don't have much, every little corner has a little something that makes it looked lived in. It's wonderfully exciting. I don't think I've ever been so happy, I think to myself, taking it all in. I mean, I do wish I had a nice area rug though. But beside that, everything is so absolutely perfect... it's a little scary. I'm just not used to everything coming up roses. It almost makes me worry this is the calm before the storm, but I push that useless thought away.

When our space is as tidy as can be, and everything is in its place, I wash some of the outer leaves of the pink cabbage thing and tuck the last of the meat inside of them like a burrito. It's a little plain, but a great starting point.

Rennek and I watch the sun dip below the horizon from the rooftop. We admire the wide flat valley behind the ruins. Rennek believes that centuries ago this was the farmland of the people who lived here. He points out the pompaya trees and the tall stalks that hold the clusters of pink cabbage flowers.

"This could be what is left of their crops, a few fruit bearing plants surrounded by overgrowth that has crept in from the forest," he tells me thoughtfully.

The moons and the stars come out and Rennek points out the different constellations he knows, though we are viewing them from a different angle than he is most familiar with. He shows me the directions of different things he has told me about: Mother Planet, Thaad, and Javan. He tells me of places he visited while he did his mandatory time with the UPC. They all sound so exotic and beautiful. He even promises to take me to some tropical beaches on a planet called Isleria. We lay for a long time on the roof, listening to the sounds of the jungle and staring up at the stars.

"We should end every day like this," I say.

"I cannot imagine anything more perfect," he tells me, his black eyes focused intently on my face. It's impossible not to smile up at him. He kisses my forehead and runs his clawed fingers through my hair. I think one of the things I love most about him is the way he is always touching me, just in the sweetest and simplest of ways. It makes me feel like he finds even the briefest of contact with me precious. He makes me feel like *I* am precious.

We head back to our room and he does his nightly check in with the others before he readies for bed and sets a latch on the door.

"That's a nice feature," I notice.

"It will keep small, curious animals from poking around, or give us a moment to ready ourselves if something larger comes knocking. It will not keep a predator out, but it might give us an extra moment to grab the guns or a knife," he tells me.

"Eek, let's hope that never ever happens," I respond.

"Indeed," he agrees.

***

The next morning Rennek hustles off into the forest and returns with two more Elysian chickens ready for the spit. We chat about building a little aviary where we can maybe raise a few of the birds and we wonder what their eggs are like. I'm happy to realize that eating eggs is another thing I have in common with my alien boyfriend. I'm happy *anytime* I discover something that seems vaguely familiar to me, to be honest.

He leaves me in charge of cooking the birds and tells me he has some work he needs to concentrate on before he heads into one of the other nearby rooms. The birds are pretty easy to cook and don't take too much attention other than a little turning here and there, so I figure this is my opportunity to check out the ruins, do a little exploring, and maybe figure out what I can do around this place to help out.

I don't bother with checking out the bathing room, because frankly, that place gives me the creeps. I don't know what could be swimming in that water. So, until we clean it out, no thank you. Instead, I walk around the courtyard and survey everything more closely. The fountains are all running now, but most of them have plants and debris in them. Rennek set up his small water filter in the main fountain and the little thing is now working to clear the last of the sediment out of the water for us. I will no longer need to manually filter our drinking or bathing water, though we will need to clean the small filter regularly to keep it functioning.

I look around and wonder what to do with myself. I feel a little bit at a loss. I could start digging all the junk out of the smaller fountains, but that would probably keep me away from the spit for too long. Plus, it would be *way* easier to do that once we have a shovel or something to scoop with. It seems all the work to be done in the courtyard is gardening related, and since I don't have any tools to help me with that, I finally decide to head over to where the fruit trees are. I'll just gather more food to make sure we're all stocked up. I grab our empty pack and start walking over. Halfway there, the unthinkable happens.

I start my mother fucking period.

I feel the telltale drop of warm to cold wetness between my legs and cringe. Why had I not even thought of this until now, I wonder to myself, cursing that I'm not more prepared.

My flow is typically light, so I grumble and curse but eventually decide I might as well continue on my errand before I head back to take care of my lady business. I had hoped to poke around for a bit longer today to see if there was anything else edible. If this was in fact once a farming area, there might be other food sources still growing here. Instead I'll have to go interrupt Rennek in his chores and ask if his super cool back world training ever covered tips on how to make tampons out of leaves and tree bark. I kick the dirt in frustration.

This is *exactly* the kind of thing I want to talk about with my new boyfriend. I grimace just thinking about it. I find the pompayas and grab only two, as we still have one back in our room. I want to grab a few pink cabbage things, but they are big and unwieldy. I think I can squeeze two in the pack and carry another. Later I'll try cooking them in the bird drippings and maybe even start experimenting with the seeds. I decide I'll go a little further into the forest first though. I'm not exactly in a huge hurry to get back and ask Rennek to help me take care of my period.

Unfortunately, I encounter a patch of thick trailing vines covered in some mean looking thorns. Just as I'm about to turn back I take a closer look and notice fat brown berries, practically the size of apples, because all the plant life is mega sized here. I tiptoe through and over some of the vines, grabbing as many as I can reach without getting stuck by a thorn. I cross my fingers in the hope that the scanner reads this stuff as edible. I see some berries on the vine have been picked at by birds, so I'm already assuming they're good to go. At least today will have one silver lining, I think to myself.

The skins of the berries are fragile, so the more I pile into my bag, the more the ones on the bottom get squished. I only gather about a dozen or so. I'll worry about getting more once we determine if they are tasty or not. I start heading back and decide now to only grab one cabbage instead of two, but when I get to the stalks I notice a horrible odor.

"Oh, barf," I cover my nose and mouth. I suddenly remember the dead animal that I had forgotten to tell Rennek about. Nasty old thing is probably rotting in the humid jungle. I look over to where I remembered seeing it and to my horror I see two more largish animal corpses. I stumble back and look anxiously around me. Now obviously this isn't the spot animals go to lay down and die in the jungle. Nope, something killed these things. My mind reels. There is a predator nearby and I'm all alone out here. I took off without telling Rennek, and unlike yesterday, I didn't even bring the charger with me.

I hear a rustling of leaves nearby and I drop my cabbage and run like I've never fucking run before in my life. I haul ass all the way back to the ruins and call for Rennek as I charge in the gate. Rennek jumps through one of the corridor windows and runs to me, searching me all over with his hands as I pant like a fool, trying to catch my breath.

"You are hurt Kate!" He exclaims. "You are bleeding! Where are you injured?" He says inhaling deeply and continuing to search my body. Alarm written all over his face.

"Wha...?" I pant, "I'm not bleeding... I'm..." Oh. I am bleeding. Then I cringe again and probably turn bright red. Rennek can *smell* my period. Most. Embarrassing. Thing.

Ever. "No, no, no." I hold my hand up, gesturing for him to wait while I suck in air. He watches me helplessly, shock and worry in his eyes. I can't help but laugh a little. "Okay, I can breathe. Not hurt. I saw a couple of dead animals in the forest and it spooked me," I explain.

"But you are bleeding Kate, I can smell it!" He says, his fears unquelled.

"Unrelated," I tell him and because it's not like I can keep it on the down low, I tell him about my period. "I just... I started my period. It's that time of the month. I'm not hurt."

"Oh." He says, clearly taken aback. He looks around, as if he wants to offer assistance in some way but has no clue what to offer me. It's not like there's a tampon tree growing nearby.

"My sister began her cycles just before I left for Javan. There are no females on Javan." His eyes have this helpless look in them that I've never seen in Rennek before. He can handle a gun fight on a space station, but tell the guy you started your period and he's helpless.

"It's cool. I can figure something out. I can rip up that shirt that's already torn, make a couple of pads I can clean and reuse."

"I will help with anything you need. Are you in pain? Madreed used to place warming pads on Kahreen. Would you like something like that? I can warm stones, we can wrap them and place them on your stomach. Do you need to lie down?" He breathes out earnestly, stroking my hair.

"No. It's just a period. I'm fine, really. Thank you though, I appreciate how sweet you're being. Let's definitely see if we can synth some tampons when the others come though. Tee shirt pads aren't going to cut it for long. Plus, I'm betting the other girls are starting to deal with this little inconvenience too."

"Why were you running?" He asks, refocusing now that he isn't worried about my blood loss.

"I saw some dead animals and I heard a noise. I figured some kind of predator was nearby." This sobers Rennek right up. He doesn't know how to handle a period, but a predator he can do.

"Come, stay close to me." He goes to our room and grabs his blaster and hands me a charger. We take a quick break to turn the meat on the spit and make sure the coals are low and cooking evenly. I also take this opportunity to change my pants and stuff a little folded square of shirt between my legs. I have to keep telling Rennek to look away and he laughs at my modesty.

"Show me where you saw the animals," he tells me and we head back out of the ruins. As we get close, Rennek stops and smells the air. He motions for me to remain silent and after a moment or two we continue on toward the tall stalks with the pink cabbages on them. I don't have to point out the obvious to him. The stench becomes palpable. I stay behind him and Rennek inches forward, blaster at the ready. His eyes move from the carrion to our surroundings. When we are right on top of the dead things he kicks at them with one of the big claws on his toes. I can see puncture holes all over the things.

"Gross," I say.

"I saw one like this on our first day here."

"So, four in the past few days?"

He simply grunts in response. His expression is severe and concerned. He studies the ground around the animals, I suppose he is looking for tracks. I look too, but I don't see any footprints, only scuff marks. He pokes at the animals again and harrumphs.

"What is it?"

"It may be nothing."

"Well tell me what it is then," I insist.

"Coincidence perhaps, but all these creatures are female, as was the one from the other day."

Gulp.

"What would hunt only females? A misogynistic panther?"

"It may not be the gender of the creatures that attracts, but rather their scent."

And Rennek can smell me… so I wonder what that means for our neighborhood predator. We poke around a little longer, but find no other signs, so we head back to the ruins.

"I will have to hunt this creature," he tells me.

"If it comes back, yeah. We should avoid it until the others get here though. I'd feel better if you weren't out hunting alone." I say, but he only grunts again in reply.

As we approach the ruins he stiffens and smells the air. He presses me close against the wall and we peek beyond the gateway entrance. Rennek is silent and still and even though I'm scared, I risk leaning forward to look beyond him. I hear the sound of something heavy scuffing against the dirt and stones. Then I see it. I don't scream when I do, but I involuntarily suck my breath in hard. Rennek pushes me back and shields me with his big muscled arm.

I can hardly believe what I saw. In the courtyard of our ruins, with half of its body hanging out one of the corridor windows, is a big--I mean *huge*, like big as an SUV, *fucking spider*. I only saw its backside very quickly, but it was dark and hairy with too many long and jointed legs. Rennek covers my mouth and locks eyes with me. I realize that I'm hyperventilating. His gaze centers me and I slow my breathing.

It's not that I've ever been particularly scared of spiders, it's more so that this thing is giant and it's been hanging around our camp for days killing animals the size of goats. By the size of it, I assume it could take down something much larger… something person sized, for example. Rennek takes his hand from my mouth and motions for me to wait. I shake my head vehemently, no. I haven't had the chance to think this through and I don't think he has either. I don't want Rennek to fight this giant thing alone and I don't want to be left alone while he does. I also don't think I'd be super helpful in a fight against a giant spider either. Instead I tug at him, hoping he gets my silent hint that we should just leave. We can come back later with the others and take this thing out with a group. But he shakes his head right back at me and motions for me to wait once more. I hear the spider moving around more in the courtyard and my heart starts pounding hard again. Rennek seems to think I've agreed to him going in there solo, so he turns and begins to charge forward. I grab for his arm to stop him, but he's too quick. I watch in horror as he bursts into the courtyard.

The spider turns and looks upon my man and I see its face for the first time. Maybe all spiders look like this and I've just never noticed because on Earth they are tiny, but this thing's face is freaky as fuck. Like, going to have a starring role in all my nightmares for the rest of my life kind of freaky. It has more beady black eyes than I can count and two long, sharp looking pincers at its mouth. It snaps them viciously when it sees my gargoyle fall into his battle stance. Blaster strapped around his chest, Rennek has dropped down to all fours, his tail whipping and his wings spread wide behind him. He appears twice his normal size, and ten times more threatening. He bares his fangs and his rumbling growl turns into a roar. The stone walls seem to vibrate with the power of it. The spider takes a few anxious steps back and forth. Its breath huffs hard, disrupting the dirt and leaves on the ground. Then, miracle of miracles, it turns and climbs over the far wall and is gone.

I run in to be by Rennek's side, but he sprints after the thing and mounts the wall like a massive, agile cat. Rennek stops at the top of the wall though, which is practically the height of a two-story building (color me impressed) and peers over the edge. A moment later he jumps back down to me. He runs his hands through his wild black hair. I notice a thin sheen of sweat glistening on him. His eyes go past me and settle on something in the courtyard. I turn to see what has caught his attention.

Laying there on the ground are the pants I was wearing earlier when I started my period. The spider had dragged them from our room. Rennek hops up and through one of the corridor windows to peer inside our room. I race up to look as well. One thing stands out clearly to me: the two Elysian chickens sit untouched, but my period pants got dragged out into the courtyard.

Rennek looks at me, but he doesn't need to speak. Thank goodness, because this is actually equally embarrassing as it is scary. Obviously, Rennek isn't the only one who can smell my period and unfortunately, it seems like the giant spider is interested in what it smells. Lovely.

Chapter 47

Rennek

"I must go after it," I tell my anxious mate.

"No! Let's just call the others and let them know what's up and start heading in their direction."

Fleeing will not work. I bite my words though, because I do not want to frighten my Kate. This thing will follow us, this thing *has been following us*. I first noticed its scent before we arrived at the ruins, I mistook it for the primates. I imagine that it has been following her scent, likely because of her female cycle. If we were to leave, as she demands, Kate would not be fast enough to outrun the beast and I cannot go days on end without sleep attempting to guard her.

The only logical course of action is that I must go after it and kill it. This is no problem though; a blaster will make short work of it. The only problem is that Kate worries over me. She has never hunted or been in a survival situation like this before. I, on the other hand, have and I know I am capable of taking this beast down. I do not worry over my ability to succeed in battle against it. I have fought and killed things this size before. This monster will be no different.

I attempt to keep the mood light, so she does not worry, but in truth I worry too. Not about fighting the beast and winning, but about all the opportunities it had to hurt my Kate before I became aware of its presence. I insist that she eat and put the other bird over the spit. She nibbles a bit, but worry still consumes her. I sigh heavily.

"My surprise will be ruined now," I tell her, feigning sadness.

"Your surprise?" She asks. I notice a little of the worry escapes her voice--not all of it, but some.

"Come with me," I tell her, leading her to an unoccupied room like ours a few doors down. Inside is what I have been working on all morning. I see Kate's eyes light up and fill with understanding. Yesterday I made much extra cord and today I have been using it to bind a pallet together for our bed.

"It is not yet finished, but if you allow me to go squash the bug I will still be able to complete it before our sunset together."

She crosses her arms over her chest and huffs at me, but I see a smile play at the corners of her pink lips.

"Come, hold our door open for me and I will bring the supplies into our room. The pallet is complete, all that is left to do is raise it a few inches so it is not in direct contact with the floor. This will keep our bed warmer and keep any sneaky vermin out."

"Ew, creepy. Okay, let's raise it up then. I'm eager to help, it'll be nice to have a bed again, especially once the others get here and bring some mattresses along. Also, because now I'm going to be thinking about vermin crawling around me while I sleep."

"You do not have to worry. I will always protect you my Kate, whether it be from eelworms or very large spiders," I say the words with a teasing tone, but it is the truth. She pinches the bridge of her nose and swats at me in mock annoyance, but allows me to pull her body close to mine.

"So gross," she says, then is silent in my embrace for a moment before speaking again.

"Rennek, this sucks! We *finally* have a bed and can consummate this damned thing... but now we have this looming threat of a gigantic spider trying to sniff out my crotch! And by the way, I forget why we even have this silly self-imposed rule about our first time being in a bed to begin with... *but,* not only do we have the spider to contend with, but my freaking period too. Thanks a lot uterus," she huffs against my chest and I stroke her mane.

"This evening we can pad the pallet with fronds and lay our blanket over them. It is not as soft as the mattress back on the ship, but it is much better than stone," I say, ignoring her words of worry.

"*Rennek*, the giant freaking man-eating spider?"

"Will have to find his own bed," I smile.

"Very funny," she squirms away. Holding me at arm's length to look up into my eyes. "I'm scared of this thing Rennek. Now, don't get all prideful about it because I believe that if necessary you would totally destroy it, but I just don't want to risk you. This is the start of... of..." she struggles with her words.

"It is the start of our lives together," I say for her. I know what my mate thinks, even if she does not wish to admit to herself that she thinks it.

"Whatever it is," she blushes, "I don't want to tempt fate. You don't have to hunt this thing alone. We can just leave and come back with our friends."

The smell of smoke and the sizzle of the fire interrupts our conversation. The drip pan has tilted and begun to overflow.

"Dammit," she says and moves to remedy the situation. I know this is not something she has ever done before and am proud at how quickly she has picked up on spit cooking.

I turn to my work on our bed. I arrange it in its space against the wall and measure out a long log from the three that I have to choose from. I find one that is approximately the same length as the bed is wide. It is thick, about ten inches in diameter. I will need to split it with my knife and a stone. It will not be simple to keep it even, but I still hope to finish my task on this day. All the while though, I am only giving partial attention to my work. I keep my ears and nose tuned in to what goes on outside in the courtyard. I think this creature is not used to a fight and I scared it away. For now.

"I will need to split this outside," I tell my mate.

"I'll come with you babe," she says and grabs her charger. "Not letting this thing out of my sight again," she says, giving it a wiggle in her palm. "Or my man, for that matter," she closes one eye in my direction--some type of human gesture, I surmise.

"You use pet names on me, it will be my undoing if you continue."

"It's called sweet-talk babe and don't worry, I don't have you at a disadvantage. It works on me too," she admits and so I close one eye at her and she nearly doubles over with laughter, which dies in her throat as soon as I open our door. "Do you think it will be back?" she asks and I notice all the lightness has left her tone.

"Not just yet," I tell her. I do not elaborate, but I know we will not be safe for long. This monster has been curious about us for some time now, following our scent, watching us. I know now that it followed us as we explored the beacon and that it has been in our courtyard before. It is becoming bolder. Today it followed my Kate's scent and came directly into our room. Next, I imagine it will test my strength. But I do not want my Kate to worry, so I continue with the day's tasks as if there is no problem.

We stand in the corridor so that I may split the log, though I did not truly need to come outside to work. I wanted to get a better scent of the area. Kate stands at one of the open stone windows looking out with her charger in hand. She guards me and I smile at how fierce my mate is. I make quick work of splitting the log. I am fairly happy with how even it comes out considering my lack of tools. Tomorrow I will take clay and use it to level any parts that are not perfect and fill any cracks in our door as well. I had hoped to do that on this day, but it seems I have more pressing tasks before me. I sniff the air. I see Kate's eyes studying me, inquiring.

"I smell it. It is not close though."

"We should leave."

I hold the door open for her. She sighs and we head back inside. Using the cords, I weave one half of the log at the top of the bed and the other half at the bottom. Kate goes to the door and peers out, muttering at me under her breath. "Typical man," I catch her saying. The final pieces are woven to our bed pallet. I test the sturdiness. It is perfect.

"I will now kill the spider," I declare. "Then we will have our sunset and make love in our bed."

"Yup, typical man," she says, crossing her arms over her chest. "Okay, you need to unpack that statement. If *we* are going to kill the spider then *we* need to discuss a plan of attack. I need to know what you think you're going to do and what I can do to be your backup."

"Is there anything else you need to unpack?" I ask smirking. She has conspicuously ignored the latter half of my statement.

"Then… uh, so you're cool with us having sex even though it's that time of the month?" She questions. "You don't want to wait a couple more days?" she says, blushing as if we have not seen one another at our most fragile and vulnerable already.

"Will you blush like this when you birth our fledglings?" I tease and she turns a darker shade of red. The expression on her face is both shy and a little bit lost… it calls me to her. I wrap my arms around my tiny human and press kisses to her flushed face--letting her know, without the words that frighten her so much, that I am here and I will always be here.

"How will we find the spider?" She asks, changing the subject.

"I have its scent now, we simply need to go to it."

"Okay, then how can I help?"

I rub my hand over my face. It is difficult. I will not leave my Kate alone here. I let my guard down once already and this creature has been stalking her. The worst could have happened while Kate wandered by herself today and I would not have been by her side to protect her. I will not allow another possibility like that to arise again. No, she will go with me. That option however brings its own obvious risks.

"It is simple. I will kill the spider with the blaster, we should not even need to get very close. You will carry the charger and one of my knives, for your own sense of safety. When we get close, you will stay behind me and I will fire at it. That will be all," I explain.

"...and in a worst-case scenario?" She asks.

"There will be no worst-case scenario," I say confidently, attempting to encourage Kate to feel as assured as I do.

"You're really sure about this?" She asks.

"We have a blaster, my sweet Kate," I tell her. "We will be back in time to turn the meat," I say, giving her my most confident smile.

"Yeah, I guess so," she harrumphs. "I forgot about the big gun. For some reason I thought you'd be wrestling it or something." She eases and I see her shoulders relax, "Sorry, you probably do stuff like this all the time and here I am making a big deal out of nothing."

"You had a scare, being alone in the forest where you were vulnerable to the creature. I do not judge you harshly for feeling this way," I tell her.

"No… it's not that. I mean, yeah that was scary…but that's not why I'm shaken up about spider hunting," she says.

"What is it then, my goddess?" I implore.

"I don't know…"

"I think you do," I encourage.

"It's just, things have been going so well. *Everything* has been going so well--between us, here on Elysia… life for me has never been this…" she struggles again to express herself. Her eyes search the room, landing on anything but my gaze. I pull her near me and press my head to hers and encircle her in my arms. She closes her eyes before she speaks again.

"Things in life just don't go this well, and if they do it means the other shoe is going to drop. Something bad is going to happen. That's just how I feel anyway, that my happiness is fragile and it's going to be shattered."

I sigh. This is a fear I resonate with. Kate is my everything. She has changed my life entirely from the moment I was blessed enough to look upon her. It is frightening to love someone so deeply, but it is empowering as well.

"We cannot let fear rule us Kate. You are a fragile and puny human, if I sat and thought on this all day I would go mad with fear and be forced to lock you in a cage so that you would never be hurt or in danger," she snorts a laugh and swipes at her eyes. "It is a fear I have, but it is irrational, yes?"

"Yes," she agrees.

"Fate has brought us together for a reason, and that reason is surely not so that we may be a spider's meal together in the forests of Elysia."

"Yes, yes. Okay. I get it. Let's go kill a spider."

We make sure the coals burn low beneath our spit before we ready ourselves to leave. I take our pack and in it I bring water and our most essential equipment: the scanner, my comm unit, and our small med pack that contains bandages, ointments, and orals which can be taken in case of illness or injury. I strap my knife to my waistcloth and hang the blaster over one shoulder. Kate carries nothing but her charger and the knife I strap to her hip.

We set off in the direction the spider fled. I easily follow its trail. I do not need to search out its scuffing tracks, for its scent is familiar to me now. We travel slowly, I do not wish to wear Kate out, we still have a busy night ahead of us. I smile to myself at the thought and my anticipation causes me to quicken our pace just a bit.

"So what, are we looking for a giant spider web?" Kate whispers.

"Unlikely, I imagine it will be a den. If it utilized a web it would not be leaving its kills around the ruins."

"Huh. Good point."

As the scent becomes stronger I know we near the creature. I ready my blaster. The land dips low here and I notice a marsh beginning to form. This area must be a tributary from the water that comes down the mountain. Unlike the flowing water that gushes through the canals at the ruins, the water here is stagnant and covered with green froth in many places. The scent of the marsh hangs heavy in the humid forest air and even still I can smell the putrid odor of the spider getting closer with every step.

We weave through places of high ground so we do not step into the murky water. I hear the call of birds and the hum of insects. Kate jumps when she notices a swarm of translucent, multi legged creatures, with spiny thoraxes and antenna that stretch out four times the length of their bodies. I try not to point out a camouflaged creature that looks much like the branches of the trees and vines around us. It walks through the water as if on stilts, looking every bit like a stick itself. It pauses, taking us in, just before a tentacle rolls up from the water and pulls the stilted creature down below. No, I do not think I will point this out to my Kate.

Up ahead, I see a swell of rocks piled near the base of a large and gnarled tree. There are gaping openings between the dirt and rocks which are large enough to fit the villain we hunt. As surely as I can smell the foul thing, it pokes its massive head out from its den. Its black eyes shine and it snaps its pinchers at the sight of us. Kate gasps when she sees it and stumbles back a bit, caught by surprise. I reach behind me to steady her.

"Sorry, I'm good," she whispers. I aim my blaster and as it emerges completely from its den. It lifts the hind side of its body in an unnatural way and I fire at it. The energy the blaster releases is like an explosion compared to the gentle hum of the marsh. It sets off a reaction from all the silent and unseen creatures in the swamp. Birds take to the air, previously unseen ground dwelling creatures scurry away, the water around us splashes and ripples wildly. Kate grips at my wing. The song of insects is suddenly silent.

A puff of smoke clears from the spider, revealing a disgusting mess of slimy, fleshy pieces sprayed across the opening of its den. All is still for a fleeting moment. Then, the body begins to move and twitch even though the front half is gone.

"What the hell…?" Kate's voice questions from behind me.

Then I see it, pushing the large body aside and emerging in a wave from the den are dozens upon dozens of spiders. Some are the size of a typical marsh rake, but others… many others, are nearly the size of the monster I just killed.

"Oh shit! What were you saying about no worst-case scenarios?" Kate exclaims.

I allow myself a silent curse before my mind begins forming a plan. The spiders are aware that we have attacked them. Hundreds of black eyes are on us, they hiss as they swarm and gnash their pincers at us.

"To the rocks," I point behind Kate and she hastily runs toward them, her own charger drawn. Once there, we climb up a few feet to gain a height advantage and stand side by side. "Aim for the smaller ones, your weapon is better equipped for them. If I tell you to run, turn and run back to the ruins and stay there."

"There is nothing that could make me go anywhere without you," she says firmly.

"I need you to trust me," I tell her and she curses, but nods assent.

"Fire," I tell her and we spray the oncoming swarm with blasts from our weapons. Their bodies begin to pile upon one another. Making some leeway with the hoard, we retreat back a few steps. I take out a dozen of the larger spiders, then a dozen more.

"Rennek!" Kate screams, calling my attention to a spider wriggling out from between the corpses of its downed brethren. It arches the rear of its body toward me, just as the larger one did before I shot it. I kick it away from me and hit it with a blast before it even hits the ground. I take a moment to look at my Kate. Her fiery mane flows behind her. There is no fear on her face, only strength and determination. Her stance is powerful and controlled. She does not blink, nor flinch, nor tremble. She simply moves her weapon from one target to the next. She is good at this. I throw my head back laughing.

"And you said you did not want to hunt on this day," I laugh. "I see the fighter in you, my Kate."

"Let's save it for the after party," she shouts, not taking her eyes off her oncoming targets. I laugh again and resume my firing. We are nearly done, when I hear my blaster phase down a setting. Luckily, Kate does not know what the sound indicates. I do not wish to worry her. This is still our fight to win. Even if the blaster doesn't make it through, Kate and I will. I reinvest mentally in the task before us, taking out the largest of the spiders. A dozen more down, perhaps twice that with Kate's contribution. The blaster drops another phase. I tally the remaining spiders. We can finish this, I think… and I may not even need to draw my knife.

But then, to use Kate's words, the other shoe drops and over the den I see the long spindly and jointed legs of another spider giant… just as massive, if not more so than the first. I don't have many blasts left. I aim for the giant.

"Rennek, eleven o'clock!" Kate screams nonsense words at me, causing me to realize three midsize spiders are closing in on me. I do not want to waste my blasts on them however. Kate sees my hesitation and fires on them. It blows the creatures back, but she has to send them each a second charger blast to end them.

I fire at the final giant, but the blast only blows off a portion of a leg. I aim and fire again, but the phase whines down to nothing. The final shot connects exactly where I wanted it to go, but without enough power to land a kill. The giant recoils at the sensation and rears its hind half. Suddenly, spines come flying at us. I look around and realize that the still oncoming swarm is firing the hairy spines at us as well. It is some type of defense mechanism.

Kate now realizes the state of my weapon. She bravely steps in front of me, firing her charger at anything that dares near us. I laugh and pull her back by the waist.

"Do not forget, my sweet Kate, the blaster is not my only weapon." Pulling out my blade, I dive into the fray. Kate curses angrily in my wake. I trust my brave and fierce female to cover me without instruction. I ignore the smaller spines that fly near me as I move in, my thick skin will not allow them to penetrate anyway. I count only a half dozen or so remaining spiders and I seek them out. Gripping each one I pass with my claws, I drive my knife into their heads. They fall lifeless at my feet. I hear the electric sound of Kate's charger as its shots fly past me.

I gradually make my way toward the last giant. The spider charges me, its gait uneven from its missing leg, it wobbles toward me at a great speed. I kill one more large spider and Kate fills the last few with multiple shots from her charger. There are a couple of small strays left, but Kate will make quick work of them. Now it is just me and the final beast.

It snaps at me and raises a leg, swinging it down on me like a spear. I dodge it. Kate runs to my side, her charger still raised, and I see the spider's eyes cloud and shift to my mate. *It smells her.* It immediately abandons its path towards me, perceptibly honing in on Kate.

"Run," I tell her. She huffs and hesitates. "Get back, now!" I roar and fling my wings open. The pack rips from my back and I hear Kate stumble and hit the ground. She scrambles and I hear her feet begin to beat against the ground. I roar my battle cry and let my wings pump just enough to aid me in a leap towards the creature.

The beast prickles at my challenge and fires more hairy spines. These are larger and have more power behind them than those of the younger spiders. I feel them graze my arm and side, but my charge is not interrupted. I land on the monstrosity's back and drive my blade into one of its eyes. It hisses and screams, bucking me off. I land on the ground in front of it, the wind knocked from my lungs. I hear Kate's screams, but cannot make out her words. Before I can recover, the spider's pincers come down on my shoulder. I imagine it will hurt later, but for now I am numb with adrenaline.

Suddenly, in my peripheral vision, I see Kate's form next to the spider. She takes her charger and presses it down into the wound my blaster gave the beast, and fires.

The thing releases me and it writhes wildly on the ground, its jointed legs frantically working to ease the pain of electrocution. I take this opportunity to drive my knife through the underside of the beast's head. It's screaming and hissing comes to an abrupt end.

"Rennek!" Kate screams. I can feel her grabbing at me and pulling me away from the spider. My feet falter and my legs feel weak, but I am beyond pleased. The threat has been eliminated.

"Rennek, come on. You're hurt. It's time to go." She tugs at me and I hear a thread of hysteria under her effortfully calm tone.

I stand and look at my Kate, brushing her hair back from her sweat and dirt smeared face. I beam at her, "All is well. I am fine." Truly, I feel fine.

"Rennek, you're bleeding. We have to get you back now," she says firmly. I laugh and look down. That's when I see the blood. I move to take a step forward and stumble again. Kate instinctively ducks under my arm to steady me.

I look down at her and see the worry in her eyes. They are wide, like saucers, and I want to tell her something to ease her fears, but it is suddenly a struggle to form words. "We should hurry…" I manage, "if we want to make it back by sunset," I tell her before the world around me goes black.

Chapter 48

Kate

I read a book once where a female character had to carry her beefy boyfriend after he got injured. She knew about hunting and stuff and made a travois to carry him. Thank god I read that freaking book. I need to get Rennek out of here in a now kind of way and it isn't like I can throw him over my damned shoulder. He's out cold, bleeding heavily from a wound by his collar bone and there are spider spines lodged in his arm and side.

"Fuck, fuck, fuck, fuck…" I mutter, assessing his large and unconscious body. I look around worriedly, making sure no predator--spider or otherwise, sneaks up on us. I decide my first course of action is to pull the spines out. They are covered in course hairs that I worry could be poisonous. I pop my shirt off without regard to my modesty and wrap it around my hand before I grab the first spine and rip it out. The hairs catch on Rennek's flesh and I wince. I pull one from his arm, two from his side, and I find a smaller final one lodged in his thigh.

I shake out the shirt, then turn it inside out, and ball it up on Rennek's collar, applying pressure while I scan the area. I need two long pieces of wood and something to stretch across it to set Rennek on. Luckily wood is something the forest floor has in abundance. I run around, kicking up piles of leaves and eventually unearth two old and weathered branches that are the right size for me to hold. Now… what can I set Rennek on? I look all around. There are huge megaflora leaves everywhere, I could use a few of those, but I don't really have a way to attach them to my travois poles.

"Think Kate, think, think." I eye Rennek's loincloth. "Fuck it," I say and work to free my man from his only piece of clothing. I spread the fabric out as much as I can and tie it to both travois poles. Now, the hard part. Or the first hard part in a long line of hard parts…

"Okay, babe. I'm sorry if this hurts," I tell his unconscious body before I start tugging him, trying to get him atop the cloth. I tug and tug and roll him, I even sit on my butt and push him with my legs. Finally, he's on top of the small piece of cloth, his arms hanging over the poles. I get up to begin our journey back, but frown at my contraption. His wings are going to get all scraped up if I try to pull him like this. I huff and decide to try to flip him. After much more work, he is naked and on his stomach atop my travois. I hitch the poles up under my arms and begin to pull.

"Ughhhh, oh my god, this is still so hard," I grunt.

I tug, pull, and drag him along and my grunts turn into sobs as we inch forward. He's okay, everything is going to be okay. I can do this. I just need to get him back to the safety of our room. I ignore the fact that he hasn't woken or even stirred. I also try to ignore the fact that the marsh around us frightens me.

When the spiders came out the other animals fled, but now, as the silence drags on, I can hear things returning. Fear builds itself up inside me. I look back at Rennek, his grey skin tone seems to be lighter than normal. It's pale and clammy. He's covered in blood, dirt, and sweat. I get about five feet and see he is sliding off the travois. I have to stop and reposition him. I get back up to the front of my poles and this time try for a running start. This extra burst helps me pull him along a little more quickly than my previous try, but he also slides down more quickly this time too. I heave at the poles, only to fall forward onto my hands and knees in the dirt and leaves.

This isn't working. I need something else. A different plan. I need help. The comm! I jump up and scan the area. Floating in the water, I see the torn pack.

"Oh shit," I breathe out and run to the water's edge. Using a short branch, I pull it towards me, rather than wading in and drenching my shoes. I'm able to get it to come close enough that I can grab it. Scooting away from the water, I dump the pack out. Scanner, comm, first aid kit. Yup, I definitely need all this stuff. I start pressing buttons on the comm, but the device does not respond.

"Hello, can anyone hear me? If you can, please, you have to come help! Rennek's been hurt! Please, is anyone there? Can anybody hear me?" I scream into the thing, just in case maybe, just maybe, someone on the other end can hear me, even if I can't hear them.

Okay, new plan. I look at the travois. The problem is the loincloth. It's too small, he keeps sliding off it. I need something big. Like a blanket. My heart pounds, rejecting the idea as quickly as I have it. I need to go back to our room and grab a blanket. I'm going to have to leave him here unguarded.

Tears spill from my eyes, but I have no time to acknowledge them. I run and rip some big leaves from a low hanging branch, this is probably stupid, but it's the best I can do. I cover Rennek with the leaves so he is hidden and say a prayer that nothing attacks him while I am gone. Just for good measure, I take my charger and find a rock covered slope near the water. I aim high and fire at it. There is a loud cracking noise and rocks tumble noisily into the water. I hear birds flapping their wings, startled by the sudden sound. I hope I scared any lurkers away…

I don't have time to waste standing around worrying, so before the rocks even finish crashing into the water, I break into a sprint. I can't leave him for long. So, over hills and rocks and branches, I run. I run until it feels like my lungs are on fire and I think I might throw up. My thighs burn and my body tries to slow down, but I push it harder. It's like being in one of those dreams where you're being chased, but when you try to run it feels like you're wading through molasses.

Finally, I get to the ruins, past the gate, go up the stairs, and into our room. I don't pause or slow down, I just grab the blanket, turn around, and keep running. On the way back to him I trip and fly face first into the ground. I push myself up, my leg protests, but I refuse to slow down. Poor Rennek is alone, lying under some fucking leaves, surrounded by piles of spider corpses. I suck air into my burning lungs. I hope we got them all. I hope he isn't being dragged into the spider's den right now.

Then, a painful thought hits me--I hope he doesn't wake up while I'm away. I feel awful for even thinking that, but I also feel ashamed that I had to leave him. He would have *never* leave me. Of course, he could carry me like a rag doll... but still, I can't stand the thought of him being alone without me by his side. Logically, I get that I had no choice, or at least none I could think of in that moment. Still, I can't stop my mind from imagining him waking up alone in the swampy marsh. I feel like I've failed him. I run harder.

When I see him still lying where I left him I feel a mixture of relief and panic. He's been unconscious for a long time. I make quick work of tying the material of the blanket to the travois. I use Rennek's knife to tear the edges of the fabric so I can secure it in multiple places. Finally, I get him back atop the fabric and start to pull. He is still heavy as fuck, and the travois is awkward and difficult to hold onto, but he isn't sliding off now and so I pull. And pull. And pull. Grunting, sobbing, and yelling my frustration into the forest as we go.

"Don't worry, Rennek. I've got you. You can count on me," I tell him... or maybe I tell myself.

I can't imagine what a mess I must look like right now, topless and sweating, fumbling over every dip and root the ground has to offer. Still, I'd be overjoyed if I stumbled upon Da'vi and Allison right now. But no one comes and the day wears thin, the sky reddens with the sunset and still we aren't back to the ruins yet.

After what seems like an eternity, I see the high stone walls peeking through the trees ahead of me. The sight of it gives me a last burst of strength and I trudge onward. It's dark when we make it inside the courtyard and I still refuse let myself slow. When I look up and see the staircase another sob escapes me. It feels like a punch to my chest. Or maybe my lungs are trying to tell me they are giving up.

"Just a little further, we're almost back babe," I tell Rennek, even though he has been still and silent since collapsing back at the marsh. I look back at him, but it's so dark and he's so still. A dark thought crosses my mind. *I wonder if he's still breathing.* I want to drop the poles and go check, but I violently push that possibility out of my mind. Of course he is, he's fine. He's going to be fine.

The stairs prove to be an issue and I have to abandon my travois and make the saddest pulley system in the history of simple machines. I use the now tattered and shredded blanket, tying it around his body and wrapping the other end around one of the window columns, then use my body weight to drag his giant ass up the stairs. I pull him on the blanket the rest of the way down the corridor and to our room.

Once inside the door I want to collapse on the ground and cry myself to sleep, but that isn't an option. It's dark in our room, the coals have died out. I feel around the floor until I find the flint and grab some tinder and a log Rennek had prepared and left by our fireplace. My hands shake, but I get the fire started quickly enough. When light fills the room, it feels like a blessing. The Elysian chicken is still hanging over the fire. It's withered, dry, and burnt on one side. I move it aside so the high fire I've built doesn't burn it further.

"I've got you Rennek, I'm here. You just stay with me and I'll stay with you, okay?" I tell him, but he just lays silent, scraped up, and filthy on the floor. Blood still seeps from the wound near his neck. My hands shake. There's a lot to do.

First thing's first. I want to get him onto the bed. It doesn't look very comfy though, and once I get him up and in I don't imagine he'll be moving for some time, so I want to get him as comfortable as possible. I grab our flashlight and run outside. I am acutely aware of the feel of my charger bouncing in my pocket as I run. I go just beyond the gates and start grabbing armfuls of big smooth leaves. I can only carry about ten at a time so I make two trips, still running, even though my legs are so sore they feel more like wooden extensions of my body than flesh and bone.

Back in the room I spread them out on the bed, making sure to scan for creepy crawlies as I do. I'm confident these leaves are safe because they come from the same type of tree Rennek used to make the cord for our bed. Wouldn't it be icing on the cake if they gave us the alien equivalent to poison oak? Luckily, I'm sure Rennek already performed a scan on them.

Once the bed looks like it has a little padding I turn to Rennek. The rest of the night passes in a daze. I wash his wounds and use a clean shirt to rewrap is shoulder. Even in the firelight I can see how filthy my poor man is. I end up having to scrub all of him down before I work to get him up and into the bed. Then I dig through the first aid kit and eye the meds. I have no clue what any of them are and again curse my alien illiteracy. If only I could read a fucking label!

"Maybe Tennir can make me a chip or give me an upgrade so I can learn to read and write in your language?" I tell my silent Rennek.

At the very least we have some ointments and creams. I smell them both before I choose a clear, sticky one to put on his arm, leg, and side. I think I'll avoid putting anything on the big gashes for now. I frown at the fresh shirt on his shoulder, already blood shines through it. I worry he needs stitches and not only do I not have the equipment for that, but I don't know the first thing about how to properly stitch anybody. Too bad I never conveniently watched a YouTube video on the subject, that sure would have come in handy right now.

Once Rennek is cleaned and cared for, I get a water pouch and try to prop his head up to help him take a drink. His head and horns are so big and heavy though and it's hard to get a good angle, most of the water I try to get in his mouth spills out on his chest and he chokes on the rest. Frustrated with how helpless I feel I wipe him down and cover him with the last of our blankets.

I look around the room. I guess it's time to take care of me now. The upper half of my body is filthy and covered in scrapes and bruises. I pull my pants off and wince as they pass my knee. It's black and blue from falling on it. I swallow a knot in my throat, determined to get done with the night's tasks. I scrub myself down quickly, not taking half the care I took with Rennek's sponge bath. I just want this all to be over with and to be lying in bed next to him. I'm dismayed to remember I'm on my period. I have to wash my "pad" and grab a new one made from my torn shirt. I only have one shirt left now. Tomorrow I'll have to do laundry.

When my tasks are all said and done I feel a bone deep kind of tired. I sit between the bed and the fire and pick at the Elysian chicken. I'm not hungry… or maybe I'm beyond hungry, but I don't want to waste the food. It won't be good tomorrow. I stare at Rennek as I eat.

"Are you hungry, babe?" I ask. My voice cracks and the silence in the room is heavy. I crawl up onto the bed with a piece of meat in my hand. Crawling close to Rennek, I try to encourage him to wake up.

"Rennek? You must be hungry, wake up and take a couple bites for me babe. It'll help you heal." I touch his cheek, but he is still except for the rise and fall of his chest.

Once I've eaten all I can I take the leftover meat and the flashlight and head out past the gate. I really, really don't want to go out into the night on my own, but I also don't want the smell of meat in our room as we sleep. I don't know what it could attract. I go as far as my wavering bravery will allow me and bury the stuff at the base of a tree. I'll have to wash up again when I get inside.

Finally, at the end of a day that has surely shaved years off my life, I crawl into bed with Rennek. I scoot close to his body and wrap my arm around his waist, careful of his injuries. Then I let myself cry until sleep carries me away from this dream turned nightmare.

***

Sometime in the night I wake to the heat of the fire. It's overwhelming. I turn to look at the flames, but they're banked low in the fireplace. I blink for a minute trying to comprehend where the heat is coming from, then I hear Rennek speak.

"Kate... my mate," he rasps. I shoot up and start sobbing all over again.

"Rennek, baby I'm here. I'm so glad you're awake!" But when I touch him I realize the heat I was feeling is coming from him. He's burning up.

"Are you well, my mate?" He manages to choke out, blinking and trying to focus his eyes on me in the low light.

"Babe, listen to me. You have a fever. We have meds here but I don't know what to give you. Which bottle is it? Tell me what will help you," I plead. He focuses on my hair and runs his hands through it.

"Fire…" he mumbles and his eyes start to roll back.

"No, no, no, no, no! Rennek, meds… what can reduce a fever? Help with infection? Or anti-venom?" I say gripping onto his cheeks and willing him to open his eyes and speak.

His eyes struggle to focus. "Red… red bottle…" I frantically scramble to the med kit, dumping everything out in haste. I find the red bottle and dump out a small spherical pill and bring it to Rennek with a water pouch. I have to slap his cheeks a bit to get him to rouse enough to take it. But he does take it and sips a bit at the water before he goes back under. I call to him, but he says nothing more. I pour water on the coals in the fire, fearful of any additional heat getting to my poor, suffering Rennek. I spend the rest of the night wiping his head with a cool wet cloth until the sun starts peeking in through the cracks in the door. Hours later, he finally seems to cool down a bit. So I lay next to him and drift back to sleep.

Chapter 49

Kate

The first thing I do when I wake is feel Rennek for signs of fever. He is warm, but not burning up like he was the night before. I eye the red pill bottle, wondering how often I should be giving him a fresh dose. Is this an every 6 hours kind of deal? Every 24? One and done? I rub my face wearily.

I think back to his words last night. They ring in my brain like a bell. Last night in his fever he called me his mate. He hasn't used that title since we had our "talk". I didn't notice really, in all our running around that he has been avoiding the term, but last night when he spoke the words it became painfully clear.

I grab water and try to get Rennek to drink, but he still doesn't rouse when I call to him. Using my fingers, I carefully dribble just a few drops at a time into his mouth so he doesn't choke on it like he did yesterday.

"We were supposed to check in last night with everyone, but we didn't. This morning too. We've missed two check-ins now. They'll be worried about us and they'll come. They might even be here today. They will be able to help you."

I stare at his motionless face, looking for any sign of recognition or awareness.

"I'm so sorry Rennek, some mate I turned out to be," I tell him and the words deepen my sadness.

"Rennek, please wake up. You have to get better. You have to. I promise, I'll be better at this whole mate thing. I was scared before, but nothing like what I feel now... the thought of you not waking up, of being without you, it's unbearable. I don't know how to be a mate or how to do forever, but for you I'll try. Every day I'll try."

Tears stream down my cheeks and I feel this sickening sense of irony, here we are on our bed, that we were waiting for, for so long, so we could finally make love… but we didn't need a bed to make love. We could have done that at any time. It was this silly, self-imposed, pointless thing getting between *us*. And all my hang ups? My mom and dad didn't have a happily ever after. My parents didn't love me the way a kid deserves to be loved. No one else in my life ever stuck around or gave me an example of what forever could look like? Well, it was all more self-imposed bullshit getting between *us*. All that junk doesn't make me incapable of having my own happily ever after with Rennek, it just makes me deserve it that much more. Laying here next to him now, like this… it's a bittersweet realization.

I hang my head, doing my best to fight off the misery creeping in at me from every angle. I need to be strong and hold the fort down until the others get here. I need to be strong for Rennek.

"Do not try and take those words back once I am well again," comes Rennek's rasping voice.

I look up to see his eyes blinking, but clear, and even a small rueful smile playing at his lips. I try to speak to him but my voice comes out a bunch of crazy barks and I fall onto him sobbing and laughing. When I feel his hand on my back, stroking me as if I'm the one who needs to be cared for, I snap back into action mode. I hurry to bring him water and this time he gulps it down. While he drinks I bring all the meds and ointments to the bed and spread them out, eager to learn all about them before he passes out again.

"What do you need, which of these will help you? You had some stingers shot into a few different spots and a bite on your shoulder here." He winces letting me know he is acutely aware of the pain coming from his shoulder. "To be honest Rennek, that one might need stitches."

"The bottle there, with the longer lid… we will have to clean the wound again… very hot water…" he struggles to explain.

I hurry to get the fire going as quickly as I can, and start to boil some water. I sure wish we had some antibacterial soap right about now. I make the water as hot as can while still keeping it bearable, before I pour it over his wound. I open the bottle Rennek indicated and realize it isn't another pill bottle, but a spray of some kind. I spray it all over the red, fleshy gash and it covers it with a plastic film, sealing it off.

Rennek tries to sit up to look at the places the stingers got him, but becomes light headed and pale. I rub some more ointment on him and he falls back into a deep sleep. I, on the other hand, suddenly have renewed energy. Seeing Rennek doing so much better has lit a fire inside me. I won't take back my words from before, not ever. I am Rennek's mate and I'm about to start acting like the mate he deserves.

I take my dirty clothes and the ruined blanket out to the main fountain and start rinsing and scrubbing them as much as possible. Afterwards I hang everything from the stone windows to dry. I take the charger with me and go stock up on more fruit and cabbages. Back in the room I take the cabbage leaves and boil them in water, remembering Rennek told me how nutrient rich the plant was. The water turns pink as the cabbage boils down. I let it cool a bit before I rouse Rennek and force him to sip at it. I offer him fruit but he refuses and soon falls to sleep again. I touch my hand to his head and am happy to feel the fever is gone. Before I know it, the sun is already going down.

The only bright side to more time passing is that we have now missed three check-ins. They must know something is wrong by now. I had hoped they would come today. I'm surprised they aren't here already. Fear and "what ifs" creep at the corners of my mind. What if something went wrong? What if the UPC found them, or bounty hunters? What if raiders stumbled across the others, just like they did with Gorrard's ship? I try not to worry though and tell myself they will be here tomorrow.

But tomorrow comes and the others do not. Another two days pass and I can't push the worry back any longer. Rennek is in and out of consciousness. His healing has plateaued. He eats nothing but the cabbage broth and his stomach turns when I have tried to force him to eat fruit.

The whole reason we had the comms and were checking in daily was to keep tabs on each other's safety, now days have passed and nothing. I worry about what my next course of action should be. Do I go look for them? Without the comm unit and the scanner I don't know how I'll find them. The only thing I can think to do would be to retrace our steps and try to get back to the pod.

Whenever Rennek is awake he can sense my tension, no matter how hard I try to hide it. He tries to joke, to lighten my mood and make me worry less, but I know he worries too. *Something* is keeping the others from joining us.

Eventually, six days have passed since the great spider massacre... though it feels like much, much longer. Rennek has been sleeping all morning and there isn't much for me to do. We're all stocked up on firewood and kindling. I can't hunt, so we've been primarily surviving on fruit. We have fruit to last for days. I'm getting awfully sick of pompayas at this point. I can't help but think back to my sad little apartment, with its cupboards filled with nothing but ramen. I would have killed for a little fresh fruit in my diet back then. Life's funny that way.

I've been able to get Rennek to eat some nuts from inside the cabbages. I cracked them open and roasted them slightly over the fire. He has eaten a few handfuls, which feels like a major triumph for me. As I tidy our supplies for the millionth time, wishing I could be more useful, I come across Gorrard's pendant in one of the pockets of our torn pack.

I play with it in my hands for a bit, studying it closely for the first time. I eye Rennek passed out in the bed. I'm beyond bored so I decide to go back to the beacon and see if maybe we missed something last time around.

I grab my faithful charger and head out in the direction of the beacon. I surprise myself by finding it easily enough. It feels like it's been so long since our first day at the ruins, and we haven't been out here since. I step into the odd clearing in the forest surrounding the beacon. There is that faint, pulsing light on the top of the device, still flashing. I squat down and stare at the designs, tracing them with my fingers, and trying to imagine what they could represent. I explore the holes that look like something you could plug your phone charger into, sticking my little finger into one, and then reprimanding myself. The thing could have electrocuted me! I don't stick my finger in electrical outlets at home, I probably shouldn't stick anything in these holes either.

Then, it's like a light bulb turns on over my head. I grab Gorrard's pendant and shove it inside one of the slots in the beacon. It fits perfectly and the light on the top of the thing raises and whirrs to the side, but does nothing else. It almost seems like it's waiting for more… maybe a second pendant? Or six? One for each little port?

"Holy. Fuck," I say, with my eyes wide, but the machine continues to wait. There is no more movement, there are no instructions and no obvious second steps. I pull the pendant back out. The beacon returns to the position it had been waiting in for the past 30 yets or whatever they call it. I do a little happy dance and then hightail it back to our room at the ruins. I can't wait to tell Rennek.

But I only make it as far as the courtyard. I hear this ungodly rumble, like the sound of a low flying jumbo jet. I look up to the skies, but see nothing at first. Then, a shadow passes over me. A large shadow. And maybe it doesn't pass over me as much as it blocks out the sun over all of the ruins. It's a ship. A *huge* ship. Movement catches my eye by the staircase. I see Rennek standing there, butt naked.

He looks up at the ship. I see him struggling to stay upright--this is the first time he has stood since his injury. I run to his side and pull out my charger. It feels feeble in my hands compared to the threat looming over us. This isn't going to be one we get out of. I can sense it deep in my heart. Maybe with Rennek at full strength, maybe if we still had a functioning blaster... but all we have is me and a charger. I look up at Rennek and his eyes meet mine. We don't have time to speak, or to say what's in our hearts. But in that one moment, when we look at each other... nothing needs to be said.

The ship suddenly becomes silent. A ramp unfolds and I see boots begin to descend. I hold my charger at the ready with my other arm wrapped around my mate. You can imagine my surprise when I recognize the face of the man, er alien, coming down the ramp. It's Gorrard! Gorrard, alive and well! Gorrard with a shining metal, robotic arm. A laugh escapes my throat and I feel like we just got rescued from a deserted island.

Gorrard steps forward and I leave Rennek leaning against the column to run for our friend, embracing him in a hug.

"My god Gorrard! You're alive!"

"I am pleased to find you are as well!" he booms.

"Don't get me wrong, we're so happy to see you, but what are you doing here?"

"We have been searching for you of course!"

"Who's we…?"

Gorrard turns and I see a woman coming down the ramp. She is tall and massive like an amazon, with cropped black hair shaved close on the sides and slicked straight back. She looks ageless and stunning… and a little bit terrifying. Her eyes are jet black pools and her skin is a cool grey, her jaw is all sharp angles. She looks like a force to be reckoned with. Her expression conveys power and makes me want to shrink backwards a little bit. I realize immediately that I know exactly who this is. This is Madreed. This is Rennek's mother.

I look back to Rennek who still clings to the column to help support himself. Then I remember he is completely naked and I'm about to be introduced to my mother in law. Lovely.

Before I have the chance to speak, a bunch of uniformed aliens, the same species as Tennir and Madreed, begin pouring from the ship. My heart pounds, I haven't exactly had the best of experience with aliens other than Rennek's people so far… but I guess these are Rennek's people too… sort of.

"Gorrard, help me with Rennek," I tell our friend. "He's been injured and needs medical attention."

Gorrard jumps into action, running to Rennek's side, unfazed by his nudity. He still bows a little when he reaches Rennek, but doesn't do the whole down on his knee thing he did the first time we met. Together we support Rennek's weight and start toward the ship. Madreed stands stoically at the ramp waiting for us, and just as we get near, I see familiar faces.

Da'vi, Allison, Reagan, April, Clark, Bossan, Kellen, and Tennir all come running toward us through the throng of aliens. I hear Reagan scream when she sees me.

"Go, I am fine," Rennek encourages me to go to our friends. I look to Gorrard and he nods, letting me know my man will be protected while I step away.

"I will help the Grey King," he assures me.

I hesitate briefly, wanting to stay by Rennek's side, but seeing humans again, particularly after so many days of radio silence, overwhelms me in a way I wasn't anticipating. Maybe it's because of all the fear I've been holding on to these past few days since Rennek's injury, but emotion suddenly overflows from within me and as I run to Reagan and the other girls. Tears stream down my face.

We all embrace and soon everyone is sharing in my tears.

"Thank goodness we found you, we've been so worried!" Clark tells me.

"What happened to you? Is Rennek… whoa, boy… okay. That's naked right there…" Reagan says covering her eyes. "Is he hurt? Are *you* okay? What happened here?"

"I'm fine, and thanks to your arrival, Rennek will be okay too. It was really scary there for the first few days, but he's been getting better, slowly," I tell them.

"How was he injured?" Da'vi interrupts.

"There was a spider. Like an *enormous* spider, almost as big as the pod. It had been following us, becoming aggressive. Rennek and I decided to kill it, but when we got to its den it wasn't just one spider, there was a swarm."

"We were doing okay though, taking them all out, but near the end Rennek's gun lost its charge. He tried to finish the last of them with his knife and he did… he did it. He saved us, but not without getting hurt in the process. I think there must be poison in his system. The wounds look irritated, no matter how clean we keep them, and even though he's gotten better, he hasn't recovered."

"Can you show me where the den was? I'd like to collect some samples to create a targeted anti-venom," Tennir implores.

"Of course, anything I can do to help Rennek. I can take you there right now."

"That won't be necessary, you can simply show me on the map. You should remain here," he eyes Madreed. "You will be needed."

Eeep, okay.

I see Madreed speaking quietly with Rennek, her demeanor cold but her eyes soft when looking at her son. I wonder if I am imagining that. He nods and they begin to move him inside.

"Allow me to take you inside Kate. There is much to discuss," Tennir tells me.

"I'll say… hey… wait," I look around the crowd of aliens who all seem to have a job to do. "Where's Vivian?"

His face takes on a weary expression and it almost seems like he is avoiding eye contact.

"Where is Vivian?" I say more firmly.

"She's gone." Reagan says, her face dropping the joy it had a moment ago from our reunion.

"What do you mean *she's gone*?" I ask, looking from one face to the next.

"Some days ago, she and Dax vanished in the middle of the night, they did not take a comm unit. Or if they did, it has not been powered on. That is the reason we were delayed in reaching you. Da'vi and Allison were to pick up the pod and transport us all here to the ruins, along with supplies, but when they arrived at its former location, it was gone as well," Tennir explains to me.

"What?" My brain can't even process all this.

"We know, right?" Reagan says.

"That doesn't make any sense. Vivian wouldn't have run off like that," I say, completely sure she wouldn't ever do something so risky on her own. Especially not without letting anyone know. *And* taking off in our only usable means of transportation? She wouldn't have done that unless someone *forced* her to. Everyone exchanges meaningful glances.

"So, he kidnapped her?" I say, almost disbelieving. "How do we find her? Is he capable of hurting her?" I'm frantic again with worry for poor, fragile Vivian.

"No," Kellen states firmly. "Dax would never harm anyone, let alone a female. We do not know why he took her, or where for that matter, but with Dax she is safe."

"Oh bullshit! He might be your friend and all, but he just kidnapped someone! What's the plan to find them?" I demand.

"Come with me Kate. All will be resolved in time, but for now your friend's disappearance is not the only pressing matter," Tennir tells me as gently as possible.

"Disappearance my ass, it's called an abduction and it's the second one she has had in as many months. This is unacceptable, if she's hurt, emotionally or otherwise, there is going to be hell to pay," I say angrily.

"On that matter we can all agree," he says calmly. I take a few deep breaths and agree to follow him. He's right, we have a lot to discuss and sitting around being angry won't move us forward.

"Okay, what now then?" I ask.

"It is time for you to meet Madreed."

Chapter 50

Kate

Tennir brings me inside the massive hovering ship and leads me through a labyrinth of corridors until we finally get to a medical bay. Off the main section are what I assume to be recovery or treatment rooms. A door whooshes open and inside on a bed lays Rennek. He is sitting up now and the color on his face is already beginning to return to normal. A doctor is working on his shoulder, but it appears to be causing him no pain or discomfort. I have to look away as the doctor stitches up the wound.

I hurry to his side. He immediately brings his large hand up to my face, caressing me.

"You look better already," I tell him and I have to blink back tears.

"I was already feeling well, I keep telling them this isn't necessary," he motions toward the doctor stitching up the nasty wound near his neck.

"Riiight, I'm starting to question your better judgment buddy," I laugh though, happy to see him joking again.

"Kate, I have to give you my deepest apologies. What I did was dangerous. I felt we were low on options at the time, but now looking back, I see that I put you in danger. I should have tried to think of another option."

"There was no way of knowing..." I start, but he interrupts.

"There are things I could have done differently. We could have scouted the den first, perhaps seen what we were up against before attacking."

"How? The thing could… you know, *smell me*." I glance at Tennir, not trying to put my period on blast. Rennek just gives a fussy little grunt.

"I should have thought of something else. You were dependent on me for protection, and I failed you. I left you alone."

"Look at me Rennek," I say holding his hand to my heart. "You did everything you could, you did your best with the information we had and you killed every last one of those spiders. You made sure I was safe. You did not fail me and you did not leave me alone. You're here right now aren't you? I don't even want to think about the alternative."

"Nor do I," he tells me.

"Plus, this is a partnership, remember? I don't mind taking care of you once in a while. Just next time, let's make it a bubble bath or a foot rub, okay?"

"You have my promise," he says while his hands roam over my arms, as if he can't bear the idea of not touching me. I can't say I mind in the least, after days of him being in and out of consciousness it feels so damned good to have him here with me, *really* here with me.

Just as the doctor finishes up and begins to leave, the door whooshes open and Madreed, Gorrard and Da'vi join us in the room.

"Madreed, this is Kate…" Rennek begins to introduce me to this alien woman towering above me.

"Yes, I am aware," she says gesturing an alien greeting in my direction. "My goodness, my sons are right, you and your people are surprisingly similar to the images of the Goddesses. While this is obviously quite intriguing on an anthropological level, I suspect it is also in part what makes humans so popular on the black market," she says.

"Tennir has sent me much information on the humans since the discovery of the trafficking ring. I am very much aware of the hardships you and your people have faced, Kate. I have been working day and night to learn everything I can to uncover all guilty parties and right this wrong that has been committed against your race. Trafficking is a violation I hold very dear to my core and I promise you, I will continue to fight for the justice and recovery of your people."

"Thank you, I appreciate that." I tell her, humbled by her clear passion.

"As I understand it, there is now more to this story than the rescue of the humans," she says, looking at Gorrard.

I see a look go over Rennek's face that breaks my heart for him. We are here on Elysia to uncover the secrets of his past, but in doing so we are dredging up the memories of his mother's rape. Though our hands are intertwined, I move closer to support him in what's about to be discussed. I just pray Madreed can offer some of the compassion I see in her to Rennek in this moment.

"Tennir tells me that you have been asking about your father?" She asks, turning her focus onto Rennek. He takes a deep breath and I worry for a split second that he is going to retreat in an effort to protect his mother.

"I have. Certain instincts have been… activated recently, and I was hoping to learn more about my sire's species and what to expect within myself. Then, in protecting Kate and her people, we met Gorrard, which was an obvious surprise."

"Yes, I can imagine," Madreed responds, smiling "I did not know you ever had an interest in learning more about your father, I will be happy to share with you all that I know."

At this point in the conversation I have to actively remember to keep my mouth shut. This isn't a soap opera, I remind myself. This is real life… no matter how juicy the details are. So, I try to put a calm and composed look on my face and hope my acting skills are up to par.

"You are aware of The Invasion obviously. I was working at the council building when it happened. Luckily, the children on planet were all placed in emergency modules, so young Tennir and Kahreen were taken to safety," she reaches a hand out to Tennir with tears in her eyes.

"The occupancy lasted months, there was no way to contact them or hear of their safety. It was terrible on the Mother Planet. Many died. Many were tortured, beaten… raped. Many were not as lucky as I." At that, Rennek begins to interrupt her, shame showing in the lines of his face, but she puts a hand up to stop him.

"I was lucky because the males sent to take our building were led by your father and some of his men. Not long before The Invasion they had been captured and forced to be mercenaries for the Invaders, but they were not capable of such evil deeds. Instead, they risked themselves to gather us and hide us in the catacombs below the council."

"For months, they were forced to act as if they were one with the Invaders, all the while bringing us food, caring for us, helping to rescue more of our people and bringing them to the safety of the catacombs. I became close to Urrek over those months," a sad smile crosses her lips. "He was brave and selfless… to a fault," she laughs ruefully, blinking away tears. "He helped me get messages to the UPC and organize the counterattack. In the short time we spent together, we fell in love. I never thought there would be another for me beyond Tennir and Kahreen's father, but Urrek awoke something in me," she says holding her hand over her heart. "And I was not the only one," she says with a nostalgic laugh. Your father's companions were… very popular as you can tell by the existence of your friends."

"After much planning, the counterattack was working, and the Invaders were forced into making their escape. That was not enough for Urrek though. There were many others still on the Invader's ship… captive, unwilling slaves. He and his men, some Vendari, some not," she says shooting a meaningful glance at Da'vi, "refused to let them leave with all those poor souls on board. They wanted to make a rescue attempt. Urrek also feared the Invaders might have information that could cause harm to other Vendari. He could not let that be so."

"I wanted to beg him not to go, I wanted to tell him that we had a fledgling growing within my womb, but I knew I could not give him such a choice. It was his nature to love and protect… his instinct. I could not make him choose between all those souls and his fledgling. So, I let him go. I planned to tell him of you when he returned. He made his friend stay with me to protect me until he did, but he never came back. The Invader's ship left and he and his men were never seen again," she stares at a blank spot on the wall and it takes her a moment before she can continue.

"After that, Urrek's friend Za'an refused to leave my side for many yets. He pledged a life debt to me. He was so saddened by my loss and ashamed he had not been on the ship to aid his friends. It was many yets before I could convince Za'an to stop guarding me like a golden fledgling," she laughs, looking at Da'vi.

"He still looks in on me from time to time, even in his old age. It was only recently he suggested his son come to watch over you. I had been so worried about you in the UPC, and then with the prospect of crossing paths with pirates while working with your brother, so I agreed," she says causing Rennek to finally break his silence.

"Da'vi? Madreed hired you to watch over me? Did you know of all this since the start?" He chokes out, in shock.

"No, I knew of nothing but the fact that my sire claimed a life debt to Madreed. I was unaware of the circumstances. He charged me with taking over that debt and so I found you. Before I could explain my role, you offered me a position on your crew, and it seemed the obvious choice to take it." Da'vi shrugs.

"You never thought to tell me?" He asks, still surprised but with more understanding in his tone than I would offer him.

"It did not arise," Da'vi says simply. With wide eyes I look to Rennek, surprised he is taking all this so calmly. He turns back to Madreed and she continues.

"In my search for you and Tennir I found Gorrard who told me of this place and the beacon," Madreed gives her son a warm smile. "It seems you and your friends are now at the beginning of your journey to discover who you are. I hope this information will help you. And I have this," she pulls out a small round disk that looks strikingly similar to Gorrard's pendant. "This was Urrek's. It is the only thing I had to remember him by, besides you of course. He told me it was a key of some sort, perhaps it may have some meaning among your people?" Rennek takes the disk.

"Now, get some rest and later we can further discuss all that surrounds the trafficking ring," Madreed tells us and she stands to leave.

"Thank you, Madreed," Rennek tells her solemnly and that's all I can take.

"Thank you? *Thank you?*" My gaze shoots from Rennek to Madreed. "Let me get this straight you're thanking her for telling you some pertinent ass shit that she should have been telling you your entire fucking life?"

Then I turn to Madreed, "I'm sorry, why are you only just now finding it relevant to inform your son that his father didn't *rape* you? That he himself isn't a product of rape? You say that Rennek is only just now beginning this journey to discover who he is, but he's been searching his entire life no thanks to you. How dare you stroll in here as if you're doing him a favor, you should be begging his forgiveness for all you've put him through. All this time he could have been proud of who he is and instead he was living with shame that not only didn't belong to him, but was based on events that never even occurred! *And* you sent him off to boarding school, or whatever, on Javan because he was a 'product of war'? He wasn't a product of war, he was a product of *love*! Seriously, what the hell?"

Madreed looks utterly taken aback and when I look to Rennek, his face conveys his surprise at how I have just spoken to his mother.

"Kate, please don't…" Rennek begins.

"No, wait," I tell Rennek and turn back to Madreed. "Did you know that Urrek was a king to his people? Just answer that for me."

"I did," she says, still with more shock than remorse.

"So, you raised Rennek to think he was the bastard son of a rapist when you knew he was a hero and a king that you loved?"

I take in this woman before me. I see she is undoubtedly strong, a woman who has worked hard her entire life and earned every bit of power she has at her disposal. I see a woman who gets her way and is not easily shaken and... I see her struggling to find the words to justify her misdeeds against her son.

"I wanted to keep him. I did keep him, two yets longer than I should have. But emotions were still high surrounding The Invasion. There was much prejudice. I thought it would be better for him to grow up with the other fledglings like him and if he entered internment he wouldn't face such harsh judgement by society," she explains. "He never asked," she finally says lamely. I shake my head at her and kiss Rennek's hand that still holds mine although the grasp is loose.

"I'll let you rest, call me if you need me. I'll be with the others," I tell him and head for the door. When I find Reagan and the others, still outside the ship and poking around the ruins, I bring them back to mine and Rennek's room. Only, I worry that after my outburst it won't be mine and Rennek's room for much longer.

Rennek has spent his whole life tip toeing around that woman, and I just stomped on her. I don't know if he'll forgive me for that one. So, I show the girls around a bit and tell them of my adventures on Elysia, all while desperately trying not to cry.

Chapter 51

Rennek

"I... I'm..." I try to begin, but can't seem to find the words. I want to apologize to Madreed, but something inside me tells me that isn't right... something inside me tells me that Kate is right. But I don't know how to say this to Madreed. My mother's story has stripped away all the shame I carried, there is nothing I need to protect her from. Indeed, why did she not think to tell me this sooner?

"We will give the two of you some space," Tennir says, and the others leave the room.

"She is your mate then?" Madreed asks, "I saw her press a kiss to your hand before she left. But I suppose I would have been able to tell by her passion alone."

"She is my mate, she too has awakened something within me," I tell my mother, placing my hand over my heart as she had done earlier.

"That is good. I like her Rennek, she reminds me of myself. She speaks truth and she speaks from her core no matter what the reactions of others will be. Which is perhaps something I should have practiced not only on the council, but with you as well."

I grunt in agreement. I still cannot bring myself to fully express my feelings with Madreed. Her omission has caused me much pain over the yets.

"People do not speak of The Invasion. It was a painful and frightening time for all who lived through it. It was doubly painful for me because that was when I lost my Urrek. It is still difficult for me to discuss. I spent many yets searching for any trace of him, hoping against hope that he was still alive. possibly being held prisoner by the Invaders...

perhaps waiting for me to rescue him." She blinks and tears spill from her eyes.

"I held my pain above yours, my son, and it blinded me to what your experience must have been. There are not enough words to apologize for this. I sent you to Javan because, ultimately, I thought you should be with other Vendari. I wanted to raise you on my own in our home, but the prejudice left over from The Invasion was too great. I tried to keep you with me as long as I could, but eventually I started to hear the comments and see the fear from other families, and I knew it was time. But please know that I did not send you away because I did not want or love you with all of my core. You are my son, Rennek. No matter what." She takes my hands in hers and for the first time since I was a mere fledgling, I hang my head and weep.

"I forgive you mother," I tell her, and she weeps alongside me.

***

The doctors tell me I must remain in this room so they may monitor my healing, so I send Tennir to bring my mate to me.

"Hi," she says sheepishly as she enters my room. My heart still soars at the sight of her, but my mate appears nervous and standoffish in a way I have not seen from her in much time.

"I see you have used the showers," I notice her shining red mane and her sweet scent.

"Yeah, I was getting pretty ripe without soap there for a few weeks. Nothing like a hot shower," she says meekly, avoiding eye contact.

"I can recall," I tell her with lust in my voice. Her eyes meet mine and she blushes, her soft smile finally reaching her eyes. This seems to jog her out of whatever keeps her from my side.

"I overstepped," she says, her smile fades and her tone is solemn. I sit on the edge of the bed and reach for my mate. I am pleased when she does not hesitate to fall into my arms.

"Are you supposed to be up?" She asks, looking ready to sic the doctor on me.

"I am feeling much better now, my sweet Kate. I wish to speak with you about what happened earlier."

"Yeah, I figured," she tells me, wringing her hands and averting her eyes again. "I *want* to apologize Rennek, but I can't. Even if you aren't hurt, I'm hurt for you. It wasn't right what she did. She should have told you the truth a long time ago," Kate says firmly.

"I agree," I tell her.

"You agree?" she asks surprised.

"I do. I was taken by surprise, first by everything my mother shared, then by your way of speaking to her..." I cannot help but laugh at the memory. Likely, no one has ever spoken to my mother in such a way. "But you were right. Her actions have caused me such unnecessary pain. I am honored you fought so fiercely on my behalf. I would do no less for you."

"I was right?" she asks, still shocked.

"Yes," I say, running my claws through her mane, distracted by its beauty. "You are as fiery as your mane, my sweet Kate." She puts her arms around my neck, holding me at bay so that she may look up at me. It feels so good to have her in my arms again, to be well enough to hold her.

I gaze into her eyes, "We came here in search of the Vendari's beacon, but *you* have been a beacon for me since the moment I saw you… you have brought me ever closer to who I am and who I am supposed to be. None of this would have been possible without you, my precious mate."

"You mean, I'm still your mate? Even after I basically cussed out your mom?"

"When will you learn? What we have is forever, my heart." Kate finally gives in fully to my embrace, pushing herself up on delicate human toes to wrap her arms tightly around my neck and to press her soft lips to my mouth. My wings instinctively encircle her.

It has been too long since I have tasted Kate's sweetness. I live for the unique and intoxicating flavor that only my mate possesses. An anger burns in the back of my mind. If it were not for my injury, Kate and I could have spent the last handful of rotations doing nothing beyond making love and reveling in each other's embraces. I growl at the frustration that I have not yet fully known my mate. All the while, her kisses become increasingly playful until I am utterly lost in the licks of her soft pink tongue and gentle bites from her rounded teeth. The sensations are bliss and soon nothing matters beyond this moment.

"I know we just spent weeks alone together in the forest, but I've missed you so much." Tears threaten to spill from her eyes. "Promise me you'll never let a giant spider bite you ever again," she asks, moving her kisses to my neck and jaw.

I bury my nose in her neck and inhale. "I would agree to anything you would ask of me, but particularly this."

I pull her up onto the bed with me and lay back so she may straddle my waist. She sits up to inspect me. "Are you sure you're okay? I'm not hurting you, am I?"

"I feel better with every touch," I tell her, running my hands up and down her bare arms. The smile she gives me tells me she shares the sentiment. Soon her hands are exploring my chest and abdomen, skimming over every muscle and pausing to lightly tease my nipples.

"There are so many things different about you compared to humans," she says.

"Oh?" I smile. I see the game she plays, I will let her list all the ways I am better than human males... exploring all the differences in the process.

"Um hmm. The grey skin for one. Obviously." She runs her nails up to my shoulders. "You're stronger and larger than any human man I've ever met," she adds and her hands run over my shoulders, pausing to appreciate my biceps. Vainly, I flex for her.

"So that I may protect my mate," I tell her.

"Oh, is that why?" She asks in a teasing tone.

"Of course."

"Then there are these... ridges?" her fingertips play at the ripples leading down to my cock, causing the drumming within me to come to life, but her fingers dance away again.

"Your ears..." she leans down to tease them with her tongue, "have the cutest little points at the tips."

"Do they?" I ask.

"They do," she assures me. Scooting up closer to my face she reaches for my horns. Her breasts press close to my face and it is all I can do to keep my mouth from seeking out their softness. She drags her fingers across the roughness of my horns, from the base to the tips.

"This is another thing men don't have on Earth," she tells me.

"That must be very embarrassing for them," I muse, causing a twinkling laugh to escape my mate.

"I'm sure it must be," she agrees. She finds my hands and traces them with her small fingers. "No claws on humans either," she says before focusing on my mouth. She drops another kiss to my lips and I feel her tongue gently graze my fangs, wordlessly highlighting another difference.

"There are the wings, but that's something you don't even have in common with the Vendari either."

"This is true," I say, shifting her hips a bit so she rests squarely on my cock.

"I've been wondering something, Rennek. There was a moment there when you were battling the spider where it almost… well, it almost looked like you flew. This may be a dumb question, I mean… with the wings and all, but… *can you fly*?"

"They are functional wings," I admit to her, laughing.

"Why don't you ever use them? It almost seems like there's been a lot of opportunities for you to fly, but I've never seen you do it."

"Hmm, I suppose it is another thing about growing up and being different from everyone else. For much of my youth I wanted... No, I *longed* to be like Tennir. And then on Javan, I longed to be like my friends. All of the galaxy told me I was different, that I was an outcast. Because of this I tried very hard to fit in, to show I was an equal member of a group, not below anyone, not above anyone. Besides, what is the point of flying if you must leave all others behind?"

"Whoa, Seriously? You didn't fly because you wanted to fit in? That might be the most tragic thing I've ever heard. Flying is a super power. If I could fly I would literally do it all the time," she says with passion creeping into her voice.

"Let me say it differently then. I did not fly because I had no one to fly with me, but now I have you Kate. Now and forever. I will take you, when I am all healed. We can fly to the shore if you like," I tell her, finding myself surprisingly excited to share this with my mate. I am pleased by the eagerness written on her face.

"I would *love* that," she whispers to me, leaning in for another kiss. Sliding my hands up her thighs I grip onto her thick hips, grinding against her core. She lets out a little gasp of surprise before I deepen our kiss.

"I am tired of waiting," I tell her.

"Here?" She jolts upright, eyes wide. "Shouldn't we at least sneak out to our room? I thought you wanted it to be... I don't know, ceremonious or something?" She eyes me as if attempting to find deception in my eyes.

"Anywhere with you is special my mate. You were correct, it does not matter where we are. I am ready to begin our forever now." A smile spreads across her lips and her mouth finds mine, she is as hungry for this moment as I am.

Chapter 52

Kate

As I lose myself in Rennek's kisses I have this amazing sensation wash over me. It is this deep and penetrating knowledge that all is right with the universe. I have finally found my home and it is here in Rennek's arms. It doesn't matter where we end up, whether it is here on Elysia, back on the Mother Planet, or traveling through outer space. As long as this wonderful alien is in my life, I am complete.

Even in the beginning with Rennek, I knew I felt drawn to him. But in retrospect, I see all the little ways I was still holding on to my tired old hang-ups... my fears about love and relationships, about letting go, and trusting in another person.

Getting abducted by aliens probably led to me learning life's greatest lesson. It isn't about your career or your education. That stuff adds to you, but it doesn't complete you. In the end, life is about the people you love and the people who love you right back.

I blink back tears of joy and dig my fingers into my mate's thick hair, savoring him entirely. To think I held him at bay, I laugh. To think I nearly lost him... I kiss him more fiercely. His hands start to pull at my clothes and I help him before his claws can do any damage to the material. We are both giggling like a couple of high school kids as we struggle with the ties.

"Is it possible that you become even more beautiful every time I see you," he asks once my body is exposed to him.

"Promise me you'll still feel that way in 20 years," I tell him.

"Kate, I will feel that way in a hundred," he says, taking my breasts in his hands. In every caress I feel pure adoration.

"And after we have a few kids... or fledglings, as you guys call them?" I question.

"Even more so then," he vows.

At first, I think to tease him a bit with foreplay before we make love, but I find that thought holds little appeal to me. All I want is him inside me, all I want is for us to be one. I give Rennek one last kiss and I fill it with all my love. Pushing him back onto the bed I take his cock in my hand and position myself over him. I slide his tip through my folds, making him slick with my desire. He breathes heavily, his eyes never leave mine.

"I love you, my Kate," he tells me as I push myself down onto the head of his cock. He is impossibly thick and I have to pause a moment before I continue.

My breaths are as heavy as his and I slide up a bit before I come back down, sinking him a little deeper into my core. I feel myself stretching to accommodate his thickness. I want more. I want all of him, deep inside me. I slowly slide up again and his hands go to my hips. He kneads my flesh and this time when I push my body down he helps guide me. I grind against him and finally feel he is fully sheathed in my warmth.

I can feel the obvious differences between his cock and a human one right away. We move slowly, delighting in the feel of each other's bodies. He is *definitely* bigger than anyone else I have ever been with, but as we move in rhythm with one another I can feel all the other differences as well. I find myself extremely sensitive to the ridges on the underside of his cock. With every movement I shudder with pleasure at the sensations they send shooting through my body.

I lean forward, sliding my hands up over his muscular shoulders. Have there ever been sexier shoulders anywhere in the galaxy, I wonder? As I lean into him my clit brushes against the ridges that trickle down below his belly button and it's like a lightbulb goes off over my head, or perhaps it's more like fireworks... Now I get what he meant when he said these ridges were for my pleasure. When I grind against him they stimulate my clit.

I grab at his hands on my hips and help him push me down harder. He takes my lead and arches into me while pulling me even closer to him than I ever thought possible. I roll my hips like a wave against his body. I can feel my heart beating out of control. The place where our bodies meet becomes increasingly wet with every movement until we are slapping against each other.

"You feel... it is so good Kate, it is beyond words," Rennek grits out. All I can do is smile. He runs his hand along my cheek, sliding it up into my hair. Grabbing a fistful, he pulls me down to his mouth and we kiss through panting breaths and moans of pleasure. I am enthralled by the sounds he makes, the masculine growl of his arousal.

I dip my mouth towards his neck, planting ravenous kisses there as I inch closer and closer to his earlobe, tonguing it upon arrival.

"Mmmm," I whisper a breathy moan. His hands go to my ass and he alternates between driving me down hard against his cock and teasing my sensitive flesh with his claws. "I love the way you feel inside me," I mummer against his ear and he growls at my words. I moan and give little squeals of pleasure with every pump of his hips. My sounds seem to be spurring him on and I decide to try to up the ante.

"I love the way your hands feel on my ass," I tell him and he grips me tighter, driving into me harder in response. The sensations are maddening, I feel myself getting closer and closer to cumming. I'm shocked because I've never been able to cum from just sex before, but Rennek has me right up against the edge.

"I love what you do to me, Rennek. You're making my pussy so wet for you," I moan against his ear. He pulls me into another kiss and I can sense how unhinged he is becoming. His kiss is fascinating to me. He is like this wild and hungry predator and I have no defense against him. I struggle to find more words, but all rational thought is escaping me in the very best of ways. He is so deep inside of me and our bodies move in time with one another. He sucks and bites at my tongue and lips. I feel myself turning to jelly in his arms. It is like every cell in my body is lost in the euphoria that is my mate.

"My mate..." I whisper into his kiss and that pushes him over the edge. A growl builds in his throat until it is an ear-splitting roar that I'm sure rocks the whole ship. He rolls me onto my back and pauses for just the barest of seconds over me. His eyes are wild with lust and love. He is looking at me as if I am the Goddess who hung the stars.

"You are so perfect, my Kate. I am the luckiest male," he tells me as his eyes make love to my body. Any other time in my life I would have felt so exposed in this moment, but with Rennek I feel emboldened. I have never felt more sexy and desired than right here, right now. His hands roam over my body as if he will not be satisfied until he touches every inch of me so I lean into his touch, giving myself up freely.

He begins to pump into me again, slowly at first. Between each thrust he pauses and I can feel my cunt throbbing with the need for release. I spread my legs further apart for him, welcoming him deeper into my body. I find I need to touch him just as much as he needs to touch me. My hands seem to have a mind of their own as they skate over his body.

"I love you Rennek," I tell him as I arch my hips towards him. His wings splay out over us, protectively encircling our expression of love. It almost feels like we are the only ones here on this planet, it belongs only to us and this moment. I wrap my legs tightly around his hips and rock into him as he thrusts.

"I'm going to cum soon Rennek." With those words he works me with everything he has and my clit grinds against his ribbed abs. I can't hold my orgasm back any longer. It hits me like a force of nature and I can feel my pussy clenching around my gargoyle's huge cock. He pumps into me hard and slow, rocking into my clit in perfect rhythm with each and every wave of pleasure that passes over me. I can tell my mate is not far behind me.

My pussy seizes him once more and I feel his coiled body release. When he cums he digs his fingers into my hair and speaks my name through gritted teeth. I can feel his warmth filling me and his cock pulses with every burst of his seed. He continues to pump into me, riding out every last bit of his orgasm and bringing a second wave to my own. Never in all my life have I ever cum twice. Not even with my trusty old vibrator. Consider my mind blown.

Rennek collapses next to me and wraps his massive arms around my small body. He kisses my shoulder while trying to catch his breath. His tail wraps possessively around my ankle. I lie there, limp--my body has no strength. A dazed and silly smile is plastered to my face. I am human jello. I try to speak, but nothing comes out beyond a few sighs. I could lay like this forever, I think to myself as my eyes begin to close.

Beep. Beep.

The door suddenly whooshes open. A strangled scream comes from my throat and I move to cover my body, but Rennek is faster. He is up and his wings are spread. He lets out one of the most menacing growls I have ever heard from him. I peek around his massive frame just in time to see a doctor turn and run from the room.

"I'll come back later," he shouts over his shoulder. The door closes again and I burst out laughing.

"Oh my god, Rennek! That was so mean! He probably needed to check on your vitals or something!" I scold my mate.

"He can do so later, after we have had the chance to enjoy our time together," he says, but the wry smile on his face and twinkle in his eye tells me he thought it was funny.

"Okay, I'm getting dressed before anyone else stumbles into your room and sees me naked."

"I will simply lock the door," he protests.

"No, I don't want you bullying all your doctors away. I need to know you are back at a hundred percent." I tell him, and I'm not willing to budge on that one. It was too scary over the past week, constantly feeling so unsure of whether or not Rennek was going to pull out of it.

Rennek acquiesces and helps me dress. As I do I feel the weight of Gorrard's pendant in my pocket. I hold it up to show him.

"Rennek! I didn't have the chance to tell you! I walked down to the beacon today while you were resting and discovered the pendant fits into those slots. I put it in and it made the light on top do some funny stuff. I wonder if the rest of Gorrard's crew had similar pieces? Maybe they all had to be inserted for it to be activated?"

Rennek goes very still before reaching over to the table near his bed. He plucks Urrek's pendant from it, rolling it in his fingers.

"Or perhaps one might work... if it is the right one? Finish dressing Kate, we are going to gather the others."

My heart leaps in my chest and I pull my clothes on as fast as I can. Rennek and I quietly move about the ship gathering the rest of his half Vendari friends, Tennir, Da'vi, the humans, and Gorrard. Then, together, we move out into the cool night air.

Chapter 53

Rennek

Presently we all stand surrounding the beacon. The pale blue light adorning the top pulses regularly. There is no telling at this point if my father's pendant will work or not, but deep inside me I already know it will. I work to savor this moment and take in as much of it as possible. I feel the crisp night air against my flesh, I feel the tender touch of my mate's hand on my arm.

I look at Kate. She is mine now, fully. She smiles up at me, sharing my joy. I look around to all the faces who have helped me get to this point and marvel at the magic of fate and the universe. It has been the wind in our sails throughout this journey. I feel a slight twinge of sadness that Dax and the sad human are not here with us to share this moment. Their disappearance is as deeply troubling as it is odd. I shake that unpleasantness from my mind, it is a problem for another day.

I bring myself back to the moment. We are all silent. Even the humans, who have no skin in this game, appear moved by the power of what is to come. They have a hope in their eyes that tells me how much they can relate to the feeling of being small and alone in the universe. If this works, and I know it will, we will be alone no longer. We will be calling all the Vendari home to Elysia.

Much will change when they arrive, I know now that they will expect me to be the male Gorrard sees when he looks upon me. I know now that though I never met my father, it is my duty to him to fulfill the role he has passed onto me. Never in my life did I seek out leadership, never did I demand to be in the spotlight, but if there is a need, and if others need my care, protection and guidance, then I will gladly be that male. I will not shirk the duties left to me. I will work harder every day to be a leader my people can be proud to follow and a son my father would have been proud to have walk in his footsteps.

Kate urges me forward and I find the slots in the beacon. My father's pendant seems to be a perfect fit. I take one last look at the faces around me. Gorrard's eyes glisten, my brother looks moved in a way I have never seen in a scientist. My friends all tense with the anticipation and my Kate smiles warmly at me, only peace and happiness in her expression. I push the pendant into the slot, a blue light emanates from the hole. There is a faint hum before the tiny pulsing light atop the beacon erupts into a massive stream, shooting up into the stars.

Over thirty yets have passed since Gorrard's crash. More than 29 since Urrek went missing. The beacon has sat in this spot waiting while the Vendari drift through space, but on this day... I call my people home.

Epilogue

Kate

Rennek gives me one last kiss before he heads to the door. "Hurry, my heart. They will be arriving shortly and I would not want to meet this delegation without my queen by my side."

"I wouldn't miss it for the world, but if I have a choice I'd rather be dressed for it," I tell him.

"Hurry," he urges again before he is gone.

I jump out of bed and walk to our wooden wardrobe. I move a few of my more practical rainforest outfits out of the way and select a high waisted and flowing sundress that Madreed sent me. Using a carved bone comb, I straighten my disheveled hair in front of a mirror hanging on the inside of the door of our wardrobe. I slip on my shoes and admire the gorgeous throw rug Rennek bought me from some Inaryan moon. It *really* does soften the room up.

Flowers fill a vase on our dining table, filling the room with their sweet scent. The counter we use as a kitchen is tidy, the baskets below are filled with food and supplies. The fire is banked and I decide I'll worry about making the bed later. Besides, I have a feeling it's just going to get messed up again before the day is through anyway.

I head out into the courtyard and see Reagan and the girls sitting around looking at a tablet-like device, they are trying to learn how to weave baskets. It's been a bit slow going on that front and they bicker quietly like sisters over technique. Their voices mingle with the call of birds. On the far end of the courtyard we have built a small aviary where we are raising Elysian chickens. Perhaps eventually we will move this out to the fields, but that won't be until we build a fence to keep predators out.

All the fountains in the courtyard run clear now. Small filters have been installed in each of them so they can be used as a constant supply of drinking water. We also use it to cook and wash clothes. About a dozen of Madreed's personal army remained behind to help with the larger projects, like clearing the farm land and cleaning out the bathing room. The difference is remarkable. The ruins were beautiful before, but now they really shine. Although, we don't refer to them as 'ruins' anymore. We all decided unanimously, that first night we were gathered together here, that we would call our growing village Beacon--for obvious reasons.

April and Tennir have been working together to plan the crop distributions and modernizing the canal's water delivery systems. The fields are already growing some of the pink cabbages, pompayas, and the big berries I discovered, as well as some other native herbs and spices. I am in constant awe of the abundance of Elysia.

I hold my dress up as I hurry up the steps to what we imagine was once a throne room but now serves as our command center. I'm panting when I get to the top. I see most of the guys are here with Rennek. Gorrard looks anxious, so I go to him first before heading to Rennek's side. Poor Gorrard has been waiting so long for this. I tell him some words of encouragement and he seems to find peace in them. We look out the massive stone openings along the back of the room and in the distance five flying figures approach.

Madreed is continuing to work on the human trafficking issue and is setting up Elysia as an official known refuge for humans. With all the media coverage Madreed has garnered, the bounty on the guys has miraculously vanished and the UPC is claiming that the men Tennir took out on his science station were working alone… but obviously none of us believe that. Unfortunately, we have no proof to support our side.

Madreed is taking names and kicking asses left and right though. She is determined to hold people accountable for the atrocity committed against humans. I know she works to gain intelligence on the location of others as well. Apparently, she is good at this type of thing because she had... *has* spent years searching for Rennek's father. She is not here with us today, but I know her ship is in orbit. It is almost as if she hopes Urrek will show up, but she refuses to speak this hope. Instead she quietly remains in orbit and offers Rennek assistance if he needs it.

Rennek stands before the windows, looking every inch a king. I admire the strength and confidence that he projects. He was born to take on this role.

I look down at the fields below us, people are working together to build something here and that's how it will be among all the kingdoms of Elysia. The Vendari race will be rebuilding their world from scratch and working to keep their culture and traditions alive. They have been given a second chance here. We all have.

Soon the other five kings land and join us in the command center. They all take turns clasping Rennek's arm in greeting and bow to him with some reverence. This is the first time we are meeting the other kings in person, though Rennek has spoken to them over the comms many times now. We have also already filled them in on all we know regarding what has occurred since Gorrard's ship was shot down.

"We would like to express our deepest gratitude to you, Rennek," a Vendari King tells him. He is the color of the night sky, so deep blue he is almost pitch black. I feel like if I stare at him long enough I'll actually see stars splayed across his skin. "Your father, Urrek, was a dear friend of mine. He championed the efforts to bring us here to Elysia. It is a tremendous loss that he is not here with us today, but fitting it is you--his son, that has delivered us all to our new world."

"I am equally grateful to be in the presence of my own people and to finally know where I come from. It is one of the greatest gifts in life," Rennek tells the Vendari.

"Perhaps only second to finding a mate," the shadowy Vendari says as his eyes shine in my direction for a split second before he turns back to Rennek. "There is still much for you to learn about our people Rennek. We will be happy to help you in this journey. I am sure each of us also have many dear stories to share with you about Urrek. He was a good male, fiercely protective, and a leader like no other."

"We do have troubling news to bare this day," a red Vendari king says, and for the first time I notice the grave expression on the other kings faces. "The ships have all arrived to Elysia now, all except one."

I see Gorrard visibly tremble at this news.

"The Grey King's ship has vanished. What we can tell, based on our linked computer systems, is that his stasis pod registered an emergency because of the attack on the scout ship. His primary protectors were awoken as well. Our sensors indicate a traveler ship broke from the central ship shortly thereafter. We assume Urrek and his protectors went to determine what happened to the scout ship. All the central ships had system links and automatically shared sensor readings, but at some point following the split of the traveler ship, the central ship vanished from our data scans."

"I would like access to your data if possible," Rennek asks the other kings.

"Absolutely, we would all like to offer you the assistance of our best data specialists, and use of our personal primary protectors as well. Your people account for a sixth of the population of the Vendari and it is a devastating loss to our culture if they are not found. We will do all in our power to discover what has happened to the ship and recover your people," the red king says. "When you are ready we will institute a search and rescue mission."

"Thank you for the resources, we appreciate it deeply," Rennek tells the others.

Poor Gorrard, I think to myself. He has waited so long to see his family, and now that he has gotten so close they have been ripped from him once more.

"There are some that knew the team on the scout ship among our people. They have inquired about survivors," another king says.

"Gorrard is the only remaining survivor," Rennek tells him and Gorrard steps up to his side.

"There is a female among my people who asks for you Gorrard. Yemala is her name," the king says.

"Yemala asks for me?" Gorrard chokes. "But I could not possibly see her... she has been in cryo all these years and is still young. I am old and scarred. I would rather have her remember me as I was when we last saw one another," he says firmly, though in a voice barely above a whisper.

"Let me know if you change your mind," the king tells Gorrard, and I'm already planning on helping him change his mind.

There are further introductions and each king dotes on me in a way that unconsciously makes Rennek growl a bit. Talks go on for a long time about plans for settling the planet and coordinating a search and rescue mission for the whole of Rennek's kingdom.

Rennek informs the others about the circumstances surrounding us humans, the kings are all much more outraged than I would have expected. They all seem to share the same deeply protective nature that Rennek and his friends all possess. Rennek lets them know we plan to continue to try and recover more humans, and any we find will be invited to join us here in Beacon, our corner of Elysia. The kings all agree and offer more of their people to aid us in that mission as well. I'm humbled by their generosity and kindness.

It must be wonderful for Rennek, it's like he gained five extra brothers in just one day. All these guys seem ready and willing to go to bat for anything Rennek needs. Finally, their talks wind to an end. There is still so much more to discuss, but I suspect there will be for some time. The Vendari all make plans for their next meeting before leaping from the windows, with wings pumping heavily, carrying them to their new kingdoms. Slowly, the command center clears until it is just Rennek and I.

"I'm so sorry Rennek," I can't imagine the weight of knowing all his people, possibly hundreds of Vendari, have simply vanished.

"I am sorry for them as well Kate, but I will do all in my power to find them."

"I know you have the help of the other Kings, but if you need me, just know you have me too," I tell him.

"Thank you, my sweet Kate. I do know this."

"There is much work to do on all fronts," he says.

"I know, I want to talk to Tennir about moving the aviary and to your mother's soldiers about building a fence. I still wanted to help out the girls with basket weaving today, to see if we can finally work the kinks out..."

"I have a much more pressing task on my agenda this day, and I was hoping you would assist me with it?" Rennek asks.

"Of course, babe, anything you need. All you have to do is ask," I tell him.

"Is that so?"

"You know it is," I tell him.

"Then I would like to ask you to join me, to watch the sun set over the shore, and to make love to me on the warm sands under the Elysian moons."

"The shore? Like the beach? I'd love to go down to the beach. I haven't been in years. Oh, but Rennek! We don't have time to go there tonight! There's so much work to do around here! It would take forever to hike there," I say sadly. It really would be wonderful to get away with my mate for a bit.

"We will not be hiking, and all else can wait until I please my mate."

"We won't be hiking? Are we going to take a pod?" I ask. But Rennek just smiles and scoops me into his arms. I only have a second before all the air is pushed from my lungs as Rennek leaps, with me in his arms, out of the window. There is the sudden terrible sensation of falling before it fades away and I feel us rising higher and higher into the sky. I wrap my arms around Rennek's neck and he holds me tightly in his muscled arms. I have no fear of him dropping me, but I still cling to him, I'm not going to drop him either. The wind is in my face as we circle Beacon. I see the other girls looking up at me and they scream and wave as we fly overhead. Rennek heads toward the horizon.

"We should arrive just in time to watch the sunset together," he tells me.

I snuggle into my mate. "I can't think of anything more perfect."

Author's Note

Holy crap, I did it. I wrote a book. This was such a long and difficult road for me. I wanted to punch this thing out like I do with the romance novels I read--with a nice healthy binge. But, having two little kids doesn't lend itself to letting me sit on my laptop for hours on end. So instead, after I tucked the rest of the house into bed, I would sit in the dark--typing away until I couldn't keep my eyes open any longer. Some nights it was only a paragraph at a time, which was maddening, but I finally finished!

As you can see, I left a lot of room for the remaining characters stories and I hope to eventually write them all. I may have left you wondering what happened to Dax and Vivian, and logically one might assume their story is next. *But*, I had a dream. A wildly inspirational dream regarding what my next book will be about--and who am I to stifle my inner muse?

The next book will still be within the same universe and we will end up back on Elysia--just with a new couple we haven't met yet. Which, is bound to happen when you think about all those cryo bags the Ju'tup had on their ship, right?

Thank you all so much for reading and I really truly hope you enjoyed the story. A special thanks to everyone who volunteered to help beta and ARC for me--particularly Kate Botting, Lyda Eagle, Cori Miller, Ronika Williams, and Laura Gail Walker. Your feedback has been absolutely invaluable. I have to say, the science fiction romance community is such a loving and generous one, and I feel so grateful to be a part of it.

An extra thanks to Amanda Milo as well. As a fan, I had been following her journey as an indie author and in no small way, it empowered me to take the plunge as well. If you are somehow reading my book and have never read

Amanda Milo--stop everything you're doing and go download her stuff now. All of it.

Please find me on Facebook at https://www.facebook.com/tracy.lauren.148 I'm new to this whole indie author thing, so I might be muddling through it for a bit before I find my stride, but come check me out anyhow. Share the journey with me. Plus, the more I feel the love the faster I might write book two! *And don't forget:* reviews make the world go 'round!

79358049R00266

Made in the USA
San Bernardino, CA
14 June 2018